W9-CMJ-396

ALL FOURS

ALL FOURS

Miranda July

RIVERHEAD BOOKS

NEW YORK

2024

RIVERHEAD BOOKS
An imprint of Penguin Random House LLC
penguinrandomhouse.com

Copyright © 2024 by Miranda July
Penguin Random House supports copyright. Copyright fuels creativity,
encourages diverse voices, promotes free speech, and creates a vibrant culture. Thank you
for buying an authorized edition of this book and for complying with copyright laws by not
reproducing, scanning, or distributing any part of it in any form without permission.
You are supporting writers and allowing Penguin Random House to continue to
publish books for every reader.

Riverhead and the R colophon are registered trademarks of Penguin Random House LLC.

LIBRARY OF CONGRESS CATALOGING-IN-PUBLICATION DATA
Names: July, Miranda, 1974– author.
Title: All fours : a novel / Miranda July.
Description: New York : Riverhead Books, 2024.
Identifiers: LCCN 2023026558 (print) | LCCN 2023026559 (ebook) |
ISBN 9780593190265 (hardcover) | ISBN 9780593190289 (ebook)
Subjects: LCGFT: Psychological fiction. | Novels.
Classification: LCC PS3610.U537 A79 2024 (print) |
LCC PS3610.U537 (ebook) | DDC 813/.6—dc23/eng/20230616
LC record available at https://lccn.loc.gov/2023026558
LC ebook record available at https://lccn.loc.gov/2023026559

International edition ISBN: 9780593719695

Printed in the United States of America
6th Printing

For Isabelle

PART ONE

CHAPTER 1

Sorry to trouble you was how the note began, which is such a great opener. Please, trouble me! Trouble me! I've been waiting my whole life to be troubled by a note like this.

> *Sorry to trouble you but it looked like someone was using a telephoto lens to take pictures through your windows from the street. If it was someone you know, then sorry for the misunderstanding, if not, though, I got the make/model/license of their vehicle.*
> *Brian (from next door)*
> and his phone number

You don't really need a telephoto lens because we have giant windows in front with no curtains. Sometimes I pause before coming inside and watch Harris and Sam innocently going about their business. Harris mutely explaining something to Sam, or lifting Sam into the air. I feel such tenderness toward them. *Try to remember this feeling,* I say to myself. *They are the same people up close as they are from here.*

We all immediately knew which neighbor Brian was. The FBI neighbor. If there's one thing we've learned from Brian it's that being in the FBI is not a secret like the CIA. He wears his (bulletproof?) FBI vest with the letters FBI on it way more than could possibly be required. It's like if someone on the Dodgers wore his uniform to water the lawn. All the neighbors would be like, We get it, dude, you're on the Dodgers.

So the first thing Harris did after I read the note aloud was scoff that of course the FBI neighbor had "caught" someone with a "telephoto lens." And the second thing Harris did was nothing. He was busy and didn't think it was worth pursuing.

"It's a little creepy, though, right?"

"People take pictures of everything these days," he said, walking out of the room.

"Do you think I should call him, though?"

But Harris didn't hear me.

"Call who?" said Sam.

I stood holding the note with that funny little abandoned feeling one gets a million times a day in a domestic setting. I could have cried, but why? It's not like I need to dish with my husband about every little thing; that's what friends are for. Harris and I are more formal, like two diplomats who aren't sure if the other one has poisoned our drink. Forever thirsty but forever wanting the other one to take the first sip.

You go.

No, you go ahead!

No, please, after you.

This sort of walking on eggshells might sound stressful, but I was pretty sure we would have the last laugh. When everyone else was sick to death of each other we'd be just breaking through, having our honeymoon. Probably in our sixties.

My friend Cassie says Love you! every time she gets off the phone with her husband. Whenever I overhear this I'm completely mortified for her.

But I do love him, she says.

You were *just* talking about how miserable and stuck you felt.

Then she kind of laughs as if it's all out of her hands. I don't expect her to be honest with her husband but at least come clean with me! Other people's relationships never make any sense. Once I got my best friend,

Jordi, to record a casual conversation between her wife and her. Jordi is a brilliant sculptor who can convincingly theorize about anything, but in this conversation she barely said a word while her wife ranted about the idiocy of a popular TV show. Only occasionally would Jordi murmur a question; mostly she just giggled at the things Mel said. I thought she might be embarrassed, but she wasn't.

"I love how sure of herself Mel is. I love opinionated people. Like you."

This was so flattering that I instantly warmed up to their dynamic.

"That show really is flawed," I said. "Mel nailed it."

My friends are always obliging me with ephemera like this—screenshots of sexts, emails to their mothers—because I'm forever wanting to know what it feels like to be other people. What were we all doing? What the hell was going on here on Earth? Of course none of these artifacts really amounted to anything; it was like trying to grab smoke by its handle. What handle?

I put the neighbor's note on my desk. I was busy, too, but I always have time to worry. In fact, I think I had already been worrying about someone using a telephoto lens to take pictures through our windows when the note arrived. Worrying is the wrong word—more like *hoping*. I hoped this was happening and had been happening since my birth, or something along these lines. If not this man through the windows, then God, or my parents, or my real parents, who are actually just my parents, or the real me, who has been waiting for the right moment to take over, tap me out. Just please let there be someone who cares enough to watch over me. It took me two days to call Brian the neighbor because I was busy savoring my position, like when a crush finally texts back and you want to enjoy having the ball in your court for a while.

"It feels funny to call someone who lives right next door," I said. "I could have just opened the window."

"I'm not at home right now."

"Okay."

He said the man had parked around the corner and that he had not photographed any other homes.

"He may have just been admiring your house," Brian suggested.

I didn't like that. I mean, it's a nice house, but come on. I didn't spend the last two days not calling because our house is nice.

"I'm a bit of a public figure," I said, going a little heavy on the false modesty. False modesty is one of those things that's hard to go easy on, like squirting whipped cream from a can. He said that's why he was concerned, because of my notoriety. I humbly replied, "Well, thank you, it's really so nice to know you're keeping your eye on things."

"It's *literally* my job," Brian said.

"*Right,*" I said, snapping out of it. I'm not a household name. I won't go into the tedious specifics of what I do, but picture a woman who had success in several mediums at a young age and has continued very steadily, always circling her central concerns in a sort of ecstatic fugue state with the confidence that comes from knowing there is no other path—her whole life will be this single conversation with God. God might be the wrong word for it. The Universe. The Undernetting. I work in our converted garage. One leg of my desk is shorter than the others and every day for the past fifteen years I've meant to wedge something under it, but every day my work is too urgent—I'm perpetually at a crucial turning point; everything is forever about to be revealed. At five o'clock I have to consciously dial myself down before reentering the house, like astronaut Buzz Aldrin preparing to unload the dishwasher immediately after returning from the moon. Don't talk about the moon, I remind myself. Ask everyone how *their* day was.

Brian the neighbor wondered if I knew anyone who wanted to buy a truck.

"It's a 2013 F-150. I'm moving and getting rid of most of my stuff."

"Oh! Where are you moving?"

"Can't disclose my next location," Brian said, and I apologized for asking.

"I guess a lot of things in your life need to be top secret."

"Yeah," he said in a soft voice. "I loved this neighborhood, though. All the trees and the way the coyotes howl at night."

"I love that, too. There's so many of them! Dozens, it sounds like."

"More."

"Hundreds, you think?"

"Yeah."

We fell silent and I didn't want to be the one to break the silence—it seemed like he, as an FBI agent, would know when it had been enough. But it just went on and on until I began smiling to myself, slightly grimacing from the awkwardness, and still it continued so the nervousness passed and now I thought of the silence as something we were doing together, like a jam session, and then that feeling ended and I grew inexplicably, overwhelmingly sad. My eyes welled up and when the silence finally broke it was because I made a sniffing sound and he said *Yeah* again, with resignation. Then, as if nothing had happened (and in fact nothing had), he went back to talking about the guy with the telephoto lens.

"I got his license plate number just to be safe. I can text it to you when I get home."

"Absolutely," I said. "That'd be great."

I knew better than to tell Harris about this exchange. He would raise his eyebrows and smile with exhaustion. What, *you* having a strangely intimate interaction with a stranger? How can this be?

I try to keep most of myself neatly contained off-site. In the home I focus on turning the wheel of the household so we can enjoy a smooth, healthy life without disaster or illness. This involves perpetual planning. For example, I cook seven waffles for Sam every weekend, filled with extra eggs, to be toasted quickly for high-protein breakfasts all week. But such forethought can feel labored, no fun—so I try to balance it out with something spontaneous, maybe an invented breakfast game or a surprising waffle topping. Harris would say mostly I just try to control everything. Who is right? We both are, but I admire Harris's old-world stoicism. He even dresses in an old-timey way, like a stonemason or some kind of tradesman. *Salt of the earth* is a phrase someone might apply to him, whereas no one would ever say I'm salt of the earth. Not that I'm a bad person, but of the two of us I'm definitely worse. Often I'm literally biting my tongue—holding it gently between my teeth—and counting to fifty. By then the urge to say something unnecessary has usually passed.

I was in bed when Brian texted me about the telephotographer's car.

It was a black Subaru hatchback, license plate number 6GPX752.

Thank you! I wrote.

No problem. Let me know if you're interested in having the plates run. I can't do it but I can connect you with someone who can. For your notes: One white or Asian male, average to above average height, slightly paunchy, with a beard. He was there around 4 pm on Saturday.

Saturday. I got out of bed and looked at the calendar on my computer. (This is the kind of thing you can do easily if you don't share a bed with your husband. He snores, I'm a light sleeper.) On Saturday at three o'clock Harris had driven Sam to a playdate, so at four I had been alone. That's right—I had dutifully called my parents, but they weren't home so I began texting friends in New York about my upcoming visit; I had just turned forty-five and this trip was my gift to myself. I was going to see plays and art and stay in a nice hotel instead of with friends, which normally would feel like a waste of money, but I'd gotten a surprise check—a whiskey company had licensed a sentence I'd written years ago for a new global print campaign. It was a sentence about hand jobs, but out of context it could also apply to whiskey. Twenty grand.

Jordi thought it was important that I spend this money unwisely. Whiskey come, whiskey go.

"Is that what you'd do?"

"No, I'd use it to quit FTC and do my art full-time." FTC is an ad agency. I immediately offered Jordi the money—It's a grant! I said. But she put a hand on each of my shoulders and looked me in the eyes.

"Think. What do you want most in the world?" she said, shaking me in a way that made me giggle.

"Uhhh . . . a good idea for my next project?"

"So do the opposite of what you'd normally do. Spend on beauty!"

Sculptors think beauty is a major theme, not a trifling indulgence. How lucky am I, right? To have a best friend like that?

I had booked a room at the Carlyle and then, on Saturday at four o'clock I had sent naked selfies to all my New York friends. We regularly send these, along with pictures of our kids and pets—it's just part of keeping in touch these days. I remembered that it had been hard to get the angle right and this was slightly disturbing. It didn't used to be this difficult to get a decent naked selfie. Maybe the quality of the light was changing; global warming.

I climbed back into bed and texted Brian the neighbor.

| How would I run the plates if that was something I wanted to do?

While I waited for his reply I touched myself, imagining the paunchy, bearded photographer jerking off in his black Subaru hatchback, my naked body glowing on his tiny camera screen. I came twice, the second time to a clapping noise, his paunch slapping my stomach. I wiped my fingers on my T-shirt and checked my phone.

| Call Tim Yoon (323) 555-5151. He's a retired cop/detective. He'd
| probably be willing to run the plates for a fee

It was too late to call so I texted and fell asleep imagining Tim Yoon running the plates.

Yoon as in noon. He ran toward the afternoon sun. Yoon as in yawn. Ran toward the sun and yawned at the edge of the Earth. Then came pounding back, a round white dinner plate in each hand.

"Shall I keep running these?" Yoon yelled as he neared.

"Yes, don't stop. Can you run them forever?"

"I can try," he panted as he sprinted past me. I watched him sink below the horizon, then I turned and faced west, waiting for him to circle the globe and reappear.

It took Tim Yoon many months to call me back and by that time I'd already figured out who the telephotographer was.

CHAPTER 2

Originally I had planned to get to New York the normal way, fly there, but then Harris and I had gotten into an odd conversation with another couple at a party. Our friend Sonja said she loved to drive; she missed having the time to drive across the country. And Harris said, Well, that figures.

What do you mean? we all said. Harris just shrugged, took a sip of his drink. He doesn't talk much at parties. He hangs back, not needing anything from anyone, which of course draws people toward him. I've watched him move from room to room, running in slow motion from a crowd that is unconsciously chasing him.

"Why does that figure?" Sonja said, smiling. She wasn't going to let this go. And maybe because it was her, so charming with her Auckland accent and big breasts, Harris suddenly laid out a fully formed theory.

"Well, in life there are Parkers and there are Drivers," he began. "Drivers are able to maintain awareness and engagement even when life is boring. They don't need applause for every little thing—they can get joy from petting a dog or hanging out with their kid and that's enough. This kind of person can do cross-country drives." He took a sip of his drink. Dogs were a hot-button topic for us. Harris and Sam wanted one; I was ambivalent about pets in general. Are we totally sure about the domestication of animals? Will we not look back on this as a kind of slavery? But how to get out of it now when the world is so populated with dogs and cats that can't fend for themselves? It's not humane to just release them. It would have to be a group decision: No more pets after this. This is the last round of them. But that was never going to happen, even if everyone agreed with me, and literally no one did. Being anti-pet (pro-animal!) was one of my least winning qualities.

"Parkers, on the other hand"—and he looked at me—"need a discrete task that seems impossible, something that takes every bit of focus and for which they might receive applause. 'Bravo,' someone might say after they fit the car into an especially tight spot. 'Amazing.' The rest of the time they're bored and fundamentally kind of . . ." he looked at the ceiling, trying to think of the right word, "*disappointed*. A Parker can't drive across the country. But Parkers are good in emergencies," he added. "They like to save the day."

"I'm definitely a Parker," said Sonja's husband. "I love to save the day."

"Wait, *parking* is exciting?" said Sonja. "That seems counterintuitive. Wouldn't driving—"

"Think about it, hon, you have to get the angle just right—"

"Okay, but are Drivers boring? I don't want to be the boring, dependable kind of person."

"No, not at all," said Harris. "Drivers can have a good time more easily. That's not boring."

"I want to be a Parker," Sonja said, pouting.

"Too late," Harris said. "You can't switch."

At this point I peeled away from the conversation. Message received. Harris and Sonja were grounded, easygoing, people who liked to pet dogs and have sex whenever. And I was a Parker. What he called disappointed was really just depressed. I'd been a little blue recently, not a lot of fun around the house. Not like Sonja. I watched the two of them chatting—his barrel chest and graying black curls somehow looked boyish and his level of animation was totally unfamiliar to me, I guess she brought that out in him. It wasn't jealousy exactly; being a third wheel is my native state. Sometimes Harris will seem to have rapport with a waitress or a cashier and I immediately cede to them as a couple—I internally step aside and give my place to the other woman, just for a few seconds, until the transaction is over.

There was a small group of people dancing in the living room. I moved discreetly at first, getting my bearings, then the beat took hold and I let my vision blur. I fucked the air. All my limbs were in motion, making shapes that felt brand-new. My skirt was tight, my top was sheer, my heels were high. The people around me were nodding and smiling; I couldn't tell if they were embarrassed for me or actually impressed. The host's father looked me up and down and winked—he was in his eighties. Was that how old a person had to be to think I was hot these days? I moved deeper into the crowd, shut my eyes, and slid side to side, shoulder first, like I was protecting stolen loot. Now I added a fist like a brawler, punching. I made figure eights with my ass at what felt like an incredible speed while holding my hands straight up in the air like I'd just made a goal. When I eventually opened my eyes I saw Harris across the room, watching. I could tell from his face that he thought I was being "unnecessarily provocative." Or maybe I was projecting my parents onto him—that's more something my mom would say—but he's always leaned a bit traditional. On our second date I began revealing my peep show past the same way I always did, like a verbal striptease, until I noticed his face kind of shutting down. At which point I immediately began reversing the story, narratively *putting my clothes back on*, as it were, and minimizing the whole thing—a youthful misstep! Ancient history!

Now he touched two fingers to his forehead and I did the same, relieved. We'd done this saluting thing the first time we ever laid eyes on each other and across many crowded rooms ever since. *There you are.* He didn't look away. Dancers kept moving between us, but he held on for a moment longer, we both did. I smiled a little but this wasn't really about happiness; it hit below fleeting feelings. At this slight remove all our formality falls away, revealing a mutual and steadfast devotion so tender

I could have cried right there on the dance floor. Sure, he's good-looking, unflappable, insightful, but none of that would mean anything without this strange, almost pious, loyalty between us. Now we both knew to turn away. Other couples might have crossed the room toward each other and kissed, but we understood the feeling would disappear if we got too close. It's some kind of Greek tragedy, us, but not all told.

I wandered off the dance floor and into the master bathroom, washing my hands with the host's facial cleanser. Of course it wasn't too late to switch from Parker to Driver—anyone with a driver's license could drive across the country. I could see myself pulling up in to the driveway with dusty tires, Sam running to greet me and Harris just standing in the doorway. He'd salute and I'd salute, but this time I'd walk into his arms, knowing I was finally home in a way I'd never been before.

By morning the idea had taken hold. Why fly to New York when I could drive and finally become the sort of chill, grounded woman I'd always wanted to be? This could be the turning point of my life. If I lived to be ninety I was halfway through. Or if you thought of it as two lives, then I was at the very start of my second life. I imagined a vision quest–style journey involving a cave, a cliff, a crystal, maybe a labyrinth and a golden ring.

"I've driven across the country," said Jordi. "It's not that great."

"It's not supposed to be! Is a silent meditation retreat 'great'? Do people hike the Pacific Crest Trail because it's 'great'? And this is even higher stakes because if my mind wanders too far I'll crash and die."

"Oh god, don't say that."

"But my mind won't wander! I'll be totally present all the way there and all the way back. And for the rest of my life I'll tell people about this cross-country drive I did when I was forty-five. That's when I finally learned to just be myself."

Of course I was always myself with Jordi; she knew I meant be myself *at home*. All the time.

Harris had found an old foldout map of the United States and was tracing his finger across it. "If you take the southern route you can go through New Mexico and spend the night in Las Cruces." I was holding a plastic hairbrush and trying to focus on all the red and blue squiggles, but my eyes bounced off them.

"Couldn't I just put New York City into my Google Maps?"

"But there are different ways to go. Different routes."

He said I should take an extra week so the drive wouldn't eat into my New York days.

"Really? That's more than two weeks without you guys." I had never been apart from Sam for that long. Each time they ran past us I tried to hand them the hairbrush; surely at seven one could be the steward of one's own tangly hair.

"Well, you don't want to drive for a week and then just turn around and come home. You should really take three weeks to make it worth your while."

"*Three* weeks? No, that would definitely be too long apart." He was being generous because I had done a lot of parenting recently while he worked with his twenty-seven-year-old protégée, Caro. Is protégée the right word? Ingenue, whatever. He's a record producer, which is actually ideal—there's no competition between us but he knows what an artistic soul needs. Early on I called her Caroline; Caro felt too intimate, like a pet name.

("Only the press calls her Caroline," Harris had said.)

("That's fine. I don't mind being like the press.")

But it wasn't just that he owed me childcare; Harris doesn't have a lot of conflicted feelings vis-à-vis the domestic sphere. I didn't either until we had a baby. Harris and I were just two workaholics, fairly equal. Without a child I could dance across the sexism of my era, whereas becoming a mother shoved my face right down into it. A latent bias, internalized by both of us, suddenly leapt forth in parenthood. It was now obvious that Harris was openly rewarded for each thing he did while I was quietly shamed for the same things. There was no way to fight back against this, no one to point a finger at, because it came from everywhere. Even walking around my own house I felt haunted, fluish with guilt about every single thing I did or didn't do. Harris couldn't see the haunting and this was the worst part: to be living with someone who fundamentally didn't believe me and was really, really sick of having to pretend to empathize—or else be the bad guy! In his own home! How infuriating for him. And how infuriating to be the wife and not other women who could enjoy how terrific he was. How painful for both of us, especially given that we were modern, creative types used to living in our dreams of the future. But a baby exists only in the present, the historical, geographic, economic present. With a baby one could no longer be cute and coy about capitalism—money was time, time was everything. We could have skipped lightly across all this by not becoming parents; it never really had to come to a head. On the other hand, sometimes it's good when things come to a head. And then eventually, one day: pop.

Harris was using a highlighter directly on the map and telling me I could always decide later to stay a few extra days.

"That's the great thing about driving; you can play it by ear." He could be generous like this for the reasons I just explained. Not me! I always wanted him back right on the dot—extended trips, school holidays, a child being too sick to go to school, these things run a chill down the spines of working mothers whose freedom is so precarious to begin with. Still, I loved this about Harris, how he always encouraged me to stay longer and have fun. I reminded him I had to be back by the fifteenth anyway. Of course, he said; obviously.

Everyone knew my meeting with Arkanda was on the fifteenth. Arkanda's not her real name. She's a world-famous pop star you've heard of. Not just famous but deeply beloved. A while back my manager, Liza, received a phone call from her people. Arkanda wanted to meet with me in Malibu at the end of April to discuss a potential project and they would let us know the details by April twentieth. All my friends were baffled by this turn of events, almost too baffled. Why, why, why would *Arkanda* want to work with *you*, they puzzled aloud. When I suggested that maybe it had something to do with my creative output they said things like *I mean, right, who knows, it could be that.* Arkanda's level of fame shifted the scale such that my work was not more notable than Cassie's work, as a graphic designer for a hot sauce company, or Destiny's work, managing an inherited apartment complex. And by choosing me Arkanda had, by extension, chosen all my friends; everyone was waiting for the end of April. *Potential project.* Of course it might be nothing, something akin to writing an essay or interviewing her. Even directing a video wouldn't be life-changing, though of course I would happily do any of these things, what a lark! But if we were to really *collaborate*, spend time together, make a shared world—an album, the lyrics, the videos, the art direction—a total creative mind meld that then entered the culture at a scale I could never reach alone . . . I splurged on a new blouse for the twentieth: silk with a deep V neckline. On the nineteenth her people called to move the meeting to early June, then the fall, then sometime around the new year, and this pushing of the date had gone on and on and on. Just when my friends and I were starting to lose hope, we were given a new date, the fifteenth, in Malibu again, at a restaurant called Geoffrey's, and something we'd never had before: a *time.* Three o'clock.

"What if my car breaks down or something?"

"One way or another you'll get to Malibu by three o'clock on the fifteenth," said Harris. And it went without saying that if Arkanda wanted me to collaborate with her we would adjust our lives to make this possible. Even Harris is a fan of Arkanda's, and not ironically, either. He would kill to produce one of her songs (which made it extra sweet that she had chosen *me*). Maybe we were both bluffing about this cross-country drive, knowing that I would ultimately back down and fly.

"Don't you worry for my safety?" I said.

"That's why I'm helping you map out your route," said Harris with his eyes on the computer. "There are definitely better and worse places to stop." He was reading a Reddit thread about queer-friendly towns and hotels, reasoning that these would be safer for a woman traveling alone. But he was confident that the trip would be good for me, for my blues, and he had faith that I would be okay. When I go out the door he always says, "Have fun!" At first I took this to mean that he really didn't care very much about me, if this was all the fear he had for my safety.

My dad always sent my mom off with a screed of warnings, reminding her of how fundamentally incapable she was of everything she was about to do. He did this for her own protection, to keep her on her toes and give her a fighting chance at survival because anything could happen at any time, even at home. For example, his mother, my grandma Esther, had jumped out the window of her New York City apartment building when she was fifty-five. No warning except she had recently been lamenting all her gray hairs.

"She couldn't bear to see her looks go," my dad always says with the same incredulous tone. Who killed themself for such a shallow reason? "And her hair was jet-black anyway—not a gray hair in sight!"

She was probably dyeing it, I always think, but I don't say this because I don't want my dad to suspect I dye my hair or that I'm like her. Harris was printing out a map of the route he recommended.

"Why would I need this when I have my phone?" I said, staring at the line across the upper half of the United States.

"What if your phone dies?"

I pinned the map above my desk in the garage, next to the note from the neighbor. If the telephotographer came back when I was driving across the country he wouldn't be able to find me with his long lens; he'd have to make do with the old pictures.

CHAPTER 3

E w," Jordi said when I told her about the neighbor's note. "Or—you probably like that?"

"Yeah. I've already gotten a lot of use out of it."

We were sipping milkshakes; mine strawberry, hers chocolate. Once a week we meet in her studio and eat junk together. Usually desserts we'd eaten as kids but almost never again since we'd discovered the healing power of whole grains and fermented foods and how sugar was basically heroin. This was part of a larger agreement to never become rigid, to maintain fluidity in diet and all things. At home I baked high-protein, date-sweetened treats. No one knew about our medicinal junk food, are you kidding? Harris and Sam would both be jealous, each in their own way. Similarly, I never told Harris what I jerked off to.

"But maybe you guys could role-play it?" Jordi suggested.

"Do you guys role-play?"

"Never."

"We don't, either."

We decided then to tell each other exactly how a typical fuck played out in our marriages. We couldn't believe we'd never done this before. If there was a good reason, neither of us could think of it.

"Who initiates? You, right?" I knew she was that sort of totally present, body-rooted lover who felt like sex was a basic need.

"Yes," she sighed, "it's always me."

"I'm the initiator, too, actually, but only because I'm trying to get out ahead of the pressure."

"How often?"

"Once a week."

"Wow," she moaned. "I *wish* I was having sex once a week!"

I laughed. We were so opposite.

"I see it like exercise," I said. "You don't ask yourself if you *want* to exercise, that's the wrong question."

"You don't exercise."

"I know, but if I did, I imagine it would be similar. I also don't love getting in pools, by the way. Sunday nights! Packing for trips! Any transition. Whatever state I'm in I just want to stay in it, if that's not too much to ask." It was, though, for a married person. Sometimes I could hear Harris's dick whistling impatiently like a teakettle, at higher and higher pitches until I finally couldn't take it and so I initiated.

I went step by step, demonstrating some movements, saying who put what where, how many times I came, how it ended.

"Geez," said Jordi. "So many positions."

"Yeah, that's more his thing. I'm completely inside the movie in my head. It's like I have a screen clamped in front of my face."

"What's on the screen?"

"Oh, you know, I'm a gross stepfather getting a blow job from my nineteen-year-old stepdaughter, or *I'm* the stepdaughter, getting tucked in. Or I'm flipping back and forth between them. There's a lot of special tucking in involving boners."

"A *step*father and she's over eighteen," Jordi laughed. "Very legal."

"It's consensual! They're mutually obsessed with each other; that's a big part of it. You probably just think about Mel."

"You don't think about Harris?"

"No, I do. Same dynamic, but with an intern or assistant. Usually I'm Harris being seduced by her. She's reassuring me that my wife will *never know* and finally I just let her suck it."

"Geez, I feel so unimaginative," Jordi said. "I'm just like, 'Body feel good. Me want.'"

"You're present—that's much better! A body-rooted fucker."

"Is there another kind?"

"Mind-rooted." I pointed my thumb at myself. "But I'm hoping to be more like you after my trip. Now *you* go."

"Oh, it's so boring compared to you guys."

I was pleased she felt this way.

"Just tell me."

She took a sip of her milkshake and twisted her mountain of black curls into a temporary bun.

"Sometimes it starts when we're asleep, we just kind of start having sex without even knowing it. So we're half-awake and sort of sloppy and then it gets more heated and . . . oh god, it's not . . . sexy-sounding like you guys."

"Keep going," I said. I was starting to have a bad feeling.

"Well, often we're in a kind of ugly position, like with both our legs wrapped around each other, kind of in this tight ball, and I really like my mouth to be overfilled so almost her whole hand might be in my mouth so there's drool running down the sides of my face and we're just, you know, humping, kind of like animals. I've actually thought about how ugly this must look, like two desperate cavewomen. Usually we're too asleep or lazy to go down on each other or use a dick so there's just, like, a bunch of fingering, or not even that, just grinding. Sometimes I will literally just hump her butt until I come, without even fully waking up. Sometimes I fall asleep with my fingers in her cunt and when I wake up they're all pruney."

I was quiet now, bludgeoned by this vision of intimacy. It wasn't a matter of having lost at this conversation; I had lost at life.

It was almost midnight. Moonlight and lamplight came through the window and her sculptures gleamed around us. They were Jordi's own body but morphed, ghoulishly skewed toward animals, cars, monsters, always headless, in wood or limestone or plaster. We wouldn't see each other again before my trip.

"You know you can just fly if you want," she said.

"Are you saying that because you think I'll crash?"

"No, no, not at all. Just that if you *don't* transform . . . that's fine, too."

I stared at her in the half-light and she looked straight back at me.

"I'm just making it harder for myself, aren't I?"

"Maybe."

I came into the house my usual way, like a thief. I turned the lock slowly and shut the door with the handle all the way to the left to avoid the click of the lock. Took off my shoes. Rolled my feet from heel to toe, which is how ninjas walk so silently. I was often two or three hours late because I had trouble admitting that I was planning to talk to Jordi for five hours. But how could it be any shorter, given that it was my one chance a week to be myself? My heart was pounding as I tiptoed through the living room. I know the quietest way to wash up, too: picking up and putting down the cup and face wash with this technique where you pretend each thing is heavier than it is. Imagine the cup is made of brick, so that as you put it down you're also lifting it up, resisting its weight—the opposite of this would be just dropping it, letting gravity put it down. When I walk past Harris's bedroom I think *glide, glide, glide.*

When Harris comes in late he slams the door cheerfully behind him. He's trying to be quiet, but not that hard. His mind is on other things, and why not? This is his house. Why behave like a thief? He doesn't see how each moment can be made terrible if you only try. There can be a problem every second so that life is a sort of low-grade torture. Then, when you are free, like when I was eating dessert with Jordi, it feels really, really good, like a drug high. So: *grit, grit, grit,* then: *release.* Joy. This works especially well for a life built around grueling self-discipline culminating in glittery debuts and premieres. *Grit, grit, grit,* then: *ta-da!* The thing that links the two states is fantasy. As a girl I fantasized about the perfect dollhouse, now I fantasize about the moment when I would finally reveal what I'd been making in the garage and be suddenly seen, understood, and adored—or at least get to stay in a nice hotel. These rewards really took the edge off life, carried me through the endless cleaning and cooking and caring and working. As a child I knew these weren't just fantasies. One day I really would leave this house, these people, this city, and live a completely different life.

CHAPTER 4

I would make the trip in six days, driving eight hours a day. I'd take the 210 to I-15 to I-70 and stay on that all the way from Utah to the Pennsylvania Turnpike and I-76, to I-276 to I-95 to I-278 to New York. I would stop in Las Vegas after the first four hours; people said there was an amazing macrobiotic restaurant there called Bendita. I would drive through Zion National Park, where there was a tunnel that had windows in it to see the scenery through. I'd spend the first night in Salina, Utah. Then Salina to Denver, Denver to Kansas, and I was already halfway. Wouldn't that feel incredible, Harris said, to be halfway—the exact middle of the country. I thought it would, but I couldn't shake the feeling that someone else would be doing the driving. I saw myself looking out the window, dozing off, unwrapping a sandwich with both hands—all things that would kill me. Harris showed me how to press the cruise control button on the steering wheel for long stretches.

"I don't see myself using that," I said. It seemed about as safe as a self-driving car.

"Okay, but you may get sick of pressing your foot down for eight hours a day."

My foot suddenly felt exhausted already.

I had PowerBars to eat for breakfast so I could always get an early start. People said you could lose a lot of time waiting for restaurants to open. Kansas to Indianapolis, stopping in Casey, Illinois, to visit the world's largest collection of world's largest objects. Indianapolis to Pittsburgh, where I-70 would end and I had a friendly ex. Pittsburgh to NYC, where I would stay at the Carlyle for six very expensive nights, plenty of time to see all my friends and all the museums and galleries and plays and have meetings for work. And then six days to drive home, which everyone said would feel much quicker, going home always feels quicker. I had twelve audiobooks and many playlists that people had made specially for me to listen to during certain parts of the drive, for example a Folkways-heavy blues compilation for the Mississippi Delta, if I decided to veer south. My to-do list got longer and longer—car inspection, therapeutic back support, withdraw cash, sun-protective driving outfits, rosacea gel, extra Benadryl, etc., etc.—but I kept at it and eventually the list got shorter and shorter. The Benadryl was for sleep, not allergies. I'd been having this thing where I woke up every night at two a.m. It wasn't a big deal unless I didn't have Benadryl and then it was a harrowing fugue state ending only when the sun rose on a fragile, weeping shell of a person, unable to work or think, much less drive safely. That's why I needed extra.

It was a two-and-a-half-week trip. The longest I'd been away from Sam or Harris was two weeks, but this was the shortest it could comfortably be. I told myself that if I missed Sam too much or Sam missed me too much then I could simply fly home at any moment and pay someone on Craigslist to drive the car back to L.A. But Sam was unlikely to miss me at all since they were an out-of-sight-out-of-mind person. As was I. The real fear was that we would forget each other. That was always my underlying fear: that someone I loved would look at me like a stranger. Or that I would take such a circuitous path away from someone that I could never find my way back to them. Even before her mild cognitive impairment my mom always introduced herself when I answered the phone. *This is your mother: Elaine,* she says, in case I can't recognize her voice or have forgotten her name. After two and a half weeks I might have to reintroduce myself to my child, but this was the heartbreaking kind of risk one had to take in life.

The night before I left, Sam and I took a final bath together. It was our weekly ritual, begun before they were able to sit, when I had to be there to prop them up or else they would tip over. Now they lay languorously between my legs, like a slipper inside a slipper, using my chest as a pillow. We kept it dark and burned a musky candle, steam rising around the flame. We ate apple slices dipped in honey, our wet crunching the only sound until one of us said something about water or time or our bodies— in this otherworldly place we had only big thoughts, like proper stoners. Often we mused about our love and how we would always take baths together like this. I knew we wouldn't, but we might always remember this feeling. Sometimes I cried, just from love, and Sam said, "Oh, *Mama*."

Tonight Sam asked if we could get a dog when I got home from my trip.

"That's the hope," I said.

"So, yes?"

"Let's take it as it comes."

"Kids aren't good at that, Mom."

Sam often explained things like this to me, as if they'd been a kid for longer than I'd been a mother.

"You're not like other moms," they'd said a few weeks ago.

"I'm not? How are other moms?"

"Well, like, you show them something you made and they're like, 'COOOOOL, I *LOVE* IT!'"

This wasn't what I had been expecting; it didn't sound so bad. My own mother was never sure how to be, what was called for in a given situation, so she often went overboard, promised the moon, then suddenly reversed course and withdrew, testily.

"I do love the things you make," I said, pushing back their wet bangs.

"I know, you just say it more like you're talking to an adult."

"COOOL!" I said, trying out the other way.

They rolled their eyes, something they had just learned how to do.

"*I* wouldn't want that. But other kids would."

"Okay."

"You should be like that at my next birthday party."

"That's almost a year away."

"I can wait."

"All right. I'll give it a whirl then."

As I dried them off we talked about how I would bring them a little keepsake from each state.

"A toy."

"Not a toy. Probably something from nature."

"A key chain would be fine."

"It might be a rock or a seedpod. Or a funny paper napkin from a diner."

"A napkin?! I don't want a napkin! Just bring me one big, good thing."

After Sam fell asleep I forced myself to walk into Harris's bedroom in nothing but high heels. The heels help me *just do it*, like ripping off a Band-Aid. Once I mutated (from intrinsically and eternally alone to sucking on another person's body) our weekly sex felt great, and by the time Harris was giving me my fourth orgasm I was sex's biggest fan, a total convert—sex is essential for a healthy relationship! But after the afterglow I withdrew into my native state and got started on dreading the next time—which wouldn't be for two and a half weeks.

In the morning the sky was gray and there was a grim feeling like this would be my last day on Earth. Which for all we knew it would be. This wasn't like flying, where you could reassure yourself that driving was a hundred times more dangerous; this was driving. I put on my white, sun-repellent car clothing and spent a long time packing the trunk and sitting in the front seat practicing reaching for things without looking at them. A woman I knew's sister had caused a six-car pileup on the interstate all because she glanced down to put in an Oingo Boingo tape. Finally I kissed Sam all over their face, but they were eager to get inside and start the screen time that had been promised. Harris took a picture.

"Call us from Utah tonight," he said, hugging me. I gave him a look that said: *If I survive, if I come back to you, let us finally give up this farce and be as one*. He gave me a look that said: *We could be as one right now, if you really wanted that*. To which my eyes said nothing.

CHAPTER 5

It was a strange indignity to be driving through familiar parts of town as if I were going grocery shopping. Even once I got on the freeway it was possible that I was only driving to visit my friend Priya, who lived in Altadena and had chickens and a long commute to work. I shifted in my seat, blindly patted my snacks, and considered starting an audiobook. But it hadn't even been ten minutes; I wasn't even technically out of the greater Los Angeles area. I tried out one of my playlists then turned it off halfway through a Portishead song. This was going to be a lot of time to think. Maybe too much time. I considered calling Jordi, but right then the phone rang, an unfamiliar number. Maybe it was someone doing a lengthy public health survey—even a solicitor would kill some time.

It was my dad. He was calling from a "loaner phone" while his was being fixed. Out of habit I started to apologize for only having a second to talk, then fell silent. He could talk for *days*. I could cross the whole country listening to my father monologue.

"It's great that you're driving," he said, "much safer," and then he launched into his news: since we last talked his original soul had wandered off and been replaced by a new one.

Uh-huh, I said, my eyes on the road.

He still had all his memories, he explained, but nothing in his life meant very much to this new soul.

"So, I'm talking to the new soul right now? It's you?"

"Well, it is and it isn't. I don't identify with myself anymore."

He described looking at my mom and still remembering their fifty-year story but not feeling anything in particular for her. A soul enters a fully grown body to save time, he explained. Rather than wait a couple decades to grow up, it can just immediately get to work.

He didn't come right out and say it, but it followed that the walk-in didn't feel anything particular for me, either. It wasn't a dramatic change—he usually asked me one question and hoped my answer wouldn't take up too much time. Today he skipped that question. The walk-in couldn't pretend to be interested in a daughter he had only just met.

"Are you still in the deathfield?"

"Of course," he said curtly. It was a rude question since he was always in it. I used to think everyone knew about the deathfield, but by around fourth grade I understood it was just his thing, although he assured me that I, too, would enter it, one day. "Probably when you least expect it, when everything seems to be going swimmingly." So far I hadn't and at this point I felt pretty confident that I wouldn't. According to him, his mother had been in the deathfield when she jumped; she had given up on ever getting out. My dad would never give up. He was a tenacious fuck. From what I gather the deathfield is what most people would call depression. Or a combination of panic and depression.

"I meditate for four to six hours a day," he said, "but I have no illusion of control; the walk-in will leave when it's ready to leave."

"Right."

You wouldn't know I had a curious bone in my body from the monosyllabic responses I give him. It feels terrible to be so cold, but it's hard to find a middle ground. There was a time I would have responded with the compliance of a mirror—his anxiety was my anxiety. Once, when I was six or seven, my mom flew to visit her sister in Boise. He kept the kitchen radio on for the duration of her flight and he didn't even have to say why—of course we were listening for the breaking news of her plane crash. At the time of her arrival in Idaho I exhaled, thinking we were safe, then he said: *Lag time*. I understood immediately. Between her plane crashing and the radio report there would be a lag. We kept listening, silently, together.

I suddenly noticed my tank was not completely full.

"Three-quarters of a tank?" he said. "That's plenty to last you for a good while."

I want to start fresh, I said. Knowing I won't have to stop again for another five hundred miles. But take care and give my love to Mom.

I exited in Monrovia. When I got out to pump the gas the tires looked low to me—not dramatically low but on the edge. I backed up into the full-service zone and while a man with a beard checked my tires and oil (both totally fine), I asked him if there were any special restaurants in the area, ideally somewhere healthy. Because now that I was doing all these other things it made sense to eat a real meal so I wouldn't have to stop all over again for lunch. The man with the beard glanced at the phone in my hand as if to say, Can't you just look that up?

"I'm on a cross-country trip," I explained. "Taking in the local favorites."

"Okay. Some people like Fontana's. On Myrtle."

I sat in the car while he filled the tank and a young man cleaned my windshield, which was unnecessary but I guessed part of the service. The guy with the squeegee had a Huckleberry Finn/Gilbert Blythe look that I used to flip out over as a teenager but with more closely cropped hair and a downy little mustache that kind of ruined the effect. He was sliding the rubber edge across the glass with long, sure, steady strokes. It was hypnotic, like being bathed. I fell into a sort of lazy trance and for this reason I was slow to realize we had made eye contact. How embarrassing. But to look away would make it seem as if I cared what this person thought—he should look away. He didn't, so we remained locked together like this as he made his way down the window. In moments he seemed to be smiling faintly at our predicament and at other times he grew deeply serious, as if this thing between us was no joke.

And I could feel my own face mirroring his, sunny and then somber, grave. I felt a little disoriented. What had I gotten myself into? Would this never end? And at the same time I had a growing anxiety about the end. I feared it would be too abrupt or that I would somehow be unprepared. It took a long time for me to notice the earbuds in his ears. He was listening to something, that's why the serious then smiling face. Probably a podcast. Could he even really see me through the glass? No, the way the light hit it made that impossible; I was just a dark shape. No matter. I'd already forgotten him by the time I pulled back onto the freeway.

I drove to Fontana's listening to Portishead at a very loud volume. This had been my main album in the midnineties when my ex-girlfriend and ex–best friend were living together in the apartment next door to me and loudly consummating their new love. The lovemaking involved some kind of hitting followed by a hoarse *uh*. It was a kind of arousal that I hadn't experienced—I'd never been hit, I'd never gone *uh*. When they had sex like this I'd put on my Walkman and listen to Portishead and try to imagine a time when this would all just be a funny story. Now was that time. My young agony was the funny part; it made me smile as I drove. Twenty years ago I'd been in my twenties; twenty years from now I'd be in my sixties. I was no closer to being sixty-five than twenty-five, but since time moved forward, not backward, sixty-five was tomorrow and twenty-five was moot. I didn't think a lot about death, but I was getting ready to. I understood that death was coming and that all my current preoccupations were kind of naïve; I still operated as if I could win somehow. Not the vast and total winning I had hoped for in the previous decades, but a last chance to get it together before winter came, my final season.

I was forgetting to be present. It seemed almost impossible to *be here now* while driving, but maybe that wouldn't be true in a few days. Right. The only way to become a Driver was to drive. I suddenly missed Sam desperately. Why was I speeding away from them when all I ever wanted was to hold them?

This had been a sad surprise about parenthood. Parents walking around with their babies always seemed to really *have* them—completely encircling them in their arms or clasping one dear little hand while crossing the street. This, clearly, was a full meal of love and intimacy. If you were willing to pay the price you would get a total love not possible with anyone else.

Yes and no. The problem began right at the start, with one of us entirely inside the other, a state that *seemed* close but was fundamentally distant. I couldn't even press my ear up against my own pregnant belly to hear them, only other people could. And the born baby was *so* soft and smooth and cute that it was frustrating, and too small to really cuddle with. I was often trying to put different parts of them in my mouth, as they did with me, but there was no way to consummate the love of your child.

With a partner you had the story of how you met, choosing each other out of everyone in the world, and the years together were chaptered with joint decisions—no one could ever say it was all a dream; both parties were accountable. Not so with a child. For the child it *was* a dream. And the unpunctuated days into years moved much more quickly (for the parent), so all one could do was free-fall through the chaos, madly making sandwiches and washing hair and hope that there would be some ritual, some time for reflection, at the end. Perhaps at their high school graduation the child would turn and say, "Phewf. I'm awake now, so I can speak about it—that was a trip, wasn't it?! What an insane number of sandwiches you suddenly had to make, having rarely ever made one before! And look at my body! Let me actually take off all my clothes and show it to you so you can get a good look before I go off into my life and never show it to you again." And they would take off everything, ceremonially, and I would admire and smell each part, touching anything they suggested I touch—a muscle, a sheen of hair—but respectfully just admiring the rest, down to the alarmingly long toenails.

Or if this was too invasive (I mean, what teenager was going to want that) then maybe just a scroll that we could both sign, acknowledging that this had all really happened and that while one of us had had no choice in the matter and the other of us had been sort of exhausted the whole time, it had, all of it, really happened. My own parents definitely wanted a scroll. I was much too vague about my childhood—at times I almost seemed to deny it had ever occurred or that it had meant anything at all. Or else I claimed it too completely, recoloring it in a way that bordered on complete fabrication. Which was actually worse—better to just leave it alone, a hallucination that I could not fully recall, an unconsummated love affair that was forever too much or too little, only being the right amount in fleeting moments, like when Sam and I took a bath together in the dark, both of us finally in the same warm watery womb. God, I missed them.

Fontana's wasn't exactly what I would call healthy. I ordered the Shrimp Diablo. The young waitress was barely civil, but I treated her warmly nonetheless; I always go out of my way to not be like my mom in these situations. She often felt she was being mocked—so she mocked back. She'd get nervous and mock a waitress, a cab driver, a neighbor. Sometimes they didn't notice, but often they did and a fight would break out, ending with her in tears. Now I'm more detached, but when she mocked me as a teenager I had to restrain myself from scratching her face or biting her. All in all, though, my mom was the cozier parent, no contest. I loved it when we cuddled; the warmth and smell of her body in a baby blue nylon nightie. Her big, soft breasts falling this way and that. Once, at around fifteen, I did briefly try to strangle her during one of those mocking episodes. That's when I discovered there's no satisfaction in violence; it actually works in reverse, making you the bad one.

I looked at my phone while eating. Someone was placing an order to go and joking with the young waitress about it being "the *usual* usual" and it occurred to me with a kind of slow horror that it was the boy who had washed my windshield. I took a sip of water and a bite of crushed ice. Of course, since we hadn't actually locked eyes there was really no need for awkwardness; it was just a surprising coincidence. He was tucking the brim of his baseball cap into the back of his jeans.

"I saw you at the gas station," I said, striking up the first of many conversations I'd be having with strangers all over the country. When you were just passing through you could really talk to anyone.

He blinked a few times. For a moment I thought maybe he wouldn't respond at all, maybe I was too far out of his orbit to even be audible.

"What?"

"You cleaned my windshield and now you're here, too. Just a funny coincidence."

"It's only a few minutes away." He looked genuinely confused by my surprise, like the idea of a coincidence was too nuanced for him. It was always like this in life. No one ever had the right reaction to anything. "I drive cars between the Hertz lots in Monrovia and Duarte, so I'm back and forth a lot. This place is right in between."

I waved my hand in front of my face, smiling, Never mind.

He glanced at my all-white clothing and said, "I'm guessing you're not from around here?"

My food came and he told me a few things about the area while he waited for his ham and cheddar melt. When it arrived he ate it standing up, answering my questions like a well-brought-up child who was poised and easy with adults. His name was Davey. I offered the chair across from me and he sort of half sat on it, while biting heartily into the sandwich and describing the history of the Hertz franchises his uncle owned. He usually worked at the counter, so moving cars was comparatively fun, "especially when I can time it with my lunch break!" He didn't question whether any of this was interesting; I supposed all handsome young men enjoyed a minor-celebrity treatment that they were unaware of. Or maybe it was young people in general these days, from being so coddled as children. I didn't mind. I actually *was* a minor celebrity so I knew what it felt like to have people be interested in the uninteresting things you said. Of course no one out here would recognize me; it was kind of liberating to know that I'd be totally anonymous, neutral, for the next 2,700 miles. His mom was a development coordinator. His wife, Claire, was a receptionist at Palaces, which was an interior design company. She was really talented—everyone said she had an eye for décor. Any siblings? A younger sister, Angela, had competed at the state level in gymnastics and then seriously injured herself. She lived in Sacramento now, taught at Planet Gymnastics.

He wasn't as young as he looked, but he was younger than he thought he was. Thirty-one is young, I said. He winced like I was just being polite. He felt like a fuckup, like he should have done more by now. He'd wasted time on stupid shit. He was working overtime these days; he needed to save up twenty thousand dollars, a "nest egg," and that would take years and years. I nodded, getting it. There was nothing on my person that revealed I'd just been paid twenty thousand dollars for one sentence about hand jobs.

"But what about you," he said, "what do you do?" Did he know this was the first question he'd asked me?

I told him what I did, in vague terms, and that I was driving to New York.

"Ah, it all makes sense, then. Will I be part of your work?"

I smiled.

"No."

"Well, I might make it in. Something you saw on your way to New York." He looked out across the restaurant with resignation, as if this was the field he would spend his whole life tilling. Then suddenly he rolled his head around and crinkled his eyes at me. For a split second I wondered if I'd been had—was this whole thing just an act? Was he entirely knowing? Did he even have a sister? But then he balled up his sandwich wrapper and shot it across the room, not making it into the trash.

"Good luck," he said. "Don't get any speeding tickets."

"I won't." I paid and got back on the freeway, sliding quickly to the leftmost lane and turning up Portishead.

Eventually the ex-girlfriend and the ex–best friend moved out, and because their old apartment was much bigger than mine I asked the landlord if I could move next door. My hands were shaking the first time I unlocked it, as if they might still be in there, still fucking. And in a way they were. They had left a big jar of rice and a long bamboo cane. *Uh.* They'd been caning each other. I put the cane in the dumpster and ate the jar of rice over the next few months, chewing slowly, looking around, making my plans. I lived there for six years. It's where I became myself—or at least a self that would last me a very long time. I never permitted any lovers to move in. I needed to eat messily while reading, to sometimes not get dressed all day. To work in bed. To wake up in the middle of the night with the edge of something brand-new and reel it in until dawn, then take a mentholated bath like a champ after a big fight. Then sleep and sleep and sleep, unmolested. Harris texted. I kept my eyes on the road and he kept texting, the number kept going up. Three, four, five messages. It was almost like I *had* to get off in Duarte, for safety, if I didn't want to make the Oingo Boingo mistake.

The Hertz lot was just right there when I pulled off the freeway so I idled in front of it. I don't like aiding and abetting coincidences so I didn't even glance around, but it would be funny if he knocked on my windshield when I was looking at my phone. The first text was the picture of Sam and me, taken less than an hour ago. And then a text that said, Could you send Astrid's mom's number. And then: Sam wants a playdate with her. And then: Just whenever you stop next. I texted Astrid's mom's number, turned the car off, and began walking around the block the wrong way. The wrong way is the opposite of the way you instinctually want to go. Maybe it sends a little kink down the wire and out into the universe—I'm here— or maybe it just makes you more alert, so you notice more. Not that I would have missed him, walking to his car. He saw me from a little way off and nodded.

"It's going to take you a long time to get to New York," he called out as he neared, "if you stop at every little town."

"I had to . . . my husband was texting—"

He laughed, meaning there was no need to explain. He was taking his keys out of his pocket.

"Back to Monrovia?" I said.

"Yep, done with my route. Home to the missus."

"Claire! Receptionist at Palaces!"

He grinned and shot me a finger like a gun. It didn't really seem like I needed to say goodbye all over again. I smiled brightly and went on my way.

I drove unnecessarily fast, merging across all four lanes. I was driving in the wrong direction, back toward L.A., but that didn't seem like too big a deal. A lot of other cars were headed this way, it's not like I was the only one. I exited in Monrovia. I drove past Fontana's and parked in front of a smoothie shop.

Who really knows why anyone does anything?

I walked around. I browsed a pet supply store and an antique mall. I touched a celluloid doll's leg and a beautiful pink silk bedspread. I got a manicure. I walked back to my car and then walked past it as if it were someone else's car and I lived here.

Who made the stars? Why is there life on Earth?

I sat in the library. I walked around the arboretum. I ate dinner at a restaurant called Sesame Grill. The waiter said something about last year's parade; he thought I was a local and I didn't correct him.

When it started to get dark I drove the car a few blocks up to a motel I'd noticed, the Excelsior.

Nobody knows what's going on. We are thrown across our lives by winds that started blowing millions of years ago.

A lit-up sign said No Vacancy, but the "no" had another "no" written above it. No no vacancy. It was like any other junky motel except for two big, dirty white columns that flanked the parking lot. The man at the front desk said, Two nos make a yes, it was a temporary fix. He looked like an old surfer. I was given a key to room 321, which wasn't on the third floor, he explained, there was only one level. I could pull my car right up to the door if I wanted.

Sam would have run around the room and instead of being disappointed by its drabness, would have ripped the plastic bag off the cup, unwrapped the tiny soap, tried out the bed, turned on the TV, and stood in the closet. I did each of these things myself, slowly. The room was surprisingly large, but this did nothing for it—a more condensed space would have been cozier. The mattress was terribly thin. Once, on a work trip, I'd been put up at Le Bristol, in Paris. As I walked around the suite I began to weep. The wallpaper had pink roses and the carpet and curtains had pink roses and the bed was a beautiful bosom you'd never want to leave. Gilt mirrors, a small marble-topped table, a pair of little Louis XIV chairs gathered in a place where you might want to read a poem. The stationery, the robe, the lotion—each of these things was thicker and more exquisite than I'd previously been aware existed. I began to panic—how would I live after this, now knowing? And then I became angry. Not at the fundamental injustice of luxuries built for an elite minority, no, just that I was only staying for two nights. In the end it was fine. I savored each meal, I took pictures like a dumb tourist, and when the time came to leave I mutely accepted my return to civilian life. I didn't get to keep the paintings I saw at the Louvre, either.

I called Harris. I told him I hadn't gotten as far as I'd hoped.

"Where are you?"

I squinted up at the plastic light fixture in the middle of the ceiling and wondered if all light, no matter its form—candle, lamp, firefly— was from the sun originally.

"I'm near Zion National Park."

"Oh, well, you made it to Utah, that's impressive."

I was getting ready to say something about seeing the view through the windows in the tunnel when I realized he wanted to get off the phone.

"I'm in the middle of something with Caro."

Harris never really wants to hear more than the minimum. Which is okay. There would be a time, after this time of formality, when we would gush to each other. And obviously right now I would only be adding more "lies." Lies in quotes because people always use the word so righteously, as if the truth is a naturally occurring diamond. But fine, call it lying. Each person does the amount of lying that is right for them. You have to know yourself and fulfill the amount of untruth that your constitution requires. I knew many women (like my own dear Jordi) who simply couldn't handle the feeling lying gave them—it wasn't their bag.

"What you see is what you get," these women said about themselves. For me lying created just the right amount of problems and what you saw was just one of my four or five faces—each real, each with different needs. The only dangerous lie was one that asked me to compress myself down into a single convenient entity that one person could understand. I was a kaleidoscope, each glittering piece of glass changing as I turned.

"Some people might say a kaleidoscope shouldn't get married, at least not to someone so traditional," Jordi had said when I told her this theory.

"But I have a traditional side, too," I said. "Must I be entirely that to marry? Do we ask this of men? No, that would be humiliating for them since they get their sense of self from their work and from the power and majesty with which they walk through this world as a self-owning creature. Same."

One day when we were both ready I would reveal my whole self to Harris; this would be like presenting a sweater knitted in secrecy.

Oh. My. God, he would say. *How did you find time to do this?!*

Just here and there, whenever I could. Sometimes even with you right there beside me.

I didn't even know you could knit!

There are a lot of things you don't know about me; that's the whole point of this sweater metaphor.

Of course if you're knitting for years the sweater eventually becomes so huge that it simply can't be hidden.

CHAPTER 6

The next morning I lay motionless on the scrawny bed for two hours. I told myself this was okay since it was easier to be present lying there than it would be back on the road; I was still working toward my overall goal. The sudden absence of responsibility was a floaty, frothy, almost hallucinogenic weightlessness. No one to make breakfast for, no need to pack a five-part bento box lunch, no need to yell Put on your shoes! Brush your teeth! (Kindly but firmly, again and again, not nagging but not indulging and always keeping in mind the future adult who was being shaped *right now*.) Why aren't your shoes on? Where are they? Here they are. That's the wrong foot.

No need to say any of these words and no one to drive to school.

There was a rap on the door and then it swung open with the shouted word *Housekeeping!* I didn't move.

"Checkout is eleven o'clock," said Housekeeping.

I looked at the clock. It was 11:16.

"You'll have to pay for another day if you aren't out in fifteen minutes."

She had a faint accent or speech impediment. Her name tag said Helen.

"I'll pay for another day."

"Okay then." She looked around the room, not even discreetly. My stuff was strewn everywhere.

"Would you like your room cleaned?"

"No, that's fine."

"Fresh towels?"

"No, thank you."

I got up and ate a PowerBar and walked back to the antique mall. I didn't go straight to the pretty bedspread because I didn't want the woman who worked there to think I especially wanted it. It was densely filled and quilted in a star pattern, satiny but not garish, salmon colored. It was the sort of very feminine and decadent thing I'd wanted my whole life; I was so good at knowing what I wanted and then choosing something else at the very last second.

"How much is this?"

"Two hundred."

I gasped.

"It's from the 1920s, in perfect condition."

"I'll give you one-twenty for it."

"Oh, that's not negotiable. It's an immaculate piece. I actually shouldn't even be selling it; it's museum quality."

Sometimes my hatred of older women almost knocked me over, it came on so abruptly. These "free spirits" who thought they could just invent the value of things.

"What museum?" I said.

"Excuse me?"

"What museum? A bedspread museum?"

She looked at me with surprise and turned away sharply. And now I felt the opposite of hatred. Who better to decide the worth of things? She was maybe fifteen years older than me. Been there, done that, nobody's fool. She wasn't even ugly, just not young, a little chubby. Until recently she had been a better-looking woman than me and she knew this at a glance.

"I'll take it. For two hundred."

She silently took it off its wooden rack and began wrapping it in tissue paper. I put down my credit card and lowered my eyes.

"One-twenty was a ridiculous counter," she said. "You should have started at one-sixty. I probably would've let you have it for one-seventy-five." She rang me up for two hundred and I made a mental note that she owed me twenty-five dollars. Not that I was going to ask for it; I wouldn't unless I had lost everything and everyone and had nowhere else to turn.

I took the bedspread to a dry cleaner because who wants to drive across the country with something musty smelling up the car. They said it could be ready by three o'clock the next day. I checked the calendar on my phone; all I had tomorrow was "Denver to Kansas City." I was given a claim stub. If anyone wondered what I was doing or who I was affiliated with I could bring out the stub: *These people expect to see me at three o'clock, or shortly thereafter.* Not an appointment exactly but certainly a commitment. Everyone thinks they're so securely bound into their lives. Really I had done almost nothing to end up here. I had walked the wrong way around the block and then gone the wrong direction on the freeway.

Since I was now definitely going to be staying another night I unpacked my suitcase and put all my clothes in the cheap chest of drawers that was really just for show. I hung my New York outfits in the closet. Using my travel steamer I steamed my skirts and blouses. Some of the outfits were androgynous—a little menswear, a little street style. I left these things in my suitcase in favor of my more overtly feminine and form-fitting clothes. Heels and pencil skirts, cropped sweaters, shirtwaist dresses with tight belts around the smallest part of my waist. Every old thing had a modern counterbalance; past age forty you had to be careful with vintage. I didn't want to be mistaken for an elderly woman wearing clothes from the 1960s of her youth. Young people especially had trouble making distinctions between ages over forty. When I got my first Patti Smith tape, *Horses*, at twenty-two, Smith was only forty-nine. But I didn't think of her as a contemporary person; I wasn't even sure she was still alive because the cover of *Horses* was a black-and-white photograph.

Instead of knowing that this was a stylistic choice, like vintage clothes, I unconsciously associated the record with the deep past of black-and-white movies. If anyone asked I would have probably managed to assign the album to the right decade, but most of life is a vapor of unconscious associations, never brought to light. A good way to check your outfit is by running past the mirror, or better yet, make a video of yourself running past your phone. How old was that blur of a woman? Was she from the past or was she modern? And where was she going in such a hurry?

I walked around Monrovia in a red shirtwaist dress and white wedge heels. The commercial areas weren't really built for walking, but there were some nice residential neighborhoods. Several times I passed teenage girls wearing backpacks, their breasts inflated by the hormones in cow's milk and barely covered by tank tops. Whenever I saw them coming I pretended I was from another country, projecting the air of someone so foreign she could not understand or be hurt by anything American. I methodically walked in every area, as if I was looking for something but with nothing particular in mind. Near the freeway there were chain stores like Michaels and Bed Bath & Beyond and it was around here that I saw a Budget Rent-a-Car in the distance. I paused and swept my eyes across the street, already knowing what would be there: Hertz. I stared at it with a funny feeling before turning and retracing my steps back to the Excelsior.

Jordi thought that it was terrific that I was already off-schedule.

"That's the whole point! Just follow beauty!"

I looked around the weirdly big, drab room.

"I'm trying."

I bought some food at Grocery Outlet. I watched TV. I took a bath. In the morning I did these same things again in the same order as if this had been my routine for years. It felt very natural. In the afternoon I retrieved the bedspread and carried it back to the motel, feeling a bit conspicuous with such a big bundle. But who was going to see me? I smoothed the pink coverlet out on the double bed and stepped back, taking in the whole picture. The maroon carpet looked more intentional now, elevated by the coverlet; too bad it was such poor quality. I could imagine a little vase of flowers on the desk. Above the bed there was a greenish-gray painting so blandly abstract it was of nothing at all. I lifted it off its clip and slid it under the bed with the original bedspread.

I felt very alive, kind of buzzy.

I had never really decorated, not with actual money. Harris already owned our house before I met him so I just moved in, which took all of twenty minutes. His dishes and furniture and bedding were of a higher caliber than mine so I gave my few things to Goodwill, installed my books and clothes, and hung my purple toiletries bag from a hook in the bathroom. When friends came over I would immediately take them aside and explain that almost nothing in this house was mine, this wasn't even my style. It was actually more sophisticated than my style; there was an enormous square, black wooden table with eight matching chairs around it. Where would you even buy such a thing? In time I just let people believe it was all mine ("ours," whatever). And some of it is: our spoons, for example. We kept losing spoons until finally there were only three in rotation. I can solve this, I thought. I can single-handedly make this problem go away. And I did. Top-of-the-line spoons, too—ten of them. Sometimes when we are in the middle of an especially bad argument I think: I'll just take my spoons and leave.

Were the nylon motel curtains intentionally ecru or just dingy? Even if you replaced nothing else, new curtains (plus the bedspread) would completely refresh the room; you didn't have to be an interior designer to see that. Although, actually, I did know of an interior designer in Monrovia—or at least the receptionist of one. I looked up Palaces. It was a strip club, but also there was a listing for *Palaces by Stephanie Rosenbaum*. The woman who answered the phone said Palacesbystephanierosenbaum with such force that it took me a moment to reorganize.

"Hi."

"You'd like to speak with Stephanie?"

I sensed Stephanie was right there and that they were both in Stephanie's live/work space.

"No, no, not exactly, no. Is this Claire?"

"Yes?"

It took a few tries to get her to understand that I wanted to work with *her*, not Stephanie Rosenbaum. Once she got it her voice dropped to a whisper and she said she would text me her number. A very discreet woman. I called her after five and gave her the address of the motel.

She was tiny and pretty with long sandy-blond hair and delicate, ringed fingers. Looking at her girlish hands I felt certain that she and Davey had lots of cuddling and special squeezes, maybe even a wrestling game they did that always left her in a pile of giggles but then sometimes led to fucking. I'm so alert to intimacy; at a glance I can immediately tell what a person's capacity for it is. Here in my room she was polished and professional, holding a notepad and pretending I wasn't her first real client. She paced around, opened the closet, peeked in the bathroom. I told her about Le Bristol in Paris. She looked it up on her phone and said, "Louis XIV, Provincial style," as if this was a snap, a style she'd done a hundred times. She crouched down and tugged on the baseboard, experimentally prying it loose and then rejoining it with a pound of her little fist. I raised my eyebrows; this was a tad invasive for my level of ownership.

"So do all the rooms have the same floor plan?"

"Oh, you'd just be decorating this one. This is the one I'm staying in. Just a few little improvements."

I watched her cock her head to the side and hold her breath. Was I crazy? she was wondering. No. Crazy was spending thousands of dollars on a hotel room and walking away empty-handed, a totally passive observer. If I canceled today I could still get my deposit back from the Carlyle, thank God.

"I really just want to replace a few things."

"And are you— Is that okay with . . . ?"

"Do you not do rentals?" I asked.

"Well, we—I—do, I do, but just to be clear, you're—"

"I rent by the day."

"And how long will you be here?"

"I mean, whatever happens, I have to leave in two and a half weeks." Arkanda.

"I see. Do you think it's . . . worth it? For that short a time?"

"I do. Do you?"

I watched her think about the nest egg.

"Yes, of course. Have you ever worked with a decorator?"

"No." In fact I had harshly judged people who worked with decorators. But I was following beauty now. "How much would it be, by the way, for this room?"

"Right . . ." She glanced around appraisingly.

There was only one correct number: I knew she needed twenty thousand, or her husband did, but would she have the guts to say it? She was taking some arbitrary measurements using an app on her phone. She squinted at the ceiling.

"I'm gonna say . . . in the ballpark of . . . eighteen thousand. That might seem like a lot, but that includes all the materials and any furniture that needs to be replaced."

Almost. She was doing that thing that women do; begging for what you want by not asking for it.

"Of course I'd need it to be done in just two or three days," I added. "So I'll have time to enjoy it. Did you include a rush fee?"

"I didn't. So let's just call it twenty."

Good girl.

Somewhat unexpectedly, she had great taste. On the first day she brought books of wallpaper with Post-its on all the rose patterns but also on rich botanical prints with jewel-toned parrots in tropical trees right out of the eighteenth century. She understood what was special about the pink bedspread against the maroon industrial carpet—in the afternoon she covered it with an even richer maroon, a Grand Parterre Sarouk carpet made of New Zealand wool. As she measured, cut, and then carefully nailed it down with tiny, gemlike nails I wondered how many seconds until someone from the motel knocked on the door. Five? Seven? Eight seconds. I opened the door on the first knock and before the old surfer could say anything Claire said, Hi Skip, and asked him to take off his shoes. He looked down at the plush carpet and then slid off his flip-flops, looking uneasy. He padded slowly around the room. Claire paused her work, hammer in air.

"Feels good, right?"

"Feels expensive," he said. "I'm not paying for this."

"She's paying."

He couldn't stop kneading the carpet with his long toes. He cleared his throat.

"In any case, this violates the terms of your guest agreement. I mean, probably. It's probably destruction of property."

Claire made an offended noise.

"Can we decide that when I check out?" I said. "After you see the overall effect?"

"There's more that you're planning?"

"It's a whole vision," said Claire, rising to her feet. "Some of our key words are Brunelleschi, burgundy, persimmon, dahlias, and tonka bean."

I wouldn't have said the key words.

"Tonka bean. Now that's . . . what is that again?"

"It smells like dark honey and cherries," she said.

"Oh." He nodded slowly, squinting. "My mom had a porcelain ball— not really a ball, more like an egg, with lots of little holes in it. It smelled like that."

"A pomander," said Claire.

"Maybe," he murmured.

"It's Victorian."

"That sounds right."

"We're gonna get back to work."

"I should get going, too," he said, and drifted out the door. Claire shut it quietly behind him. Her power was impressive, probably Daddy's little girl.

At the end of the day she dragged the horrible mattress off the bed and we carried it to her hatchback.

"I'll be right back with the replacement. It's really nice—memory foam." She scanned my face to see if I knew what that was. For some reason she thought she was more worldly than me.

"I know what memory foam is."

"Okay. So then you know it takes about a week to completely off-gas."

I didn't know this, not the exact time frame. I mentioned I was very sensitive to smells.

"Of course," she said. "The one I'm bringing now has already been off-gassed; in a week or so I'll switch it out with your one. It's breathing in my backyard right now."

What a complicated mattress plan.

"So the one you're bringing . . . why can't I just keep that one?"

"Well, you probably want the brand-new one since you paid for it."

"Right. Thank you." It still seemed overly complex.

She toddled off with the old mattress and in less than twenty minutes came back with the memory foam one. It was considerably heavier. We dragged it awkwardly onto the bed and remade it with the thick white sheets she'd brought that morning.

"Try it out. You'll love it."

I sat on it gingerly. It was very nice; I couldn't help smiling. She smiled back.

"It's my own mattress."

I stood up immediately.

"Oh—I didn't think you would mind," she said, "since the motel one was filthy."

I stared at the bed.

"Where will you and . . ." The name Davey seemed overly familiar, as if I really knew him. ". . . your husband sleep?"

"Oh, we're easy," she said. "We have an air mattress—it'll be fun! Like camping."

———

That first day of the renovation was day four of the trip: Kansas City to Indianapolis. As Harris noted, I had made up for lost time and was back on schedule. He asked me if my neck was aching and I said it wasn't. One fine day I would tell him all about me, and this trip would be one of my stories. We would be holding each other in bed, saying everything, laughing and crying and being amazed at all the things we didn't know about each other, the Great Reveal. Sometimes it would be painful, like if he told me about fingering his assistant, but none of it would be threatening because our current level of intimacy would be so high that there was no room or desire for anyone or anything else. We would just want to hold each other for the rest of our days (which might not be that many, depending on when this happened). Even though the amount of catharsis would be off the charts Harris still might get lost in the weeds so there should not be lots of little inventions for him to comb through; he shouldn't have to say, "But what about the light on the wheat in Kansas? You just made that up?"

I didn't go on about wheat or my aching back or anything else. He said something general about work being hard. It was possible that he, too, was sparing me lots of made-up specifics to paw through later when he revealed what his "work" really was.

"Sam wants to talk to you," he said, and the child came crashing on the line. They wanted to know if I had a present for them already. Had I gotten them something giant at the museum of big things?

Caught off guard, I said I had. This was a mistake, obviously. (One that would never quite go away.)

Can I see it? they said, suddenly switching to FaceTime with the horrifying technological fluidity of a child. I quickly surveyed the motel parking lot where I was pacing. It could be anywhere.

Look at you, I said. I miss your wonderful face. My eyes filled.

Is it a big pencil?

No.

Can I see it? Why is it so dark there?

I'm outside.

Where's the pencil?

It's not a pencil. You'll see it when I get home, it's a surprise.

Come home right now! they squealed.

I thought about it. For the record: on the evening of the fourth day— the first day of renovation—the pain was so sharp I briefly considered driving home and telling the whole thing like a funny story. If I had actually been driving across the country the pain wouldn't be this bad; what made it excruciating was how innocently Sam and Harris were going about their lives, unaware of my nearness. Why do such a thing? What kind of monster makes a big show of going away and then hides out right nearby?

But this was no good, this line of thought. This was the thinking that had kept every woman from her greatness. There did not have to be an answer to the question why; everything important started out mysterious and this mystery was like a great sea you had to be brave enough to cross. How many times had I turned back at the first ripple of self-doubt? You had to withstand a profound sense of wrongness if you ever wanted to get somewhere new. So far each thing I had done in Monrovia was guided by a version of me that had never been in charge before. A nitwit? A madwoman? Probably. But my more seasoned parts just had to be patient, hold their tongues—their many and sharp tongues—and give this new girl a chance.

I told Jordi, of course.

"So you're staying there . . . for the whole time?"

"Well, I'm taking it as it comes. But at a certain point there won't be enough time to make it to New York and back."

"There's a fabricator in Monrovia," she said. "I used to go there all the time when I was working in fiberglass."

"Then you know it's close."

"Real close."

I told her about redecorating the room, the wallpaper, the carpet.

She said I sounded excited.

"Do I?" But now I could hear what she meant. My whole body felt like it was vibrating with nonspecific anticipation. I wanted to break out into a high-pitched keening noise.

"But why there?" she said. "Why not a prettier place at least?"

I said I didn't know. I had stopped for gas, and then lunch . . .

"There was one funny thing, actually."

I told her about the boy I'd seen on all three stops. It was his wife who was doing the room.

Jordi told me about a folktale where a troll appears three times. She's always bringing up things from mythology and history. If it was anyone else I would be so bored by this, but with her I kind of like it. In the folktale it's ultimately not the troll himself who is important, it's the number three. Maybe this was like that?

I said I thought maybe it was. We mused about if she should come visit me; she shouldn't because that would make her complicit in a lie. My friend: she's very good. Like a nun or a saint—not a prude, just kind of holy. Now she was telling me a dream she'd had about chiseling green marble.

That night I lay in the pitch-black room on Claire and Davey's marriage bed, under the star coverlet. It felt like I was lying in the center of a ritual offering, an elaborate spell. In two more days the room would be ready. Ready for what? I tried to make the high-pitched keening noise, but each time it came out too mournful, like a wail, the bleat of a lost goat.

Claire did this thing where she knocked *as* she was opening the door with the key I'd given her, so I was always scrambling to pull myself together, wiping my face, tucking in my shirt, while she said Hi, hi, hiii! Today she hurried into the bathroom, where she placed a glass bottle of tonka bean bodywash and some lotion made by Italian nuns. She pulled the thin hotel towels off the rack and replaced them with new snowy white ones that came from a giant canvas tote.

"Touch," she said, pointing at the new towels. I politely patted one and then rubbed it with both hands and pressed my face into it. It was the nicest towel I'd ever felt. So thick and absorbent it made all previous towels seem like sad little rags. There was a giant bath sheet, a hand towel, a washcloth, and another one that Claire described as a "demi-towel"—it was for anything truly dirty, like a toothpastey mouth or hair with conditioner in it. "The demi-towel preserves the other towels for your face and body," she said, placing it beside the sink.

"Did you make up 'demi-towel'?" I whispered.

"You can just leave the towels wherever and Helen will replace them with a clean set every day, just the same as usual." I noticed Claire ignored about half the things I said to her, which made me feel a little like I was talking to my hard-of-hearing mother.

While Claire and a plumber replaced the little bathtub with a different, better bathtub and "rainshower" head I sat in my car, making calls. I told my manager, Liza, to cancel the reservation at the Carlyle and my meeting with the feminist shoe designer and to try to get a refund on the tickets for the one-woman off-Broadway show, although, I emphasized, that was less important than canceling the hotel, which, alone, ate up more than half of the whiskey money.

Liza didn't ask why. She wasn't someone I ever had to explain myself to or be embarrassed in front of since she had no actual interest in my field; she was just someone I'd gone to high school with. During a rough, postdivorce financial patch, she'd reached out to our entire class, and even though I had never once talked to her in school I said she could assist me for a few months until she got back on her feet. During those months I finished the body of work that would make my name, and Liza, I guess, managed things. In any case it had gone well and now that she was everyone's point of contact it never felt right to ask if she could move on, especially once she was diagnosed with fibromyalgia. Harris loves to speculate about how much money I could have made over the years if I had a real manager instead of Liza.

I can never quite explain how the terms of my success are built upon an agreement to carry this person on my back for the rest of my life. There has to be a burden to keep everything in balance. (Needless to say, a man would never get bogged down in this kind of weird financial penance.) Also everyone likes Liza. Everywhere I go, all over the world, people ask *How's Liza?* and are slightly disappointed that I'm not as gregarious as she is. After events, if I'm made to go out, I usually wind up answering their questions about Liza and kind of elaborating on our relationship, making it sound like we were lovers in high school and now that I'm married, we persist, slightly tortured by our attraction, forever bound. This isn't at all true. But there is often one masc-of-center woman or nonbinary person among the faculty hosts and they blink as I tell this story, take a sip of their sober beverage, look at their shoes, and when they look up I meet their eyes with a hot *yes*. I don't take it further than this. I only need my lesbianism held and kept, like a person who buries little bits of money all over the world—it's never on me, but it's never far.

"Where are you now?" Liza asked before we got off.

"Almost to Pittsburgh."

"So, tomorrow New York."

"Tomorrow New York," I said, watching a fellow guest clean something off the back seat of her car with wet wipes. Probably child's vomit.

I canceled all my friend dates with a text explaining that I'd had an artistic revelation and was going to use my time at the Carlyle as a solo writing retreat but I'd reach out next time I was in town. One friend wrote, Go get 'em tiger / can't wait to see the world you are conjuring! I tried to let the self-loathing blow past me like a cloud. There was only one friend, a woman named Mary, who I was too close with to do this, so to her I just said I was having a bit of a crisis but I couldn't go into it now.

"As in . . . midlife?"

I laughed, no. Although maybe midlife crises were just poorly marketed, maybe each one was profound and unique and it was only a few silly men in red convertibles who gave them a bad name. I imagined greeting such a man solemnly: I see you have reached a time of great questioning. God be with you, seeker.

"Are you having an affair?"

"No, no, nothing like that."

"Menopause?"

I laughed. Mary was older than me and obsessed with hot flashes. She took the opportunity now to tell me a story about putting her head in the freezer at a party, and I laughed again. I kind of liked not knowing anything about this stuff. My ignorance made me feel like a sweet little sister, practically a child.

"But if it ever comes up, we had lunch, okay?"

"We had lunch and it was delicious and I loved seeing you," Mary said.

This made me whimper. Probably I should have just driven to New York.

"I love you."

"I love you, too. Good luck, sweetie."

After lunch Claire breathlessly wheeled in a heavy box on a little collapsible luggage trolley.

"This is the last of these. Completely discontinued, vintage from Portugal." She threw her purse down and began puzzling hexagonal tiles together on the bathroom floor. "First I went to International Stone and Tile and they were so overpriced that I thought what the hell, I might as well take a look at Radwill's."

Radwill's. I passed that sign every day on my way to Sam's school. I wanted to believe that we were farther away than that, but of course we weren't. Should I drive past the school to maybe catch a glimpse of recess? No, that would be creepy.

I knelt beside Claire and started fitting the hexagons along the edge of the bathtub.

"Use these ones for that." She pointed toward a stack of half hexagons. Not sawed in half, but ingeniously designed for edges. The tiles were pale green with gold stars formed by joining with two others. Each hexagon had the possibility of creating three stars if it could be completely encircled by six more, a mathematically expanding galaxy. We moved quickly across the floor, our patterns occasionally joining in the manner of people silently collaborating on a giant jigsaw puzzle. We wanted to know if there would be enough to cover the whole floor and as the stacks dwindled it seemed less and less likely . . . there was a hurry to the finish, both of us sweaty now. I handed her the final tiles. She pressed them into place.

"Almost. Just three or four short," she said, sitting back on her heels and blowing air under her bangs. "I can get a few solid green ones; I'll hide them behind the toilet."

I stood and took in the whole floor, hypnotized by the repeating design. It was giving me a peculiar feeling.

"If we'd had the exact amount," I said, "like if the pattern had been complete, doesn't it feel like something might have . . . *happened*?"

"I'll prepare the floor and cement them down," she said. "You'll have to be a little careful for forty-eight hours."

I was thinking of illusions that become so complete they actually opened up into other dimensions. I tried to think if this ever really happened or if it was just something I'd wanted for so long that it felt familiar. A mean little tap on the door startled us. I hurried across the room and peeked out.

"I'm good for towels, thanks."

"She'll be using her own towels, Helen."

The woman eyed Claire, who was shamelessly opening the door all the way.

"Starting when?" said Helen.

"Starting now. You can wash them the same as the others."

"Not if they're not white I can't. We bleach them."

"They're white." She handed Helen the canvas tote. "There are three sets so there's no reason she shouldn't always have clean towels."

Helen took the bag and looked huffily down at the new carpet, the wallpaper, the vintage coverlet.

"I can't be held responsible for any damage to the coverlet."

"No, of course. You're not to clean that."

I blushed. She was treating Helen so poorly. But maybe this was just a fuller, more honest expression of my own classism.

"Helen was my uncle's wife," said Claire. "But she cheated on him, so he divorced her."

Helen nodded in agreement and opened her mouth to add something.

"It was a long time ago," said Claire quickly.

"Not so long ago," said Helen, sort of brightening and softening. "You girls are too young to understand, but you'll see."

"I'm forty-five," I said.

"Oh. Then you know all about it." She gave me a warning look that meant we wouldn't say more in the presence of the young woman. I couldn't tell if this was to protect Claire from the horrors to come, or because there was a real secret we were keeping for ourselves. I was pretty sure I *didn't* know all about it.

On the third and final day Claire made me stay out of the room all afternoon while she "QCed" it.

"Quality control," she explained.

"I know," I said.

I walked around and called all the friends I could think of. They were lonely conversations because I could reveal almost nothing about my current situation, so I only asked about them. Some people are authentically like this, always asking another question, dodging anything personal. What a miserable life, or maybe it's fine for them. I went to Grocery Outlet and came out with just enough food for that day. No point in robbing myself of tomorrow's shopping trip since I had no other plans. As I walked I became aware of a car rolling slowly alongside me.

It was Davey. He didn't seem overly surprised to see me with a bag of groceries on my hip.

"Change of plans?" he said, lowering the window.

"Yes."

"It is pretty great here." A joke. We laughed. I shifted my groceries to the other hip and looked toward the Excelsior.

"I won't keep you," he said. "Just wanted to say hi."

I started walking again and he drove slowly alongside me. I couldn't quite remember why I was in such a hurry. I almost had the urge to run.

"If you're still here on Memorial Day you can see the parade. It's not much, but if you like that small-town stuff. Or I could give you a tour, show you around."

"I don't know if I'll still be here," I said, ignoring the part about the tour.

"No?" he said, and I shrugged like a person with no ties, a drifter. There was something weird about this conversation, I couldn't put my finger on it. He drove off with a wave and I kept walking. Trotting along. There was no mention of his wife's renovation. That was the weird thing. Neither of us had brought it up.

Claire made me hand the groceries to her and wait outside. The room was done and even though I had slept in it every night and participated in its progress, she wanted to give me a tour at the end as if it were all new to me. I think she got this from home transformation TV shows that end with a breathtaking reveal. She had me get in my car and then get out again as if I had just pulled up; she videoed me walking toward the shabby, pale-yellow stucco motel. I fumbled with my key and she stepped forward, zooming in on my face-about-to-be-transformed-with-joy. I swung the door open and I actually didn't have to pretend. Somehow Chopin was playing and with all the finishing touches—framed Audubon prints, a marble-topped desk—the motel room's tasteful opulence was shocking. Not as extreme as Le Bristol, but I was moved. The new sheer curtains let light in like the old polyester ones but were framed by chintz drapes patterned with pink peonies and apricot dahlias that picked up the same peonies and dahlias buried in the wallpaper, between the birds. How was this possible? Were they made by the same company? I touched the fat golden tassel at the end of a hanging cord.

"Pull it," said Claire.

I pulled it and the drapes glided shut, filtering the daylight into an otherworldly rosy-gold. Claire tiptoed around, pointing things out, her face glowing angelically in the golden curtain-light. She showed me how I could hook up my phone to a sound system that was "just a notch below Sonos." In the closet, next to the safe, was a sleek black toaster oven.

"The top of the toaster oven is a hot plate, see?"

I could have looked at it forever, so shiny, but she kept moving. There were two pink velvet chairs I hadn't seen before, intimately angled toward each other. I sat in one, fingering its dark carved wood.

"These are special," Claire said, smoothing the velvet. "I've saved these for a long time, under plastic, in our garage."

"Oh. You should keep them!" I stood up.

"No, no, they don't fit with our style—I was saving them for the right client."

Our. The style of her and Davey. I imagined IKEA shelves and the easygoing crappiness of a young home. I mean, I'd never lived like that, my crappiness was always labored and striving, but I could see how you wouldn't want these two stolid chairs crowding the living room like judgmental parents.

"They're called 'great chairs.'"

"Well, they are great."

"No, like great-grandparent, or . . ."

"I get it. I was making a joke."

Claire smiled, a demi-smile, preserving her real one for things she really thought were funny. We had never clicked, but it didn't matter. I took out my phone and she told me her Venmo and I sent her twenty thousand dollars, at which point we learned there's a limit of $4,999.99 on Venmo so I found my purse and dug out my ancient checkbook. The receipt of the last check I had written was for a massage two years ago.

What would the next check be for? And what would I feel when Claire stepped out the door and I was suddenly alone, not in New York with all its possibilities but in Monrovia, where I already knew every major street and store? I could already feel depression coming on, its tsunami wall rising up. Claire left and I folded to the floor and then she came back— she forgot to return her room key—and I quickly tried to swing myself upward, but it wasn't really worth the effort. I sank back down and she said bye again but not without a little fear, I was crazy after all, but what did she care—she'd been paid.

CHAPTER 7

The finished room was hard to leave and not because it was so beautiful. I stayed in for the next two days, mostly under the coverlet, mostly watching TV. Harris texted and I replied that New York wasn't so great, I missed the drive, which probably wasn't what a real cross-country driver would feel, but I was trying to be honest. He said he was kind of relieved I'd gotten there safely and I wondered if I would have or if I would have crashed somewhere along the way. As the sun set it seemed I had, that I was stuck in some terrible purgatory, neither here nor there, not home but not really anywhere else. The room being so beautiful only made the fugue louder, worse. Was I supposed to work here? Finally come up with an idea and then throw myself into it for the rest of my time, inspired by the setting? I imagined telling the story of the room renovation to interviewers. Wow, they would say, you have so much faith in your practice. Not really, I would say, and then I would describe this very day, how lost I felt. I knew no one in this town. I had run out of most of my food except for several bags of trail mix, so I just ate that, for every meal.

I planned on sleeping as much as possible the following day, but in the late morning there was suddenly a tremendous racket as if the whole town were gathering outside my room. Shouts and metal chairs dragged and music turned on and off and then on again. I peeked out between the curtains. Booths were being erected, platforms. It was as if the locus of an event was right in front of the motel, and it was. The parade. It was Memorial Day. I lay in bed with the trail mix and listened with an achy feeling in all my limbs.

At ten a.m. Harris texted: Happy May 31

My stomach lurched. Sam's due date. One of us always texted the other.

Seven years ago, eight weeks before May thirty-first, I had been sleeping soundly when, just before dawn, a very, very young voice cried out.

Wake up wake up wake up, it said.

But I'm so tired.

Wake up wake up WAKE UP! WAKE UP!

I sat bolt upright with one hand on my massive belly and shook Harris awake. We moved elegantly like astronauts who had spent years training for this outer space emergency and now here we were, wordlessly putting on our shoes, getting in the car. Dr. Mendoza, my ob-gyn, began a sentence with the words "I know you wanted a natural birth, but—" I stood up and began walking out the door in my gown and bare feet.

"Where are you going?"

"To surgery," I said. "Where's the room? We don't have time for this conversation." I would've cut myself open if that's what it took.

A male nurse told me to arch my back "like a scared cat" while he did the spinal tap to numb me from the waist down. There was no pain, but I could feel Dr. Mendoza cutting open the dull meat of my uterus and shoving things around; it took some muscle, like opening and emptying a pumpkin. I squeezed Harris's hand the whole time and from the silence in the room I knew things weren't going well. *Oh*, I thought, *this is the great trauma of my life. Here it is, finally.*

I turned my head and saw a tiny but perfect paper-white baby on a tray. Was it dead? No one seemed to know or be willing to say.

Just minutes later I was sitting in a mechanical bed, abruptly empty and stapled shut. The tiny baby was in the NICU being intubated and receiving blood transfusions. Outcome TBD.

As she hooked me up to a catheter a nurse described how at some point almost all the baby's blood had drained out through the umbilical cord, into me. Fetal-maternal Hemorrhage.

"Sometimes it happens because of a sudden impact, like a car crash. But not always. Sometimes it happens for no reason."

No reason. Well, that wasn't going to be good enough to last me for the rest of my life. Even if this baby lived I was going to need more reason than no reason. The nurse squeezed my bag of fluids and started to leave.

"Wait."

She paused wearily.

"Will Dr. Mendoza come in and explain all this?"

"Explain . . . ?"

"Fetal-maternal—what just happened."

"I told you pretty much everything. You should try to remember if there was an accident."

"No accident," Harris said.

"But is there a pamphlet or something?" I said. "A piece of paper about it?" We had collected lots of these handouts during the past seven months—about diabetes, preeclampsia. Harris nodded. We needed a handout, given that there was no baby here.

"No. Nothing like that for this," the nurse said. "Because it's very rare."

"How rare? Like, do you know the odds?"

"No, you'd have to look that up."

Look it up, right. At some point I would reconnect with my purse and phone and I could look it up.

"Do you know if there's an online . . . like a chat room for women who've been through this?"

She paused in the doorway and looked at me as if I really wasn't getting it.

"That would be a chat room of mothers with stillborn babies."

The nurse left and Harris and I looked at each other from opposite ends of the small room, his face a sunken gray mask. We said nothing for a few minutes, our new reality descending like night falling forever. Then he brought two fingers to his forehead, our old salute. I saluted back from my metal bed.

Yes, same to you, I texted. Happy due date.

Our elegant choreography, our duet, had continued as we drove back and forth to the hospital for the next seventeen days in a shared nightmare so inconceivable that we told almost no one. We didn't want intruders clumsily trying to comfort us. Our pain was ecstatic! We were of one mind, waiting and praying in concert; us against the surreal world we saw out the car window. People were waiting in line for brunch while we waited to see if our baby would live or die. Every stupid song on the radio was vivid and moving to us—*our* songs, all of them. And even after we brought the tiny baby home, the oneness continued. We had sex at strange hours and a little sooner than was advised because we could not wait; once we did it at the foot of the bed while the baby slept up near the headboard. It was a wartime romance: fucking in the face of death, amid the rubble.

It didn't last. No. On or around May thirty-first Sam achieved a very basic milestone—bringing their small fists near their mouth or something—that was cause for celebration. We began, on this day, to think Sam might be basically okay, and so with no acknowledgment or goodbye, we returned to our posts. Harris, relieved, became calm and composed again and I, though also relieved, kept one hand on the fire alarm and missed my wartime lover.

But we had once been close and so we could be again, though I shuddered to think what kind of cataclysmic event would be required to bring this about.

The Memorial Day parade was never-ending. There were hours of megaphone narration and cheering and music—sometimes marching brass instruments, sometimes rock played through a PA. It seemed like it had gone on for five or six hours. Was I sick? My face was sweating, my eyes were moist. I held my head over the toilet as if I was about to vomit but didn't.

And then, seemingly with no warning, it was over. Everyone went home. I hobbled to the window and peeked out through the curtains. A man was collecting trash, otherwise everything was back to normal. It was a perfect late afternoon. I straightened up and suddenly felt fine, just hungry. I bathed quickly, put on a pencil skirt, and went out. I ate at a Japanese restaurant: miso soup, agedashi tofu, spicy tuna rice cakes. I kept ordering more and more items and drinking tea and adding rice to broth and slurping it up. I was free to do anything I wanted. I went back to the room to brush my teeth and then I walked across town to the area by the freeway with the chain stores. An electric gong chimed four o'clock. The Hertz lot was fluttering red, white, and blue flags, but it seemed like nobody was there. No one was at the counter. I dinged the bell and a groggy-looking old man wandered out. Happy Memorial Day, he croaked. His name tag said Glenn-Allen.

"Is Davey here?"

"He went to the parade."

"It's over now."

"Oh, is it? Then he'll be coming back any second."

I sat in a row of connected chairs. Was this a bad idea? Should I leave? Glenn-Allen raised his eyebrows and pointed at the window: Davey was coming. I wasn't going to turn or stand up, but the old man kept pointing, he wouldn't stop, so finally I turned and looked, but I didn't say hi or exclaim and neither did Davey. He went straight to the counter and picked up the company phone.

"Can I take off?" he said in a low voice. He looked at me, blankly, as people do when they're on the phone. "No, there's no one here. It's dead." He said okay a few times and then hung up. "Let's go."

Go where?

"How do you know I'm not here to rent a car?" I said, as a joke, but it was unclear where the humor lay. My mom often flirted with whatever young man happened to be around—it was horrifying to witness. Hopefully Davey and Glenn-Allen didn't think I was flirting.

I followed him out and on to the main street, Foothill Boulevard, past the dry cleaner, past the antique mall.

"What kind of tour would you like?" he said. "What would be most helpful for your work?"

A tour, right. My "work."

"I guess, just, the area . . . ? From a local's perspective."

So he pointed to things and told me what they were and his relationship to them.

"Church, but not the religious kind."

What?

"My mom has her gatherings there."

"What kind of gatherings?"

"Uhhh, they're women's . . . maybe crafts? That's the pool."

As if I wouldn't have known the pool was the pool. Despite the area's obvious limitations, he couldn't help but feel that everything that had to do with him was a little bit interesting and unique, and after being so alone it was a relief to be guided. We hiked up into the hills, a fancy neighborhood called Hidden Valley, like the salad dressing, and he explained that he had a calling, not renting cars, something else that he would tell me about another time. He felt he was ten years behind in terms of this calling. Did I have any advice for him on that?

So I was in a position to give advice. Of course he could see I wasn't his age, but just how old did he think I was? His mother's age? If his mother had had him at twenty she might only be fifty-one.

"Is your calling tennis?"

"No."

"Music?"

"No. Could you not try to guess?"

"Sorry." We walked in silence, watching overly large crows land on a fence. "I guess any calling, no matter what it is, is a kind of unresolvable ache," I said, giving in to knowing more than him. "It's a problem that you can't fix, but there is some relief in knowing you will commit your whole life to trying. Every second that you have is somehow for it." You could also apparently lose your calling and wind up wandering around with a guy who worked at Hertz.

We walked. He said nothing for a while and I wondered if my little speech was the kind of lofty-yet-humble way of talking that made more sense if you knew I was semi-famous, which he didn't seem to. Maybe he'd looked me up and been impressed to see I was legit—but the scope of the whole thing was probably lost on him. He was like my dentist who every time told the same story about his daughter having heard of me. *What are the chances?* he always said, shaking his head with amazement.

"I do it whenever I can," Davey said finally. "Whenever I don't have to be at the lot or moving cars."

"Or walking with me."

He smiled at that.

"If you're practicing your . . . *oboe* then maybe you're not behind," I said. "Do you need to be an oboe star? Or is it the kind of thing that you need to be part of a team or group to really do properly?"

"No. I don't need a team. But I'd like it if some people heard me play my oboe."

"Wait," I whispered, "is it really the oboe?"

"No, of course not. I would have said something if you'd guessed it."

"Right, you would have cried out. Exclaimed." I made a noise of surprise, not a very good one. He did one, gasping.

"That's more like a cry of ecstasy," I said. Now he acted out a series of sexual noises, like a stupid teenager. It was so dumb, so silly that I felt embarrassed, as if all the people in my life were watching and couldn't believe I was hanging out with this person. *I know, I know,* I said to Jordi and Mary and Priya and Harris and even Sam. *Don't worry—I know. He's a ridiculous person.*

The next day I walked to the Hertz at the same time, four o'clock, right on the gong. He didn't seem surprised to see me again, just lifted his chin in hello and said he'd be done in one minute. I discreetly held my hand out level to the floor, curious if it was steady or not. Not steady, fully shaking. I couldn't figure out why that was. Often these days I was shivering as if from cold but if anything I was warm. It was an excess of energy, maybe I needed Reiki healing or a cranial sacral massage. For now I slapped the backs of my hands on my thighs.

"Ready?" he said.

We walked in silence for a long time. No more tour guiding. It seemed like he was getting up his courage to say something. He cleared his throat a few times and I wondered vaguely if I was about to pass out—the shaking thing was suddenly out of control.

"I think you're right," he said, very seriously. "I haven't committed my whole life to trying, not really."

For some reason I was crushed with disappointment. What did I think he was going to say? That I was the heir to a fortune? It was a compliment that he took my advice to heart. We talked about our love of the craft and I jokingly guessed that he made bowls out of tree burls and he ran with that, going on and on about how wooden bowls made him feel. More and more I found myself siding with him against all the people in my life. *Sure, he's dumb, but is dumb bad? What even is dumb?* He had been with Claire almost as long as I had been with Harris—puppy love. Did they plan on having kids? Yep, absolutely. We stopped and got bottles of water. Picking out the water, standing in line, him paying with his debit card—these simple things were such a pleasure for some reason, they stood apart from all the many grocery experiences of my past. We drank the water in the parking lot and it seemed to be drawn from the deepest, purest crack in the world. I drank and drank and when I could drink no more I just held my mouth open and let the water pour over my lips and chin and down my dress, the whole while smiling at him while he smiled at me. When the bottle was empty I daintily put the cap back on. He took it and threw it in the recycling for me. A different kind of person would have commented on what had just happened, made a joke or offered to get me napkins. By not doing any of these things, he was complicit, inside the performance with me. But it wasn't a performance, was it? No, nothing I did ever was. It was only ever the truth of the moment, coming out freely and expecting to be understood, not made much of, just taken seriously like any honest speech. It was dumb, but anything smarter would miss the point. I was speaking now to all my friends and family: *You have all missed the point of me.*

I have a friend, Dara, who is always going after younger men. I thought of her often during these walks with Davey, imagining that she would think I had finally seen the light, come around to her point of view. In my head I would argue back just as vociferously as ever. I wished I could really call her and raise my voice, but I couldn't risk telling another person I wasn't in New York.

The women I had dated were often my age, that was fine. But the men always had to be older than me because if they were my same age then it became too obvious how much more powerful I was and this was a turnoff for both of us. Men needed a head start for it to be even. Once, for just a few months, I had a boyfriend who was my exact same age. He was cute, but he didn't know about obscure music from the eighties, he only knew the same Top 40 eighties music I knew because we'd both been stupid little kids in the eighties. What good was that, the blind leading the blind? I felt embarrassed for Dara. What did these little pip-squeaks have to offer her? I personally wasn't interested in fighting this particular double standard, gender-wise. What about Davey? Dara would ask, if she knew. And I would say, I'm glad you brought that up. Do you know how many times an hour he checks Instagram? He has his phone in his hand and he pulls it down to refresh the way a person might unconsciously flick a lighter, and then he glances down to see the new posts, even if he's in the middle of a sentence! He seems to have no idea he's doing it or that it's rude. You can't take a person like that seriously. Sometimes Dara pressed me, Why hang out with him, then? But because I wasn't really talking to her, I didn't have to answer. I didn't know why, only that it wasn't *that*. It disturbed me to think that she would be all over him. She'd lean her bosom against the Hertz counter and giggle. The next day Davey and I took another walk and nearly the whole time I was mentally wrestling with my whorish friend Dara, which is maybe why I didn't see it coming until it was right in front of me.

We'd hiked up into the hills again, chitchatting the whole time about air travel, then TV shows, then funerals. We stopped to look at the view and catch our breath and he took his sweater off, and as he pulled it over his head his T-shirt lifted, too, and in front of me was his chest. I don't want to describe it. I'll just say that there were only a few hairs around the nipples. That's all I want to say at this juncture. Skinny but muscles. That's all, enough. The word *ripped* comes to mind, The End. I was alone with it because for a moment his head was covered by his lifted sweater and he was busy getting untangled. He wasn't very or unusually tangled, this wasn't a kitten hopelessly tangled in a ball of yarn—no, this was an ordinary brief moment of covered face. For a few seconds I was alone with his chest, his nipples, the hairs, and it was a hallowed moment. The urge to kiss his chest was very strong. But somehow this felt understandable, like if you were in a similar situation with Jesus, if Jesus had his sweater over his head and you were suddenly facing his chest, well, you would kiss it. You would not miss this chance for the whole rest of your life to be blessed by the experience. Then he pulled the T-shirt down and I quickly turned my head toward the view and he tied his sweater around his waist and glugged some water and we started walking again. For the rest of the walk I looked down or away.

That night, by myself in 321, I faced him like a new bride, nervously, not sure, after years of being mentally molested by so many stepfathers and CEOs and doctors, if I could join loins with this boy, his chest, the nipples, or were they too sweet and sacred?

They were not. I lay down on the bed and touched myself while thinking about us taking off our clothes and him pushing his cock into my pussy, which was so wet right now as I came for the first time, and then he was fucking me from behind, and now in my ass (*Claire never lets me*), as I came again, and then I was sucking him, and I came again, and then he was licking my pussy as if he'd been dying to and I came again, for the fourth and last time, and lay exhausted, in his imaginary arms, both of us sweaty and sticky and spent. It was the kind of totally present, animal sex that Jordi had. But wait—no sooner had I stopped than I felt the need to start again, rubbing myself and writhing around on the very mattress that he had ejaculated on many times. It was a bottomless fuck, excruciating like an itch that couldn't be scratched. I had done this before, become infatuated and gone on fantasy benders, but this was specific and apart from anything previous, and there were two reasons for this.

1. I was so surprised. I had been caught off guard, his body had snuck up on me, and this made me feel as if I was not entirely the author of my fantasies. They seemed to be happening *to* me and this gave the internal romance a quality of realness that was very, very poignant because
2. (and this came like a blow to the head in the middle of the night) I was too old for him.

This was my first experience of being too old. I had not always gotten exactly what I had wanted—men had been unwilling to leave their wives for me or to do more than flirt—but even in these humbling cases I hadn't questioned my right to feel desire. Now suddenly my lust was uncouth, inappropriate. I was powerful and interesting, perhaps funny and unique; I took him seriously in a way he wasn't used to—but he was not jerking off to me. Just a few years earlier, at forty or forty-two, I would have been a contender, but now it was too late. And he was just the first one. From now on this would be the norm. And not just with men younger than me, but with all men. I would never get what I wanted anymore, man-wise.

Before my grandma Esther jumped, she emptied all her pill bottles out the window, right onto Park Avenue. The doorman later described them to us as "raining down." We had to keep returning to this building because Aunt Ruthie, her daughter, inherited the apartment, so there were many opportunities to go over the details with the doorman. Mrs. Migdal tipped him big that day, he recalled. Then, after dumping the pills, she put herself in a trash bag, a black plastic garbage bag, so that, you know, it wouldn't be a mess for whoever had to clean it up. I'm not quite sure how she got herself out the window while still in the bag, but it reminds me of the way girls know how to take off a shirt or change their clothes *inside* a sweater, without ever being indiscreet. She managed.

Twenty-three years later, Ruthie jumped out the same window. She hung in there longer than her mom but not by much. This happened seven or eight years ago, before it had really occurred to me that I was next in this matriarchal lineage.

I got up and washed my face, the star tiles cool underfoot. How crazy and vain did you have to be to kill yourself when you found out that your main thrill, the thing that really got you going, was gone forever? Maybe not so crazy. If birth was being thrown energetically up into the air, we aged as we rose. At the height of our ascent we were middle-aged and then we fell for the rest of our lives, the whole second half. Falling might take just as long, but it was nothing like rising. The whole time you were rising you could not imagine what came next in your particular, unique journey; you could not see around the corner. Whereas falling ended the same way for everyone.

I paced around the new carpet, remembering when my friend's eighty-year-old dad had winked at me while I was dancing. This wasn't a funny anomaly; this was the order of the day. In the future I might be grateful when this happened, even if the man was ninety, one hundred, one hundred *twenty*. A man of any age. Trans men, women, and less gendered people were another story (always), but if my hetero tale mattered (and suddenly it seemed like it did) then this was a very abrupt conclusion. I had not seen this coming and so I had not lived my life accordingly. I had not gone out and done all the straight things I wanted to do while I still could. I had sat on my nest like a complacent hen, certain that when I felt like strutting about again everything would be exactly as it was before.

But to be clear, I had not, at any age, desired a specific male body in the way I did now. While all my boyfriends and crushes had been reasonably good-looking, my attraction hovered up near their face, where they kept their talent and power. Lusting for the whole length of a person, head to toe, was what body-rooted fuckers did, Jordi, and men. Now, for the first time, I understood what all the fuss was about. How something beautiful could strike your heart, move you, bring you down on your knees and then, somewhat perversely, you wanted to fuck that pure, beautiful thing. Sex was a way to have it, to not just look at it but to be with it. I suddenly understood all of classical art. The endless carved nudes, Venus in her shell, David. And sexy clothes. I had worn them without really understanding why, thinking of sexy as one of many styles, not realizing it was the only style. You should always be emerging from a shell if possible. Without knowing it, without really understanding it, I had been a body for other people but I had not gotten to have one myself. I had not participated in the infuriating pleasure of wanting a real and specific body on Earth. I lay in the center of the bed, unblinking.

Wanting a body had a seriousness to it. When you said you might never recover, you really meant it. This kind of desire made a wound you just had to carry with you for the rest of your life. But this was still better than never knowing. Or I hoped it was.

Because in truth it was like a bad dream, a nightmare. Life didn't just get better and better. You could actually miss out on something and that was that. That was your chance and now it was over. I wondered if I would continue with my work and then I realized that my work was all I had now. I had gotten it completely wrong—I thought I was laboring toward a prize, but the prize was right there, I already had it, and work was something I could do afterward, after I was no longer young enough to be beautiful and could no longer be wanted by someone beautiful.

How's New York now? Harris texted. Better?

I'd been in New York for five days already. But I still had a full day left and then another week to drive back across the country. There was plenty of time for more walks. I looked at the clock and added three— two a.m. was pretty late to still be awake in New York, but not if I was living it up.

I texted the party emoji, heart eyes, the Statue of Liberty, and asked how Sam was.

He texted a thumbs-up and a picture of Sam in the bath.

I sent three hearts, which he knew meant the three of us.

At two a.m. PST I was still mourning and jerking off, but eyebags weren't going to make or break anything at this point.

The next afternoon, just before four o'clock, I walked to Hertz shaking like a person heading to their execution (who, though terrified, wanted to be executed more than anything else in the world). There he was behind the counter; he smiled and gave a little nod—he was real and wanted to take a walk with me and this was enough. And even if it wasn't, well, it would have to be, for the rest of my life. I was sexually tormented and I was mourning, *but* (and I held on to this like a buoy) I didn't *really* care about him. I did not want to share my life with the boy who worked at the Hertz in Monrovia.

"I have a theory that it's technically in Arcadia," he said that afternoon. "It's on the border but they call it Arcadia to avoid an encroachment case, you know?"

We walked down and tried to find the line between Monrovia and Arcadia. We decided it was an invisible line in the air in a particular spot—we drew it with our hands and both began to feel it very strongly.

Here, watch me walk through it, he said. He wanted me to look really carefully and see if I noticed something pressing against him briefly when he passed through. I stared with all my might and then he said, You walk through it, and he stared at my body to notice if the cloth, my thin sweater, if it compressed against me. As he stared so hard at my chest in broad daylight my eyes filled with tears because one would only play such a game with a child or someone similarly neutral-bodied, an old woman.

On that day we walked mostly in silence. Was he bored? Had we run through all the possible topics? Would this be the last walk? He took me to a particular wooden fence and leaned into it, inhaling. I gave the fence a sniff. It smelled warm and sweet, almost alive.

"I fucking love it," he said.

We tried to put our finger on what it was about the smell, something to do with childhood, contentment. Oh. Pussy. That's what the fence smelled like. I blushed and hoped he wouldn't have the same thought. Had he taken Claire here? Her renovation still hadn't been mentioned, but he brought her name up casually all the time, so I began to think maybe he hadn't connected the dots. He might have been one of those husbands who doesn't listen very hard to what their wife says.

The next day Jordi suggested I bring it up, maybe tell him what a nice job Claire had done. I hadn't said anything to her about his chest yet, the hairs around his nipples. My little crisis.

"Otherwise it's kind of weird, right? I mean, you loved her! You're so happy with the room."

"I didn't *love* her," I said sharply, and she went quiet. There was a long, tense silence. I thought about saying I had to go. But I had nothing to do until four o'clock.

"Remember the folktale about the troll who appears three times?" I said finally.

"'Soria Moria Castle'?"

"Is that what it's called?"

"Yeah. It's Norwegian."

"Okay. But remember how you said it's not the troll himself who is important, it's the number three?"

"Yeah. Three is body, soul, spirit. Heaven, earth, water."

"But not in my case."

"No?" There was a little quiver to her voice.

"No. In my case it *is* the troll himself who matters."

"The boy."

"Yeah."

"I thought maybe."

"Did you?" And I saw then that she had. She had done her best to lead me toward other possibilities, interpretations, but of course there was only one way this could go. I told her about the sexual turn things had taken in my head. She said, Well, of course. A young hunk, who wouldn't? She was very healthy about sex, kind of Swedish. It was something you did to get your blood moving, like saunas and cold plunges. I spent a good thirty minutes trying to get her into the bent, hung-up place I was coming from, but she was a sculptor, so physical beauty was too basic for her to puzzle over. She had always known. Also, she was used to my crushes. I almost regretted how much I had told her over the years; it made it harder to convey how this one was different.

"I get it. He's playing your part. You're the objectifier!" She still thought I should bring up Claire. "People always like to hear nice things about their partners. Think if it was Harris, you'd be proud." Would I be? "I ran into him," she added grimly.

"Oh no."

"Yeah. I was worried I was going to have to lie. I don't like lying. I'm not like you."

"I don't like lying!"

"No, of course not, I didn't mean that. I mean I can't compartmentalize. You're good at keeping everything separate."

"Hm."

"You're bolder. You take on more risk."

I laughed nervously. "Not a liar, just more incredible."

"Anyway, I didn't have to. You didn't come up."

"Oh, good."

"We talked about Lore Estes. It was actually a really great conversation."

"Who?"

"Lore Estes. There's a big show about her at MOCA and we both bought the book. It's such a gorgeous book, you would love it. You can see it when you get back."

I looked at the great chairs and they suddenly looked very strange. Alien. What sort of silly mess had I gotten myself into and why wasn't I in New York? Or working on a new project? Or home looking at this gorgeous book with Jordi and Harris? But I hadn't done anything really wrong; I was fine. Everything would be fine. This little masturbation problem would go away as soon as I got home. In fact, what was I even talking about, what was this revelation about physical beauty? It was just a drug state that would wear off. And thank God! Because I did not want to live in a world where I had missed my chance! Soon enough I'd be home and it would be like none of this had ever happened. Harris had such exquisite taste. I really wanted to see this book. I spent the rest of the afternoon planning the rest of my life. I made lists of the different areas and how I could throw myself into them. They included Family and Marriage and Work but also Service. I had not been of enough service in my life. I could see getting deeply involved in all sorts of helping. The image that came to mind was scrubbing gutters by hand. That wasn't a thing, but maybe there was something more useful but similarly exhausting I could do. After scrubbing I would shower and then rest.

And.

And I could go home *now*. Before this perspective wore off. I could go home and tell the truth about everything I'd done and it would be bizarre but also entertaining and kind of endearing because I had failed so completely. For years Harris and I would tell our friends the story of when I was too scared to drive across the country and hid out in a motel room instead. It would fit right in with a couple other tried-and-true stories of me doing loony things. There was something kind of cozy about being a funny little wife; it was snug. It didn't take me long to pack. I called the front desk and explained I was checking out.

"Hold on," said Skip. He hung up and a moment later there was a knock at the door. He took off his flip-flops without me asking. His eyes darted this way and that, taking in the finished room. "I have a business proposal."

"Okay."

"You leave the room like this."

"I was going to."

"Oh, you were."

"What's the business proposal?"

"Well, basically just that I don't charge you for destruction of property. You get your deposit back."

I thought about telling him how much all this had cost. Also: what deposit?

"You can charge a lot more for this room now, if you want," I said.

"You know, I thought I might do that, actually, since you mention it. I might call it a *suite*."

"I guess technically it's not a suite," I pointed out. "Because it's just one room, the same as the others."

"I don't think people will get hung up on that. They'll know what I mean."

"If I ever come back here, like with my family, I'd like to stay free of charge."

"Certainly I could give you a generous discount. You could pay what you paid this time, instead of the new rate."

Just then the town clock made its four p.m. electric gong sound and I froze. Snakes can swallow and live off the same mouse for days, but once it's been digested they begin to starve almost immediately. If they don't eat within an hour, they'll die.

"Skip. I'm afraid I have to go."

"Oh, right now. Should we use the credit card on file?"

"No, not— I'm not checking out. Change of plans."

I quickly unpacked and re-dressed myself and hurried to Hertz. He had just left, Glenn-Allen said. I didn't have his number. I had Claire's number, but that was no help. I walked back outside in a daze.

Someone called my name.

It was him; he was standing by his car. I jogged over. I had to jog because walking was too slow.

"Should we go?"

"I wish I could." He held up his phone apologetically. "Claire needs me to do some house stuff."

I nodded. I didn't think I would repack carefully this time. Probably just throw everything in my suitcase. Also the rest of my life would be a slog and then I would die. Which is the case for many people. It's no big deal.

"But hey, if you're free later maybe we could meet up."

Behind him, in the back of the parking lot, a woman was struggling with her child.

"In the evening?"

"In the evening," he said.

The child was refusing to walk and the woman was demanding that he come, *right now*. The child sat down. What would the mom do? Would she hold her ground? Or give in, forever spoiling the child? It wasn't my problem. I turned my body so that I couldn't see how it resolved.

"Do you know the Buccaneer?" he said.

"I've seen it. It's a bar."

"It *is* a bar. That's correct."

He walked backward toward his car without looking away from me.

Now he was opening the door with his hand behind his back. "Eight o'clock?"

He tipped an invisible hat through the window before driving off. The child was on his back now, lying on the sidewalk. The mom was at her wits' end. She was about to lose it. I turned and walked away. What would I wear? Or was it better not to change? KIERAN, she bellowed. THIS IS YOUR LAST CHANCE.

CHAPTER 8

I was a little early. I walked around the block very slowly so I wouldn't work up a sweat or create a breeze that would mess up my hair. I was wearing tight blue jeans, a tiny yellow sweatshirt, and brown wedge heels. Low-key but flattering. As I rounded the corner I saw him waiting by the entrance. He had changed, too. He looked freshly showered, with an untucked button-down shirt stupidly buttoned under his chin, skater-style. Just before I got to him a couple appeared, a young man and woman, and Davey and the man did a quick and elaborate handshake. It was too late to retreat or circle back around the block.

"Hey," he called out to me. He gave me a sort of pat on the back and introduced me to his friends. "She's passing through on her way to New York."

"Hey," they said. The young woman in the couple had hair down to her butt and wore a bra that was somehow a shirt. She looked me up and down not understanding that my outfit was sexy, too. We all went inside. Were we going to spend the whole night with this couple? I wanted to cry. The girl tossed her hair over her shoulder and mimed holding an invisible pool cue.

"Gonna clobber him," she said, and the couple headed down a hallway to the right. Wonderful people, loved them. Davey guided us into the main room. I walked around the bar. It was so clean. I supposed the last time I'd hung out in bars was before indoor smoking had been outlawed. Young people sat in amiable groups and pairs with seemingly no intrigue surrounding them.

"Where are all the drunks?" I said. "These people all seem like co-workers unwinding after work."

"Yeah, that's what they are." He squinted at me. "You maybe . . . don't go out much?"

"Oh, I go out," I said too quickly, as a joke. "I'm constantly out." No, of course I didn't hang out in bars. I had been in my converted garage for the past fifteen years, working at the table with one short leg. And when I had gone out, it had been to attend my own events or the events and openings and premieres of my friends and peers. The bar was having trivia night and people were excited about that. They had time for that. I hadn't planned on becoming this rarefied; I had just spent every waking moment trying to get across what life seemed like to me, only allowing undeniable things—the child, a bad case of the flu, hunger and thirst—to take me away from this trying. And apparently time had, meanwhile, been passing—great swaths of it, whole decades. Indoor smoking had been banned and this young man was leading me to a table outside. The air was perfectly warm. We drank tequila and I wondered if the upside-down triangle of his upper body—his bony but broad shoulders narrowing down to his small waist—was perhaps a classic proportion with a kind of ancient resonance. Something to do with Michelangelo's drawings or Da Vinci or whoever it was. The Da Vinci code. Like if you measured the angles of his upper body would you discover those same measurements in the Bible or inscribed on a Greek vase and would they also correspond, if scaled up, to a larger, cosmological measurement, perhaps between stars? Celestial music—what was that? If I'd been at home, working, I'd pause to look it up. But, stunningly, I wasn't at home working and I wouldn't look it up and I didn't really want to look anything up, ever again. We were sipping our drinks and talking; I was trying to explain what my work meant to me. How life, usually so frustratingly scattered and elusive, came under my spell; I could name each thing, no matter how obscure, and it would open to me as if it loved me. Working was a romance with life and like all romances always seemed on the verge of ending, was always out of my control. I said this last part half standing, with my arms grasping the air as if to catch a bird. I really got why people drank to unwind after work, this was great. I tried again to guess his secret passion.

"Chef?"

He shook his head.

"Some kind of sport? Baseball player? Boxer? Racehorse . . . rider?"

He didn't bother with these.

"Singer? Rapper? Rock star—"

"I'm a dancer," he said abruptly. "Not like a ballet dancer but more what you would probably call hip-hop. Street."

I laughed and he smiled.

"Why is it funny?"

"It's not. I'm just trying to picture . . . is it like break dancing, or . . . ?"

"We don't need to talk about it."

"Okay."

"I guess from your perspective I must be kind of silly."

"No, not all." Now I was thinking of those boys, or groups of boys, who danced for tips on the Venice Beach boardwalk. He was like them. I was pretty sure I'd had a smooth, unjudgmental reaction. Maybe I shouldn't have laughed. But wait.

"What do you mean 'from my perspective'? What's my perspective?"

He looked at me like, *Come on.*

"When you were my age you'd already made"—and then he said the name of my big breakout success. "I was sixteen. It rocked my world."

I looked away, my face a smiling mask.

Why did I think this young man was hanging around me? Because I was such a great beauty? So magnetic and witty? He knew exactly who I was. He was a fan. I could be ninety and he'd be eager to sit across from me. This is what fame had bought me: a disciple. But not the kind famous men had, not a young woman eager to suck the wisdom out of my dick. My fame neutered me. He was grinning.

"You recognized me," I said tightly.

"Well, sure. I saw you talking to that guy at the gas station and thought I was going to have a heart attack. Then we had the thing when I cleaned your windshield."

"But you couldn't see me, the glare—"

"What are you talking about? We were looking right at each other."

I felt like I was moving in slow motion, underwater.

"So when you came into that restaurant, Fontana's—"

"I knew you'd be there. Because you'd asked the gas station guy where to eat."

Not just a fan, a stalker.

"You really seemed like you didn't remember seeing me," I said evenly. "That was a good performance."

"But I thought we both knew. We had had the crazy moment through the windshield, and now we were playing a kind of game. You asked me so many questions. And I kind of spilled the beans when I said I worked at Hertz."

I didn't see how that was spilling the beans.

"Oh my god," he said, covering his mouth, "you're so . . . You think everyone's job is to clean your windshield."

I shook my head. "No—you were cleaning another car, too."

"A Hertz car. You do understand that I don't work at a gas station?"

I turned red. There *was* a little vagueness around car-related jobs.

"Wow," he said, shaking his head. "So that one went right by you."

"Sorry."

"Anyway," he said, recovering. "Despite everything, you stopped in Duarte. That blew my mind and I thought that was the end. A story I'd tell myself for the rest of my life."

That should have been the end.

"Then I saw your car parked at the motel. And I knew. This thing was on."

"On?"

"Or did I read you all wrong?"

If this age, forty-five, turned out to be the halfway point of my life, then this moment right now was the exact midpoint. A body rises, reaches an apex, and then falls—but at the apex, the peak, it is perfectly still for a moment. Neither rising nor falling.

"Why did you come back?" he said. "Why are you here?" He waited, his sharp, dark eyes on mine. "You came back for me. You're here for me."

"Why would I do that? That's crazy. That would be crazy."

He smiled a little, sympathetically. "Yep. But that's what people do."

We sat in silence. I wondered if I was misunderstanding. He reached across the table and touched the back of his hand to the back of mine, ever so gently. There weren't very many ways to take that. Just one, really. He said, Can we get out of here? He stood up and walked inside to the bar. He was settling our tab. I walked unsteadily to the bathroom with my purse in my hand. I put on tinted lip gloss, smoothed my hair, and washed my hands. A pale woman was applying concealer under her eyes.

"Would it be possible for me to get a dot of that?"

I held up a finger and she dabbed the sponge-tipped wand against it. I rubbed my fingers together and patted them around my nose. Our eyes met in the mirror and I could tell she was hoping something good would happen to her tonight, but it probably wouldn't. Not that she wasn't cute and there wasn't someone for everyone, but what were the odds? Mostly you put concealer on and then later take it off and nothing life-changing happens in between.

I, on the other hand.

Suddenly I could not leave the bathroom quickly enough, I nearly ran to him. He put his arm around me and we walked out into the night.

After a minute he wisely dropped his arm and we walked side by side, but clumsily close, so that our hands and arms irregularly bumped into each other. This occasional bumping was so consuming that it was hard to think. It went without saying that we were headed to the Excelsior.

My hands were shaking as I unlocked the door. He slowly walked around the room and I took in the grandeur all over again; the colors and textures were like nature when you're tripping. I plugged my best playlist into the stereo. He touched a bird on the wallpaper. Did he understand that his wife had picked it out? He stepped into the bathroom and stared down at the tiles. After a minute he said, "I could look at this forever."

"I know." I pointed to the three solid green tiles behind the toilet and explained how if there had been the exact right amount, if the pattern had been complete, another dimension might have opened up, a portal. He moved one of his socked feet so it was touching mine.

"We can't do much more than this, you know," he said, letting his arm hang against my arm.

I was so overwhelmed with the foot and now the arm, and the fact that he was naming it, acknowledging it. "As much as I want to," he added, his voice kind of husky. He gave the front of his pants just the briefest flick of his eyes, just enough to direct me down there. Oh. He had a huge cock. It was stretching mightily against the front of his pants. In the larger scheme of life I didn't care about a big penis; it was just a punch line or an annoyance. Once I'd had a boyfriend whose penis was so big we couldn't really have sex that way. But this thing held in by his pants . . . this was quite sobering. I was moved. I wanted to genuflect and kiss it, or heartily shake his hand in warm and sincere appreciation. He had said something just now, what was it? Oh yes, about not being able to do more than touch his foot to mine. We were already light-years past feet—although feet still mattered, star tiles still mattered. The air smelled of dark honey and now we were walking back into the main room and the streetlight came through the pink and gold curtains like a blaze of fire; it would always be sunset in here.

He ran his hand over the silk coverlet.

"It's very girly," I said.

"I love it."

We stared at the bed like it was doing something interesting.

"But maybe," he added, "we shouldn't lie down on it. That might be too tempting. For me." Also it was his mattress, under there. His marriage bed.

We sat in the great chairs. We pulled them together and held hands and kind of leaned together.

Every few minutes we shifted our position, like I put my leg over his leg, and this new information left us speechless for a while. The proximity of my leg to his cock. The way it made us both imagine me sitting entirely on his lap, straddling him, facing him. I described this position and he said he'd already pictured that days ago.

"When you thought about these things, did you . . . jerk off?"

"What do you think?"

A synth song with a very slow beat was playing. Sometimes we would look at each other and be amazed, that this had happened, that we both felt the same way. Our eyes would meet and then they would take a little walk around each other's face; I stared at his dark lashes, the freckle under his left eye, his full lips. People look at each other's lips before they kiss them. When he stared at mine I almost began to lean forward, but then we both looked away, a new song was coming on, we shifted our hands, met each other anew. Time passed. We weren't saying much, but every once in a while I'd ask him about something—the day we bought water, the day he told me about the parade, and he'd tell it back to me as a courtship. There was another version of life where I wasn't siloed off within my brain; an invisible dance partner had been there all along, mirroring all my movements from afar.

I thought we were going to do this forever. I had entirely forgotten that things end, this night would end. When he, after four or five hours, said something about needing to go, it was a slap in the face. Real cold water. Then he showed me his phone—3:27 a.m.—and I laughed. What a time! We would both be fried tomorrow; he would have to come up with an explanation for Claire and these problems were a comfort. We exchanged numbers and after a long, dangerous hug goodbye I shut the door, waited a few minutes, and then went out myself. I ran. I ran as fast as I could through the warm California night.

I knew I wouldn't sleep and that I had to, to look rested tomorrow, so I took an extra Benadryl. What a treat not to have to contend with myself; I simply passed out under the silk coverlet. Just five hours later I woke up exactly as I had been the day before, having wrestled not at all with the shadows, still high on astonishment. I picked up my phone and texted: I adore you. I don't regret anything. I want to put every part of your body in my mouth. I wrote exactly what I felt. This was foolish and risky and I would never text so freely again. But that is what I wrote to him on the morning after our first night.

He did not write back.

What had I done.

I began shivering. I couldn't eat my usual breakfast and my body immediately began hollowing itself; I shit out anything that could come out. Every few seconds I checked the phone and everything rectangular or shiny seemed to be a phone illuminating—the back of my hairbrush, a plastic box of almonds—I twitched, glancing this way and that at glints of light.

He texted at noon.

| I feel the same way.

I sank to my knees and pressed my forehead against the carpet. I ate half a piece of toast. I tried to take my time writing back. After twenty minutes I wrote:

| But you probably got more sleep than me.

He replied immediately, one word: Doubtful.

If I had tried to cash that word the bank teller would have said: We don't have enough money. There was not enough money in the world to cash that one word, *Doubtful.*

I spent the day preparing to see him, cleaning and smoothing my body. I pushed my finger deep inside my pussy and tasted it, as if his tongue would soon be in there and I might be able to adjust the flavor. But it tasted fine. I thought a young man with a hard dick would find the taste satisfactory. I wore a nude thong and a soft, cream-colored silk jersey dress, suitable for a safari in the 1930s, and the same brown wedge heels. The dress was casual but held my waist and clung slightly to the swell of my ass, the bare tops of the cheeks. I made myself eat a slightly toasted Gardenburger, so that I wouldn't risk getting a headache with him. I didn't want anything to interrupt us.

Harris called while I was recurling a lock of hair.

I stared at the name on the phone, petrified. What if I couldn't get the tone right?

He had some things to say about the roof and a playdate Sam had with a girl whose family we'd always been wary of.

"Instead of dropping her off the mom just *stayed.*"

"Oh god, what a nightmare."

"It ended up being fine. I learned a lot about nineteenth-century Russian literature. She's a teacher."

As per my habit, I immediately saw Harris and this teacher-mom as a couple and silently deferred to them. He asked if I was okay.

"Yeah! Why?"

"You sound a little quiet."

"Well, I miss you." A panicked guess at what might be appropriate. Then out of nowhere I began weeping. "It's strange to be on my own for so long."

"You're doing great," he said. "It's going to feel weird or wrong at first, but you just have to push past that."

"Yeah?"

"Yeah."

For a moment I almost felt like he knew and was really trying to encourage me to be brave, as if this romance was an agony I was shouldering for both our benefits. It often was my job to go out on an emotional limb for us, to be the unhinged, messy one—the one who acted out. Or re-enacted.

After our post-NICU honeymoon ended—on or around May thirty-first—I watched Harris become a goofily warmhearted father. We were no longer in the seventh ring of Hell together so he could not be blamed for resuming good cheer; it was in everyone's best interest that he did. I tried to do the same.

The first flashback came in a public bathroom in Griffith Park. I had just done the awkward maneuver of peeing with the baby strapped to my chest and now I was waving my hands under a faucet trying to activate the sink's motion sensor. After a moment I realized there was a foot pedal to start the water. Where had I seen this before? I mused, but the flashback had already begun—there's always a moment of neutral disorientation before it takes you down. In the hospital was where. And now I was there with Harris, wearing the white gown, pressing the pedal with my foot to wash my hands, sanitize them, but hurrying, hurrying, because I couldn't wait another second to see my tiny baby—it was too horrible that they were all alone, just lying there in the clear plastic isolette. But even worse than that: the cold fear of what might have happened since that morning. Had things taken a turn for the worse while we were at lunch? Were we back in the red zone? We never should have left. *Hurry!*

All this in a second or two. Then I was back in the restroom, sweating and weeping with Sam safely swaddled to my chest. I met my own eyes in the mirror.

So. It wasn't over. The past could come back, fully formed, at any moment, unlocked by a random combination of sounds and movements. It was all still with me, down to the smell of the antiseptic soap. I looked at Sam. They seemed unconcerned, gnawing on a small rubber elephant and watching me blow my nose.

"I felt so much that I cried. I'm done crying, but I still feel sad. It's okay to feel sad."

That would have to do for now. I drove us home.

For the rest of the day I was so exhausted I could barely move, as if all my energy had been used up in a single second. Eventually I told Harris about the flashback and this was like pouring a cup of water down the drain, no comfort whatsoever. Which wasn't his fault—imagine every person who has ever greeted a time traveler upon their return home. There's no way to ask the right questions, being so filled with a belief in the present. *What did the horses smell like?* That would be a good question.

"What are you going to do tonight?" Harris asked now.

"I'm having dinner with Mary." It came out fully formed, no forethought. And with this lie my heart began to pound. It was almost four o'clock.

I arrived at Hertz on the dot and Davey behaved as he had on the previous days. His face betrayed nothing. As we walked I waited for a signal that we could pick up where we'd left off last night, but he seemed breezy.

"Feel like getting a smoothie?" he asked brightly. I didn't say anything. "*I* do," he said, steering us into a place called Nekter. With a mango smoothie in hand he began whistling through his teeth as he headed toward the bathroom. I was uncertain if I should follow. He whistled right past the bathroom, past the cleaning supplies, and right out the back door. I hurried after him into the alley—he strode across it, toward a low, pale-yellow stucco building. It took me a moment, not being from here, to get my bearings. This building was the Excelsior, the back of it. That window was my window, a little too high to climb into. But there was a faded pink canvas deck chair down at the other end of the alley—he was already walking to get it. I ran around to the other side of the building and let myself into my room. I pulled back the curtain and slid open the window. Standing on the chair he heaved himself up easily, jumping through with one hand on the sill. He turned and shut the window and curtain and then immediately put his smoothie on the side table and pulled me to him. If this had been a movie he would have kissed me now; instead he put both his arms around me and stood very still, like he was righting something that had been wrong all day. We just stood, breathing deeply, recovering from all those seconds of not being together.

"I can't ever come in the front again," he said, stepping back a little.

"It was so late last night . . . I think you're fine." I hoped we could go back to holding each other. He studied my face.

"So, what's your . . . marriage arrangement?"

"I mean, I'm married," I said. "That's the arrangement."

"But it seems like that maybe means something different for you, based on . . ." He gestured vaguely at me; I looked down at my dress.

"Based on what?"

"On this. Me being here. But also, I guess, your work?"

My work was full of unlikely couplings, unauthorized sex, surrealism, and a shit ton of lesbianism. Apparently he had taken all this quite literally. I tried to imagine myself from his point of view, a married mother somehow living completely off the rails. She was literally toppling over some kind of railing, legs in the air.

"I'm the same amount of married as you," I said. "We're in the same boat."

"That's sort of a relief. How guilty do you feel?"

Guilty? My head swam for a moment trying to quantify the amount of guilt I'd felt, second to second, every day of my life. Such that now, in this moment, I felt only justified. I was owed.

"I guess guilt feels like a waste of our time," I said. "I'd rather feel guilty when I'm alone."

He nodded, seeming to take the hint, and began syncing his phone to the stereo. Some smooth R&B sounds came out of the speaker. He lay down on the carpet and patted the place next to him; I lay down on my stomach.

"I wondered if we could—" And he showed me, turning onto his side and reaching for me. I scooted backward into him. He folded his arms around me, we lay like a married couple in a bed and the song went, *I've been thinking 'bout you, you know, know, know.* When he got too hard we rolled apart. Our hands found each other; I pulled one of his fingers to my lips and he pushed it into my mouth. Throughout my life men had been pushing their big fingers into my mouth and although I went along with it, I always thought, *Are you out of your mind? What should I put in there next? Your shoe? How about I just lick the pavement?* But this was entirely different. I wished it was a little *dirtier.* I wanted to eat his day; everything he had done that day. He groaned and pulled it out, but I couldn't have that—I reached for his thumb with my lips and caught it and held it, sucking like a baby, until he pulled that one out, too.

"Best few seconds of my life," he whispered, but sat up, forcing himself away from me. "When do you go?"

"In a week."

It seemed like a long time to me. Think of how much had happened in just twenty-four hours.

"You should have come sooner," he said. "It took you nearly a week to come to me."

I lowered my eyes. I couldn't have come to him because I had to make this room with his wife. I didn't say that. The R&B had changed to hip-hop. He suddenly jumped to his feet and turned up the volume. Was he about to start dancing? I casually rose and made my way to the bathroom, shutting the door behind me. I rubbed lip balm on my lips and cheeks and fixed my hair. He was definitely dancing out there. Which was a little awkward. What was I going to do—stand there and watch and then clap when he was done? Or maybe just pretend it was normal. Yeah, that was the way to go with this.

I glided out, smiling casually as I made my way to the minifridge. I watched him with my peripheral vision while I made some little snacks with crackers and avocado and olives. He was good, but he wasn't incredible. Sometimes on Venice Boardwalk you saw a dancer who made your jaw drop and dollar signs spin in your eyes. Every single person felt they had personally discovered the dancer and once in a while the dancer would appear on a late-night talk show. Even out of the corner of my eye I could see Davey wasn't at that level. Which was a good thing. If he had been truly talented I might have fallen in love with him; I would have felt I had a God-given right to.

He turned the music down and we ate the snacks I had made. For some reason they were especially delicious and I had trouble convincing him that I wasn't a good cook. We listed off all the things we liked to eat. He didn't really know anything about health. He checked Instagram for the millionth time and I chided him.

"You're on it. I follow you," he said defensively.

"But I hardly ever look at it."

"So you don't have *any* internet addiction?"

"I read the news a lot." This made me sound old. "And I do look at this one message board."

"*There* you go—everyone has something!"

I held up both my hands like, *Guilty as charged*, and hoped he wouldn't ask me what the message board was for.

"What's it a message board for?"

"Shoes."

It was a message board for mothers. Mothers who all had one problem in common. But I didn't want him to think of me as a mother with a problem.

"Shoes?"

"A certain kind of rare high heel."

He wrapped his hand around my foot in its white anklet and we fell silent.

Despite what the nurse said, I had scoured the internet for Fetal-maternal Hemorrhage, looking for someone who had been through it. I learned how to spell all three of those words, not just the easy word, *maternal*. Unlike some topics, which went on and on, there was a very finite number of internet pages that contained all three together as one thing. There were a few scholarly scientific papers and a tabloid article about a "ghost baby" who had survived, thanks to Jesus. That baby's mom was already pregnant again, she'd moved on and was doing great. Which wasn't what I was looking for. I needed a mom who had flashbacks that knocked her off her feet in broad daylight.

My mistake (always!) is in *laboring* when actually the opposite is called for; it took me two years to think of simply typing "FMH." And there it was: babytalk.com/fmhmomschat. My heart was pounding as I slowly scrolled. The nurse wasn't wrong: it was all mothers of stillborn babies. Some of them wanted to know if this would happen again if they tried again. Most were just posting to say WTF. WTF just happened? And since science didn't know, there were no answers—just the echo of other mothers who had also posted WTF on another night, often in another year. There was no actual dialogue, only solitary women putting their candle on the same altar. One husband was writing on behalf of his wife who was too wrecked to even type FMH or WTF. He wanted to fix this, he wanted answers. He didn't understand that we never expected answers or for anything to get fixed. The most we ever hoped for was fellowship. It obviously wouldn't be appropriate for me to post. My story was so different that it was actually the opposite—a miracle—and there was no breakout thread for mothers of stillborn babies who then lived. So each time I was knocked out by a flashback I returned to the chat room and just scrolled. Maybe it was creepy to lurk anonymously, but there was nowhere else to go and it was much, much better than nothing.

Davey slipped his finger into my little white sock and then kissed the back of my hand; I was surprised that was allowed. He shrugged and said, People used to do that all the time.

"Sure," I agreed. "And they do still kiss the queen's hand."

"What queen?"

"The queen of England."

"Do they?"

"I'm pretty sure."

He kissed it again, slowly, and I thought: At this rate we'll be having sex by the end of the week.

That evening I walked back to the store and bought Brazil nuts, a tin of sardines, a dark chocolate bar, and two avocados. Beauty foods. Also several boxes of baking soda and a neutral kind of lotion that you can find at any drugstore, Vanicream. I rubbed every inch of my wet body with baking soda then rinsed it off and slathered myself with the white cream and put on cotton pajamas. By morning the lotion had all absorbed and after a couple days of this my skin became smooth and soft like a child's. It didn't seem possible that this whole time I could have had skin like this if I had only tried harder, no, there was something chemical happening, biological. It reminded me of the pregnancy glow. When I went one way, my clothes went the other way, a constant, slippery motion that made me feel undressed all the time.

And now that I knew he was jerking off to me, my fantasies became more intimate, specific, as if he could feel me touching myself, too. Often I rode him slowly for a very long time, like an old hunched man on an exhausted pony with a steady gait, riding and riding until I c-a-m-e. I had a brand-new need for deep penetration; I wanted him, or something, up inside the center of me. I had a black rubber dick at home. I knew exactly where it was—the vitamin drawer—and considered sneaking home to get it, but when I googled sex shops it turned out they were everywhere, like low-profile drugstores. The dick I bought in Monrovia was a dumb glittery purple. When I fucked myself with it waves of sensation radiated upward, warming my chest all the way to my chin. The feeling was so acute that I suspected I had a polyp on my cervix that was getting bumped in just the right way. Or else it was Davey; he'd made me bloom in there.

I didn't tell him these things because he was always trying to maintain a boundary, an invisible line like the one between Monrovia and Arcadia. ("You must have known on that day," he said, "from the way I looked at your tits in that little pink sweater." And I shook my head no, I had no idea, but I didn't explain why because I didn't want him to see me from a new angle, suddenly aging before his eyes like in a horror movie where the beautiful girl's face crinkles into that of a wrinkled hag, then a skeleton, and finally a pile of dust.) He could tell me that he'd jerked off, but he wouldn't say specifically what he fantasized about. He could spend four hours a day with me, from four to eight p.m., but when he had to leave he couldn't be even a minute late.

"Where does she think you are?"

"Dance practice with my friend Dev."

"Does Dev know about us?"

"No, god no. He wouldn't get it. He'd say, 'Don't be a loser, D. Keep it in your pants.'"

"You are keeping it your pants! You're doing a great job of that."

But our moral codes were entirely different. He keeled over, like he was having an ulcer right then and there. And he actually might have been. He had never done anything like this, never even been tempted.

"It's only because it's you. Anyone else I'd be able to resist."

This was meant as a great compliment, but it felt impersonal to me, like he'd been caught in the snare of my work. Whereas my feelings for him were totally pure, I'd simply been drawn to him.

"To my pretty face," he said glumly. We each worried that the other one adored something that wasn't really us. He wondered if I had told anyone and I said I had. He had told someone, too. This was both incredible (it could be *told*, it was real) and worrisome.

"Does the person you told . . . know who I am?"

"No."

Being only a little famous was a constant lesson in humility. I often chastised myself, saying, *Look who's getting too big for their britches.* But no matter how small I made myself I was always too big for them. They must have been very small britches to begin with.

"Maybe we could keep it to just one person each," I suggested. "I don't need to tell anyone else, do you?"

"No. This person can be my one person."

"What did your one person say?"

"Well"—he smiled shyly—"my one person knows me really well so they were really happy for me."

"I like your one person."

"What did *your* person say?"

Jordi had been beside herself. She said I sounded completely different, utterly changed.

"I do?"

"Yes, the quality of your voice, it's all opened up."

"Open, open, open," I said, trying to hear the new quality of my voice. "Test, test." I asked if she judged me and she said, How could I judge you? For what? It's brave to feel so much.

"Brave? Why?"

"I guess because it could . . . end in pain."

I couldn't imagine what she meant. Now that I knew it was mutual, no pain was possible.

On Sunday he couldn't stay quite as long.

"We kind of have a ritual where we watch—"

My hand shot up in self-defense and he stopped short.

"*Sorry,*" he said. "I'm just trying not to rock the boat, you know?"

I had Sunday night rituals, too. Hair washing, cutting tiny nails, bedtime story; if I could keep all this at bay then he could spare me the name of their TV show.

Then, as if this would comfort me:

"I made a dance for you."

Oh no. He hadn't danced again since the first attempt and I thought he understood it wasn't the best use of our time.

"You did?" I said.

"You look concerned."

"No, no! I'm not!" I pulled up a chair. "Should I sit?"

He laughed and made sure the curtains were fully shut. He took off his plaid shirt. He found a song on his phone and I sat and then realized he was just warming up so I stood and then he changed the song and I could tell it was about to start and had the sudden feeling of wanting to run out of the room, like I'd been strapped into a ride at an amusement park that was more than I could handle. He began moving slowly—slower than slowly, he was doing some trick that made it look like a fast movement played in slow motion. I smiled and then frowned. I felt unsteady, like I was becoming ill or there was something wrong with the air. What bad timing for something to have gone wrong with the heating and cooling system in the room. No—false alarm—it was just me, holding my breath and tensing up. I was clenched like a fist, braced against what he was doing. Now he was speeding up. Going faster and faster. I didn't want him to embarrass himself in front of me. But he wasn't embarrassed—he was airborne. He was in a reverie, moving around the room with an impossible buoyancy that made it seem as if he were slowly flying. He touched the floor only once in a while, and each tap of his foot propelled him as if he were lighter than air. It dimly occurred to me that this was the first time I'd seen him dance—last time I'd been too busy protecting him from humiliation; or maybe I'd seen and been afraid. Because in a million years no one would ever call this guy second-rate. Dance was his calling. *I* was the amateur whose dancing was an embarrassment. The instinct to video him was strong, to somehow have or keep what was happening, but of course that was a pedestrian thought. We were outside the internet, it had never been invented, there was only now. I just had to take it. Stand there, with one hand on the chair, and endure the beauty of what was happening. The very second I succumbed to it, tears rose to my eyes in sharp points. Because I could suddenly see that it was about us, he had figured out a way to show the feeling between us. When he leapt and turned in the air like that it was ecstatic and obsessive—he did the move again and again like some kind of endurance art and it only became more exactly the truth the longer he did it. He was pouring sweat. I was entirely known and I thought: *This is the happiest moment of my life.* And with that sentence came tremendous sorrow because nothing was more fleeting than a dance—dance says: joy is only now. So I gave up on everything but now. Every opinion and judgment I had ever had, my entire past including my child and husband and parents, my future, my career, my eventual death—I let all of it go. Or I did nothing, for once. I just watched the dance. Still moving, he caught my eye and nodded ever so slightly, as if I had just arrived.

He was panting hard and glossy when he finished and his eyes were unfocused, like he couldn't really see. I opened my mouth, getting ready to praise, but he held up a finger and kind of limped to the bathroom. I heard the shower go on. I sat on the bed like a person in a foreign waiting room.

"Where are you?" he called out.

I shyly peeked into the steamy little room. He was obscured behind the rippled glass, just a shape soaping itself. He was ready for my response now.

"I don't even know what to say." I hated when people said that to me—*Well, you better come up with something,* I always thought.

"It was the most incredible thing I've ever seen. I don't even know if I would call it good."

He paused in his lathering. "You don't?"

"No, of course it was good, it was incredible. But I felt like it was beyond good and bad. Like a new thing altogether that needs new words." This was getting too complicated. "I loved it. Watching you dance was the happiest I've ever been in my life."

Now he laughed, boyish glee. "I had a fantasy that you would talk to me while I was in the shower afterward. I mean, I pictured this."

"I feel like we live together and I do this all the time."

"Yeah." He squirted out more bath gel. "This stuff smells amazing." It did.

A very specific tonka bean that Claire would immediately recognize.

I wondered how I would warn him without saying her name. But I didn't have to.

"Do you have another kind of soap?" he said with sudden urgency. "Or some shampoo or something?" The mood had changed. He was rummaging around in my shampoo bottles, smelling each one. "None of these are gonna cover, they're not strong enough."

I looked around the bathroom in a panic. Toothpaste, rosacea gel, Vanicream, mouthwash. Mouthwash.

He made an oof noise when I handed him the big bottle of Tom's Wicked Fresh mint rinse aid and then began pouring it all over his body. The minty clouds were so overpowering that we both began coughing. He said, "I'm coming out," which I understood meant I should leave the bathroom. I sat back on the bed and after a minute he emerged, hair slicked back, his pants and hoodie back on, but not his sweaty shirt, which he laid over the back of one of the great chairs. He came over and stood between my knees and kind of wrapped his arms around my head and I felt like I was inside of him, a minty world. My mind didn't wander. That was the thing with him—I never wanted to be anywhere else or think about anything else. I was entirely present, if that mattered anymore. He whispered into my hair that he had to go. I said okay because I didn't want to be a grasping, clawing sort of person.

I told Jordi everything that had happened and she said she had suspected that he was a good dancer.

"You did? Even when I said he wasn't?"

She said I could be a tough crowd and she guessed a white boy would have to be pretty good to even show his face in that world. Sometimes when she spoke about him I felt jealous of the two of them—Jordi and Davey—even though they had never met. When she sympathized with his guilt I felt like a wild animal among humans, missing the qualities that make a thing civil.

Just as I thought we were finishing up, meaning I had worn her down with my single, relentless topic, she asked if I was in love with him. I laughed out loud.

"No, no," I said, "it isn't like that. He's fundamentally kind of goofy. Oh—he left his shirt here." I pressed it against my face and breathed deeply.

"I guess from what you said—"

I couldn't even let her finish. "If you met him you would actually laugh. I mean, almost anyone you picked off the street would make as much sense for me to fall in love with as him. In fact, he is literally a person I met on the street, at a *gas station*." I stopped, letting the words *gas station* sink in.

"I see. Okay."

There was a distance now between us. Was she angry? She said she was just tired. She was making a new sculpture, something in green marble.

The next day Davey could hang out only for about an hour; he had to help Claire with something. I was aghast but smiled and nodded passive-aggressively.

"Don't be like that. It's just as bad for me."

Was it? I would have loved to have seen a graph of the relative bad-nesses.

We huddled around the hour like a flame and then he left. It wasn't good to have extra time alone. Until four o'clock was the exact right amount of hours to eat and masturbate and watch a rom-com or two—I didn't need the whole evening as well. I ordered a giant spoon for Sam from a company called greatbigstuff.com. At five thirty I put on my sneak-ers and loitered around the arboretum, alternating between thoughts of Davey and picturing giving this giant spoon to Sam, their delight. They would be with their after-school sitter now, Leila. If I called her she was unlikely to ask me anything at all before putting Sam on. Leila was a "do no harm" nanny—she didn't exactly cultivate or inspire Sam, but they were safe with her. Our first nanny, Jess, had meditated with the baby, cooked macrobiotic meals, and given Harris and me shiatsu treatments. She was too good for us and we knew it. After a year she was poached by a family who could offer her a 401(k), healthcare, and full-time pay for part-time work. Who had that kind of money? Jess couldn't say, she'd signed an NDA, but we thought it was probably someone high up in local politics since her mom worked in the mayor's office. Whoever it was didn't last very long because Jess opened her own restaurant in Sonoma only a couple years later. Sometimes we still called out *Jess!* as a joke, when everything was falling apart or we were too hungry to cook. Sam also yelled *Jess!*, which was funny because they had no memory of her. Meanwhile Leila had forgotten that I was out of town and not in my garage studio.

"You thought I was in the garage this whole time?"

"I don't usually see you—I go when Harris comes home."

I went through great measures to not have to go into the house after school. I even had a pee jar in the garage.

"Right. Well, I'm not back there." I didn't say where I was; this new generation had a kind of deadpan psychic quality. "Can you put Sam on?"

She gave them the phone and they asked immediately about the big thing. I was glad to be able to give in.

"It's a spoon."

"How big is it?"

"About the size of my leg."

"That's not very big."

"How big did you think it would be?"

"Like . . . to the ceiling."

"But how would I get it in the car?"

"You could tie it on top like camping stuff."

We talked about how great this would look, like something from a Richard Scarry book, and then they asked if I felt like we would be getting a dog when I got home.

I'd forgotten about that, about becoming the kind of easygoing person who likes to pet dogs. Instead of becoming a Driver (or driving across the country), I'd doubled down on my Parking. Literally.

"We'll have to see when I get home," I said. "It's hard to make that decision from where I am."

"Can I see New York City?" they said, suddenly calling me on Face-Time. I answered, keeping my face squarely in the frame as I scanned the area. Nothing very New Yorky around here. I headed toward a tall-ish parking garage across the street.

"I'm in an outer borough right now."

"What's that?"

"It means it's quieter, no taxis and things." I huffed and puffed up the stairs to the top of the parking garage. From there was a rather striking view of downtown Los Angeles. I flipped my camera.

"Manhattan."

"Wow," they breathed, taking in the skyline. "I can see the Empire State Building!"

"Yep."

Not only the wrong city but the wrong time of day. It would be inter-esting to see, karmically, how this would come back to me. What lies Sam would tell me down the road to protect their morally questionable secret passions. In case karma worked this way, I shut my eyes and men-tally tagged my untruth with a little note: *Please be safe, sweetie.* That was to Sam, in the future, when they lied to me.

They asked how many more days until I got home and because I had just negotiated a few extra days, I knew the number well: five. Which seemed like a long time to both of us, too long, but the moment I got off the phone it seemed much too short. As I neared the motel Davey texted: Sorry, I thought she only wanted help getting it in the car. I looked up and saw Claire waiting by the door. And a mattress. And Davey.

She was so tiny next to him, one of those tall man/little woman cou-ples. When I sat on his lap I had to kind of hunch over to bring my face down to his height. She must tilt her face up to his like a child. I waved and she waved and he nodded carefully. *Do no harm,* I said to myself. *Do no harm.* I unlocked the door and said thanks for waiting. Claire started to introduce Davey and then stopped.

"I guess you've already met," she laughed.

I thought she was going to help him, but she just pointed and he dragged it inside. She seemed to be the boss of the relationship, but it was probably more complex than that. He had probably saved her from something and she had saved him, too. I took off the covers and pushed while Davey pulled their mattress off. Then the two of us put the new one, our mattress, in its place. Claire helped me remake the bed—we stood on either side, smoothing and tucking. Anything can be a ritual, you just have to name it before it ends. This was a Ritual of Permission. I permit thee to fucketh my husband. We finished with the many and flowered pillows, one after another.

CHAPTER 9

The next day he was busy when I arrived so I had to sit beside a customer in the row of connected chairs while he rented a car to a woman my age. I tried to figure out from her back if she was flirting with him. It made me crazy, other people around him; he gave himself so freely to these customers. In some alternate dimension I engaged with other people, too. And I had stature! Sometimes people wanted my autograph! But I couldn't even hold that idea in my mind for one second before it was overwhelmed by a new and much more profound thought: Who cares. None of that had any impact on what was going on in this Hertz on the Arcadia/Monrovia border. I looked at the ceiling, took smooth breaths, and pulled my shoulders back. The gray-haired woman sitting next to me chuckled a little and said something under her breath that weirdly sounded like "You're admiring him" but obviously wasn't that.

"Excuse me?"

"You're admiring his . . . physique," she said, adjusting her turquoise necklace.

My right ear generated a high-pitched tone and I pressed on it while smiling and blinking.

"Who?"

"Davey."

I wasn't sure if I could perform a believable denial and also, why should I have to? What a preposterous thing to say. One didn't have to respond to lunatics. I kept smiling and nodding politely like I couldn't understand a word she said, total gibberish.

"I won't tell anyone," she said with a wink.

I laughed and for a split second I wondered if I could kill her, just quietly press on part of her neck until she slumped to the ground and then push her under the bench with the back of my heels. Davey looked up and I smiled hi. He looked alarmed, rattled by the gray-haired woman, and turned sharply back to his customer, using a pen to explain a map.

I leaned away from her. Who was she? A witch? Had she given him something and now she was owed his soul or firstborn child? She had some kind of terrible power over him. She extended her clawlike hand in my direction.

"I'm Irene. His mother."

Or, she was his mother.

"I've seen that look before," she said. "It always surprises me because he was late to puberty, still looked like a little boy until he was sixteen or seventeen. And then all of a sudden: women in the grocery store, girls on the street, *grandmothers*."

My face. I wasn't being careful with my face. Jesus Christ. Who else knew? Everyone who looked at me? He was dying—sweating and disassembling before his customer. He knew exactly the kind of embarrassing mom things she was saying. I stood up, turned my back on her, and walked out of the franchise. It was an act of solidarity. She doesn't matter, it said. She's nothing. He immediately texted prayer hands and said he'd be done in a second.

When I looked up she was beside me again.

"I heard about your four o'clock dates," she twinkled. From who? Oh. His uncle who owned the Hertz, that was probably her brother. "Shall we go have a bite to eat and chat?" she said, taking my arm. I turned and looked at him helplessly through the window. How could I refuse his mother? Wide-eyed, he watched us walk away.

We went to Sesame Grill and both ordered the minestrone soup. "It's the only thing I can digest here," she said. "You know he and Claire will be having children soon."

"I know that's the plan."

"It's more than a plan, he's totally bound in. He'd be lost without her."

I was offended by this characterization of him.

"He doesn't know the first thing about taking care of himself. He wouldn't know what brand of toothpaste to buy. How old are you? Forty-five?"

"Yes." It was disappointing that she had nailed it.

"And you have a husband and a child and you're successful in your field. Fields."

She, or Glenn-Allen, or the uncle, had read up on me. "You read up on me."

"No, Davey told me."

I put my spoon down.

"*Davey* told you."

"I know everything. I'm the one person he's told."

At first I didn't believe her. Because this would be a good way to get a person to spill the beans if you had a suspicion.

"I will say this: he's deeply aroused by you." She paused to take a long slurp of soup. "In terms of eros, this surpasses any experience he's had so far. I've seen it myself, when he talks about you."

She was bursting. Dying to dump out her whole barrel of cracker-jacks and rusty springs. I kept my eyes on the table in a posture of un-willing submission.

"Luckily he knows kundalini so he doesn't have to waste that energy in release—he can transform it and use it. For his dance. Do you know kundalini?"

I didn't feel like this was a real question so I didn't answer.

"Don't worry—*I* didn't teach it to him." She chuckled at this prepos-terous idea. "I could have, though! I've been studying it for thirty-five years! But I got him a great teacher—a disciple of my teacher, Suraj. Is your child a girl?"

Don't gender my child.

"Well, when you have a boy there's this heavy responsibility to make a good man. A man who knows what to do with his sexual energy. The day I saw stains on the sheets I called up my best friend, Audra—you guys would get along, she's super artistic. I said, 'Audra, Davey's having wet dreams. It's time.' We had talked about this for years, we had an agreement and she made good on it. The very next day she invited Davey over and they talked and she became his lover. She had him explore her body, she explained all the parts of her vagina and vulva. Vaginas are *complicated*, right?!"

My stomach was in knots and I was kind of hunched over, my forehead almost touching the table.

"They watched pornography together and he learned how unrealistic it is. And he had so much sex that it became ordinary for him. He wasn't like other teenage boys, running around causing mayhem because of their clogged-up fourth chakras. He came into his beauty during this time. He got serious about dancing, he began dating Claire. That lucky little girl, to this day she doesn't know what hit her. You know she just lies on her back and lets him do everything? I don't believe she's ever fellated him. She's not cold—I mean, I love that girl to death, so gifted—but I always told him that she wasn't the end of the story. There were other sexual horizons. You've been great because he's gotten to use his kundalini. Obviously there can be no sex, not with you being somewhat of a public figure and married, but I think you know that and are maybe just having a little crisis because of your age and all. I've been there."

This was the last straw. I looked her dead in the eyes and shook my head: No. No more. As I stood she began fussing with my soup, trying to summon the waiter.

"She wants this to go! Can she get this to go?" She was pouring the bowl into a plastic container when I left. I stood on the sidewalk for a moment and looked back at her through the glass. She held up the container of soup. I thought about shrieking at the exact pitch that would shatter the window, it coming down like rain. I walked back to the Excelsior and got in bed. He had texted, many times.

"What did she say?" was how he answered the phone. My heart dropped; this was exactly how you would answer the phone if your mom was inappropriately involved in your sex life.

"She's your one person? The one person you told?"

He was quiet.

"You know who my one person is? My friend Jordi. She's a *friend*. Who she isn't is my mom. Or my dad. Or my mom's best friend Audra."

"She told you about Audra?"

"Oh no. That's *true*?"

"Don't make me feel like a freak," he whispered.

I hadn't thought of it that way. He was just a kid when it started. If he had been a girl with an overly involved father I'd consider him a victim of abuse. This was no different.

"Sorry."

"Everyone has their shit, right?"

"But why would you tell her? Shouldn't you be making a boundary?"

"Who am I gonna tell? A guy friend? She takes this stuff really seriously, she's respectful, you know? I can really explain how, like, profound our thing is and she gets it."

After a moment he added that he was working on changing their relationship.

"I have to get out of this place. That's the problem."

I liked it when he said *I* not *we* about things that probably involved Claire. He was starting to do that more often. I wondered if it mattered. His mom would never be my in-law, that was Claire's problem. But how skilled *was* he? An overly skilled lover was kind of icky—desire should make you clumsy. I always imagined us tripping all over ourselves with hunger.

"So, you're doing some kind of kundalini—"

He laughed. "Well, no, since I jerk off after every time I see you."

This made me feel better, that she didn't know everything. I laughed a little and he quickly said, "So can we drop this? My mom's weird, and I tell her too much, but I'm still just this fool who can't stop thinking about you."

"Okay."

"Thank you."

"Just one more thing," I said.

"Oh no."

"Is it possible you have a thing for older women because of Audra?"

"No, you're not— She was way, way older. I think of you and me as almost the same age. Roughly."

"But she was probably my age when you were— Wait, you don't still . . . ?"

"No, no. No. She's like . . ." He started to say how old she was now, but the number was apparently too preposterously high to say. "*No.* Not since Claire. Claire fucking hates her. And she agrees with you that I'm too close to my mom."

I didn't want to be the same as Claire so I said, Who am I to judge? And that I hoped when my child was grown they felt even half as comfortable telling me things (or exactly half as comfortable, that would be a good amount).

"It's funny that we're talking on the phone," he said. "We've never done that. Am I coming over?"

"Where are you?"

"In front of the smoothie place."

I considered saying let's skip it today, as if I had other things to do or self-control.

"I'm opening the window."

Almost immediately he was climbing in and then we were holding each other, flooded with sensation and relief. We didn't play games because we didn't have to. I made our snacks, he put on a new playlist, we lay on the floor. An Arkanda song came on. It was the one where she sings about what sex with her is like.

"You picked this or it's random?"

"I picked it," he said.

I let that throb through my body for a moment before showing off.

"I'm actually supposed to meet with her when I get home, to talk about a potential project."

He half sat up.

"You're shitting me."

"No. She reached out. Or her people reached out. June fifteenth, three o'clock, at Geoffrey's in Malibu."

It was unnecessary to mention the many, many postponements.

"That's in, like, a week!"

Fucking Arkanda. I could have added a few more days onto my trip; Harris had even said this was the great thing about driving, you could be flexible. Would it be crazy for Liza to push the meeting? Had anyone ever done that to Arkanda? No. And it wouldn't be appropriate. Oh, life! Such a trickster! Always teaching you a lesson! I didn't bother working out what the lesson was.

"Maybe I can come," Davey said.

"You can! It's a beautiful cliffside restaurant—the three of us could have drinks looking out over the ocean."

"I was kidding, but man. What a picture. Won't be forgetting that anytime soon. Text me after."

This was nice because we didn't talk much, really at all, about our relationship after next week. What form it would take. When or how we would see each other.

"I'll text you a picture of me and Arkanda."

"Unreal."

I could probably do more than send a picture. Arkanda worked with dancers all the time; depending on what we were meeting about, it might even be my job to gather dancers for her. I didn't want to get his hopes up, but it was a comfort to know this was one way the future might un-fold. He slid his leg between my legs. That was new. I slowly ground against it, an automatic response like how a newborn baby squeezes any finger that touches its palm.

It was my last night in New York. After Davey left I made a video for Sam and Harris with the exquisite wallpaper behind me: *I'm sad to leave this beautiful room but SO excited to be driving back to you!* I knew I was pushing my luck, passing one hotel room off for another. A therapist might say I *wanted* to get caught, but I don't think that's it. I just wanted them to see the wallpaper—to know me, a little bit.

The next afternoon Davey jumped through the window and immediately began walking around the room, shutting the curtains and turning off the lights until it was pitch-black. I laughed in the dark. Then there was the sound of a lighter, that unmistakable crunch and snap. His face was lit up, he was cupping a joint.

"Do you smoke?" He exhaled and passed it to me. This was unex-pected. Pot didn't always agree with me, but this was its own sexy little deal. How casually he'd done it. I took a puff. The cigarette was the only light in the room and keeping my eyes on it made the dark darker. He put on a hip-hop song about stars I'd mentioned liking. I could hear him moving around in the dark, dancing.

"You ever dance to this?" he called down to me on the floor.

"All the time," I said, not moving.

"You know I can't see you."

So I stood up. I shut my eyes and imagined I was back at home, watching my reflection in the windows. What were the things I did with my body when I was pretending I was in this exact situation? That I was the best dancer in the room, a professional, a devastatingly sexy mother-fucker. I bent my knees, squatting low, and rocked my pelvis with both arms hanging straight down, my hands shaking like I was about to throw dice. And this move, when it really got going, transformed into a thing where I leaned way back, from side to side, isolating each shoulder and rolling them separately. *Fishing,* I said in my head, I felt like a hot fishing rod, bending and reeling in.

"That's cool," he said.

He could see me.

"Sorry. My eyes adjusted."

My eyes had, too, and I saw that he was doing my move, not a silly imitation, but out of interest, and he was adding a little more lower body, so it wasn't all shoulders, and maybe it was the cover of darkness, but fishing suddenly seemed like something special. We both did it until it changed naturally to another thing and then another; at times we were very close together, I could feel his hot breath and then we'd let the whole room be between us, a trippy, consuming gray, through which he looked like a painting, and then we made our way back together again.

I put my hand to my mouth.

Sometimes when a cock was in my mouth or pussy I touched my lips, just to feel how tautly stretched they were, how tight the fit was. This was like that, but with happiness. I knew I was smiling, but how big? And it was then, with my fingers to my lips, that my eyes fell through the dark onto his stupid, soft little mustache. And then to his shirt buttoned all the way up to his thick neck. I stepped back and took in the whole of him. He was doing something particularly goofy in that moment, dancing with his arms dangling like a monkey's. Maybe my jaw dropped— still dancing he yelled What? over the music and I yelled I'll tell you later! And he yelled Something good? And, still smiling, I yelled Probably not!

The second he left I called Jordi. She wasn't there so I texted that I needed to talk to her right away and then I called again, no answer, so I just lay perfectly still on the bed, waiting. When she finally called back I answered the phone on the first ring and she said, Are you okay? I started crying with hard, involuntary sobs.

"Of course I love him," I gasped. "I'm so crazily in love with him."

"Yes," she said quietly.

I described his mustache, his buttoned top button. "All the things that I thought would keep me from falling for him suddenly flipped around and became the things I love most. What is that? How did this happen?" I said, as if she had been the one responsible.

"Is it the kind of love where you can't sleep?"

"Well, it would be if I didn't drug myself with three Benadryls every night."

"Wait, you take those *every night?*"

"Otherwise I wake up at two a.m. and am a total wreck the next day. Let's talk about this later."

"But is that healthy? To do that for years? I'm looking it up."

"I think it's okay. It's over-the-counter."

". . . significantly higher risk of developing dementia," she read.

This wasn't great news, given my mom's mild cognitive impairment, but dementia was the least of my problems right now.

"I'll go off them when I get home." Home. Fuck.

"Arkanda will probably have something."

I laughed through my tears, but also: she probably would. For this and love.

"Do you want to be with him instead of Harris?"

"No." That was still easy and true. "He's not a rock like that. I love him as my lover. I just want to dance with him, I don't want to raise a child together."

"So maybe it's okay."

"And fuck him. And kiss him. And lie in bed in his arms all day."

"If you were a French man this would all be perfectly acceptable," Jordi said.

She was a really good friend.

Everything would be fine. My last few days would be incredible days and then I would go home and have my meeting with Arkanda. I'd text the picture of us to Davey. Maybe she would hire him as a dancer or maybe I wouldn't even bring that up. My life was going to keep changing and expanding. The thing with Arkanda might require me to travel. I imagined calling Davey from hotel rooms, the actual Le Bristol. Arkanda might feel that the thing we were working on (album? movie? book?) was really as much mine as hers and she might stand there with her hands on her hips as her lawyer signed over half the credits and royalties ("I just like for things to be done right," she would explain, "all the *i*'s dotted and the *t*'s crossed") and then we would go on tour together. And it's not that Davey would stop mattering, it's just that all of life would be one long ride of new experiences so I would have had my fill by the time I finally came home; I'd be glad to land. The particulars of my weeks in Monrovia would have been buried by so many other exquisite experiences. Arkanda would arrange "massages" for us and I would be surprised to discover that this was a discreet way of saying sex. It wouldn't be polite to decline. And the beautiful men and women who made us come would be professionals, with clean sweat and cocks and afterward, as we showered, Arkanda would say they were the best, all the female pop stars used them.

Okay, the part about her signing over half the royalties would never happen. But I was really meeting with her and I wouldn't be surprised if female pop stars had these kinds of massages. The point was, I had it all. Or I had a lot of things, including a meeting with someone who had it all.

CHAPTER 10

Thursday was Pennsylvania to Indiana. I forced myself to glance at my itinerary each day so I would have some sense of my journey; I should at least know I'd *been* to Indiana. More important, it was Davey's day off so he came over a little earlier and we drove up into the hills. We hadn't been there since before the Buccaneer. He drove and kept one hand on my thigh the whole time and I kept my hand on top of his. There was no path in the obscure place where he pulled over so we had to pick our way over some rocks, but then it opened up into a pretty little field of dappled sunlight and tiny flowers. The ground was pokier than it looked so he walked back to the car to get something to lie on. He returned with his arms full and paused, at a distance, looking at me. I was stretching toward the sky, my cropped shirt floating high—I stopped, letting my hands fall. We'd never had the opportunity to see each other from a distance. Bees buzzed around us, the air was hot and green-smelling.

I laid out the various old jackets and towels he'd brought, puzzling them together in a patchwork. We stretched out next to each other and he put his hand on my stomach. For a long time we were quiet and then he surprised me.

"Every day she came home and told me about the room." So we *were* going to talk about it. Now that we weren't in it. "What you liked, what you didn't like."

I moved his hand just slightly higher.

"Did she think I had good taste?"

"She thinks you're . . . a character. But those pictures—she's going to get clients from those pictures."

What pictures? But it made sense, she had probably documented every inch of the room while I was out walking.

"And what did you think?"

"Me?"

"When she told you about it."

"I wondered what you were doing. What you were up to. It seemed like you were trying to . . ." He stopped short.

"Trying to what?" I really wondered.

"Trying to tell me something."

I thought back to that week, squinting as if it were decades ago. It had been a kind of brainless mania.

"It seemed like maybe"—he laughed with embarrassment—"maybe you were getting ready for me. Getting our home ready."

I blushed.

"You must have thought I was ridiculous," I whispered. "Batty."

"No. No, it was the most romantic thing. I couldn't believe it. And it let me know you cared about us. Me and Claire." Now he sat up. "I mean, that twenty thousand dollars . . . I had told you we were saving up . . . and what you did for her career? It was the right thing. I appreciated you reassuring me like that."

"Reassuring you?"

"That we could hang out without me having to worry you were going to fuck me over. You're a good person. I needed to know that."

My eyes were shut against the sun so I just kept them shut and lay there. A good person? What a preposterous theory. But there was joy in believing him; I tried to give myself over to the idea that I was good. I sat up and picked a piece of grass by sliding it slowly out of the ground.

"Saving up for what?"

"What?" He looked away.

"What are you guys saving for?"

He really didn't want to say. I laughed. It was funny to see him looking so cornered. He laughed, too.

"A house. And then a baby."

"Oh!" I said very quickly. And then I said *congratulations*, as if they had just had the baby. He said *thank you*, nervously scanning my face.

His life was so pungent and real. He seemed to have no trouble recalling his plans from a couple weeks ago, while mine had become very vague to me. I was like those poorly attached kids who would sit in any mom's lap at the potluck, whereas Davey had been thoroughly, perhaps overly, loved, and so Claire had stayed in focus. His restraint wasn't a form of flirtation that would eventually evolve into sex; it was actual restraint, he was sacrificing something he wanted for Claire. And now, thanks to me, her career was launched and they could buy a house and have a baby.

I stood up abruptly and started folding the towels and jackets.

"I think you maybe just jumped to a conclusion that isn't true," he said.

"You're not having a baby?" I was being crazy. What did it matter? I already had a baby and here I was. But all that was still ahead of him, all that shared hope and togetherness. I gave up folding and tramped away. Claire would probably push it out of her vagina; the baby wouldn't bleed out inside of her. I thought of telling him to remind her to do kick counts in the third trimester to be sure the baby was still moving.

"I have very strong feelings for you, if that isn't clear," he yelled.

I stopped and looked up at him from my part of the field and he just stared back, a face of pure misery.

"I can't say the thing I want to say to you, I need to save some things for Claire. But . . ."

"I love you," I yelled back. And then I said it a few more times. It wasn't something I needed to save for one person. He groaned and bowed his head over his hands and knees.

I saw his point. The words, though old-school, had a weird power. A few seconds ago we had been in a play and now it was turning into real life. If you wanted to be sure the play would end—the curtain would fall—then you shouldn't say those words.

He waited until I had slogged back through the grass to ask his question. It was really more of a statement.

"You love me but you wouldn't leave your husband for me."

I stared at him, agog. Was he insane? Just switch horses? And Sam would be his, what—stepchild? Harris was an adult, *my partner*. I didn't respond. It was like a ghost asking you to leave your husband for them—there was no kind way to say But you're *see-through*. He got the message anyway.

The next afternoon (Indiana to Kansas) he brought something in a little paper sack that he said was for later. I hoped it was a sex toy.

"You can't put your dick in me, but you can fuck me with the thing in that bag?"

He laughed and said no, he would show me later.

"First," he said, taking my hand, "let's lie on this bed."

I couldn't believe it.

"Are you sure?"

"I'm not as much of a free spirit as you, but I'm trying."

Oh. He was worried he was going to lose me if he didn't up the ante. And maybe he would! One day. If it stayed like this for years.

I lay with my head on his chest. He said he couldn't believe this, that he was lying with his dream girl in his arms. I saw us lying like this for the rest of our lives, profoundly married to other people but always knowing we could return to our shared world. This was what I had always wanted; he was real enough to love and love me back but not so real that I couldn't desire him. No matter how miserable I was, there would always be this to look forward to. I smiled, thinking of Parkers and Drivers. Now I could live a full and complete life as a Parker, rather than becoming a Driver, like Harris. And I would probably be a better wife and mother now that I had a lover. An almost lover.

Physically we were always on the edge of something new. That night of the paper sack I lifted his shirt and kissed his chest. The tiny nipple hairs. Then slowly I moved all the way down to the band on his underpants, which I thought would be boxers but which were white and tight and made me lose my mind a little. I unbuttoned his jeans and he only said *Fuck* under his breath. His big, hard shape was barely contained. I kissed the waistband and breathed deeply into the fabric. I couldn't believe I was down here and I wanted to stay forever. Just build a little hut right by the side of his dick and live there for the rest of my days. One might wonder why I didn't just start sucking him? Was he really going to stop me? Well, yes. He might, and that would be humiliating. I pressed my lips across his cloth-covered cock and it was right after this that he pulled me up, looking stern. By now I knew this was the look he got when it was taking all his will not to give in. He seemed on the verge of punching himself in the face or banging his head into the headboard. It was really painful for him, whereas for me it was an elaborate Victorian game. We would touch a little bit more each day, drawing it out as long as possible, and then one day we would allow ourselves to be overcome. And it would be real life. Real smells and wet tongues and cum and pubic hair and this would be astounding. The crossover into this land of physical intimacy would be like breaking the sound barrier or a plane lifting off, babies learning to walk. A new world would open up and yes it would be rife with new problems but oh the joy that would come from pausing, midsentence, to kiss.

"Time to get up," he said, rolling away from me.

What was in the bag was a strobe light. I laughed out loud. What?

Trust me, he said, it makes things more intense. As if I didn't know what a strobe was, as if I'd never attended an eighth-grade dance. He turned out the lights and turned up the music to the loudest point Skip would allow, then clicked the thing on. We started dancing. By now it didn't bother me that I wasn't at his skill level; I understood that total commitment was the only thing that mattered. The room appeared in shattered pieces, we saw each other and then we didn't. In the brief instant when the strobe caught us we were just souls, meeting each other's eyes, dead serious. This wasn't possible with language. Words always took things down a notch with their supposed *knowing*, their elaborate *trying*. Words kept you in two separate brains. Dance was the way to close the gap. What gap? How could there be a gap between any two living things when every living thing was so obviously one thing. It was handy that we were both human, but not essential, no, not essential. The beat was pure communication, there could be no misunderstanding and it could only draw things together. Here's what humor was: syncopation. Opposing the beat was a way to get fancy, show off, like a toddler daring to walk away from their mom, all the while knowing that their mom was everywhere and everything. Sometimes I danced like an old woman, barely moving, just swaying a little. Sometimes my ass swelled up like those red monkey asses and mated with the air, pumping it. Nothing was embarrassing, that's the thing you have to remember: there was no shame. Like taking Molly but we hadn't taken it.

Also this: he was glorious in what he could do. He could hang horizontally in the air for a strangely long time, sometimes strumming his fingers, making a joke. He could become entirely feminine, not only in essence, but actually seeming busty, cunty. I made a gesture with my fingers like I was sliding them between his wet labia and in the moment I was sure we both knew what I meant. Mostly he was just a really good hip-hop dancer. A strong, tireless body that wouldn't quit. When we were finally spent we threw ourselves down on the great chairs or the floor and he'd open the minifridge and take out the carton of orange juice he'd brought. We'd pass it back and forth and as it hit my tongue I'd decide that this was in fact the best part. Being so physically exhausted and drinking the cold orange juice together.

If life was completely incredible, if every moment was a perfect 10, then we'd all be totally present all the time. I know because the past and the future were of no interest to me in Monrovia. Thinking about them seemed like a waste of now. When I wasn't with him I just luxuriated in my beautiful room, sleeping late and anointing myself and having orgasms and listening to music and eating only the foods that appealed to me: hot dogs and puddings and orange Popsicles and things with peanut butter on them. Sometimes I watched a TV show or read a magazine. I didn't work or try to think of an idea for my next project. I didn't feel guilty. I didn't tiptoe or walk on eggshells. My system of *grit, grit, grit,* then *release* didn't apply here—it was all release. I was happy.

Only sometimes, when I first woke up, I had thoughts in an entirely different voice. It was cold and unimpressed. It said, *What are you doing. You're betraying your husband. You miss your child.*

I did. When the voice said this I suddenly missed my child with the incoherent, howling ache of that other time I'd lived twenty minutes away from them, the NICU days. I'd woken each morning touching my empty tummy in horror: Where was the baby? The baby was lying alone in an isolette on the fourth floor of a hospital near the freeway.

This is nothing, the voice said. *None of this is anything. Why are you hanging out with a stranger?*

It was chilling that some part of me was unmoved by Davey, but it seemed to indicate that there was a core self in there; someone was leaving the light on for me should I ever have to retrace my steps and find my way back. In the meantime I could push deeper into the woods without worry of getting lost.

Then at some point, without my noticing, the voice stopped. The moment I woke I thought of Davey, before anything else, every morning. Also, there had been warm and caring nurses in the NICU, I reminded myself. The baby wasn't alone.

CHAPTER 11

He'd had a sex dream about a boy he went to high school with.

"Aaron Bannister. He was the sweetest kid. Kind of fat. You have to picture his face—like the kindest, most innocent face."

"Was he into it?"

"Totally into it."

"And was it the kind of sex dream where you're so turned on you almost come in the dream?"

"Oh yeah, for sure. I did come."

I took this in.

"What were you . . . doing? Sex-wise?"

"Well, I was, you know, sucking him." He looked only embarrassed to have to state the obvious, to spell it out. I loved him so much in this moment. No man I had ever been with had admitted to a gay sex dream. If pressed, and I did, they would say they didn't have such dreams, which was even more disappointing. I wasn't asking them to be bisexual, just to inhabit the full range of their manhood. But I had been drawn to older men. You go back a generation or two and the cost of being gay is steep enough that it's not something you toy with if you don't have to; you just don't remember those particular dreams. The stakes were ridiculously high, vis-à-vis their manhood—it was often in peril and the threat was real; every one of my boyfriends, even Harris, had been beat up in high school for being "arty." So me purring about gay eroticism was just annoying, as if I didn't know them at all.

Davey was this same kind of man, old-fashioned and principled, but he was of his time. It just wasn't as big a deal, gayness, and so he remembered the dream and the reason he was telling me wasn't even that—it was because, *Aaron Bannister.* He knew I loved to hear about the people he'd gone to school with, the original cast, the archetypes.

"We should look him up. I just want you to see his face."

I had never opened my computer in his presence and it seemed like a funny little machine. My fingers were all over the place like wild spaghetti and the feeling made me giggle. I couldn't even sit up straight.

"Do you not know how to spell *Aaron?*" he laughed. *"A-a.* What is your problem?" He shook his head at me and took over typing.

"Look at that face"—he pointed to the slightly pained smile of Aaron Bannister—"I should have had sex with him in high school. He was probably gay."

My eyebrows shot up. Maybe all young men were bisexual now. Did Claire know? Sure, he said, but it wasn't something they had in common. He asked me to show him people I'd dated and I looked up my first girlfriend.

"So sweet," he said. "What a cute couple you must have been."

It was the only time I really cried with him. I just put my head down and bawled for absolutely no reason I could think of.

The closer we got to having sex the more clear it became that we really weren't going to.

"We can do anything else," he said softly.

"What if we just kiss," I said.

"If I kissed you I'd have to fuck you."

That didn't sound like such a big problem to me. Not that it wasn't frightening to really cheat, it was, but this was that rare situation where you should just go ahead and enjoy it and then have it in your heart for the rest of your life, a sort of vaccination against other less extraordinary affairs. And bitterness.

I watched him walk to the bathroom. *I'm thinking something,* I thought. *What am I thinking?*

I jumped up and before he completely realized I was behind him, I stuck my open palm in the stream of his hot pee, catching an overflowing handful. He made a kind of laughing bark of surprise, then fell immediately silent—it seemed to take all his concentration to keep peeing now that it was into my hand. He had a lot, it kept coming in a hot, steady stream that smelled like cereal. The smell and the heat of the urine were disorienting; one is instructed so firmly to stay away from pee and yet there is no actual law or punishment, being peed on *is* the punishment. But you don't die when it touches you and surviving pee makes you feel mighty. He was done, shaking the last few drips. I had been careful not to look at his penis. He tucked it away and I carried my hand to the sink. He watched me rinsing it off for a moment and then came over and squirted soap on his hands, lathered them up, and washed my palm and wrist, forearm and fingers. He did this with great focus, as if my hand was something very dear, a treasure.

"Is that a thing you like?" he said seriously, not meaning the hand washing.

"Oh, no—I've never done it before. I'd never thought about it until right then."

"Did it turn you on?"

"No, not exactly. But I really liked it." Now he was drying my hand with the bath sheet. "Did it turn *you* on?"

"Yeah. Couldn't you see I was trying to stay soft?"

I hadn't allowed myself to look.

"Do *you* have to go?" he whispered.

It moved me that he wanted to switch. The bright, focused look in his eyes said that none of this had ever crossed his mind before but now that it had he was one hundred percent onboard. Innocent yet totally committed, this was his essence.

"I don't think I have to go."

"Maybe later."

"I do need to change my tampon." I meant this as a warning that I needed a minute alone, but he took it another way.

"Okay." He glanced around. "Where are those?"

I mean, I was horrified.

"Oh, I don't think . . ."

He looked hurt and then suddenly self-conscious. He smiled, blinking, looking away. I'd just broken a beautiful spell. He was reaching for the door.

I took the small box down from a high glass shelf.

"Here they are."

I didn't want him to see my vagina. All vaginas look great if you're about to push your dick into them, but here, dripping blood over the O of the toilet—what good would that do either of us?

"I didn't look when you were peeing, I was facing the same way as you."

"I get it, but how will I . . ." He was holding the tampon wrapped in plastic, tilting his head, trying to understand the logistics. "Maybe if I sat down first . . . and then you sat on my lap." He mimed reaching the tampon down between his legs in a gesture that was slightly disturbing to me; I wanted to laugh but didn't.

"Okay."

He sat down in his jeans on the open toilet seat.

"Those might get bloody."

"I need to keep them on. Don't want to poke you."

I slid down my underwear and scrunched my skirt around my waist as I sat down on his lap, carefully lining up my thighs along his thighs. He put a hand on my stomach and exhaled a long, controlled breath. He was calming himself down; maybe some of that kundalini training.

"Do I open this now?" he whispered, holding up the o.b.

"The old one has to come out first," I said, reaching down mechanically. He pushed my hand away. I sat there, feeling his big fingers fish around for the string as mine usually did. It was pressed up against the labia, which were probably not entirely free of blood. I felt close to tears, some combination of shame, excitement, and an unexpected kind of sadness, as if this were coming after a lifetime of neglect. I had been so completely alone with my period all these years. He found the string, wrapped his finger around it, tugged, and seemed surprised that it didn't just pop out. With his breath heavy in my ear he gave it a long steady pull and very slowly it came into the light. He was so hard under my right thigh. He held it in the air by its string, the almost black creature from Middle-earth. I pulled off a long piece of toilet paper, ready to take over, but he wrapped it up himself with intense concentration, making various rookie mistakes and surprising choices, such as doubling up the toilet paper to begin with.

"I just put it in here?" he said, and dropped it into the tiny white porcelain trash can. Now he worked at opening the o.b., finding its little pull tab like a pack of cigarettes. He uncoiled the blue string.

"There's no . . . I thought there was, like, a holder . . ."

"I don't use that kind."

I could almost feel his thoughts rolling around like metal balls. No holder. With his face right against the side of my neck, he reached down between my legs again and slid the tip of one finger inside me. I shut my eyes. He was finding the hole. Now, with the other big hand he pushed the tampon in.

"How far?" he whispered.

"Pretty far."

He pushed it—and his finger—deep into me, the rest of his whole hand cupping my cunt. He was very careful not to move his finger or palm, but neither could he seem to leave. We sat there, breathing hard together, for a long minute. Then he withdrew and I wiped with toilet paper and stood, suddenly clumsy as if I'd already forgotten how to do anything for myself. There was only a very tiny smear of blood on his jeans, no one would ever notice. He washed his hands. We looked at each other in the mirror, very seriously and then slowly smiling. Sex was great, but this. This was something we'd never do with anyone else. Our thing.

We were getting down to the end. My reversed driving route was hard to keep track of but I planned to push my return by one day, because what was one day in the scheme of Sam's life. We stopped dancing and just lay together, spooning or holding hands, looking at each other's faces. We didn't talk about Sunday, that would only hasten it, but finally, that evening, he said, This has been the most beautiful time of my life.

"I'll only be thirty minutes away," I said from within his arms.

He was quiet. Not just quiet but unmoving. He seemed to be holding his breath.

"What are you picturing?" he finally said.

"Well, just that if we really want, we can see each other . . ."

Again, quiet. I turned over so that I was facing him.

"I mean, I'm not going to *never* see you again," I laughed.

"Right, maybe . . . at some point."

I could suddenly see that while we had been very, very intimate, we had not communicated very thoroughly. That part of us had not been called to the table. And now it seemed a little uncouth to get so specific. So I left it. We could get into the details tomorrow when we were really out of time.

On Saturday I called Harris and said I was getting close but that I wanted to spend the night in Monrovia.

"But that's less than thirty minutes away—you should just come home."

"I'm a wreck, I've been driving for days. I just need a night to pull myself together. When you drive it's like you need a vacation after your vacation!" There was some weird logic at play. I thought if I could put a little bit of truth at the end maybe all the other days could kind of hide behind it, like a bush.

"Where are you staying?"

Was he going to come here? Surprise me?

"I forget the name . . . some motel. The room isn't so bad actually."

He told me Sam couldn't wait but didn't say anything about if he could. I guessed he was a little put out that I didn't want to come right home; that I wasn't absolutely dying to.

"Can you take them to school on Monday?" he asked. "I have a nine a.m. call."

I almost laughed. It just sounded so foreign to me, like a parody of a life. But I would only have to live this way for one day; my meeting with Arkanda was on Tuesday.

"Yeah, of course. You'll have drop-off on Tuesday, because I have Arkanda."

"Oh, I thought that wasn't until later in the day?"

Well, yes, but I would want to wake up in a leisurely way, bathe, take my time anointing myself . . . Oh. It was only here that I lived like that.

"Right, I'll do drop-off on Tuesday."

I slept in a motel in Monrovia, as I had said I would. In the morning I called the front desk and asked for a late checkout.

"How late?" Skip asked.

"Two."

Davey would take a long lunch at noon. I couldn't very well justify taking a whole day to drive home from Monrovia.

"That should be okay," Skip said. "Just drop your keys at the front desk. Don't drive off with them like some people do."

I packed. It was surreal, pulling out my familiar suitcases from under the bed and taking my clothes off the gilded hangers. Were the hangers mine, too? Yes, technically I could take everything in this room. The porcelain trash can, the towels, the bedspread; I had paid for all of it. But if I piled everything into my car then it wouldn't be here to come back to.

Leaving the room intact was some kind of insurance that Davey and I would meet here again, at least a few more times. I folded my clothes carefully, pretending that I would be unpacking them in Arkanda's guesthouse, maybe with her watching. Of course things wouldn't move this quickly—I would have to unpack at home and repack—but this performance made it possible to stay in motion. I folded his soft plaid shirt and placed it neatly on a great chair. I put a stack of twenty-dollar bills on the marble-topped table for Helen, one for each day of my stay. I bathed and slid on the same soft, cream dress that I had worn on our first real day in this room. I was glowing in the mirror, there were little pulsing dots spinning around my head, either something mystical or I wasn't breathing enough. My phone rang; it was Liza.

"I'm in the middle of something," I said.

"I can text it."

"Okay, let's hang up and you text it."

"I'll just say what it is, in case you have any immediate questions, and then I'll hang up and text the details."

This wasn't even close to how a real manager would act.

"Okay, say it quickly, like a text."

"Let me think of the shortest number of words." She paused. "Okay, here it is: Arkanda canceling. Call me for details."

"What."

"Should I hang up?"

I paced around silently for a second.

"I don't understand. There was a time and a place—three o'clock, Geoffrey's."

"I know. I told them that."

"What did they say?"

"They said, We're really sorry."

"And what did you say?"

"I said, Let's just put something on the calendar."

"That's good. That's a good way to phrase it."

"It's how I always say it. And it usually works, but this time her assistant said they would have to circle back because Arkanda's whole schedule was changing because she had to go to Beijing for three months. She also said every day is Tuesday."

"What does that mean?"

"Well, I said, Are Fridays generally good? And she said they don't use days of the week, just the numbers. So Sunday is no different from Tuesday. Every day is Tuesday. I thought that was interesting."

I got off the phone at that point.

I stared at my suitcase and duffel bag lined up by the door. Maybe something else would come up; maybe I would need to go to New York for work. No, of course not, because *I had just been there*. I wasn't going anywhere for a long, long time. That had probably always been true. I had a bad feeling, my tongue tasted sour. Was an alarm ringing in the distance? A very loud but very faraway alarm? No. There was no alarm, it was just the sound one's own ears make in silence, churning.

Right before he arrived I had the sudden, weird hope that he would reach into his pocket and pull out a gift and it would be jewelry. I would have this necklace or bracelet and no matter what happened next I could touch it throughout the coming days and feel okay. He did reach his hand into his pocket, but then he just left it there. He stared at my packed bags and then at his folded shirt on the chair.

"I hoped you would keep that."

It wasn't really the same thing as a locket, but I unzipped my suitcase. He knelt down beside me and laid the shirt on top of my toiletries bag, giving it a pat. Then he ducked his head, tilting sideways to look under the bed.

"What's that?" he said, pointing.

I pulled out the painting I'd slid under there so long ago. "It's one of those pictures that's of nothing, so it won't offend anyone. I think they're made especially for motel rooms and doctors' offices."

He stared at it. "It's a woman. See?" He outlined a gray figure with his finger. "She's walking into the woods or some kind of cave or . . ."

Why were we wasting our precious time on this? I slid it back under the bed. We stood and he held me and I thought, Good, let's begin. Because there were only a couple hours to process everything that had happened between us and discuss how we would integrate each other into our lives going forward. I could see meeting once a month or even once every two months. And I had some ideas about dance opportunities I could help him get in New York. Or London. Somewhere far away where we could, eventually, no rush, consummate this thing.

He kissed my forehead.

"I wish I could carry your things to your car for you."

I stepped back, aghast.

"We have almost two hours. We can do anything we want for two hours."

"We can't say goodbye for that long. That's just going to make it more painful."

"But we have to . . . talk about everything," I said. "What are we going to do? Are you going to call me?"

"When?"

"When? I don't know, to see if I got home safely? Or to check in tomorrow?"

"That's probably not a good idea. That will start a whole calling and texting thing. Better to go cold turkey."

Cold turkey.

"What about texting after Arkanda? The picture of me and her I was going to send you?" I could text him to say she had suddenly canceled; that would be something.

"You'd better not, but I'll be thinking of you at three on Tuesday. Hoping it's going great with her."

I said nothing. He held my head.

"It was perfect," he whispered. "Nothing like this will ever happen to me again."

My eyes were open and wild against his chest.

I had miscalculated, made some kind of basic, dumb error. Nothing said now could save me; it was suddenly and overwhelmingly clear that it was much, much too late. Something very bad was coming next and the only way I could have avoided it would have been to not stop for lunch in Monrovia two and a half weeks ago.

I became numb and orderly. I said I wished him the very best. He looked around and said he was going to miss this place; I said me too. This was a terrible exchange, but what did it matter. Bullets fired into a body already dead. He said again that he wished he could carry my bags out and I said it was really no problem. He climbed out the window, first one leg, then the other. There was an opportunity to do something romantic with the open window between us, but I just gave him a tight smile and drew the curtains shut. I turned and went right to my suitcases and began rolling both of them out the door and toward checkout. I didn't turn to see if Davey had circled the block and was going to chase after me and in a short amount of time it became evident he hadn't, wasn't going to. As Skip took my key, a middle-aged couple came in, sweaty and disheveled from the road.

"We weren't sure, from the sign . . . 'no no vacancy.'"

"Two nos make a yes," he told them, running my credit card. "We actually have a new suite."

"Oh, a suite!" the woman said, turning to her husband. "That sounds nice."

He nodded. "I think we can splurge for one night."

"It's just being cleaned right now, if you can wait a few minutes." Skip had handed me the receipt already and now gave me a look like, *Is there anything else I can help you with.* The couple also now looked at me. I opened my mouth to say something about the suite, about it really being mine—but it wasn't. If you wanted to own property you went about it in a completely different way. Escrow, things like that. I wheeled my bags out to my car, tears openly running down my face. Helen was carrying clean, folded towels to room 321, but she paused to watch me load up.

"I don't regret what I did," she suddenly called out. I was startled;

my weeping paused. "If I could go back, I wouldn't do anything differently. I would do it all exactly the same."

It seemed like she had committed a terrible crime and somehow thought I was the right person to hear she was unrepentant. I nodded as if I understood and, now somewhat self-consciously, got in my car and began backing out.

Her affair. She didn't regret cheating on Claire's uncle. I looked back at her in the rearview mirror. With the towels clutched to her chest, she watched me drive away.

PART TWO

I drove past Monrovia and the exit for my friend who keeps chickens. I kept glancing at my phone, but Davey didn't text. People were right about the drive home feeling shorter than going the other way; in fewer than fifteen minutes everything around me was alarmingly familiar. In twenty minutes I was almost home. I was gasping in a strange way, a fish on land. I pulled over. Of course it wouldn't take me a week to drive home, but this was ridiculous. This wasn't enough time to even plan what I was going to say, how I was going to be. I stared dumbly at my mileage. I watched a YouTube video about how to hack your odometer, but it was too complicated for a modern car. He never drove my car anyway; I was being paranoid. Or paranoid about the wrong things. Like, was the car even dirty enough? Did it look like I could have driven across the country in it? I turned abruptly to look at the back seat and did something to my neck; it seized up painfully. Good. This was good. "I did something to my neck," I would say, coming in the door. And that would explain everything. People were always acting the wrong way because of things like a pulled neck. It was a drag when someone was like this, but not a crime. I glanced at myself in the rearview mirror. How could anyone see this face and not think: *that person is in love?* But luckily life wasn't like that. No one would guess that instead of going to New York for two and a half weeks I had hidden out thirty minutes away with a boy who worked at Hertz. That would be an absurd conclusion to jump to. I pulled back into traffic. In no time I was on our street. God, look at it. So utterly the same, like a diorama of itself. And there's our neighbor, Ken, waiting for his dog to poop. He waved and walked up to the car. I rolled down the window.

"Hi, Ken."

"Haven't seen you around for a while!"

"Yeah. I took a road trip."

"Just you?"

"Yeah. I drove across the country."

"Wow, you must be exhausted! I'll let you get in!"

I hesitated. Why hurry when this was the last moment of my freedom. I imagined telling Ken about my situation, how nervous I was about re-entering my home, given the chaos in my heart. He might suggest that I spend a couple of nights with him and his wife, Ann, or whatever her name was. *Think of our home as a halfway house,* they'd say, making up the guest bed. *A chance to pull yourself together.*

God, this is exactly what I needed, I'd say.

Just eat and sleep and let your unconscious do the work. While you're sleeping we'll say prayers and do various energy-moving rituals to help you with the transition.

"Thank you," I said. Ken stepped away and I pulled into my driveway.

They weren't home. The scooter was gone; they were out at the park. I brought in my suitcases and washed my hands and quickly began putting away my clothes. I wanted to be in the middle of something when they came in. But they were taking a while. I walked around the house, noticing small changes—new drawings on the refrigerator, the Lore Estes book, a weird purple cardboard box on the coffee table. Things were fundamentally dirty in a way I wouldn't have allowed, but I was in no position to complain about anything ever again. I carried my empty suitcases down to the basement. I rolled them into their place and then I froze, listening: They were home. They were opening the front door.

"Mama?" Sam ran around the house; the scooter rolled on the kitchen floor above my head. My heart shattered at the sound of their little voice. Whatever I had been doing to minimize this pain abruptly ended—I was desperate to see my child. But I couldn't move. I was immobile, stricken. The transition was simply not possible for me. Someone got a glass of water from the faucet. The toilet was flushed, loud in the pipes. Harris called out my name. Sam shouted, Where's my big spoon? They knew I was home, but where was I? How much longer could I stay down here without it being hard to explain? Not much longer. I was crouched between my suitcases and a mini trampoline on its side. I wasn't dead, but I was too much a soul. I had weighted things too heavily in the direction of music and poetry, and my spirit, thusly animated, had come to think of itself as a full person. It did not understand how misshapen it was. Now they were looking in the backyard for me. Other people knew how to merge things; I was forever running back and forth between opposites, never in any one place.

I could not be found.

They could not find me.

I pounded up the stairs in what felt like the very last second; the last train home.

"I was in the basement!" I yelled. And though this didn't quite explain everything, it seemed to be enough. Sam jumped into my arms and I carried them to the couch and rocked them and kissed them like a giant baby. I was weeping when I looked up to see Harris taking our picture; without thinking I threw my hand up, blocking my unreliable face.

"You'll thank me later," Harris laughed. "Welcome home."

I stood and hugged him; Sam wrapped their little arms around the two of us. My dear family. Thank God for it. There was no problem. I had everything anyone could ever want.

The next morning I woke up doubled over, gut-punched. Before even opening my eyes, it was obvious that I had experienced too much joy in the Excelsior. Regular life—my actual life—was completely gray, a colorless, never-ending expanse. *Just get through this one, first, day.* But that was too long. An hour was too long. My system of *grit* followed by *release* was completely broken—this was too hard to grit through and there was no future release to look forward to. I didn't even have a project to hide inside of, a premiere to work toward. There was only now. I told myself that all I had to do was get up and make Sam's school lunch. After that I could die or go crazy. I got up. I splashed water on my face and walked into the big kitchen with the big family-sized refrigerator and began ripping up kale for the kale salad that went in one compartment of Sam's bento box. My face contorted into tears while I did this. Not a small cry but heaving sobs. After a minute I wiped them away and put olive oil and salt and nutritional yeast on the salad, massaged it, put the lid on. Part one done of a five-part lunch. The problem wasn't the lunch, it was what came after, the whole rest of my life.

Sam stumbled sleepily into the kitchen and I quickly wiped my eyes and kissed their sweaty, sweet-smelling hair and warm face.

"Your cheeks are so cute, I might have to eat them!"

"*Your* cheeks are so cute, Mama!" And they pretended to gnaw messily at my cheeks, making animal sounds. They were fine. Not traumatized by my absence; enough love and stability in the bank to cover two and a half-ish weeks.

Harris woke up. We didn't gnaw on each other's cheeks because that wasn't our dynamic; he nodded hello and asked me how I had slept, like a coworker in the staff kitchen, but less neutral. There was already something I should have done but hadn't. What was it? Initiate sex on my first night back? Yes, I should have done that before I had a chance to get my bearings. But also my movements around the kitchen were too tense and erratic, herky-jerky. I put a glass in the dishwasher before he was even done with it. Why was I being this way? If only he could have seen me in Monrovia! So relaxed. I froze, seeing Davey climbing in the window. Pulling me to him. How we just stood there.

"I know what you're thinking," Sam said.

"What am I thinking?"

"That I'm going to ask if we can get a dog."

Good God.

"We will get one," I said. "We *will*. But this isn't the right moment."

"When will it be the right moment?"

"We'll just know. It will be obvious to both of us."

I drove them to school, a twenty-three-minute drive that I had histori-cally tried to use for conversations that benefited from no eye contact. (Did you maybe *borrow* the teacher's stopwatch and forget you borrowed it? And that's how it ended up in your backpack?) But Sam was in luck, today it was okay to listen to the same song on a loop for the entire ride. I glanced at my phone every few seconds. No texts. Had it even really happened? I saw us dancing to the strobe, spooning on the floor, his finger pushing in the tampon. Yes, it had. It had all really happened. Maybe that was enough and I could be grateful for the experience. I imagined a heroin addict saying, "I will always treasure the memory of being high. I am grateful for the experience."

In the rearview mirror Sam was quietly talking and gesticulating. They hadn't yet learned to keep the dream inside. I briefly met their eyes and they looked at me absently, as if over someone's shoulder.

How do you know if you're in the deathfield? I texted my dad from the concrete floor of the garage office. I wondered if this would come across as a cry for help and got ready to insist that I was *fine*. The hair around my ears was soaked through from crying on my back.

You're not in the deathfield if you're asking that question, he texted back, and then seven pictures, all of rocks. He is an amateur geologist.

By evening I was no longer so emotional. Emotions seemed com-paratively fun, florid and poetic. Now I was more like a machine need-ing a part it couldn't function without. There was a coldness to my mind, it could only drill down into a single repeating thought. I had to talk to him. That was all. Nothing else was of interest to me. I wasn't allowed to call or text, but he never said don't come back.

I cuddled with Sam, read Narnia, kissed them in all the funny places they pointed to. I sat in the dark until their breaths were sweetly deep and even, then I crept away and began my preparations with the precision of a suicide bomber. Everything had to be in place for the next day: Tuesday. Harris still thought I was meeting with Arkanda; my plan was to tell him later that she'd canceled at the last second. For now it explained why I was so nervous, why I was trying on so many different outfits, why I would wear makeup to take Sam to school. The trip would be timed with Davey's lunch break. *Are you in agony, too?* I would ask him. *Or was it like summer camp for you? Fun but it's nice to be home.*

After morning drop-off I thought the words *It's showtime* and broke into a grim, cold sweat. I thought of calling Jordi on my way to Monrovia, but then I'd have to call her again afterward to tell her how it went—better to just tell her the whole story at once. It was shocking all over again how close it was, even quicker when you knew where you were going—twenty-seven minutes with no traffic.

I parked across the street from Hertz but at an angle so he couldn't see my car through the big front windows. My heart was pounding so hard I could hear it, there was a clicking noise. He wasn't at the front desk, but unless his schedule had changed it was ten minutes too early for lunch. He must be moving cars between lots or in the bathroom. I watched Glenn-Allen spray down the front counter then look at his phone. I sat in my car for twenty minutes before realizing. It was his day off. How could I have forgotten. He didn't work on Tuesdays. I fell back in my seat and looked all around, reeling. So he could be anywhere. But almost certainly he was at home. I couldn't go to him there because I didn't know where he lived. I sat for a few minutes, just adjusting. Recalibrating. I certainly couldn't turn around and drive home; he had to know I'd been here. I would leave a note. What would the note say? The note would say: *Call me.* I looked at Glenn-Allen again and imagined him asking if I wanted to add my name and me saying Davey'll know who it's from and that seeming very negative, like he'd knocked someone up and now he had to pay the piper. I was going to have to leave it in a language that only Davey understood.

I drove the two blocks to the Excelsior. It was startling and painful to see my old door. It had been less than forty-eight hours, but it felt like years. I parked near the alley. I put the pink canvas folding chair in my trunk and drove back to Hertz. Glenn-Allen was on the phone now. I wouldn't put it right in front of the building, where it might get cleared away, but across the street, next to the city trash can and the bus bench. In that kind of setting no one would be in a hurry to remove it, it was more seating for the elderly and disabled. It almost might be too subtle. Would Davey even notice it? Probably. He would recognize it as very similar to if not as the same pink canvas chair he used to step on to get into my window, but would he pick up on its meaning?

It wasn't a hardware store, more of a garden supply place, but they had spray paint. I had to ask the clerk to unlock the case. It was hard to shake the sensation that Davey was watching every move I made, but I pushed forward. For all anyone knew I was a local woman who needed to paint something black.

"Is it quick drying?"

The clerk, an older man, put on his glasses and read the label. "Dries in thirty seconds on most surfaces."

"Wow. No going back," I said.

"No," he agreed. He looked at me over his glasses. "You ever used this type of paint before?"

"Not recently. Not that I can remember."

"You might want to practice first, on a piece of newspaper or something. Until you get the hang of it."

He actually wasn't that much older than me. A kind man. He probably thought I was touching up my garage door or something. For a moment I longed to be a woman with that kind of concern and a normal, everyday feeling in her chest. Nothing exciting happening but nothing really wrong. I used to have days like that. Did I? Maybe not.

The clerk was right, it took a little while to learn how to form the letters, you had to keep your hand moving, you couldn't stop or it would pool. I practiced on the free weekly. I wrote CALL, CALL, CALL, turning to a fresh page each time, followed by the shorter but trickier ME, ME, ME. Then, without further ado, I tilted the chair onto the ground and sprayed CALL on the backrest. Counted to thirty. Then set it upright again and wrote ME on the seat. It was perfect, almost like art. I quickly set it up next to the bus stop. He would see it in the morning when he got to work. Then he would call me.

Jordi picked up on the first ring.

"I'm just leaving Monrovia," I said, merging onto the freeway.

"Oh my god," she said. "You went back."

"Just wait." I told her the whole story, ending with putting the chair across the street from the Hertz.

She didn't say anything. As I sped down the freeway the sky seemed to broaden and sharpen. I felt a little like I was waking up from a dream.

"You think I should go back and get it."

"Maybe." She said this very, very gently and then kept talking in the strangely careful, calm voice—*What you guys had was so special and so . . .* mutual, *but this is kind of . . . stalkerish . . . I'm just worried you might regret*—but I had already exited and gotten back on the freeway in the other direction. I said I understood and I thanked her.

"I'm sorry," she said.

"No, no need to apologize. I'm really grateful for this perspective." There was an odd civility between us. It was sobering to realize there were limits to our cheering on. She would not cheer me off a cliff. Right before we hung up she asked if I'd stopped taking the three Benadryls every night. I had forgotten about that. I touched the side of my head as if I could check for dementia that way.

"I'll stop now. Starting tonight."

"It might be a good time to take really good care of yourself."

"Okay."

"And your family."

That was a slap in the face. But she was right. Very right. I hoped I wasn't too late. And the chair. I didn't know how to dispose of it. Its desperate message made putting it back in the alley too risky; anywhere in Monrovia was dangerous. So I returned to L.A. with it in the trunk like a dead body. A few blocks from our house I pulled over and put it in the park. There was a grassy area where people liked to sit or picnic and sometimes they even brought camping chairs. I set it up in the shade. Someone would probably swipe it in the night. I'd left countless things in this park—my sunglasses, Sam's hat—and nothing was ever still there when we came looking for it.

As I crossed the grass to my car it became 3:00. I stared at my phone for the whole sixty seconds, knowing almost for certain that he was thinking about me. Me and Arkanda. Having drinks cliffside with the ocean view. Then it became 3:01 and the rest of my life without him unfurled, endless and bleak.

Then a text came.

It was a video shot at night—I had to cup my hand around the phone and hunch over it to block the glare. He was lit only by his car headlights. It took a little while for me to notice them: the columns. He was dancing in front of the Excelsior. He had gotten up in the middle of the night, slipped out of their bed, driven back to the motel, parked the car just so, and done this dance. There was no part where he touched his heart or enacted heartache in an explicit way—it was just the whole thing. His whole body was desperate and writhing and occasionally climbing an invisible thread, seeming to rise, and then falling as if down a well. He did it in slow motion so I could see each frame, the terror of falling. Some movements he did again and again, like a repetitive thought or a human trapped in the limits of this fucking life. At the end he walked toward the camera, his sneakers crunching on the gravel, broad shoulders heaving breathlessly, and for a moment his whole face filled the screen. He looked wrecked.

Men gave jewelry when they couldn't give a song or a dance about their love because they couldn't sing or dance. But he could. I stared at the name Davey on my phone, blood pounding in my head. I thought: I should do some breathing exercises first but I didn't have the discipline to take even a single long, slow breath before I called.

"I have to call you back," he whispered, no hello. "I'll call you right back," and he hung up. I dissolved into a pool of narcotic relief. The effect his voice had on my nervous system was so powerful and immediate that I felt like I was going to pass out as I waited. I steadied myself, putting one hand on the smooth trunk of a tree. Maybe a sycamore. Maybe this moment would spark a lifelong interest in nature. Probably not. He called back.

"What's up," he said. My heart fell. What was *up?*

"Well, I got the video. I loved it. And I really, really miss you."

He was silent. Maybe I had misunderstood the video. I would never call him again after this. He could call and call and I wouldn't answer.

"I miss you, too," he said. "This is harder than I thought it would be."

I touched my forehead to the tree.

"Yeah."

We were silent together for a long time. I blinked and fat tears rolled to my chin.

I could hear his breathing. It sounded strange. Oh, he was crying. *He* was crying.

"I shouldn't have sent you that," he rasped. "It's just gonna set us back."

"I made you something, too, but I"—I glanced at the Call Me chair in the grass—"didn't send it."

"You're a better man than me. Stronger."

He had such a sexy way of putting things. Other people disappointed, but he, surprisingly, never did.

"But this is the end," he added, taking a breath. "This has to be the real end."

"I know."

"I need to be starting my life now. I want all the things you have—a child, a house—"

"Where do you live now?" Too prying. "It's not big enough?"

"We rent a guesthouse; it's basically one room. We could never afford a real house this close in. So that video was goodbye, okay?"

"Okay."

"No calling or texting after this. That was our time and I'll never feel like that again but I can't think straight when you're in my life, you understand?"

"Yes." He couldn't think straight.

"So if you want me to be happy—not happy like I was with you, but happy in a normal way that I can, like, build a life on—then you won't call."

"Okay."

"Or text."

"Or text. I get it. I love you and I want you to be happy."

"I want you to be happy, too. You know I'm not going to say I love you."

He kind of just had.

"Sorry," I said.

"Don't say sorry. Thank you for understanding."

"I want the best for you."

I felt so jolly and generous I almost added *You're gonna be a great father*, but I didn't. We got off the phone warmly, almost laughing, saying I'll see you when I see you.

I texted Jordi that the most magical thing had happened—I forwarded her the video—and that now it would be no problem to let go and that I loved her and I was getting off Benadryl and also What is going on with you??? Tell me everything! I wrote. I feel as if I've been gone for years.

That night I made my famous grain-free blueberry pound cake and cut fat slices with a steak knife and regaled everyone with the story of Arkanda canceling at the last minute.

"Again! Can you believe it?"

"You don't seem very disappointed," Harris noted.

"I guess I just feel like what can she give me that I don't already have, you know?" I looked around fondly but mostly meant the video on my phone of Davey dancing. I had to make sure to download that and back it up.

After dinner we played a made-up card game using many random, incomplete decks of cards combined. I had the energy and focus to invent fun rules like if you got an ace you had to pretend to be an object.

"Mama has an unfair advantage," laughed Harris. "This is her area of expertise."

"Unfair advantage!" yelled Sam.

I giggled, unsure what my expertise was (being something I'm not?) but feeling proud. And the whole time I wondered, Is this real? Despite all the lies leading up to it, was this moment of pretending to be a pepper grinder—rotating my hips—real? Maybe it all began now, my life as a wife comfortable in her own home, a real wife. I tried to remember how Pinocchio had become a real boy. It had something to do with being in a whale, maybe saving his father's life; I hadn't done anything like that. But surely a woman was more complex than a puppet boy and she might become herself not once-and-for-all but cyclically: waxing, waning, sometimes disappearing altogether.

I glanced at the sex high heels before bed, but there was no hurry now; there were still four days to initiate before the week was up. I did an algae mask and skipped the three bright pink Benadryls. I had a hunch that I'd sleep very soundly tonight. Good night, everyone! Good night, Sam! Good night, Harris! Sweet dreams!

At two a.m. I was wide-awake as if it were the middle of the afternoon. My ecstatic relief was completely gone; it had seeped out during my few hours of sleep. Of course I would always be okay when I was listening to Davey's voice and I would always get progressively less okay each hour after that. As I lay in the dark the full severity of my fixation came into focus. There weren't minutes in between my thoughts of him, just breaths—sometimes two or three, but never more than that. How had this happened? It made no sense. And now I was masturbating without even deciding to. His dick was pushing into me while he kissed me and we were looking at each other with disbelief that this was really finally happening; he said my name again and again while he pumped harder and faster and his dick was my clitoris; I was fucking my own hole with his/my giant hard clit, the glittery purple dick, and it felt absolutely incredible—probably the polyp, hopefully benign.

"Mama! I'm awake!"

It was six a.m.

I rose from my grave. I made a smoothie, toasted a waffle; I explained things and made laughing sounds at the end of jokes. I found I could talk to Sam and think about Davey at the same time. I sliced my finger open while chopping a carrot and for a brief, shocked moment— as I stanched the bleeding and got the Band-Aid—I was present and whole, total mind/body integration. *Your entire life could be like this*, I told myself. *Just let him go.*

The week ended and I did not initiate sex with Harris, which was like being past due on a bill. I knew it would feel good to orgasm, cry; certainly sex would reconnect us . . . that was the problem.

Sam graduated from second grade and summer camp began, with its crude, random schedule. *Pickup at 2:25? Why not just 2:30?* I needed those extra five minutes for my FBI-level, hyper-focused internet dives. Over the years Davey's mom and uncle had posted pictures of him and his sister, Angela, and these were often exquisitely raw and unflattering images. I loved seeing him this way. The razor burn or acne and longer hair. From there I went to Angela's timeline; occasionally her brother had visited her in Sacramento and I liked to see them hanging out together, without Claire. Did Angela even like Claire? Certainly Angela would have preferred me as a sister-in-law if I had been presented as an option. I also looked at the timeline of Angela's boyfriend, scrolling deep into his attempt at getting a carpentry business started. Davey had Liked his post about replacing a countertop. Whenever I saw his full name in the wild my heart nearly stopped: Davey Boutros. But for every piece of gold there was a scorpion to step on. In Angela's boyfriend's grid was a carousel of family photos from a hike. In slide three Davey was standing behind Claire, his hand wrapped around her waist from behind. It was the most violent and obscene image I'd ever seen—a knife to the gut would have been gentler. I tried to calm myself with Dev's feed, Davey's dancer friend, our alibi. He only posted dance videos and historically many of these had included Davey—but none since my return. Maybe Davey was too sad to dance, just as I was too sad to talk to God or work or do anything but scroll.

Each night I came in from the garage as late as possible, the evening hours with Harris and Sam being the most treacherous as I mimed my way through interactions that should have been second nature, a perpetual houseguest nervously trying to demonstrate how at ease she felt. And then it was the dead of night again and I understood how truly forsaken I was, having lost my bond to my actual family and formed an alliance with someone who might as well be fictional.

I spiraled until dawn, wondering if my dad's soul had come back and if it was possible that his walk-in had walked-in to me. Not literally, but my dad and I shared an ability to become untethered from our surroundings, creeped out by the familiar. It was really a shame that I had to keep such a strict boundary with my father. He would never know how successful his grooming had been! How often I still saw the world through his eyes. Which in my youth had ensured a certain intimacy (with him) but now seemed to stand in the way of intimacy a lot of the time.

"Mama! I'm awake!"

On the weekends, I was expected to be present and engaged for many hours in a row, which needless to say I couldn't do. I couldn't even stand up completely straight; I was always slightly doubled over with loss. Harris sipped his second cup of coffee and said something about mugs in a funny accent; when I didn't laugh he grew silent, watching me make the seven waffles.

"I thought we'd hear more stories about your trip," he said between sips.

I immediately straightened up.

"What do you mean?"

"You usually have a story when you come in the door, even just from the grocery store."

Did I? Yes, of course, I was always wanting to tell him more than he wanted to hear. It was especially annoying when I recounted an interaction with a fan, sort of downplaying it as if I didn't live for that. I poured the batter, thinking.

"There was a waiter in Indiana who knew my work. He talked my ear off about what an incredible hip-hop dancer he was and then as I was walking to my car he ran out to the parking lot and tried to *show* me. It was so awkward."

Sam rushed in, hating to miss anything.

"What? What was awkward?"

"Mama met a dancer in Indiana."

"And he talked my ear off! I can tell you anything about his wife! His sister! His overbearing mother."

"These people always think they really know you," Harris said, ripping off a piece of Friday's waffle and putting it in his mouth. "They can't separate the actual person from the work."

I was suddenly overwhelmed with the urge to slap him, hard. *The real me is in my work. Any fan of my work knows me better than you do.* But whose fault was that? I hunched over my crossed arms.

"Still carsick?"

That's what I'd said on the first night, what a weak excuse.

"It might be more intestinal."

"You should go lie down," he said. As if a person who'd just been on vacation for almost three weeks deserved to go lie down—ha, nice try, buster. I remade waffle seven.

Jordi was my only escape, my one person. I dressed for her as if she was Davey and sometimes arrived in such a state of desperation that I couldn't talk for the first few minutes in her studio; I just walked around gasping, as if I'd been holding my breath since we'd last spoken. If before the trip I had looked forward to our dessert dates, now I lived only for them. Once she'd canceled at the last minute (to meet with an important curator) and I lost my shit like a devastated child. Far from becoming a Driver I'd become such an extreme version of myself that I couldn't tolerate anything that fell outside my extremely narrow interests, which were all memories.

"Once I was telling him something and he asked me to repeat it because he'd been distracted by my jawline. And then he traced my jawbone." I showed her, dragging my own finger from my ear to my chin. "Like that. Also, I think I forgot to tell you that once we went to a Middle Eastern restaurant in broad daylight, like a regular couple."

"You did tell me. Right after it happened."

"Oh, that's right."

Jordi put both her hands flat on the table and took a breath. Uh-oh.

"I want you to know that it's okay if you want to leave Harris. It's not a crime. People do it every day—"

I cut her off.

"That's not the issue."

"It's at least a *little bit* of the issue."

"I don't want to be married to Davey or even be his girlfriend! It's not that kind of love."

"Okay, but it doesn't seem like you want to be with Harris eith—"

"I *do*." I reminded her how Harris was a balancing force, the yang to my yin. "I just got out of balance in Monrovia. It's like I did ketamine every day for two weeks and now I'm hooked and I have to get unhooked or it will destroy my life. *That's* how you should be thinking of this."

"Okay. How many times a day do you think of him?"

I did some quick mental math, taking the estimated number of times per hour and then multiplying it by the twenty hours I was awake every day.

"Between three and four thousand?"

Jordi nodded calmly as if this wasn't a completely unhinged amount. She fished around in a drawer until she found a rubber band and then showed me a trick that had helped her stop smoking. I put the rubber band on my wrist and snapped it a few times.

"Only do that when you think about him; it's negative reinforcement."

"I *was* thinking about him."

I snapped it again.

"Do you still look him up?"

"What do you mean *still*?"

"I thought you were trying to get over it."

"I am. It's hard."

"But do you notice anything you do that makes it harder? Or easier?"

Looking him up was only ever agitating, this was obvious. I checked everything one last time and then she showed me how to put blocks on my phone and computer so I couldn't do that, something she'd learned when she was semi-addicted to porn.

"Now, what makes you think about him less?"

There were really only degrees of more, but I tried to think of what was the opposite of looking him up.

"Maybe your work?" Jordi suggested.

"What work?"

Our eyes met; she looked quietly terrified for me. Obviously a person like me, like us, could only find salvation in her work.

"Cleaning. Maybe when I clean I think about him a tiny bit less."

"Perfect," said Jordi, "and think how nice your house will look!"

I scoured and polished like a woman who had only her floors to be proud of. I attacked the refrigerator and freezer, our closets, junk drawers—all the places a happy person would never go.

Wow, said Harris. I guess we never lifted up that rug.

I simply told myself what I wanted to have done and I obeyed, with no feeling about it one way or the other. I went room by room: every drawer, floor, cabinet, shelf, window. I wasn't fast or energetic, just methodical—the dutiful servant of a future, unheartbroken self. Some weekends I was so wrecked I could only manage one wall of a room, very slowly. Because it was undesirable work, clearly no fun, Harris and Sam could only stand by.

"Are you going to clean out the drawer under my bed?" Sam asked, nude except for a digital watch.

"Not today. I'm only doing this wall. Anything that's along this wall will get cleaned out. You should get dressed."

"What about the toy bucket?"

The toy bucket was in the corner, where today's wall met next weekend's wall.

"I'll do the toy bucket today."

"What about the middle of the room?" said Sam, standing in the middle of the room.

"Once I'm done with all four sides then I'll vacuum the whole room, including the middle."

Sam sat down in the center of the rug, prepared to wait several weeks for me, then grew impatient and positioned themselves against the wall I was working on. They shut their eyes and wrapped their arms around their knees, waiting.

"What is this thing?" I said, talking to myself. "I've never noticed it before, but it's against this wall so I have to clean it." The thing giggled in anticipation. I pulled it out from the wall and leaned it back onto the rug. Its eyes were still closed. I took a clean rag and gently wiped its face, behind its ears, between its fingers. I cleaned each knee, which made it laugh. I turned it over and cleaned its butt cheeks and the bottom of its feet. When I was done the thing opened its eyes and, mixing its metaphors, now seemed to be a person who had slept for a hundred years.

"Who I am?" they said. "Who are you?"

"I'm your mother."

"Mother? What's a mother?"

"It's a person who takes care of you because you are their child."

"Child? What is child?" They walked around the room touching all the familiar things with wonder.

"A child is a younger person."

"Is this a child?"

"That's a bed."

They teetered out the door to discover the rest of the house.

Every day there were opportunities like these. Every day Sam and Harris extended their hands and said, Come in from the cold. But I could not come in.

CHAPTER 13

It was easy to fool Sam because they operated in terms of the things they wanted, moment to moment—not that they weren't affected by emotional undercurrents but that they couldn't call me on it very specifically. Harris, on the other hand, was starting to sense that something was up. I now owed him several weeks' worth of sex; I mean, he would never put it that way, he's a good man—but my mood was impacting the household, its smooth runnings. We watched a TV show about a travel agency and midway through he pressed pause.

"Are you crying?"

I hadn't even realized.

"Their plight is very moving to me," I said, quickly pulling myself together. "A business . . . struggling to keep up with the technology . . . online booking."

Harris, no idiot, didn't say anything to that. I let out a sigh and shut my eyes.

"I'm just wiped out from my drive. Exhausted."

"Sometimes it's hard to come back," he said slowly. "Really hard."

Did he know? On some level? Maybe he did. Maybe he was about to confess something and then I would confess and this would be the start of us finally breaking through. Unfortunate timing, since I wasn't in the mood to break through right now. But I might feel differently in the moment, the way people who suddenly accept Jesus Christ into their heart were like, Jesus who? just seconds before being born again. I sat up, bracing myself. He was finding the words.

"When I get home from Olympic"—Olympic was a recording studio in London—"it always takes me a couple days to readjust."

"Yeah," I said, waiting for the confession.

"To get back into the swing of things."

"Right."

"But then I do."

Oh. No confession. He was saying there were limits to how long one could mope around and apparently he did it the right amount.

"It's a little more than that," I said sharply. "What I'm going through isn't the same as when you're making an album."

He turned off the TV, took a long, slow breath, and waited. For my big reveal.

Good God, what had I done. This was not the plan. I was supposed to clean and snap the rubber band until I got over Davey.

"You wouldn't understand," I muttered, trying to wiggle away.

"Try me," he said with a cold little smile. He was already furious about whatever I was going to say next.

I bent my head and drew my knees to my chin, desperately trying to come up with some event or condition that would shut this down, something frightening but not too extreme; a conversation ender.

"It's . . . *menopause*."

"Oh!" His face completely changed, softened into a mild discomfort.

"Yeah."

As lies went this seemed okay. Historically there were so many women who hadn't spoken up about their biology, it was all right to err on the side of overspeaking. I could get some details from Mary, my older friend who was always talking about hot flashes.

"Menopause. I'll need to read up on that."

"That would be great," I said, although hopefully he wouldn't read so much that he discovered I didn't really have it. I started crying now, surprisingly easily. He put his arms around me and said we'd get through this. There was a feeling of generosity between us. He was genuinely sympathetic and I was able to channel this sympathy toward my actual pain, the mayhem in my heart. He seemed about to start a kiss, which would have been a stretch for me, but then he thought better of it. He patted my back. Maybe I could live my whole life this way, counterbalancing each lie against the next one, nothing ever falling.

We took a walk after dinner. Sam liked to visit the dogs at the dog park and rinse out the bowls by the spigot and fill them with clean water and encourage other people's dogs to drink.

"Come on, boy," Sam said, "it's time for your water."

"I'm afraid she's not thirsty, honey," a woman answered for her dog. "Which one is yours?"

"I don't have one yet. We're waiting for the right moment."

The woman glanced at me, a mother who obviously cared more about pet hair on the sofa than my child's joy level. *It's not only the pet hair!* I smiled pleadingly. *It's more that I'm already operating at my emotional edge! Help!* But for the rest of our time in the dog park I tried to be wholesome. Each time Davey came to mind I snapped the rubber band and forced myself to say Hello, gorgeous, or Hi, sweetie, to a dog. I greeted almost twenty dogs and every one really liked me. You've made a friend, Harris said when a dog licked my hand.

On the way home Sam raced ahead of us through the grass, stopping abruptly in the picnic area.

"Call me," Sam said. "What's that mean?"

I looked up with horror.

"It means *Call me*," said Harris. "Someone wants someone to call them."

"But why is it on a chair?"

I shrugged, like God only knows.

"Is it free?"

"Well, it might belong to someone who put it here—"

"It's kind of cool," Harris said, plopping down in the chair. "Maybe we should grab it. For the backyard."

I cocked my head: *Really?*

"What?" he said. "You love stuff like this." Sam sat on his lap.

I didn't say anything. It was hard for me to gauge the translucency of the situation. How obvious was it that this was the chair my lover used to step on to climb into my window? That I—I, Mama—had painted CALL ME?

"We can put it under the linden tree," I said.

Each morning I switched the rubber band to the other wrist to keep the lacerations equal. I alternated between masturbating and cleaning. I bought special wood polishes and dusted *behind* the books in the bookshelves. I filled up eleven black garbage bags with everything I hadn't worn in a year and a few things I wore every day but which were depressing: some clogs, my cheap pink bathrobe. Ten bags barely fit in the car. I would have to make a second trip for the eleventh.

It was on one of these cleaning days that a glossy, oversized real estate card came in the mail. We got a lot of these ads for houses on the market in our neighborhood, which used to confuse me—why would we want to buy a house a block away? But Harris had explained that it was to show us how much other houses were going for so we might get the idea to sell ours through them. Which was probably true. What did I know about the ins and outs of real estate? I'd never bought a house in my life. I put it in the recycling and started mopping again.

Then stopped. Walked back to the trash can. Took the card out.

It was *our* house, the house I was standing in right now. There was my car parked out front. A big asterisk next to "$1.8 million" indicated the *estimated market value based on houses in your area.* "Thinking of selling?" it said across the top. "Let's talk!" I squinted at the picture. The printing wasn't great, but there was plainly a woman standing in the window and it was me. I was wearing my old pink robe, the one I'd just given to Goodwill. When had this picture been taken?

Oh. The telephotographer.

I studied her little face. Even low-res you could tell she'd never held her hand in someone's hot pee. She'd had crushes, but she'd never been a body wanting a body; she'd only fantasized and worked. But she'd made some good things! People liked them! Davey liked them. I pinned the card above my desk in the garage, next to the map with my route to New York, next to the note from the neighbor. I wondered if the telephotographer had even noticed me in the window and if I would ever masturbate about that kind of thing again or if it would be all Davey from here on out. In any case, mystery solved. No need to run the plates.

I cleaned around all our doorknobs with boiled dough made from an early settler's recipe. I rubbed the dough all over everything like a big, soft eraser, kneaded the dirt into the dough and rubbed some more. When the dough ball became black it was time for a new one; they lay on a tray in the refrigerator, pale, inedible buns.

"You used to make cupcakes," Sam said, poking a doughball.

"I'll make cupcakes again."

"When?"

"Well, depending how things go, maybe in a month."

"That's like a year for a kid."

"I'm sorry."

We looked into each other's eyes, mine welling.

"Is this the moment?" Sam asked.

"Yep. This is it."

We all drove out to a rescue shelter in Torrance. It smelled like hell. The chosen puppy was utterly bereft, shattered like me but fresh off the original trauma rather than re-creating it. He was a shaggy little mutt with poodle hair we were told to brush every day.

"That's very important," the woman said, handing us a cheap, temporary leash. "Some people adopt this kind of dog not realizing the daily upkeep."

"I've had dogs my whole life," Harris said, offended.

"I know nothing about dogs and am kind of afraid of them," I added.

Sam named him Smokey the Bear. Almost immediately Smokey broke his leg. Now we had a puppy with a cast and a cone who shit and peed indoors. This was all fine with me. If I'd been asked to carry a giant wooden wheel on my back, that would have been okay, too; external obstacles kept me busy. Smokey brought incredible joy to the people I lived with. Many songs were sung about Smokey, not by me. He was lovingly brushed every day (until the wire brush fell behind a dresser) and given a bangs trim so he could see. When the man and child were out Smokey wailed loudly and I tried to comfort him, but the wound was too deep. Also, the dog trainer said not to soothe but to just model how actually fine everything was—a tall order. I paced around the living room yelling on the phone so Jordi could hear me over Smokey's whining.

"DO YOU THINK HE STILL THINKS ABOUT ME?"

"Of course."

"REALLY?"

The dog shifted his whining to a higher pitch.

"How could he help it? Hey, have you tried CBD for sleep?"

"DO YOU THINK HE STILL MASTURBATES THINKING ABOUT ME?" Having to yell was making me sound extra deranged.

"Yes, but even more than that, I'm sure he was transformed by you. Think of it as a beautiful gift you gave him. Are you still snapping the rubber band?"

"I'M SNAPPING IT AS WE SPEAK, NONSTOP. I DON'T CARE ABOUT TRANSFORMING HIM; I NEED HIM TO JIZZ THINKING ABOUT MY ASS."

Smokey watched me uneasily from his dog bed as I paced around yelling and snapping. Our eyes met and I flashed forward ten years to a time when artificial intelligence allowed dogs' thoughts to become words. (*It was easy*, the scientists would say. *They were nearly verbal already, we hardly had to use any AI—just a smidge to get them going.*) The dogs immediately start speaking about all the horrific things they've witnessed—crimes, violations. Turns out they are a garrulous species, won't shut up, and have incredible memories. Unlike humans, who could never remember what they'd been subjected to as babies, the dogs easily recall events from their puppyhood. Smokey recounts this particular day—mimicking me with a cruel, uncanny accuracy. "'I WANT HIM TO JIZZ THINKING ABOUT MY ASS,'" he growls. I'm horrified, terrified. But instead of exposing my depravity to the world, he narrows his black-rimmed dog eyes at me and asks Why? Why would a person want that so bad? And because I've had a decade to think about it, I know the answer.

An hour later the dog was still wailing so I went against the trainer's advice and tried to comfort him with hugs and pets and scratches. But he was inconsolable, he wanted his mama, Harris. So I wailed with him. I sang the low, mourning song of a sailor's wife. *Come back to me, big dick, please take this heartache away. He is lost o'er the sea, my big dick.* I cried with my mouth hanging open, the sad, empty place where the dick should be, and then, after a while, I just silently held the crying dog but left my mouth gaping like a distended stomach, loose and dumb.

CHAPTER 14

Praise God for the dentist, the eye exam, the yearly oil change, all the appointments I'd scheduled before Davey, back when I could do more than rub between my legs. There were two other women in the waiting room when I signed in for my yearly gynecological visit, one was young and pregnant and the other looked about seventy-five. I watched the pregnant woman committedly read her magazine, snug as a bug in a rug, the very center of the universe. To the degree she saw us older women, she pitied us. She was in the midst of something very exciting, very right, and after this phase there would be a *baby*, and it was unclear what would happen to her after that but probably more good stuff! Better and better! And the woman in her seventies, well, nobody except the doctor knew—or could even conceive of—what was going on between her legs, though I tried and saw gray labia, long and loose, ball sacks emptied of their balls. How did it feel to still be dragging your pussy into this same office, decades after all the reproductive fanfare? She was scrolling on her phone, seemingly unbothered or unaware that she had nothing to look forward to, cunt-wise.

There was something wrong about all of us sharing the same room. At the pediatrician's there was one waiting room for sick kids and another for the healthy ones and a big fish tank in the shared wall so you could stare through the glass at the other kind of kids. They were a little distorted through the pale green bubbling water and occasionally a fish glided by; this would have been a proper veil through which to see the other generations of women. Maybe three rooms/two tanks through which we could peer wordlessly at one another, knowing each age was an evaporating dream we'd either had or would eventually have and there was no way to penetrate each other's sphere.

I watched the receptionist typing. These were the longest non-Davey thoughts I'd had since he'd lifted his shirt on the hike. I quickly got back to work, sucking on his fingers—unfortunately my name was called before I got to the part where he said *Best few seconds of my life.*

Dr. Mendoza washed her hands after shaking mine. I was already in the paper gown so I spread my legs and put my feet in the stirrups; I knew the drill. Only she wasn't quite ready for that yet, she was looking at my chart and asking me general questions about my well-being. She's a naturopath, a midwife, *and* an ob-gyn MD, which is something you can get in Los Angeles if you're able to pay out-of-pocket. I remained splayed while we talked—I didn't want to appear self-conscious about my exposed crotch.

"How is Sam doing?" she said with a special intonation to let me know she remembered the birth. FMH must be right there in my chart.

"Fine, great!" I called out from between my knees.

"Still having flashbacks?"

I'd forgotten I'd told her about those.

"Not for a while, actually."

"Good," she said, which surprised me—not very holistic. Even this witch couldn't quite understand what it meant to give birth to a stillborn baby who then lived.

For seventeen days there were two babies: one floated in darkness, fairly free and unbothered, and one was laboring in an isolette in the NICU, their tiny body filled with tubes and tethers to beeping monitors. I loved both babies dearly, passionately, and for those seventeen days I did not play favorites because regardless of the outcome I knew I would always have two babies. I sang and talked to the one in the NICU, letting them know I was there. But I also talked to the soul in darkness because I didn't want them to feel scared or alone or that I would ever abandon them. Two and a half weeks later we were released with the living baby. Now more than ever I felt it was important not to play favorites, but devoutly tending to death was increasingly maudlin, ungrateful. So, though they were upsetting, it was always a relief when a flashback came over me. I hadn't forgotten; I was still a good mother. The baby—then and now—was safe. Dr. Mendoza was asking about my cycle now, How were my menstrual cramps? Fine, fine. A flashback was actually a lot like a period. Involuntary, not easy, but still a relief, to be unexpectedly pulled into something so primeval, almost cozy in its leveling pain.

"Any changes you've noticed? Unusual discharge?"

"I think there might be a polyp in there. Maybe on my cervix."

"Why?"

"There's been some irregular bleeding?"

"That could be your age; your period becomes erratic. Let's take a look."

She let the front part of my chair drop on its hinge, an embarrassing vagina-dump-truck feeling, and inserted the cold metal beak.

I didn't mention the actual symptom, the deep arousal, but I got ready to ask if I could perhaps *keep* the polyp, if it was benign. Was there really anything wrong with letting it be?

But there was no polyp.

"Really?"

"Totally clear down there."

I couldn't believe it. I was like Dumbo thinking the feather made him fly but really it was just him all along. Or Davey. Snap. Dr. Mendoza's eyes briefly narrowed at the rubber band, my red wrist.

"Do you menstruate regularly besides the spotting?"

"I think so? I might not even be spotting."

"Any hot flashes?"

"What? No, no, nothing like that."

"Insomnia?"

"No . . . sometimes I wake up at two a.m. and can't fall back asleep, though."

"How often does that happen?"

"Most nights?"

"For how long?"

"A year? Or two?" It had to be annoying that I was answering every question with such uncertainty, but anything more confident would be inaccurate. She was asking me to describe myself as if I was a horse I owned when actually I was more like a radio program, an ongoing narration that I could barely recall.

"Any vaginal dryness?"

"No?"

"Are you sexually active?"

I tried to remember the last time I'd had actual sex, before Monrovia. "Yes?"

"And you're doing weight-bearing exercise?"

She'd had a thing about this ever since I turned forty, which made me feel like she didn't really get me. Athletes exercised, poets and prophets could just drift around. I said I'd danced a couple months ago.

"What really matters is how you're feeling. How are you feeling?"

I looked down at my lap, suddenly overcome.

"My emotions just go on and on like runaway trains," I whispered. She was a lot of things but not a therapist so it wouldn't really be appropriate to cry. I rode out the emotional wave by discreetly digging my fingernails into my thighs and mentally counting to one hundred while she said something about estrogen, a blood test. She handed me a tissue. Now she was drawing a serpentine shape in the air to describe fluctuating hormones. I felt strangely seasick, my ears roared. She said hormone replacement therapy at my age could help decrease my risk of heart disease, osteoporosis . . . the jingle for Tums came into my head—

tum-ta-tum-tum-TUMS!!—which reminded me of Aunt Ruth. I was squeezing the tissue into a smaller and smaller ball and she was holding a bottle with a blue cap, showing me how the cap clicked as it turned.

"We'll see where your levels are at, but you'll probably be taking one click of Estradiol once a day. Or two clicks"—she clicked the cap two times—"once a day." This clicking was putting me into a trance. "You'll rub the cream onto the inside of your thigh or your arm. And then we'll add progesterone and you can see how you feel. We'll adjust as needed."

My ears popped.

"My thigh?"

"Or your inner, upper arm."

"Wait. Are you saying I'm in 'menopause'?" She glanced at my air quotes; I had no idea why I was making them or this funny face of horror.

"*Peri*menopause; menopause is next." She said this briskly while snapping off her gloves. Now she was saying I'd get a call about the results of my Pap smear and here was the order for my blood work, something, something, bioidenticals, patient portal.

"Do you have any questions?"

"No?"

I sat in my hot car, stupefied. I couldn't believe it. A classic case of the boy who cried wolf. I had brought this on myself by using menopause as my alibi. Or, more likely, I was suddenly and officially old. I stared dumbly at the blood-work order. I pulled up WebMD on my phone and searched for "perimenopause." It took me straight to menopause; I clicked Symptoms.

- insomnia
- vaginal dryness
- depression
- anxiety

- difficulty concentrating
- racing heart
- weight gain
- memory problems
- dry skin, mouth, and eyes
- increased urination
- reduced libido, or sex drive
- urinary tract infections (UTIs)
- reduced muscle mass
- painful or stiff joints
- sore or tender breasts
- headaches
- reduced bone mass
- less full breasts
- hair thinning or loss
- increased hair growth on other areas of the body, such as the face, neck, chest, and upper back

At first glance the list seemed to describe a horrible disease, possibly fatal, but reading through it again I realized most of these symptoms were already familiar, they regularly came and went and came back again. So, okay, the concealment and containment that had begun at puberty would need to ramp up if I wanted to keep presenting as feminine in the mainstream; big deal. Vaginal dryness? I'd been using lube for thirty years, ever since my second girlfriend (a sex-positive butch with balls of steel) had said *It makes everything hotter.* It was only on the third read-through that I spied the buried lede.

- reduced libido, or sex drive

Reduced . . . forever? This couldn't be; I would have heard. I knew about Viagra. I would know about this if it was common. Someone would have told me—my mom. Although my mom hadn't told me anything about sex to begin with; why would she start now? I turned on the air conditioner and started dialing. I had to spread the bad news immediately.

Jordi was skeptical.

"Reduced according to who? The old men who straight women eventually get sick of servicing? Science doesn't know anything about women's libidos."

I tried to explain the dropping hormones, estrogen, but everything Dr. Mendoza had said was already out the other ear. I searched my phone for some kind of summation or chart.

"I'm sending you a graph," I said, "tell me when you've got it."

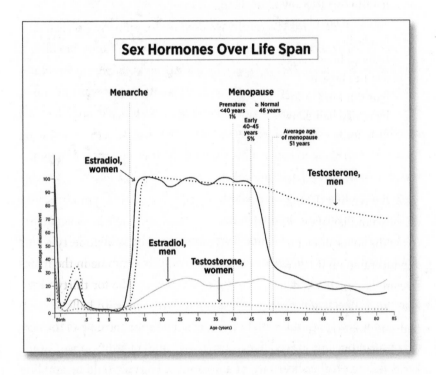

We stared at the nonsensical lines and numbers, waiting for them to come into focus.

"*Wait,*" I cried out, "this is worse than I thought. Look how sharply estrogen drops. That's libido."

"It is? Isn't libido sort of a combination of—"

"We're about to fall off a cliff. We're going to be totally different people in a few years."

"I already feel like I'm different people at different times of the month, depending on where I am in my cycle."

"Sure, sure, but this is a *dramatic shift* smack in the middle of our lives. Look, it's almost as sudden as puberty. The line goes up at age twelve, then it's basically steady—that was our whole adult life so far—and then it drops. That's it. It's over."

I couldn't believe what I was saying. My mind clawed around frantically for a moment, trying to find a way out, a loophole . . . then a terrible, familiar bravery descended.

Brave was the word Harris always used to describe my stoicism during Sam's birth. Bearing the unbearable. But it wasn't only bravery, it was also submission. *This is happening and my only option is to accept it.* I cannot fight it. I can only move through it. Menstruation was like this at first and now menopause—rides that began with a jolt and that one could not get off. What were my options? Become wild-eyed and bang on the doors? Make a scene? This would only draw attention to my misfortune. Better to be brave and silent.

A sour unease flooded my chest.

I stared at the cliff on my phone.

Grandma Esther and Aunt Ruth were already falling off this cliff when they jumped; that was one alternative to brave submission. Jordi was still studying the chart, making observations. *How weird,* she said, *that men have almost the same amount of testosterone forever.*

I expanded the graph with two fingers. The slight decline of the dotted testosterone line looked like a change one might hardly notice. While I was falling off the sheer face of a mountain, Harris would be ambling along a gently sloping country road with a piece of straw in the corner of his mouth, whistling.

When I got home there was a giant bouquet of tropical flowers in the dining room; they fanned like birds and tentacled all over the table. I approached it cautiously, having learned from past flower assumptions.

"They're for Caro's birthday," Harris said. "Her assistant is going to pick them up later."

"Beautiful. She's gonna love them."

The bouquet was so big that I had to kind of talk around it at dinner when I shared my news—the cream for my thigh, insomnia. Not the part about libido or the cliff.

"But you already knew this was happening," Harris said.

"*Right*," I said, shifting my tone to one less shocked. "This was just the official confirmation." I didn't say that I had only just come into my sexuality about two months ago and so the thought of losing it . . . A sob escaped me. Harris asked if there was anything he could do to help; I met his eyes and for a moment it was like looking at my true love after I'd already swallowed the poison.

"No," I whispered. "There's nothing you can do."

"Can I see the blue thing with the clicking cap?" Sam yelled from behind the flowers.

"I don't have it yet."

"When you're done with the bottle can I have it?"

"It isn't safe for children." Although this particular child might need their own estrogen in a few years; age outed all of us. So much of what I had thought of as femininity was really just youth.

"Maybe it won't be as bad as you think," Harris said. "What was it like for your mom?"

I rolled my eyes; my mom couldn't even remember what had happened last week, never mind thirty years ago.

But there was only one thing I really needed to know.

"Libido?" she said, writing down the word *libido*. She can follow the conversation fine as long as she takes notes.

"Yes, would you say you still . . . have some?" I turned on the white noise machine and faced the back of the garage. "It probably dropped after menopause."

"I don't remember that."

"Oh?" I perked up; maybe it wasn't so extreme for the women on this side of the family. "So, you still have orgasms and everything?"

"Orgasms, hm. You know, I'm not one hundred percent sure I've had one of those."

This didn't surprise me very much. Once, when I was eight or nine, my parents had sex right next to me in a hotel room. I had lain there, paralyzed, as she tried for a moment to protect me—*Let's wait a little longer*—and then gave in and let him do it. From what I could recall, she didn't move or make a sound. I had always assumed this was for my sake, but maybe she never did.

"In any case, menopause wasn't a big deal for me," she added breezily.

"Really?"

"Well . . . do you remember my little surgery?"

She'd had a cyst on an ovary and scheduled a routine surgery to have it removed. When the operation was over the doctor reported that they'd taken out her ovaries, too.

"He didn't like the look of something. Better safe than sorry."

I knew this story but only as a disinterested teenager. Now I found myself sitting down.

"How old were you?"

"About your age?"

"And . . . how did you feel about that?"

"I was glad he didn't have to go in twice!"

"Sure, of course," I said, wondering if it was legal to remove someone's ovaries without their consent. "So you just woke up and were in menopause."

"Was I? I never thought of it that way. Are you wanting me to check my journals?"

She had hundreds of journals. As a teenager I had secretly read them, skimming the endless thinking layer beneath the daily events. But what was under that? Who was she? Once in a while she would write, *I should leave*, but didn't elaborate.

"Or maybe you can just ask Robert," she added testily.

"Dad? About your menopause?"

"Yes, since his memory is so much better than mine."

I couldn't tell if this was passive-aggressive or if she was serious. Either way, it would be rude to keep pressing her about libido. I needed someone for whom this was recent history.

"How's your midlife crisis or affair or whatever that was?" Mary said; we hadn't spoken since I'd canceled on her.

I laughed dismissively, then lowered my voice. "I have some questions about menopause and libido."

"Where is my Lego book?" Sam screamed outside the garage door.

"Under the couch! Sorry, Mary."

"Perimenopause," she said. "That's what you're in."

"Right. Basically, just—"

"I can't hear you."

"Sorry! I guess I'm wanting to know . . . is this the end?" I stage-whispered. "Is that what you've been saying? That I won't be able to feel this way, this desire, in a few years?" *Say no. Say no, no, you totally misunderstood me.*

She sighed.

"Just be glad you can still feel it. I feel a little . . . *numb* now. Dead down there." I wondered if she was making it sound worse than it really was. Sometimes I did that to compensate for people's lack of imagination. But I had plenty of imagination so maybe I should take all of this down a notch. "There's no hormonal drive now so it all becomes mental," she continued. "I have to create a narrative that makes it possible, otherwise it starts to feel like rape."

This was new for her? I'd always had to get out ahead of sex, dig an inclined trough so it could flow easily downhill. Being walloped, pounded by lust was very recent. Very. I told Mary about body- versus mind-rooted arousal. "It sounds like you used to be body-rooted."

"Oh, definitely," she said, laughing, "but I don't even recognize that person now, my old lustful self. I can't imagine doing the things I did."

I saw her bent over a car. Being licked by a dog. Her bare ass slammed against elevator buttons. She had done it all so she could afford to laugh.

"And now you're mind-rooted," I concluded.

"I guess so. What kind are you?"

"I was mind-rooted until . . . a couple months ago."

"So maybe this won't be such a big change for you," she said. "You'll just be going back to normal. And at least you got a last hurrah? It sounds like?"

I said nothing.

"We should all get a—what's that thing Amish teenagers get?"

"Rumspringa?" I said.

"Right, rumspringa. We should be allowed one year during peri-menopause to be free, knowing the end is coming." She laughed at a high pitch. "It's such a dangerous time, right before the window closes."

"Dangerous for marriages, you mean?"

"Well, that, too. I was thinking for us. You really have to know who you are and what is ending so that you can decide what to do when you come to the fork in the road. It's like pregnancy in that way."

Fork? What fork? Was there a choice to make? Were there two kinds of postmenopausal women? Mary's son started yelling in the background, something about a toaster, she was sorry but she had to go.

I immediately took the rubber band off my wrist. I couldn't believe I'd been trying to kick my desire—the last precious surge of it!—like a bad habit, an addiction. The exact opposite was called for.

CHAPTER 15

I would drive back to the Excelsior, set up my headlights the way he had, and hit record. I wouldn't be naked, but I'd show more of myself than he'd seen before; my ass, for example, he didn't really know the full extent of it. It would be arching in the moonlight. I'd be dancing between the columns. An incredible dance that said it all—no labor for him, nothing to consider, just straight to the cock. I wouldn't text it. I wouldn't break the rules; I wouldn't have to. I'd post it. He never went more than fifteen minutes without checking. A short wait for him to come fuck the shit out of me. And if he was still too moral I'd explain my situation. That I wanted to have sex with him before I died, because after I died I'd have to go on living for another forty-five years.

I locked the door to the garage and set up my phone on the desk with the too-short table leg. I had a lot of fond memories of my butt, but I hadn't looked at it recently so I took off my clothes, turned my back to the camera, and did some experimental shakes to get inspired. I played it back and then watched again to be sure my eyes weren't deceiving me. I recorded from a different angle, but it didn't help. Something had happened back there; there was no way to know exactly when. It was like when you can't find your purse and then realize it's been stolen. My butt was long where it used to be round; it looked like a pair of fat arms. And there was a tushy on my front side, below my belly button. This wouldn't do. No, this was a real situation. The dance was my one shot; I had to bring it.

Exercise-wise I'd never done more than buy ten yoga classes and take two of them. I was so weak that sometimes my arm got tired brushing my teeth. I nodded instead of waving—hands are heavy! No one wants to admit it! And heads. Just keeping the whole contraption upright was a lot. I was almost always leaning on something, sharing the burden with a counter or a doorway. There was nothing really wrong with me, exercise just seemed like a lot of investment in a temporary body. Wasn't it smarter to spend your time making things that could live on after that body died? That had been my stance until now. The internet said it would take three to six months to train and condition my abs and glutes. Did I have that long? And the willpower? I zoomed in on the hormone graph. The numbers got a little fuzzy, but measuring scientifically with my fingernail it seemed like I was about four months from the cliff's edge. I considered Mary and the fork. The two paths were suddenly obvious:

sex with Davey   vs.   a life of bitterness and regret

The dance had to work; if it failed to summon him the consequences would be dire and lifelong. Of course I would train for three months; I was lucky to still have enough time.

A basement in the neighborhood had been remodeled into a small gym with three lifting stations. It was run by a husband and wife, Scarlett and Brett, who stood around looking at their phones and sometimes ordering people to push from their heels or isolate their glutes. Brett asked what I wanted, body-wise. I hesitated—just say it? I described the butt in my mind's eye and he nodded seriously, as if I was describing a brand-new thing that no one had ever put words to before.

"So, lifted?"

"Uh-huh."

"And rounder?"

"Exactly."

I explained that I hadn't slept well lately, "that's why I'm so weak."

"This'll give you energy," he said confidently.

In old sweatpants and a T-shirt I heaved black metal balls and barbells around, dumbly lifting and lowering however many times I was told to, my face bright pink with heat and embarrassment. Wasn't this basically what Hell was? People forced to endlessly lift and lower heavy things for no reason? The men at the other two stations grunted and bellowed with abandon while they raised massive barbells over their heads. The phrase was "go 'til failure," which meant keep lifting until you couldn't lift anymore and then lift a couple more times, ugly. *Ugly* was the actual term for the final lifts that were lopsided and incomplete because your muscles were failing. You succeeded by reaching failure again and again. Whenever it started to get easier Brett or Scarlett moved the goalpost, adding weight or reps so that it was never possible to succeed or finish, there was only the repetition toward an ever-growing challenge.

The whole time, every lift, I thought of Davey. At the start of a session I focused on the body I wanted to present to him, how it would look and feel in his hands, his arms, underneath him—as if he and I were one person and my body was for our enjoyment. When that got blurry I switched to saving his life: I squatted and lifted boulders he was trapped under. Sometimes Claire was trapped under the boulders; I saved her and this act of valor meant Davey and I could spend a few days alone together—morally no one could object. Or with the dumbbell balanced in the crook of my knee I did glute curls out of sheer rage, fury at what he had done to my life. I would get strong and then I would destroy him, beat the crap out of him. Finally, in the last few minutes of the session, my body began to give out and my mind just stopped. Time went by with no thoughts, just the sound of my breath, the clunk and clink of the weights; my bright, burning muscles. I floated home, high on endorphins.

"So let's say you do have sex with him," Jordi said, scooping vanilla ice cream, "what then?"

"What do you mean?"

"Well, what happens after that?"

I laughed. It made me gleeful to imagine this time *after*. We were eating the ice cream with artificially colored rainbow sprinkles.

"Seriously, though," Jordi said, "take Wile E. Coyote and the Road Runner. If he gets the bird, then *who is he*? What's the cartoon about? Maybe Davey is supposed to be a chimera."

"A chimera?"

"An impossibility, an illusion."

I made a sour face.

"The cartoon is about a coyote who finally gets what he wants and is able to move on. Now he can order from companies besides Acme, order things that aren't to kill the Road Runner. All because of this one little, harmless fuck."

I could hear myself. I sounded like other people, believing sex could save me as opposed to knowing that only my work could save me. What work? I had no project beyond preparing for the dance; my calendar was blank except for my gym days.

"What about Arkanda?" said Jordi. "Is she back from Beijing?"

This surprised me. Jordi was the one person who'd been immune to Arkanda. Did I really seem that far gone?

"I wouldn't even have time for a potential project right now," I snipped. "I mean, I have the time but not the mental space."

I called Liza on the drive home.

"How long is Arkanda in Beijing for?"

"Three months."

"Then she's coming back soon. They're probably planning for when she gets back right now."

"Back where?"

"Home? Does she live in L.A.?" I'd seen paparazzi pictures of her two kids, Smith and Willa, drinking smoothies in Malibu.

"She has a lot of houses," Liza said. "I think she has a place in Beijing."

I tried to imagine home being wherever you were. Money did this, but it wasn't just that. She had so much permission to be Arkanda that she didn't need to go somewhere or do anything to be *more* herself. I was making this up. Projecting. The gods; that's what they're there for.

"They should know that we can't just keep rescheduling forever," I said, exiting the freeway. "I mean, don't say that, but they should get the sense that we might be at the end of our rope, in terms of rescheduling."

"I think I've given them that sense," Liza said.

"But you didn't say that, right?"

"No."

"Because they should also know that we totally understand her lifestyle, we get it."

"I think I've been striking the right tone; Kiley knows we get it."

"Kiley?"

"Her assistant. Her new assistant. Kiley isn't as great as Tara, but no one was going to be and finally Tara just had to start looking out for herself. She's about to have a baby."

"Okay, so that's an example of something I didn't really need to know."

Liza was silent. She was doing the thing where she tells me something by not saying it.

"What? Just say whatever it is."

"Nothing."

"All right then."

"Just that it's been a while."

"A while since what?"

"Since Arkanda first reached out."

"Well, sure, these things can take a while. She's busy."

"Before Tara she had an assistant named Zoe. Zoe was the one who first contacted us."

"She was pretty eager, too, if I remember."

"You had just won the Blinken Prize."

"No, it was after that." The Blinken Prize was a prize for a debut, a first work from an emerging artist. I worked in so many mediums that I was able to debut many times; for about fifteen years I just kept emerging, like a bud opening over and over again. But that was a long time ago now.

"It was probably because of the Blinken that she'd heard of you," Liza said quietly.

I stared at the woman in the car to my left. She was trying to fluff her hair in the rearview mirror.

"If that's true then it's been too long." A real manager would have given up years ago. Only Liza would have kept the appointment afloat for such a ridiculous length. "You can just let it go."

The loss seemed enormous, damaging, hardly survivable. And the shame of being so many years past when the first assistant, Zoe, had reached out.

"Maybe you'll win something like the Blinken again, down the road," Liza said.

I made a scoffing noise. A prize for people twenty years after their debut?

"I mean, much further down the road, when you're in your eighties or nineties. If you're still working."

"Of course I'll still be working."

"Well, it sometimes happens, at the end . . ."

I saw what she meant. For women. If you kept going. There could be a little flurry right before you died. But until then . . . wilderness.

CHAPTER 16

There was no reason Harris shouldn't work with Caro and the London Symphony Orchestra for a week and a half.

"Right?" he said. "I mean, you're not doing anything?"

I looked at him with undisguised terror. Alone with Sam I would have to be present and responsible around the clock; I couldn't live in an agonized dream world, masturbating toward the dance. Sounds good, I whispered. Have fun.

He ignored my dramatics because honestly, what the fuck? After how supportive he had been of my cross-country trip? And he was right. In a court of law I would be on his side, against me. These days nothing I felt was admirable or defensible. My entire inner life—my soul—was disgusting, vain, profoundly selfish. Only by lifting actual blocks of iron could I redeem myself for a short time. Harris left for the airport in an elongated black SUV with dark windows; that's how Caro rolled. On Wednesday camp let out early so Sam sat in the corner of the basement gym with their iPad, glancing up every once in a while to say, You can do it, Mama, you got this. Which just about made me cry.

In some ways it was easier to parent alone. I could run a very tight ship. I had Sam making their own bed and folding napkins, both of us running on a perfect schedule. But the days were somehow anemic, hollow, even with made-up games and foods, riding bikes, and long baths; I couldn't seem to generate a healthy, hearty family feeling on my own. It felt like an act.

"Maybe it is," Jordi suggested. "Does Sam really know you?" Only a person without a child would ask such a question. She was sitting in the pink Call Me chair, under the linden tree. We watched the child rip up a leaf across the yard. "If you're lying to Harris aren't you lying to Sam?"

Not when we were in the bath together, but yes, I supposed that most of the time I tried to present myself as more even-keeled than I actually was.

"More hormonally one-note," Jordi said, referring to the graph. "Imagine what it feels like to be a man. No cycles. No deaths-within-life. No transformation from one kind of person into another."

Every time Jordi and I met, the premise was that we had changed radically since the last meeting, and would again and again. This churning was, frankly, painful. But also exciting because we never could be sure what was coming. Our constant transformation was a big secret, of course—for the world, even for Sam, we performed sameness.

"Maybe we shouldn't do that," Jordi said. "Flatten ourselves like that. Erratic doesn't have to mean crazy or irresponsible. Shouldn't we be normalizing change?"

Now Sam was talking to an imaginary rapt audience of thousands. We watched them make some flourishy gestures.

"Let's come back to this," I said. "But not forget." Forget what? Suddenly it took all our effort to even remember what the fuck we were talking about two seconds ago.

"Not performing sameness," Jordi said quickly.

"Right. Oh, I have a good placeholder," I said. "A bookmark."

I told her about how Arkanda didn't use days of the week, just the numbers. "So Sunday is no different from Tuesday. 'Every day is Tuesday.'"

If you had hormonal constancy, as men did, you might not be taking your cues from your body about when to rest. You would have to build that in: Sunday is the day we don't work, God's day. But if what defined the days was *you*, your biological clock and calendar, then every day might as well be Tuesday. Perhaps you wanted to work for two weeks solid, recording a hit #1 album, and then rest for one whole week, while you were bleeding.

"Every day is Tuesday," repeated Jordi. "Got it. It's a bumper sticker in my mind. Any updates on the potential project? Sorry. Never mind."

I showed her how to do ass squats (straight back, weight over your heels) and we talked about her work situation. She wanted to quit the ad agency; Mel was supportive and telling her to "carpe fucking diem." Somehow this made me tearful, Mel saying this dumb phrase.

"Maybe you just miss Harris," Jordi ventured, cautiously.

I stared her down. I ached with missing, not him.

Though when he finally came home—wearing a new baseball cap and smelling like the airplane—it was obvious how Sam and I benefited from the counterpoint of a different kind of person. A Driver. He messed up all our systems and interrupted our daydreaming, but then he immediately wrestled Sam and the dog wholeheartedly, with total commitment. Or at least it seemed that way. Maybe he was acting, given that he'd said it always took him a few days to get back into the swing of things.

"Doesn't it feel strange," I said, watching him unpack, "to be part of a family again, after being on your own?" He said nothing in return so I just yakked on and on until I saw myself: a spewing electric popcorn popper with no bowl under it.

"Anyway," I laughed, crossing my eyes and twirling my finger to show I knew I was cuckoo, "welcome home!" I went straight to my bedroom before I could become any more annoying.

Sex, I remembered. But I stayed put.

When I woke at two a.m. the light in his room was also on. Jet lag. For the next three nights we were both awake in the middle of the night, reading in our respective rooms. Then his internal clock adjusted and it was just me again.

"I don't want to take estrogen out of vanity, but does it really keep your skin thick and moist?" I asked Dr. Mendoza. "And if so, what's the time frame on that?"

We had just gone over my hormone panel. I would start with .25 milligrams of Estradiol bioidentical hormone cream twice a day and a progesterone pill at night. I hoped to be dewy, almost reborn, in time for Davey's dance.

Dr. Mendoza smiled.

"Vanity is a great motivator because you can *see* the outside of your body. But remember that the same changes are happening on the inside, too. Your cartilage is drying out, just like your face. Exercise, a Mediterranean diet, replacing your hormones—that's how you reduce inflammation and protect your joints. And brain! Bioidenticals lower your risk of dementia by a third. We want you to be living independently in your eighties and even nineties."

I wasn't sure I could look that far ahead. On the other hand, I'd been thinking of myself as "mother material" since age twelve when I held my baby niece and my aunt cooed, *I spy mother material.* So maybe projecting myself into a future biological state was nothing new.

I filled the prescription at Rite Aid, just like allergy medication or antibiotics. Every morning and night I turned the blue cap of the Estradiol bottle and a single, precise spurt of white cream was ejected. I swiped my finger across to pick it up and rubbed it into my inner thigh, alternating thighs.

"And I stop taking the progesterone pill right before the full moon," I explained to Jordi, "so I can get my period." She opened the bottle, sniffed the pills. She was on the fence about HRT for herself and I had no agenda. I just didn't want her to get mad at me later, when we were in our eighties, if she had a third more dementia than me. *Some friend you are!* she would say. *And another thing: who are you?*

It took a month for the hormones to kick in, then one day I made up a silly little song for Sam about a baby named Bibby. The hormones didn't make me sing, but they helped me regulate stress the way I used to so that I wasn't living in a never-ending crucible at all times. I still cried easily, but I didn't worry I was going to cry on and on forever. The runaway trains of emotion became ordinary trains again, turning with the track, making stops. And with progesterone I now slept the whole night through, the warm, deep, dreamy sleep of a pregnant woman but without the enormous belly that makes it impossible to sleep.

Bibby the baby, I sang while doing the dishes, *was a very big baby / bigger than Bobby* . . .

But it wasn't just the hormones. This time of preparing my body for the dance was delightfully finite; it would end in sex with Davey, which was even better than a premiere. With something to look forward to I was perfectly fine, almost chipper. Harris snapped along to my Bibby song.

". . . *a littler baby,*" he said.

"What?"

"I was adding to the song: *bigger than Bobby / a littler baby.*"

I'd forgotten how he used to dignify my dumb songs like this, taking them seriously.

I re-soaped the sponge.

If perimenopause had caused my unrest, my turmoil, and taking hormones was the solution . . . then there was no turmoil, all was well. We were singing the song together from the top now, *Bibby the baby,* but I kept my fingers secretly clenched around the sponge, a signal to the audience, God, anyone who might be watching. Don't miss this claw.

I stopped mentally kicking and screaming before each workout; like a broken horse I went along with the program. I saw the same people from session to session and we nodded at each other in passing, winded and dripping with sweat. They didn't realize this was temporary for me. After the dance I would never lift anything heavy again, at least not over my head and fifteen times in a row. I began to work on my moves. I wasn't choreographing it exactly—I wasn't a dancer like that—but I had a battery-powered record player and a stack of 45s I'd inherited from my dad when he went digital. I played each one, listening for something extra, not just a good beat but something that would call Davey out of his house and into the night. The winning tune was by a '60s band called Hedgehoppers Anonymous, chosen for their lyric about love. Are you afraid of it? the song teases. Afraid of love?

"Do you remember that song?" I asked my dad. "Did it mean anything to you?"

"I've never heard of it."

I asked if this was still the walk-in.

"What?"

"Am I talking to the walk-in or is your original soul back?"

He changed the subject. Either that theory hadn't stuck or he couldn't be held responsible for a conversation I'd had with someone else. I listened for about thirty minutes, then, right before we hung up, I asked him about his mom and sister.

"You always said they killed themselves out of vanity. What does that mean exactly?" No one's despair was that simple. How do you get from the mirror to the black trash bag? Whose voice in their heads said *Jump*?

"They lived in a fantasy!" he said. "They both thought someone would come sweep them off their feet and when it finally hit them that this was just a dream—"

"Wait—why was it just a dream?"

He seemed surprised to have to spell it out.

"They were too old."

I did a very loose-legged, full-body shimmy until abruptly lunging to the record player and catching the needle just before the word *love* was sung. Then I rewound the record with my finger—vvvvp, vvvvp, vvvp—back to the start of the song, and resumed dancing. The plan was to do this again and again until finally I would dance too hard and wouldn't make it to the record in time and the word *love* would be sung and I would give up. I'd fall to the ground and then I would crawl to the camera, to him.

This crawling seemed to be the end, but really it was the centerpiece of the performance because as I danced and lifted weights and jerked off the larger implication of the hormone graph was dawning: only bad stuff was coming. The next big milestone, after the Coyote got the Road Runner, was her own death. This dance had to work because generally, going forward, things would *not* work out, disappointment would reign. My grandmother knew this, and her daughter. Everyone older knew. It was a devastating secret we kept from young people. We didn't want to ruin their fun and also it was embarrassing; they couldn't imagine a reality this bad so we let them think our lives were just like theirs, only older. The only honest dance was one that surrendered to this weight without pride: I would die for you and . . . I will die anyway. You can do that with dance, say things that are inconceivable, inexpressible, just by struggling forward on hands and knees, ass prone.

I spent weeks writing and rewriting the caption so I would have it ready to paste in; something that would let him know I had just shot this and was still there, waiting for him, in room 321. Finally I had it: rn. Everyone under thirty-five knew what that meant.

CHAPTER 17

H ow are you feeling about your progress?" Brett asked one day, as I was midlift.

"Okay?" I puffed. I wasn't sure how he meant that. Was it possible they needed this station, my time slot, for a more serious lifter?

"Yep. Looking good," he said. Scarlett nodded in agreement and gave me a thumbs-up with her little manicured thumb. I looked at myself in the mirror. Sweat was running down the sides of my face. I was wearing black spandex shorts and a jogging bra; the baggy clothes were too hot and I needed to be able to see exactly what I was doing. The loud animal noises that had at first alarmed me? They came out of my mouth now, involuntarily, on especially excruciating lifts. My free weights had gone from eight to twelve to fifteen to twenty. I was dead-lifting the heaviest kettlebell, the eighty-pound one. And now that they mentioned it, I began to notice little things. Like carrying in the groceries—I could hold one bag in each arm, even if they had jars and bottles in them, and it was kind of pleasurable, the bags bounced. And the weight of my own body seemed less arduous. I floated around as if gravity was balanced by an equal and opposite lifting force.

That night I took off all my clothes and stood in front of the mirror. Sam looked curiously from me to the mirror and back again.

"I'm changing," I said.

Sam took off all their clothes and nudged into the reflection. We turned this way and that, looking at ourselves.

"I'm changing, too," they said.

"*You* definitely are."

"You are, too," they said politely.

"How so?" I asked.

They looked at me, squinting. "You're . . ." They placed one gentle little hand on my tummy. "Taller."

I called the Excelsior and asked Skip if the room was free on Wednesday.

"It's all yours," he said.

This time I told Harris where I was going. He was wearing giant headphones so I waved to get his attention.

"I can hear you," he said, not taking off the headphones.

"Okay. Remember how I stayed in Monrovia on the last night of my trip?" I said loudly and clearly.

"You don't have to talk like that. The technology—listen."

He slid off the headphones and put them on me.

"You can hear me perfectly, right?"

I could, it was amazing.

"I thought I'd spend the night there, to work. I can wake up early and get right down to it." Down to what? What work? I was counting on the arm's length with which we held each other's careers. He took the headphones back and stared at them, blinking.

"Just one night or, like, as a regular thing?"

It hadn't even occurred to me to ask for more than one night, but this was shortsighted. If it happened once it would happen again. There would be an affair, a last hurrah that spanned a few weeks or months, and then we'd be done. Davey and Claire would go have their baby; my libido would drop and I wouldn't mind because I'd taken care of myself. Harris and I could break through. In a way I was doing this for us, for our future.

"A regular thing. I'll be home by the time Sam gets home from school. I'll tell Sam." I said this in an overly firm voice, ready for whichever tactic he used to change my mind. But he didn't. Harris wasn't controlling. At worst he was like a king who wanted his subjects to think he was fair. At best he wanted me to be happy.

"Have fun," he said.

When I handed Skip my credit card he told me to put it away.

"Funny thing about that room. When I explain it's a special suite and that a prominent person helped to design it—"

My eyes widened.

"—not mentioning your name, of course," he hurried to add, "but, well, I can't charge enough for it." He started out charging double what the other rooms cost, a hundred a night. "Then I tried saying one fifty. No one balked. Two hundred. Nobody batted an eye. I'm up to three hundred a night."

He handed me a key.

"It's yours. Whenever you want to stay just call me and if it's available you can just let yourself in. No charge."

This graciousness was a surprise. I wasn't sure how to respond. I pointed out that my free stays, at three hundred dollars a night, would eventually, one day, add up to the total I had spent on the room.

"Should I give my key back then?"

Skip looked at me like I'd said something rude and I suddenly felt very hung up, very square, about property and ownership. It seemed I could not handle the fluid sense in which this room was mine and always would be. As if I didn't trust myself, my ability to be moral, unless I was legally bound. I put the key on my ring and said I might actually need to come back regularly, if the project I was here for went well today.

"Is it a different one from the one you were working on last time?"

"Same project, actually. A continuation of what I started."

"Try to keep it to Wednesdays if you can. We're never fully booked midweek."

"So if I come every week that wouldn't be a big loss for you?" I loved talking about this; the affair was getting more and more real. Skip waved me around to his side of the counter. I laughed. There was something funny about standing in his spot. He brought up the reservations screen and typed my name on next Wednesday and then ticked a little box that said "recurring reservation" and my name filled every Wednesday on the screen. He scrolled down to show me there was no end to the Wednesdays, which was actually too much sex with Davey. "Thank you," I said. "This means a lot."

"I think you'll find it as you left it."

The room was immaculate, a time capsule. The salmon-pink coverlet, the drapes with their dahlias and peonies, the rich wallpaper. I threw my bags down and breathed in the warm smell of tonka bean and wool carpet, nearly weeping with relief. This room was real. I wasn't crazy and he felt very near. In the memory of all the places we had sat together and lain together and danced together but also geographically. Posting the video almost seemed unnecessary, as if just being in this room might draw him to me. But the sun was setting, the time was drawing nigh. No more waiting and preparing. A stoic calm flooded my body. I changed into his plaid shirt. I rolled up the sleeves and tucked it into the big beige panties he liked but had only seen the waistband of, then I reached up and pulled the shirt's hem out through the leg holes, making a plaid ruffle over the top of each thigh. As far as I knew no one had done this look before. My hips were banging side to side—boom-boom—champing at the bit. I looked at the coverlet. Tonight I was going to fuck under it.

I stepped outside.

I reparked the car so my headlights would shine on me as his had on him.

I set the record player on the gravel and my phone on my bumper.

I tapped the red record button and started the record player, turning it all the way up.

The drums rolled and I danced as if my whole life depended on it, shaking the ass that had lifted so much black iron. *The moon is shining in the sky above,* the singer crooned, *are you afraid of*—just before *love* I dove down and rewound the record back to one. And again the drums rolled, the guitars jangled and thrummed, I shimmied and shook, and interrupted the song—pounced on the record and spun it back, vvvvp, vvvvp, vvvvp. I did this over and over, becoming wilder and more full-bodied each time, throwing my head back, arms into the night sky. It felt so goddamned good to do something besides lift weights or live life. I almost laughed because *this had been the plan*—the goal of the past three months—and while I'd never doubted it, I'd also never really believed it would happen the way I dreamed, yet here I was! Flying. I missed my cue—*love*—diving down, and knocking the needle off the record a second too late, just as planned. The record clicked, skipping as I crawled on hands and knees toward him—looking straight into the camera knowing he was looking back. I had not forgotten us and I was not letting go; I was holding on, holding on, holding on. Blinded by the headlights I barely knew where I was headed, this part had not been rehearsed but when I played it back it was perfect. I simply disappeared into white, faded out. I was prepared to do as many takes as needed, to bloody my knees, but that wasn't necessary. It was perfect. I posted it: rn.

Knowing how often he flicked to refresh, I reparked the car and hurried back to the room, washed my knees, fixed my hair. I was light-headed, breathless, getting ready for the knock.

Every few seconds I refreshed. Not that he would heart it before coming over, but he might. I imagined him flicking, double-taking, turning away from the people he was with. Maybe he was at the Buccaneer and he would walk here from there, slightly drunk. I hoped he wouldn't text first, I wanted to skip the whole back-and-forth about if he should come to the room. Of course he should. Other people were Liking the dance, hundreds of them. They thought it was part of my work, a new direction but not entirely surprising. Jordi hearted it, but she knew. I had told her I would call her as soon as he left. Or the next morning, if it was too late.

Very slowly, over the next hour and a half, I realized my plan was not quite as airtight as it had seemed. I had thought the dance had actual summoning powers, like a Ouija board or something done on an altar. But that was just one way of looking at life. The other way was coming into focus now, very sharply.

I pulled on my jeans and left the room. I wasn't looking for him but if I ran into him, well, fate. He'd never said exactly what part of town he lived in so really any house could be his. I walked past a lot of them and the Buccaneer and the Hertz and then I began bargaining. I don't need to spend the night with him, I just need to see him. I don't need to see him if he'll just text me. If he would just fucking heart the post, that would be enough. Anything, I begged, just give me a sign. My legs were exhausted, but I couldn't return to the room alone, I couldn't stop walking until I had something. I walked past the smoothie shop and then a street that was doing wine and cheese outside as if they were a gallery but it was just the antique mall and a pet supply store that had kittens up for adoption. People were eating cheese and petting the kittens; a girl in an apron was carefully handing them to people. The older, chubby woman who I'd tried to lowball for the coverlet was pouring wine into plastic cups. I turned away and took a kitten. She was hugging people she knew and offering them wine and saying, *Everything is fifteen percent off.* A woman approached her and said, *Audra! What a beautiful night!*

I froze, looking into the kitten's round eyes. It blinked and I blinked. Audra, a very uncommon name. Not many people in Monrovia could have it. Probably just one: Davey's mom's friend who taught him about sex.

There was my sign.

I carefully handed the cat back to the girl in the apron and took a cup of wine from Audra's tray. I drank it down like water. She remembered me, I could tell, and this was good. Because she owed me.

"Excuse me," I said, "I'm a friend of Davey Boutros's. I was supposed to meet him, but . . ." It was kind of astounding that I hadn't paused to think before beginning this conversation. ". . . I can't find him. Could you tell me where he lives?" That last part sounded especially bad. "I'm from out of town," I added.

"Maybe you can text him," she said.

"He mentioned you're *friends with his mom*."

This gave her pause. Obviously I knew him. But how much did I know, she wondered. She poured out a cup of wine and handed it to a woman in a batik blouse.

"He doesn't live here anymore. He and Claire moved to Sacramento two months ago. They bought a house up there."

I stared at her, blankly.

Dazed and dumb.

It was as if she'd pulled back her arm as far as it would go, wound it up, and then punched me in the stomach. Rubber-legged, I walked myself off the street, all the way to the back of the antique mall. I lowered myself onto a fainting couch with a stain.

They'd moved, together, and bought a house: together. They'd packed boxes and this had been laborious and they'd done it: together. There had been many logistics, as first-time homeowners, and they had figured these things out: together. In Sacramento they had walked around the house, room by room, marveling that it was theirs. The porch, the cupboards, the closets. They couldn't believe it. They felt so grown-up. The first night they giggled in bed, saying Is this real? and We'll never forget this. And they wouldn't; they would never forget it.

All this had happened while I was snapping the rubber band and cleaning and training. There was something very wrong with me. I was somehow outside the fold of life, crawling on gravel, dancing, and stopping the song as if those were real things, as if that was how people communicated.

It was okay to cry and let my makeup run because he was nowhere near. He was in Sacramento. Where his sister lived. They probably started looking at houses the moment my check cleared, before I'd even left. Snot dripped from my chin onto my thigh. I rubbed it in. Audra sat down on the other side of the couch. She scratched at the stain between us.

"I thought this was a water stain, but it's protein based. Probably milk."

I looked at the blotch, trying to dry my tears with my hands.

"I have some incredible pear tea at home."

I nodded, wondering how tea could help a milk stain.

"How about a cup of tea? I can get someone else to lock up."

We walked in silence. I didn't really want tea but I couldn't drive home or go back to the motel alone. And she knew him; she knew him well. This made her charismatic. The same was probably true for her; a mutual ex always draws women together like magnets.

There was a giant bed in her living room, covered with pillows and velvet throws.

"This is a bed," I said stupidly. Had Davey been in that bed?

"Yes, so much better than a couch! Sometimes I even have little dinner parties and we eat in that bed, so fun."

It went without saying that she lived alone. Bed-in-the-living-room or marriage—you couldn't have both. She pointed me toward her bathroom so I could clean up. As I blew my nose and wiped off my face I peered around. Beside the tub was a big cozy armchair. I stared at a glass rack of essential oils and wondered which one was for what I had.

She made the pear tea and toasted biscuits. I sat at the kitchen table and watched her do these things; now she was washing cherries. She asked me how I knew Davey and I said he was a fan of my work and we'd become friends last spring. I said the part about my work so she would ask about my work.

"What is your work?" she asked, putting down a dish for the cherry pits. I described it, trying to regain my dignity and let her know that tonight was a low point for me. Some people—not her—would have given a lot to have me sitting in their home, all weepy. She said she'd have to look me up and I winced, remembering that some people thought they were enough without reeling off their credentials. Most women, actually. Fame really made you act like a man.

Why pretend. I was here for one reason only.

"So you . . . taught Davey . . . ?"

She reared her head back. "What do you mean 'taught'? Is that how he put it?"

"No, he didn't want to talk about it. That's what his mom said, that she asked you to . . ." I looked at the floor, blushing. ". . . guide him in the sexual arts."

Her laugh was throaty and went on for a long time. She sat down heavily and bit into a biscuit.

"She *asked* me? That's what Irene said? No, she didn't have the slightest idea what was going on for a good six months. I didn't know how to tell her. I mean, I felt terrible. What a creep. Who sleeps with their best friend's son?"

I tried to imagine sleeping with my friend Priya's son and it was impossible; I had seen him born. A bitter look must have crossed my face. She straightened up and took a sip of tea.

"He was helping me with my cat. I had a big old tomcat that needed medication three times a day and he would come after school when I was at work. He was supposed to just give Alfie his pill and make sure he was okay. But I'd get home and see little bits of my food missing—my fancy granola would be almost gone, or, I make this gingerbread with sliced pears on top? Candied pears?"

I nodded impatiently.

"He practically finished that off. He was clearly hanging around until just before I got home. Watching my TV, looking at my books and not even putting them back. I should have hired Tamika, my friend Adrian's daughter. Girls nose around, too, but they're desperate not to get caught, right? They leave everything exactly as it was. They're more conniving in that way, I guess."

I put my cup down heavily.

"Okay. One day I got home from work and he was still there and he was watching an old VHS tape of mine. It was racy. In it I'm basically nude except for a little tuxedo collar and belt, a black leather belt—it was a gift for a boyfriend but then we ended things before I could give it to him."

She seemed on the verge of telling me all about this boyfriend. I widened my eyes.

"Anyway, I was so embarrassed! For both of us! I snapped off the TV, and he . . . he was a stupid teenager, eighteen years old, and actually a little mean. He was laughing. He should have felt caught, guilty, you know? But he still had that slightly cruel side—they get that from their buddies at school. Mean whenever someone is vulnerable. He was laughing as he got his stuff, his backpack, and I was furious now, ashamed I guess, and exhausted from work, and right in the middle of laughing he saw my face and stopped. It was like he saw I was a real person all of a sudden. He started apologizing, which only made it worse. I said, 'Don't worry about it,' and shut the door. And I was actually fine. After I'd eaten and had a bath I was sorry I'd made any kind of big deal out of it. It wasn't even worth mentioning to Irene. I texted him something about Alfie, you know, *make sure he has water*, just so he'd know we were all good and he still had his job. Do you want more tea?"

I could have killed her for stopping right then.

"No? Okay. Where was I. Oh, right. The next day when I get home he's still there. He's waiting for me. And he's so sorry. It's like he's been entirely reformed, he's woken up. I'm reassuring him that I'm fine, it's not a big deal, but he's nervous, ranging all around the house, looking at everything. 'You've got so many little things,' he says. He's picking things up and putting them down. I'm following him around with the cat in my arms, explaining my knickknacks, but he's always on to the next thing before I can finish. It's like he's looking for something. He's standing outside my closet, peering in. 'Lots of dresses,' he says. I start to explain that they aren't all dresses, there's a blouse section and a skirt rack—but he interrupts me, he's holding up a black leather belt. 'Is this the belt?' he says.

"It takes me a second to realize which belt he means. And I just stand there, holding the cat. I'm thunderstruck. He's not apologetic, I had completely misread the situation. He's on fire. He's been thinking about the video nonstop and he's back to *have* me. Or something. He doesn't know what he's doing, but he's not leaving. We stood there for a long time, then I put down the cat. This was all the permission he needed. The way he took off his clothes . . . it was like a kid late for gym class, in such a hurry. And, well, his . . ."

"I know."

"Oh. You do." She tilted her head, looked at me anew.

"I mean, not— I don't know him as intimately as you do," I reassured her. "Go on."

"Where was—"

"He had undressed."

"Right. He's standing there naked and . . . *at attention* and he . . . hands me the belt. Like I'm going to put it on! Just take all my clothes off and put it on." She took a sip of tea. "So I did. With all kinds of warning bells going off in my head. But also it's clear as day that I'm not going to have the level of resolve required to kick him out. I'm a highly sexed person, always have been, and it's already begun between us—no one is going to applaud me for my restraint if I do it with more clothes on rather than less. And another thing: I was forty-seven. How old are you?"

"Forty-six. Just turned."

"I might have even been forty-six. I know it's not correct or whatever, but being objectified turned me on; it was my main turn-on. I wasn't sure what came after that—maybe nothing."

She paused to pick up a fallen cherry pit. She put it in the pit dish and continued.

"Of course, he was so young that the difference between forty-six and fifty was lost on him, but I was convinced that in just a few years fucking me would not cross his mind. He would have played with himself watching the tape and that would've been that. But I still looked youthful. Like you." She smiled and I knew she was being polite. I was vaguely young for my age, thin, but she had obviously been a true beauty, with a heart-shaped face and bouncy boobs and the whole nine yards. The kind of top lip that naturally flips up at the cupid's bow. All those things were in evidence still, but they were . . . pulled down. Jowls, breasts, everything soft had fallen. She left the kitchen and came back with a photograph.

It was painful at first, to see him again. He had his shirt off and one arm around her. He looked like her child, but his posture was so possessive, like a skinny boy pretending to be a man. She was in her bra and they both looked slightly drunk or something. Maybe just very, very happy. I felt winded with envy and she was drinking it in. I knew enough about conversations between women to know that telling me this story and showing the picture—her prized possession! her best antique!—was thrilling for her. Nothing could bring him back, but this spilling was a real treat. And was it over? Or would she go all the way? Because I wanted it all. It would hurt, but at least I'd know how he was. What he did. What it felt like. Not firsthand, like I'd planned, but from the horse's mouth.

"Then what happened?"

She bit into another biscuit.

"What do you mean?"

"You put on the belt and . . . ?"

"And we became lovers. We were lovers for the next two years. Then he started getting serious with Claire and it just . . . came to a natural end." The measured way she said this brought the opposite to mind. High drama. Tears and pleading and fighting. A heart never entirely mended. But still, they'd been together. For two years! And now she had the gall to suddenly get *discreet*.

"Oh, come on, tell me all the details," I said chummily.

"My, you *are* eager, aren't you?"

My smile evaporated.

Here I was, with nobody and nothing. She owed me.

"Do you remember that you sold me a coverlet?" I said. "Pink with a quilted star?"

"Yes, of course. A beautiful piece. In perfect condition."

"It wasn't, actually. It had some small holes in it."

"Well, it's more than a hundred years old, so that's to be expected. Are you using it or keeping it as a display piece?"

"I'm . . . using it. I have a place here."

"Oh! Where's your place?"

This conversation was headed in the wrong direction; answering that was going to open a whole can of worms. But maybe this was a quid pro quo situation. I had my own Davey story to trade with.

"The Excelsior."

"That motel?"

Well, of course she wanted to know; she was all about decorating. As it turned out Claire had bought a number of pieces from her over the years—Audra had tried to sell the great chairs for almost a decade before she finally unloaded them on Claire.

"They're handsome, but no one wants to sit on them."

"Davey and I sat on them."

"I'd be curious to see what she did to the place. Can I take a peek?"

Did it even fit in her mouth, that's what I wanted to know. How did he fuck. What did his body feel like against hers. I just had to play my cards right, not seem too eager again.

"Ohhhhh," she said, walking around. "Ohhhhh."

This was gratifying.

She bent down and touched the carpet, turned in a circle studying the botanical wallpaper and light fixtures. She breathed in the tonka bean soap and lotion made by Italian nuns. She ran her hand over the coverlet.

"You know, this belonged to a friend of mine. She was always planning on using it but wanted to get the right bed first. Poor Dottie. It was in a storage bag and when I started to unzip it the whole bag just crumbled into little dry pieces of plastic. But it had done the job of preserving the quilt, the quilt was perfect. So you came here to do this . . . *installation* with Claire, and that's how you met him?"

That made a lot more sense, but I explained the gas station, stopping in Duarte, doubling back to Monrovia. Her eyes widened.

"You made this room for the two of you; a nest. Like a bowerbird."

I paused in case she wanted to tell me about the mating habits of bowerbirds.

"Sorry," she said, "go on."

I told her everything. About the cross-country drive, about the walks and the date at the Buccaneer and dancing and the tampon, every single thing. I had told Jordi most of these things, but in pieces, as they happened. Never had I unrolled it as a single story, and she—knowing him as she did—was an incredible audience. The Rolls-Royce of audiences. She could mentally fill in details that I was missing, but her own story had stopped more than a decade ago. She was dying to know what kind of man he was, how he had turned out. Was he different from other men? Yes, is what I seemed to be saying. And was it because of her? How could it not be. She was like a mother talking to her son's girlfriend, but since she wasn't his mother and I wasn't his girlfriend neither of us had to avoid any particular taboos. It was a free-for-all, with both of us feasting as we liked. I wondered if there would be anything left for me, if I was spoiling its sacredness, but she assured me my problem was the opposite.

"You haven't indulged *enough*. You're anemic." She looked me up and down with a sympathetic frown. "You poor thing, you made this whole place and didn't even get what you most wanted. Just a fantasy, a tease. And now you're going to think about it over and over again for the rest of your life." She shook her head, tsk tsk.

I protested. Real things *had* happened in here.

"How long was it again? That you were here?"

"Well, three weeks, but I spent half the first week redoing the room. Also," I added, "the experience with him inspired my new project and *that's* real." Because this wasn't at all true—there was no new project—I elaborated, explaining how my work was a kind of lifelong conversation with God. She cut me off.

"The room is good. That's tangible and you still have it. In terms of your work . . ." She shrugged. "It sounds like you had a good thing going, but obviously it's not enough anymore or you wouldn't be here."

I laughed. What a thing to say.

I started to quietly hyperventilate.

Audra watched me fall apart for a little while, then she suddenly grabbed her purse and stood up.

"Hey," she said. "All is not lost. I want to do something for you— wait here."

Just before she shut the door behind her she gave me an encouraging smile and a thumbs-up.

It was probably a food she wanted to give me, something like the pear tea. Or a coupon for a facial. I paced around in anguish. Sacramento. He was gone. They'd planned this all along. I'd been their mark: a wealthy woman helpless against his attentions. Maybe he hadn't even wanted to hang out with me but Claire had said, You have to, otherwise she might suspect. Or worse: they had not consciously conspired; they didn't have to. They were two young people making a life—they naturally made choices that ensured their survival. Even loving me had been part of this larger story about them, a test of his devotion. I had given him a shining opportunity to prove to himself how very, very much he loved his wife. This might have been shaky or in doubt before I came along. Now they were rock solid.

I checked my phone. Many thousands of people had Liked the dance video, none of them him. Sacramento. Had there ever been a more romantic city. Where the fuck was Audra? What if she didn't come back? I remembered what Mary had said about the rumspringa. I'd had my chance and I'd missed it. I looked around. What a bunch of crap I'd wasted my whiskey money on, like a drunken fool. I'd probably never come back here; I could hand in my key. I looked in the mirror, a mess of red eyes and streaked mascara. It didn't matter. I thought about young Davey watching not my dance video but hers. And getting so aroused he had to come back the next day. What did they do? What the fucking fuck did they do with each other?

She returned with a cloth farmers' market bag over her shoulder. I wasn't hungry and my patience was spent.

"You never finished your story," I said flatly.

"Oh, I know," she said, reaching into the bag with coy eyes. It was strange to see that sort of impish look on an older face; I made a mental note to stop looking coy in the next three to five years. Like a magician with a snake, she slowly pulled out a black leather belt. The belt.

"Which one of us should wear this? You pick."

I laughed out loud, I couldn't help it. Her expression changed.

"You wanted details. For what? So you can go home to your house with your husband and child and fantasize about me and him while you fondle yourself for the next twenty years?"

I said nothing. What did she want me to do, beg? Because I would. But she was on a rant now.

"Fantasies are all good and well up to a certain age. Then you have to have *lived experiences* or you'll go batty. Which is the normal thing: dementia, memory loss, Alzheimer's—all more common in women. Fantasy consumes them until they can't tell what from what."

"Aren't those things . . . genetic?" I said weakly.

"Exactly. It's passed down through the generations." Now she was taking a flask out of the bag and two little cut-glass shot glasses. "You think those cotton-candy dreams aren't hurting anyone"—she handed me a shot—"but *they are*. You and everyone around you. Cheers."

She clinked her glass against mine and we both swallowed, tequila, but there was no way I could do something sexual with her if that's what she meant. There was no attraction between us. In fact, I felt a little panicked at the thought of her in this belt, now, at sixty or however old she was. She had no waist for it. Maybe she would agree to answer just one question. What would it be? Did he make a sound when he came? No. What was his favorite thing to do, sex-wise? No, too general.

She was studying me, her arms crossed.

"You want graphic? I can tell you everything. *Everything.* But maybe I don't want to. Maybe I'm not interested in contributing to your sexual frenzy."

"I'm not sure I would call it a—"

"Yes," she interrupted, "you're completely caught in it. So what you want to do is come into reality any way you possibly can. *Any which way.* He asked me if I could move like I did in the video, that's what happened next. Do you want to wear the belt or should I?"

She was kind of yelling like a person commanding that you come to God. I thought of the estrogen cliff and my grandma and aunt; Audra's theory was frighteningly close to my dad's—either they were both crazy or I was, for not grabbing her outstretched hand. It might be the last one. She shook the belt impatiently.

"What if I"—how did she put it?—"*fondle*"—I accidentally yelled the word, "myself . . . while you tell me." I could go no lower, I was at the bottom. She perked up like I'd finally said something interesting.

"Have you done that before? Do you do that with your girlfriends?"

God no, I said.

She turned off the overhead light and stared at me on the pink coverlet. She poured herself another shot. I wondered if she'd been with women; her agenda seemed more self-help than sexual. She leaned against the wall and sipped from the tiny glass.

"I danced the way I'd danced in the video for my ex-boyfriend, naked except for the belt."

I waited to see if she was going to do the dance, but she didn't, thank God, and so I shut my eyes and I licked my hand, which was unnecessary.

"He said, 'Could you do the thing you did at the end. With the wall.' At the end I kind of fell and caught myself against the wall with both hands. So I stood like that, with my naked back to him and my hands on the wall above my head. He was quiet, just looking I guess, and then very slowly I could hear him making his way to me. He was so, so nervous. He wanted it the way it was in his head, probably aggressive, macho, but I could feel him shaking. So I turned to him and just put my arms around him and we stood like that, naked with his boner between us, and then we started to kiss."

It was very strange, having it told to me instead of telling it to myself. She put each image in my head so I didn't even have to think. At first I jerked off presentably—the way I thought other women masturbated—but ultimately I gave up, tensed my body into an ugly rigor mortis, and let my hand go frantic. The first time I came, after she described him hungrily lapping at her pussy, she paused in the story, which kind of threw me—*is she waiting for me to recover? ew*—but we kept going. I flipped over onto my stomach as I often do when I imagine using my cock on someone. I'd been Davey many times, fucking not just Aaron Bannister but so many different women and men; now I got to hear exactly how that felt. She sat down on the edge of the bed and spoke more quietly. She told me how entirely he filled her mouth and how he sometimes became confused, wanting it in her mouth and on her tits at the same time, and this was great; because, unlike Davey's cock, mine actually could be in two places at once, I doubled it, and was about to crest again when I noticed the bed was moving ever so slightly, rhythmically.

Okay, so she had become aroused, that was human. Still, I was put off. This wasn't part of the deal and I found it icky to be jerking off side by side like that. But she kept narrating, more breathlessly now, and after a moment of self-conscious rage, I started touching myself again. Stopping wasn't really an option and the bed absorbed the worst of it. Tempur-Pedic.

She described bouncing on top of him and how he would leave school during lunch, how insatiable he was, how he dry-humped her in the guest room during a potluck with Irene—her best friend, his mother—in the next room and this memory in particular seemed to move her because she fell silent then, just breathing hard beside me as her hand worked double time, and I turned to her, it was impossible not to, she was so horny and warm and close, and she immediately gripped me and I ground into her, feeling her big, soft tits under my chest, the same ones he'd felt. Did I want to kiss her? There was no way not to, the way our faces lined up. I pushed my tongue in while pulling up her skirt and down her underwear and she said *Please, please* in pouty begs that were silly but also worked; they were so debased. I'd never touched a body this big and rounded; I gripped her thighs, then her enormous ass, then her thighs again; I cupped her swollen cunt, squeezed her big arms—apparently my hands couldn't get enough of all this flesh. Her skin was beginning to thin with age, like a banana's, but instead of being gross it felt incredible, velvety warm water. *Well, knock me over with a feather,* I thought. *Who knew.*

What I had thought of as a stomach was actually an extension of her pussy, like on a Kewpie doll. I hoped she wouldn't notice I was riding a little high, trying to occasionally feel the rise of the cunt-belly against my clit, which led me to discover that her tits, the way they hung down, connected everything. It wasn't pussy/blank space/tits—it was pussy all the way up to the tits. The whole body was tits. I had a vision of trying to put it all in my mouth, trying only for the thrill of failing to contain her, everything overflowing and spilling out. Of course that would be too craven, but the urge lit up new neural pathways, as if sex, the whole concept of it, was being freshly mapped. Because despite everything that had happened in this room, hers was the first new body I'd been with since I met Harris. It was like breaking up through the surface of the water after swimming blindly for fifteen years. I could suddenly get my bearings in relation to land, see where I had been all this time, and it was somewhere totally different from where I'd thought.

I wanted to slide my finger along her wet slit—just to feel it, that's all—but right before I reached down I remembered an item from the WebMD list—the slit might not be so very wet, because of her age. Licking her was too intimate and licking my hand seemed gross, so in an action so quick as to be involuntary I dipped my fingers into my own cunt—it was right there—and transferred what I had to her. I did this a few times, my fingers going back and forth with a teasing syncopation, and now, given my personal investment, I wanted to make her come. It would be so easy, she was right on the edge. I waited until she was kind of writhing and then I began circling her clit. It wasn't so easy: I'd forgotten how long some women take to come! I pretended I was young Davey, learning. I wondered vaguely if she was vibrator-tuned, if this was a fool's errand, but like dawn slowly breaking, her breaths became subtly harder and harder until she was finally bucking and stamping the bed with one fist. Then still, with aftershudders.

We lay on our backs, panting. One of my arms lay across her waist. My mind was a swirl. How awkward was this going to be? Would feelings develop? What if she fell in love with me? One step at a time. Just be tender.

"You were right," I whispered. "It was better to have something real than—"

"Nothing? I was better than nothing?" she said at full volume, and then laughed, reaching for her blouse and bounding out of the bed.

I blinked and sat up, watching her pull down her skirt. Now she was wiggling her foot into a shoe. She wasn't going to fall in love with me; that was an idiotic thought. As the postcoital haze dissipated I flashed on the woman who'd held out the belt, poured the pear tea, sold me the bedspread—from the start I'd been thinking of her as fundamentally pitiable, a sad character. But that beautiful bed in her living room . . . she probably fucked or fondled or kissed people on it all the time. She wasn't lost in the past—her tryst with Davey had been followed by many others. The sad character was all in my head.

My face reddened. It wasn't just Audra I'd dragged through the mud; it was every woman old enough to be my mother. Including—just recently—myself.

What a pickle, I thought, seeing my situation from afar. *Quite a conundrum. A catch-22.* It didn't seem possible to drag oneself through the mud (one's hand on one's own collar), but neither was it possible to throw oneself out the window in a trash bag.

I watched Audra get a glass of water and neaten her hair with a brush from her purse. So smart to keep a brush in your purse.

"You look beautiful," I said from the bed and Audra humored me with a smile, like I was a very mixed-up little girl. Her work here was done. She was ready to go home.

I got dressed and walked her back to her place.

"Thank you for an incredible night," I said at her door.

"I'm sorry you've got it so bad," she said.

I nodded, hangdog, and stumbled off in the direction of the motel, but after turning the corner I one-eightied and set out into the night.

I walked with giant strides and marveled, almost laughing, that I'd actually had sex with someone—the dance had worked!—and it was the woman from the antique mall who wasn't even my type! I sashayed down the middle of the street. With the moon an almost-ball above me I scanned the lit windows hoping someone might witness me out here alone and so free. I turned the corner and spotted a woman getting out of her car. She was rummaging in her trunk now. Would she look up? She did—an admin type with gray curly hair—but briefly; she was focused on the thing in the trunk. Perhaps it was some black leather belts, a slithering mass of them. Maybe she, like Audra, had just come home from an unusual sexual experience. Or something else, something I couldn't picture. It seemed unlikely that my entire view of older women could be changed by Audra. On the other hand, people were always referring to the *one* person—the gay teacher, the animal rights activist—who had changed everything. Wasn't this the great hope and folly of humans? That we were all so influenceable? Not weak or flimsy but actually interconnected at the root level, like trees—we took everything personally because it was personal. I inhaled my fingers, her warm, buttery cunt smell, and kept them under my nose as I walked.

It was two a.m. I'd left the known world and hadn't died, in fact I felt fantastic.

Was this the secret to everything? This bodily freedom? It felt intuitive and healthy, as if promiscuity was my birthright as a woman. Maybe it was. Was this the skeleton in civilization's closet? The reason why men had come down so hard on us since the start of time? I had the urge to call my mom and tell her the good news—but no, it was too late in every way. The moon! So huge! It suddenly seemed natural and sweet to fuck all my friends. But also my lawyer, who I couldn't remember the face of because we only communicated through email, and everyone else I worked with, regardless if they were someone's assistant or the head of a company—what better way to understand other people's realities? I should have sex with both my parents of course (it was only a matter of time), and obviously my cousins, wherever they were, should all be fucked. I lamented the relatives who had already died before we could share this tenderness. Children weren't a part of this, but the parents of Sam's friends should be brought in, especially the mothers I had nothing in common with—fisting would cut right through the politesse. And who else? Like God making a new civilization I tried not to leave anyone out.

Forty-five minutes later I was still walking. I no longer wanted to fuck everyone in the world—that was lunacy, ha ha!—now I wanted to *eat* the world like a giant fruit. I wanted to go to other countries, yes, but also how come when I dropped Sam off at school I always hurried home even when there was no urgency? What was keeping me from taking a different exit? Why didn't I throw themed parties or run an artists' salon? I should have a lover, sure, but also other specialized relationships—someone who I only cried with, someone for mutual back-scratching, artistic pilgrimages; I could be the part-time child or pet of a lonely adult, how interesting for both of us—and each of these people could be anyone, from any walk of life. I had always done this kind of thing but in secrecy (Davey) or in my work (harmless make-believe) or while belittling myself (what a kook!) when really this was no trifling matter. A person with a journeying, experimental soul should be living a life that allowed for it. The past wasn't my fault; of course I had been using prefab structures—not knowing any better—but now I was older and could see my new path clearly, extending from tonight and ending when I died. *I get it,* I whispered into the darkness. *And thank you,* I added, because we hadn't talked in a while.

I was far outside of Monrovia when I started walking back to the motel. As I came down to Earth I wondered if I'd misunderstood the fork in the road Mary had been talking about. I'd thought the two paths were:

sex with Davey   vs.   a life of bitterness and regret

But maybe the road split between:

a life spent longing   vs.   a life that was continually surprising

like this night had been. While I didn't have the narcotic high Davey gave me, there was another kind of elation and it was, among other things, *weirder.* I felt untethered from my age and femininity and thus swimming in great new swaths of freedom and time. One might shift again and again like this, through intimacies, and not outpace oldness exactly, but match its weirdness, its flagrant specificity, with one's own.

What a relief it was to not have to tiptoe into the house but just swing open the door of my perfect room, throw the key onto the floor, pee loudly, drink from the tap. She'd left the belt for me, neatly coiled by the sink. I smiled, honored, and threw myself down on the carpet with my aching legs up against the wall. How many miles had I walked in the dark? Five? Six? What time was it? The streetlights glowed through the curtains, that hallowed forever-sunset. Davey and I had spooned on this carpet like two babies in a womb—suspended, feeding off each other but never with a goal. We didn't orgasm, we didn't produce anything, we had no practical needs, only the demands of our expanding souls. I would have many relationships like this; some might only last a few hours, like Audra, or might, like Davey, be sexual without sex. From where I was lying I could see the old motel painting was still wedged under the bed, along with the original bedspread. I slid it out with my foot.

He was right, it wasn't abstract, there was a figure. The green and gray daubs formed an old woman standing before a darker area, a thicket, a hollow. A cave.

After floating in the womb with Davey, I only wanted to know that I would get back there again one day. But the woman was just hovering by the cave's entrance, which was sealed off—you could tell if you squinted. It had sealed up behind her years ago, when she was my age. She hadn't been bold enough or she maybe had, maybe she had gone home and changed everything and the cave had closed anyway.

A cautionary portrait for women, issued to motels like Bibles. I swallowed, pushing it back under the bed.

CHAPTER 18

There was a pizza box crammed into the refrigerator, otherwise everything was exactly the same as when I had left the day before.

"We had a sleepover!" Sam said, holding their arms out like ta-da. "And watched half of a documentary about jazz!" I hugged and kissed them, smelled their cheeks. How would this child fit into my new life structure? Not to mention this husband. Slow and steady. Do no harm.

"Did you get a lot done?" Harris asked.

I'd forgotten to feel guilty walking through the front door; now I waited for guilt but it didn't come. This particular sex had been a matter of life or death, not a romance but a ladder thrown to me.

I buried myself in Sam's hair and murmured, Yes, it was very productive.

Harris went for a jog, which was funny because he doesn't jog. When he got back I went to the basement gym. I dead-lifted eighty pounds, hinging at the hips, core tight, heels down. The dance was done, but obviously I would keep training. I needed my strength, *my bones*, for the ten million things I would do in the next half of my life. My eyes in the mirror were severe, unyielding.

Get 'em, killer, said Brett.

After Sam was in bed, Harris called me over to the dining room table, to his computer. I thought maybe he wanted to play me something, a new mix, and I was going to be enthusiastic because I had bigger fish to fry.

But it wasn't a mix, it was *me* on the screen, dancing in a video that seemed a hundred years old but was actually taken last night.

"What are you"—he leaned toward the screen—"wearing?"

"A plaid shirt?"

"But what's on the bottom?"

Muted, my rocking hips looked especially sordid. Music makes everything acceptable.

"Underwear."

I was scared; it was scary to be busted. Next he would ask what or who the dance was for. And so it begins, right now. I pulled my shoulders back. Journeying spirit.

"What if one of Sam's friends' parents saw? Or their teacher?"

My jaw dropped a little.

What will people think? That was his point? I was a throbbing, amorphous ball of light trying to get my head around a motherly, wifely human form. Wearing clothes at all, at any time, was my concession to Sam's friends' parents. I laughed and said, "You can take the stripper out of the bar, but . . ." The end of that sentence wasn't going to make sense, but he got the idea. I was unapologetic. "Surely you can't be trying to control what I wear?"

"Seriously?" he said. "You think that's the issue here?"

"Well, it is my body."

"Jesus. Of course, 'your body, your choice,' I get it, but doesn't it seem a little inappropriate, given that you're married? A little disrespectful?"

"Disrespectful to who?"

"To *me*. Especially given . . ." He paused here and I knew what he meant. If I had also been privately dancing in my underwear for *him*, fucking *him*, that would be one thing, but given that I hadn't been, the video was particularly painful. He didn't say that, though. Especially given . . . *everything* was how he finished. What a relief. It would have been hard to ignore the feelings of my comrade, my pal—but a controlling man? I rolled up my sleeves.

"Okay, see, because what I was thinking . . ." Yikes, I was speaking as the ecstatic creature who roamed the streets. Was she a succubus, hellbent on destruction, or my true self? Either way it was too late—rage was coursing through me. I raised my voice. "What *I* was thinking was that the entire system that I live within is disrespectful to me, to people like me—"

"People like you? What kind of person is that?"

I tried to think of how to sum myself up in a way that wouldn't be incriminating or start a gender war.

"A Parker," I said, using his own word.

He rolled his eyes. "Okay. That's not exactly new information."

"The new part is that I'm done trying to be the other kind of person. A *Driver*." I spit the word. "I'm not ashamed anymore." But I was, deeply, so I launched into a speech, a rallying cry.

"Must I become this other kind of person to be good? To deserve pleasure? Should I just never have desire? Or always be ashamed?" *No! I say no!* And I was just getting started. "Do you understand that I only have three years before my libido drops? Your testosterone goes like this . . ." I made a near horizontal line. "And my estrogen goes like this . . ." I drew the cliff, angrily chopping the air with the flat of my hand—furiously actually, I was FUCKING FURIOUS about how unfair this was. "You have all the time in the world, but I'm about to *die* in here, in this house!"

Harris was staring at me like I was deranged, a maniac. I'd stopped talking, but my words rang on and on. The implications were vast and horrific.

"If you told me I had done something that hurt you"—he was speaking very slowly, holding the side of his face as if I'd just punched him there—"I think I would at least consider not doing it."

"I've been not doing it this entire time," I said. "This whole marriage."

The words just flew out of my mouth like a bird.

His response was straightforward.

"Fuck you for wasting what should have been the best years of my life," he said. "My *one life*."

He was right. What was I even saying? Our old devotion suddenly swelled in my chest, an agonizing burn. Why would I risk my longtime companion, my one true home, for an unnameable energy?

Panic leapt at my throat.

I took his point of view immediately, a total one-eighty. *Sorry, sorry, I'm sorry,* I said, *I love you, please, I'm sorry,* like trying to wind up a hurled roll of toilet paper. It was not possible to take it back; the damage was done.

He closed his laptop, walked to his bedroom, and shut the door.

I lay on my bed with wide-open eyes, shivering but somehow unable to get under the covers. I could hear the murmur of Harris's voice on the phone; he was telling someone what had just happened. I imagined getting up right now, slipping out the front door and finding that all the women in the neighborhood were also leaving their houses. We were all running to the same field, a place we hadn't discussed but implicitly knew we would meet in when the tipping point tipped. We ran like horses, but we weren't horses, so after the initial hugs there wasn't anything to do there in the grass. Everyone started checking their phones to see if their partners were calling and they weren't. Not yet. We hadn't been gone long enough. Soon it was just a million women waiting for their mates to call, to be needed, and then to fall into panic and guilt, to be torn, which was our primary state. Start the revolution here, now, in this field? Or drive home and slip back into the fold, use the electric toothbrush, feel grim and trapped? Of course there was no decision to make because we were all already home, not in a field. There was no collective tipping point. Most of us wouldn't do anything very different, ever. Our yearning and quiet rage would be suppressed and seep into our children and they would hate this about us enough to do it a new way. That was how most change happened, not within one lifetime but between generations. If you really wanted to change you had to believe that you were both yourself and your baby; you had to let yourself be completely reborn within one life. Of course the danger was in risking everything, destroying everything, for nothing. As I had done tonight.

PART THREE

CHAPTER 19

In the morning Harris and I made breakfast and Sam's lunch in a terrible, polite re-creation of our former life. *Do you want to drive them to school or should I? / I'll do it. / Thank you.* What had once seemed like formality was, in retrospect, a secret, special marriage language. Our new, cold vacancy: *this* was formal.

"I wanted to let you know that I'll be spending one night a week in my office," Harris said, putting on his jacket. "Just like you."

"What night?" I asked dumbly, as if this were just a scheduling matter. His eyes landed on my new belt. There was a brief psychic tussle around the belt, its energy, but neither of us had access to this level.

"I was thinking Mondays."

Mondays. We sounded like people talking about custody.

"But who would he be starting an affair with," Jordi said, "so suddenly?"

"Caro."

My mind had seized on this idea and it was a strange relief, a bone to chew on.

"A twenty-five-year-old pop star?" she laughed. "Wait—is that *the* belt?"

"Yeah. I'm wearing it so I don't forget which fork of the path to go down. She's twenty-eight and he spends a lot of time with her. A lot. It's okay; no one understands more than me how these things happen—there's probably a side of him that can only come out with her." I.e., the side his dick was on. But why shouldn't he transform through sex, too? Everyone should; a psychosexual democracy. I wiped my eyes and blew my nose.

"Just give him a second," Jordi said. "*The initial reaction isn't the eternal reaction.*" This was a thing from a Jungian self-help book that we often told each other when our partners fucking hated us.

"Or," I said, "everything is about to get really bad. This is the moment after the plane has crashed but before the breaking news." Jordi knew the story of listening to the radio with my dad.

"*Lag time,*" she said.

"Exactly."

Alone on Monday night I threw myself into mothering. Sam and I tried to do all the boring things differently, sliding around in Tupperware shoes and eating dinner in the backyard, in the dark. We were scared inside by coyote howls, a whole pack shrieking at once.

"That's *hundreds* of them, not dozens," I told Sam, quoting the FBI agent who used to live next door. Tim Yoon had never called me back; for a moment I pictured asking the retired detective to follow my husband like in the movies. He could take pictures with a telephoto lens, full circle.

"Let's do bedtime differently by not going to bed!" Sam suggested.

"Sorry, sweetie"—I held out their pajama pants—"a certain amount of boring things just have to happen or there will be chaos."

"I like chaos," they said sleepily.

The next evening I studied Harris, looking for signs that he'd been with Caro on the foldout couch in his office. Not bags under the eyes or strange perfume but perhaps an effort to appear *good* by doing something thankless, like folding laundry. Or replacing the dead lightbulb in the hallway. But there was nothing like that. He missed Sam, that was all.

When I didn't pack my bag for Monrovia on Wednesday morning (why would I go?), Sam and Harris both seemed disappointed. Sam wanted another pizza night and Harris wanted a break from our silent, relentless war. Fair enough. As I drove I suddenly realized these nights apart were probably the first steps toward divorce. Divorce, *of course*. I gasped alone in the car. I had truly believed we would break through at some point. I could still imagine the older versions of us, laughing fondly about something the other one always did.

The room was flawless again, no upheaval in here. Just one week ago Audra had been ordering me to come into reality any way I possibly could. *Any which way.*

And I had. Here I was.

I tried to watch a TV show everyone was talking about, but all the references to sex and marriage and infidelity made me weep and that's what the show was about. I almost wished for an FMH flashback just to be taken out of the present, even for a second. The NICU was hell, but we were together in it, it was part of our long history. Even if I started a new, more open relationship immediately after the divorce and stayed with that person for fifteen years, it wouldn't be the same stretch of life. Coming into ourselves as parents and adults—none of that would happen with anyone else. If there was anything meaningful about aging, it was tunneling backward in time together, holding memories as a couple so they made a kind of safe basket in a rough and arbitrary world—not just for Sam but for us.

Around midnight I searched "Sacramento Hertz." It felt good to play with fire, regress. There were three in the area; Davey was almost definitely working at one of them—a comfortingly pathetic lateral move. I read their Yelp reviews. Particularly good or bad customer service was sometimes described, but he was never mentioned by name. Then, all of a sudden, I stumbled on a comment about an employee at the airport location: *Denise*. She was called out for being "a very rude young woman," which was a lot for me to take in all at once. Denise. Young. Rude. Whereas I had primly accepted Davey's personal boundaries Denise probably just started sucking his dick in the staff bathroom, and what could he do? Pull her off?

I touched myself against my will, sickened. It was like having just one drink and ending up pantsless under a bridge.

On Thursday afternoon I dressed and repacked my things and drove to pick up Sam from school. I was desperate for their little face but knew the desperation wouldn't be mutual, thank God. They walked up to the car holding the giant metal spoon and insisted on buckling it into the seat next to them.

"I brought it for show and tell."

"And how did that go?"

"Pretty good. For my show I showed how you can really eat with it. I ate my yogurt."

"What about for your tell?"

"I told about how you drove all the way to New York and back."

I worked to keep my face solid. The worst part was that they would actually love the motel room and the story of what I had done to it; it was right up their alley. Every day they woke up and bravely lived according to who they actually were, not what already existed. They had parents who affirmed this, but they could probably already feel the ways in which we were less daring than our child—feel but not articulate. Not yet. In a matter of months, maybe just days, they would turn slowly, point their finger, and say *You weakling. You hypocrite.* As I had with my mom.

Now Sam was describing a cupcake another kid had in her lunch.

I tried to imagine a woman just like me but without secrets. Unapologetic. Would such a woman be acceptable or would she be cast out like a witch? And why such a fear of being cast out when that wasn't even really a thing anymore? Because we were all witches until very recently. We were cast out and burned at the stake only three hundred years ago. That's nothing. No time at all.

"It had frosting and sprinkles on top and cream in the middle," Sam said. "How did they get the cream in there?"

"You make a hole with the handle of a wooden spoon; you poke down and then you squirt the cream in. Then you frost the top."

"Can we do that?"

"We can do that."

Harris walked into the kitchen as we were finishing up. He paused, watching us smooth on the monkfruit-sugar frosting. I held my breath.

Almond cookies with jam in the middle, grain-free banana muffins, carrot custard—even when they turned out all wrong Harris always gobbled them up, which was the highest praise. Praise I maybe couldn't live without. I was suddenly united with a long lineage of women who fixed everything through food; terror can really strip you of your modernity.

If he eats a cupcake we're going to be okay.

He paused.

"There's cream in the middle," Sam said with great urgency. We were both praying.

But Harris was only looking for something and it wasn't in the kitchen after all.

CHAPTER 20

It had been two weeks since I'd said all those terrible things. This wasn't like other fights; it wasn't a matter of pride and one of us eventually apologizing, tears, kiss and make up. I had most likely *meant* all the terrible things I'd said and we both knew it. When I imagined proceeding with life as usual, "getting over myself," a familiar hopelessness engulfed me. But setting up some sort of new, unleashed life as a divorced mom sounded like a punishment, someone else's story. As for Harris, he couldn't even look at me. When he had to pretend to, in front of Sam, I noticed he was actually looking at my forehead or cheek, any part of my face that couldn't look back. Stalemate within, stalemate without. It wasn't a healthy atmosphere for a child, but we probably had another two weeks before Sam's future as a drug addict was locked in. Two weeks for one of us to make a move.

"We're all so siloed," Jordi said, "that's the problem. No one can see inside anyone else's relationship so we're all just casting about in the dark ages. Think of tech! It advances so quickly because people are pooling their knowledge. Open-source software and all that."

I nodded, agreeing with the words I was most familiar with, and quietly looked up "open source" on my phone.

It was software *developed in a collaborative and public manner.* That sounded hopeful. Could one open-source a marital crisis? I scrolled.

There were *faster project starts* (great, the sooner the better), *robust community support* (please!), *easier license management* (okay, that didn't apply), *without being contractually locked into work with a single vendor* (Harris).

It was worth a try.

That night I texted all my married friends in their forties and fifties (and a few younger ones as a control group). What are you doing on Wednesday? I asked. I scheduled them one by one, sending the address of the Excelsior. Room 321. There will be snacks.

"Are all the rooms here this nice?"

Cassie, fifty-three, only had a second while her daughter was at ceramics.

"No, I had it redecorated. It's part of a . . . never mind." The room wasn't the point. I described my situation, Audra, the fork, the urgency.

"So this is all based on one fun night?"

"No, the night with Audra was just the breaking point," I said. "I think I've been conforming this whole time."

"Sure," Cassie said, "we all have to conform a bit. Compromise."

I opened my mouth to ask if compromise was really the same thing as conform—

"Okay, here's my take," she said. "*Just ride it out.* A lot of women destroy their lives in their forties and then one day they wake up with no periods and no partner and only themselves to blame."

That had the ring of truth to it.

"So, you think I should just smooth things over?"

"I know that's not the hip thing to say, but yes."

"I don't know if I"—I gasped—"can physically do that. Swallow my desires like that."

Cassie sighed.

"Remember the Simone de Beauvoir quote," she said, "'You can't have everything you want but you can want everything you want.'"

"And what is it *you* want?" I whispered, leaning toward her.

She shook her head.

"Just hold it together for a few years and you'll thank me when you come out the other side."

Want without having. Hold it together, I typed in my notes, trying to remember the other times people had said, You'll thank me later—did I ever thank them later?

"Wow, these curtains. What kind of flowers are those?" said Nazanin, forty-nine, looking around the room.

"Dahlias and peonies." I hurried her over to the refreshments laid out on the marble-topped table; there were still three more women coming today.

"Are you recording this?"

Nazanin had once indulged me by recording a typical conversation with her nanny back when I was pregnant and couldn't conceive of the nature of this relationship (though between the FMH and Jess, our wonder-nanny, this anxiety quickly became moot).

"No recording. Prosecco?" I asked her what she would want, relationship-wise, if she could have anything. Assuming most people were living like Cassie, I needed to know if my wants were any different or larger than other people's. Was everyone grit, grit, gritting?

"What would I want . . . you mean, theoretically?" Nazanin was the butch to a very traditional femme, a twenty-year marriage.

"Put Kate out of mind. Imagine there's no way to lose or hurt her."

"Okay. Well . . . in addition to Kate I'd have someone in another city," she said, glancing around, as if the room might be bugged. "A trans guy or someone masc like me."

I nodded. Didn't see that coming.

"One-eighth of me is probably a gay man. But I wouldn't want that part of me to run the show, you know? I can just jerk off to pictures of Lore Estes."

Lore Estes; the book on the coffee table. I'd never opened it, but for some reason I'd assumed the artist was dead. I said an eighth seemed like kind of a lot, in terms of desire.

"It's probably more like one-sixteenth," Nazanin said. "Not enough to risk anything for."

1/16th = not enough. >1/8th = maybe worth the risk, I typed afterward, then took the belt out of my bag and held it across both palms like a boa constrictor. My hidden part wasn't a sexual orientation like Nazanin's—what would you call it exactly?

"The divine feminine?" suggested Isra, fifty-one. "And yes, she can absolutely run the show. Trust her. Visualize her."

I saw an unreliable hippie mom running off to India with her lover.

"You remind me of me before I transitioned," Isra said. "That sense that time is running out but you're too chickenshit to explode your life."

I laughed nervously. Chickenshit? I was known for my fearlessness; my work was always being called daring. Isra was still best friends with the woman she used to be the husband of; this ex-wife and her new partner spent holidays with Isra and her girlfriend.

"So there's nothing you still yearn for?" I prodded. "You're just completely self-actualized?"

She looked away.

"Have I told you about cryo?" I shook my head. "Well, one of my goals is to get signed up for cryogenic preservation. It may seem ridiculous, it may be impossible, but if it works out you get a second chance at having the youth that you wanted. That's what I yearn for, a childhood that is authentic to me."

"Okay, wow. Is it expensive?"

"You basically buy a cheap life insurance policy to pay for it, and then a maintenance fee."

Coming from Isra this didn't strike me as off the wall; she'd always lived ahead of the curve. Science had been wrong about her gender, maybe it was wrong about death, too.

Opposite of Simone de B, I noted. *HAVE what you want—do not be stopped by what seems to be reality.* I checked in with my email, the nurse at Sam's school had sent an "Ouch report." Sam had fallen off the jungle gym and had a small scrape on their left knee and were given a Band-Aid and ice pack. Harris had replied with thanks and said he would ice it again tonight. I wanted to add that I, too, cared about the knee and I wasn't here in this motel just fucking around, I was trying to figure our shit out.

Shareen, forty-seven, was my last official interview for the day. She was married to an unusually great man, Ari, a labor lawyer. "But Ari is my second husband," she reminded me. "Flip over."

She was giving me a mini bodywork session on the bed, lymphatic drainage.

"But don't you pretty much have to hate your partner to get divorced?"

"No. There was nothing really wrong with Steven, my first husband. I just didn't know myself when I met him. I was only twenty-four."

I had been thirty when Harris and I met. I'd known myself well enough to know I was too far-fetched for any admirable person to commit to. So I had changed, matured, and that had turned out very well. Mostly.

"Steven. I've never even heard you say that name."

"I almost never think about him."

So a person could be completely disposed of, without a trace. It was like a horror movie.

"Do you know you have a giant ball in your throat?"

"Literally?" I said, clasping my neck.

"No. It's anger."

Anger, I wrote in my notes. Jordi was due any second.

Anger. I always lost coherency, intellect, when it came to root anger, that is, anger at one's parents. My hands hovered over the keyboard, stumped. A sad-sack pulling up empty pocket linings: I got nothin'.

Though perhaps that was the point.

Nothing, a void, would be impossible to dredge up or articulate. Only something—an event, a trauma—could be remembered, survived, wailed about. I tried to connect the dots to Harris and me, our situation, but here she was.

Jordi walked around pointing out all the things I had described over the past six months. It was even more beautiful than she had imagined.

"How the light . . . the curtains are . . ."

"Glowing, yes, a perpetual sunset."

"And . . . this soap. How does it smell so good?" she asked, lathering her hands.

"Tonka bean."

"And wow, these towels. Would it be weird if I took a bath?"

Through the rising steam I told her about my day of open-sourcing. I wasn't sure I had learned anything at all, except that my friends were very comfortable in this motel room. I described how they lounged around, spoke freely, massaging me and eating butter cookies.

"I can't picture any of that happening in my actual home, even if I were alone there. You've never taken a bath at my house, for example."

"Maybe you would like living on your own," Jordi murmured from the tub, her moon-face sweetly flushed.

Maybe. Or maybe I was like a person on vacation in Hawaii who gets the dumb idea that they should move to Hawaii so they can feel like they're on vacation all the time. Once settled into the Big Island I would quickly discover that the devotion between Harris and me was the secret linchpin of my life. Suntanned and wearing a lei, I would lose my mind, enter the deathfield.

Jordi complimented the star-patterned floor and I described

fitting the tiles together with Claire and the sense that if there had been the exact right amount of them a portal to another world would have opened.

"And there was the right amount?"

"No, we were three short. If you look behind the toilet . . . there's three solid green ones."

She slid over, sloshing water, and squinted past my shoulder.

"To me it looks like they match the others." I turned slowly, almost frightened. "See?" she said.

Yes, the three solid greens that interrupted the star pattern were gone; the pattern was magically complete. Someone had completed it.

"Claire and Davey," said Skip, when I asked him the next morning. "They told me the floor was unfinished."

"They both came?"

"Yes. Well, maybe it was just him who actually installed them. It was a while back, right before they moved up north. A lot of young people leave because of inflated property values and—"

Another dimension didn't open up, but knowing he'd cared enough to go through so much trouble was very soothing, narcotic actually. I took a picture of the place behind the toilet. A little backup plan. If things got very bad (deathfield in Hawaii) I could always send Davey the picture and walk through the portal into his arms. It would start with sexting; he had to be pretty bored up there in Sacramento.

I smoothed the coverlet and laid out the remaining butter cookies. Everything was riding on today's data—my younger friends.

Destiny, twenty-nine, was newly engaged.

"I might be a bummer to talk to right now," I warned. "I'm a little unsure about the institution of marriage."

"Same," she shrugged. "Marriage is a vestige of the slavery mindset, people as property." Which was why she and her fiancé had very bespoke vows. "I told him, 'I want to be married to you for my whole life.

I love that idea. And I want to have sex with other people; I find that exciting.'"

"You said that?"

"Why should I be ashamed about what I want? Shame says: 'I'm bad.' I'm not bad." She was training to be a therapist; this sounded like something from one of her classes.

"I really am bad," I said.

"I wonder who taught you that?" she mused, taking a sip of sparkling wine.

"Just that I'm here in this motel room"—I gestured around—"is evidence enough."

"As opposed to where?"

"My parents' house?" I said as a joke, because it's always about the parents in therapy. But she just nodded.

Wow, she's a natural, I thought as the notion landed. *My parents' house.*

"Hey, you know who you should ask about this?" Destiny said before she left. "Arkanda. I'd love to hear her take."

Bespoke vows, I noted. *Me bad—who taught?* And: *Leaving parents' house = bad.*

"I've always known I was nonmonogamous," Caitlyn, thirty-two, yelled from the shower. She was sweaty from her morning stroller run; I held her baby, Sophie, on my hip.

"You know what a cuck is?" she asked, stepping onto the thick bath mat.

It took some discussion with their couples therapist, but now Caitlyn and her husband had a good thing going. They picked the women together.

"The hotter the better," she said, doing an elaborate patting and scrunching thing to dry her hair. "At first he would try to include me, pull me in. But now he knows I prefer to not even be in the room. Spying through a crack in the door is best."

"And this turns you on?" I asked, transferring Sophie from my hip to hers. Only the words came out mangled because I had too much spit in my mouth; I had forgotten to swallow the entire time she was talking. Caitlyn's eyes sparkled. Oh. This was how she got the women.

I switched gears, asking if she was body- or mind-rooted when it came to sex. "Or do you find that distinction too binary?" I added, off her eye roll.

"Sounds like you're not smoking enough weed before fucking," she said, bouncing Sophie. "Try Dutch Treat or really any indica-dominant hybrid."

Drugs, I wrote down, while waiting for the next woman. *Cuck.* Caitlyn was so matter-of-fact and orderly about her desires, nothing like an unreliable mom running off to India with her lover. Of course that mom was no one in particular, just someone I'd cooked up to scare myself with. Like a Beware of Dog sign meant to scare people off the property when really there was no dog. Or witch. A very cheap and effective security system.

Talia, a thirty-seven-year-old historical biologist, was my last hope. She said that marriage wasn't the problem, it was the social ecosystem around it.

"For example, dances. They once fulfilled an important function in society—court dances, barn dances, ballroom dances—they allowed people to legally touch someone who wasn't their husband or wife."

"That's . . . healthy?"

"Yes, biologically it's important to feel different arms and hands . . . smell strange bodies. A diverse human biosphere makes for a healthy marriage."

She said this last part with exhaustion, as if she'd made this argument a hundred times. Maybe she had. As far as I knew, she and her partner did not attend barn dances.

Some customs have remained—monogamy—but not all the microtendrils that actually made it possible: the community, the dances, and God knows what else.

This was my final note, the open-sourcing was done. It didn't seem to amount to much, but of course it wouldn't, not here. I waited until the last second to leave, then drove home at top speed. *Mama's coming!*

CHAPTER 21

While I squeezed our child and brushed hidden clusters out of their hair, Harris informed me (my forehead) that he would be throwing a brunch next Sunday.

"To celebrate Caro's new single ahead of the release."

"Of course."

I couldn't believe it. This was where his focus was?

"Do you want me here for it?" I asked, trying to imagine Caro and me in the same room. This brunch didn't really fit into the theory of their secret affair, unless it was a "hidden in plain sight" kind of thing. Still, wouldn't he have a better time without me there? "I could help set up and then leave for a few hours. What kind of food were you thinking?"

Harris looked up at the kitchen ceiling and shut his eyes as if I'd just said something beyond the pale.

"I'd like to be with a person who actually wants to be here," he whispered. Not to me but to himself or the gods.

But did he still want that person to be me? With my journeying soul? Or was this a future person who liked gardening and spread all her stuff around the whole house rather than keeping everything near her? I could picture her sleepy, smiling face in the morning. Who wouldn't want to wake up beside that? Tendrils of hair escaping from a messy bun, laugh like a bell. Harris put his earbuds in. Sam was lying facedown on the heater vent, mainlining the comfort. There was a pile of pee sheets on top of the washing machine; they were starting to regress, bed-wet, the way kids do when they have no other recourse. Either that or they'd just drunk too much water last night.

On Monday Harris had his overnight again. Sam didn't seem to question our need to work "too late to come home." After they were asleep, I masturbated angrily to the thought of Harris fucking Caro on the foldout couch in his office. How long can we go on this way? Or is this just our new life? I texted Jordi. She called me right back.

"I actually slept over in my studio, too, last night," Jordi said. "I'm going to do it every Thursday—you've started a trend."

"Where did you sleep?"

"The loft. I made it all cozy." She texted a picture of herself in the loft. Her face was lit up, like me after Audra. On *her* the exhilaration looked bold, interesting, not tawdry or selfish.

"I guess it's different for you two; Mel trusts you. You're trustworthy."

"I don't know . . . the danger is inherent. It's a more promiscuous construction than sleeping in the same building every night. And that one night off somehow shifts the whole week, right? *Oh.*"

"What?"

"We're reshaping the calendar. The bookmark worked. *Every day is Tuesday.*"

But I couldn't remember why this had seemed so important; it sounded like something a crazy person would say. I saw myself staggering through the city in the dark, a toothless, ranting woman who had once had a good home with a husband and child but threw it all away for . . . no one can even remember. Something about pleasure.

"Still there?"

"Hi," I whispered gravely.

A long, sad silence, then Jordi asked if Harris and I had a special place.

"Somewhere you could go and talk about your problems directly? Maybe in nature?"

"No," I said, "we don't have anything like that."

"Or, not a place, but maybe a special—"

"We do this saluting thing."

"Saluting."

"Like soldiers. We did it the first time we saw each other, which didn't feel like the first time. It was like, *Oh, there you are.*"

Jordi made mm-hm sounds, like this was the ticket.

"Salutes began as gestures of trust to show you weren't holding a weapon," she said. "So that's a good start."

I planned on saluting him from across the classroom at Parent Night, but Harris couldn't get away from the studio, he and Caro were working with a cellist from Japan. Where's Harris? everyone kept asking and each time I explained about the cellist—to a teacher, to another mom— it sounded more and more like a cover story. Some parents were already divorced and Parent Night was one of the few times they had to come together and be civil. I imagined Harris and me like this, silently noticing each other's new haircuts while looking at Sam's work. The work of our child; our incredible child. Sam hated their drawing of basalt and wanted to rip it up.

"You know who will love this picture?" I said, kneeling with my arm around them. "Your grandfather."

I texted my dad, the amateur geologist, Sam's drawing of a gray rock.

You wanted to know about Elaine's menopause? he replied the next morning.

I had never followed up on my mom's suggestion because it seemed unlikely—or maybe just too sad—that he would remember more than her about this. But I guess she'd told him.

"She said it was nothing? Ha!" my dad barked. "That's convenient."

"I think she just couldn't remember."

"She remembers. She moved out! You know that."

I remembered there was a studio for a few weeks—

"It was a month. She lived there."

—but the timing wasn't so clear in my head.

"It was right after her surgery; a direct result of her sudden menopause. She said she'd had enough—you know, 'Enough is enough'—and she found some sad little apartment and lived there until she got her arrhythmia diagnosis and came to her senses."

The arrhythmia didn't turn out to be a big deal, as heart things go, though now it seemed it actually had been life-changing. I could only recall her showing me the cupboard of canned soups in her tiny studio. *So simple to make and clean up,* she'd said proudly.

The house without her in it, that I remembered. While she was gone I tidied and made my dad's bed and cooked us food like a little sixteen-year-old wife. One night I couldn't find him—I looked everywhere, called his name inside and out. Finally there was some rustling in the corner of their bedroom; he was wedged between the dresser and the wall. His face emerged from the shadows and he asked for a glass of water.

Why are you speaking like that?

He was speaking strangely.

Oh! His eyes lit up. I can sing now! he exclaimed. Perfect pitch!

Both of us had terrible voices, couldn't hold a tune to save our lives. He explained how with this new voice, this *Slavic accent,* he could sing. It didn't sound regional to me, just mangled like there was something wrong with his tongue. From the corner he began singing (or chanting, really) "Ol' Man River." He stopped a few times, overcome with emotion, but drew out the last line—*Just keeps rolling along*—like a grand finale, going extra hard with the accent.

"Juuuuthwts karpz raring alaaaarrrng!"

After that I stopped cooking and cleaning. I was incapacitated with guilt about abandoning him in the deathfield, but at sixteen I was too old to keep him company in there. I'd heard perfect pitch and he didn't have it.

"Can you put Harris on for a sec?" my dad asked now. "Roger's son wants to get into the music business—"

"He's not here," I said sharply, as if this was my dad's fault. "He spends Monday nights at his office now."

I added a day to my workout schedule. If my butt got any more lifted it would choke me, but now I was going for sheer strength, as if I were preparing for a wrestling match. Wouldn't that be a hoot, if Harris and I just wrestled it out, perhaps to the death. I watched myself in the mirror, split-squatting with twenty pounds in each hand. I looked different. Was I bigger? Or smaller?

"Sometimes people add a day before an awards show or their wedding or something . . . ," Scarlett mulled out loud. She could be a little nosy.

No wedding, no awards show, I said.

"Or right before they start dating again," Brett chimed in, raising his eyebrows like *Hubba-hubba.* "A lot of our clients end up back on the market."

Scarlett shook her head: *Don't listen to him.*

"It's true!" Brett insisted. "We've seen it a million times: someone starts working out, gets hot, and then they're like, *Dude, I could do better! Time for an upgrade!*"

"We have different theories about this," Scarlett said evenly. "I think it's the mind-body connection. Lifting puts you in balance—like yin-yang, you know? That symbol?" She drew a backward S in the air. "And that helps you bring your life into balance. Which *sometimes* means relationship changes."

I didn't say anything to that, just kept going with my reps and Scarlett wandered toward a beefy, grunting man.

But she was right. Yin-yang and the whole thing. I wasn't fatter or thinner; I'd incarnated. Of course I had always been in here, but so gingerly, like a person never wanting to unpack even though they're obviously going to be staying awhile. Now my brain was spread out over my whole body, not just in my head. I had achieved this through this brute, relentless lifting and lowering, which made sense—you couldn't think your way to a physical place, you had to go there. This reminded me of when I discovered that most people were in some form of recovery; it was the secret undernetting to the world I lived in. If you didn't know about recovery and exercise you were out of touch with the human plight. There were only so many ways to lift yourself back up—and falling down, well, it's what we do. My heat radiated against the night air as I walked home.

Harris decided on Mediterranean food for the brunch.

"That's good," I said, "something for everyone."

No response, as usual. He had told me I didn't have to stick around, but obviously I *was* going to stick around if it was the last thing I did. The guests, friends of Caro's and industry people, milled about the house with little plates and mimosas, seemingly with no inner challenges. Sam walked from guest to guest offering mints that they had bought with their allowance money.

"Altoid? . . . Care for an Altoid?"

Harris and I put on a great show, tidying and tending like a couple so overflowing with love that we had to share it with everyone—through food and drink! Have seconds! Thirds!

Caro was wearing a dress without a back, more like an apron-plus-shorts. It was easy to avoid her by hanging out with the most boring people at the party. Why would anyone describe a trip they had just gone on unless it was to Hell or the center of the earth?

"Have *you* been anywhere fun lately?" a long-haired man asked me after describing Cancún.

"No," I said, "but I'm just realizing this dynamic I have with my husband where I express my problem so dramatically that *I* become the problem, which makes me desperate to win back his favor. It's a cycle that keeps us from ever moving forward with our issues. I think my mom did this, too."

"Sounds like you could use a vacation!" said the long-haired man, smiling and moving away from me.

"This all *started* with a vacation!" I called out, but he was already in the garden.

"Does a giant with a heroin addiction live here?" our friend Dan said, pointing at the oversized spoon lying by the couch.

"No," I laughed, picking it up, "just a normal-sized person with a giant addiction."

I stared at the utensil bought a lifetime ago. Forks branched apart; spoons gathered together. And a really big spoon—

"He's the best, right?"

It was Caro; she meant Harris. We both watched my husband/her maybe-lover as he made a little plate of food for a woman holding a baby. Hummus? Do you like hummus? What about baba ghanoush?

"He's my voice of reason," Caro confided. "I can be a little crazy. I'm a 'crazy genius' or whatever."

She said it like she was quoting. I must have missed that particular article about her.

"I know my energy is sometimes hard to be around, but it's who I am," she said, poking one nostril with a dainty finger. I'd never seen a grown woman openly pick her nose. "*A little toughie,*" she said under her breath, referring to her booger, I guess, or maybe herself. She wiped it daintily on a tissue from her purse, then Purelled her finger. She glanced at the giant spoon I was holding and then my face.

"You have great skin," she said flatly. There was no rhythm to this conversation.

"Thanks."

"I'm gonna have great skin, too, because I have literally not once been outside without sunblock. Lots of people my age haven't. You can't tell right now, but you'll notice when we're old. We're gonna have no wrinkles. *What about laugh lines and worry lines,* you might be thinking—"

"I guess I was about to have that thought."

"But we're low affect—either because of autism or other stuff, emojis. I'll smile if it's, like, a friend's birthday, but otherwise it feels over-the-top, you know? Kind of fake."

I considered mentioning that I wouldn't actually be alive to witness how unwrinkled she was in her old age, but I didn't want to say anything that could be construed as competitive or aggressive because it was turning out that I liked her. She was a lot stranger than I had ever realized and I could see how she and Harris made a successful team. She didn't give a fuck and he did. She had a dark energy and one of Harris's gifts was organizing other people's darkness into something very winning. Literally. They had won many prizes together.

I said her skin was incandescent and she asked me if I thought the straps on her dress should be up or hang down. I said hang down and she wandered off to look for a friend.

I watched her pause as she passed by Harris. He put his hand on her naked back and bowed toward her to hear what she was whispering. I put the big spoon down. Envy passed through me like nausea. Not because they might be fucking but because they were committed to each other for such a clear purpose and yet she remained free. Whatever she had going on with him she was also associated with a steady stream of beautiful young men and women and nonbinary people. Many of the women were from the hip-hop community and previously had been considered straight. She seemed to be having the best time, all over the world, and Harris *admired* her for this—far from judging it, her sexual freedom was part of the material he got to work with. Now she was talking to the one other guest at her fame level, a man who had invented an app we all used.

By dusk everyone had left. I thought there might be a reckoning after the brunch, but instead we simply dropped our act and resumed the deafening silence. Sam watched TV while we cleaned up. Throwing out half-eaten pitas, my heart suddenly started to hammer. With one hand on my chest I tried to stay calm, but I couldn't breathe. It was all the working out—I had overdone it. I leaned against the wall; the tray slid into the trash. Okay. I'm dying, I thought and wondered if I could make it to Harris in time. He was in the backyard picking up cups. If I died halfway and fell down in the hall Sam would find me first. Now sweating and shivering I forced myself to keep cleaning up because, as I'd realized ten or fifteen seconds ago, this was just a panic attack. With rattling hands I gathered up little plates and napkins; I still wanted to stumble to Harris and fall at his feet, but now there was no reason to, no reason good enough. When he came in with the stacked cups he saw only that I was moving slowly as if the task was very arduous, as if I hated to help him. *Quite the opposite!* I wanted to shout. *In my final hour I only wanted you!*

And total bodily freedom, now that the urgency of death was fading.

I smiled to myself, weeping and tying up the trash bags.

This standstill between us was just life, that was suddenly obvious. There was no way to fix it, nothing to open-source; life was just a struggle. It was supposed to be.

I carried the trash and recycling out, a big bag in each hand. Before going back in I paused outside our house, looking at the lit windows. Harris passed by holding a plate in his hand, his eyes briefly flicking toward his own reflection.

This was the night before Tim Yoon, the retired cop, finally called back.

Yoon as in moon; he ran through the night. Yoon as in spoon, like a fork but to hold.

CHAPTER 22

He said it didn't usually take so long, but his daughter had just gotten married.

"It was a big to-do. Destination wedding. Anyway, you had some plates you wanted to run?"

"No, not anymore. I figured it out." I told him about the telephotographer and the real estate card.

"Why the telephoto lens, though? Is it a close-up photo?"

"No. Brian just thought that."

"Who?"

"Your friend Brian who used to be my neighbor. He gave me your number. He works for the FBI?"

"Oh. You know he died."

I gasped. "I didn't know that. Oh my god. Was it . . . in the line of duty?"

"What do you mean?"

"Did he get shot?"

"No, no, he had something wrong with his kidneys. I think he was only in the FBI for about a month before he got his diagnosis and had to quit."

That's why he was selling his truck. He wasn't moving; he was dying.

Tim Yoon asked if there was anything else I needed.

"People finding? Anyone you're having trouble tracking down?"

I said no.

"Yeah, there's a lot less need for that service now, with Facebook and everything."

That night I told Harris about the telephotographer, the real estate card, and the death of our neighbor. I was glad to have something major to report on; he had to say something—a man had *died*.

"That's sad. He was a young guy." Each word said like a dollar he wished he was spending elsewhere.

"So he wasn't even in the FBI anymore," I said.

"Right."

"But he was still wearing his uniform."

"Yep. Heartbreaking."

It seemed like the conversation would end there, but then, incredibly, he asked what they'd priced our house at. I couldn't remember. I ran out to the garage and came back with the card.

"One point eight," he read. "Okay. Good to know." Then he leaned in, squinting. "Is that you?"

"Yeah."

"Huh. Creepy. He probably shot it from his car."

"That's what I was thinking," I said. This was almost an actual conversation. And there was a strange feeling in the air; I couldn't put my finger on it. Now he was just sitting there, not speaking.

"Maybe go put that robe on," he said finally, very tersely.

"My robe? Why?"

He glowered, said nothing.

"I gave it to Goodwill."

He stood up. I guessed that was that. But before he left the room he said, "Just wear something else."

The front door slammed shut as I stared at my dresser. Did he just leave? I put on a short, sheer nightie and stood half-naked in the living room for what felt like a year, but if this was a test then I would stand there for the rest of my life. After a while I peeked out the front windows. He was sitting in his car. Should I go out there? I went back to my spot. Eventually there was a quiet knock at the door.

He didn't do a whole lot to get into character so it took me a moment. I invited him in, we sat on the bed. He took out his phone and showed me the pictures he'd just taken; our big curtainless windows glowed in the dark and my nightgown was completely translucent. This made me stupidly wet, but he seemed unmoved. I folded my hands in my lap.

"What else do you like to take pictures of?" I asked the telephotographer.

"Nature scenes mostly."

"Have you ever been to Zion National Park?"

"Nope."

"I'm gonna pass through there," I said. "I'm about to drive across the country." If I was playing myself in the real estate card then I hadn't gone on my trip yet. Not that historical accuracy necessarily mattered here.

"I wouldn't let you drive that far alone if you were my wife."

"No? Well, I want a challenge, an adventure."

"I can give you an adventure."

Even still I wasn't sure.

"He'll never know the difference," he added.

"Who?"

"Your husband."

He unbuckled his pants and let his heavy dick fall out. Okay then. I went down to my knees, shut my eyes, and got started thinking about the telephotographer, who had ended up Asian in my mind, like Tim Yoon. He said something I didn't catch.

"Excuse me?"

"You're a real 'good-time girl,' huh?"

"A real—?"

He slapped my ass. Yow. He was really committed to his role. He even looked a little different, the way his mouth was hanging open and his eyes were kind of mean. He pulled me up and onto the bed. Oh: he was still furious at me. And with his eyes boring down I couldn't shut mine, which was a problem—how could I *think* with him right there? A crisis actually, because suddenly it was clear that everything depended on this; I had to fuck the telephotographer without shutting my eyes. I tentatively ran my hands over the salt-and-pepper hairs on his barrel chest; he shifted and an acrid scent rose from the sheets, slapping me in the face. This man, this erect photographer, was really here, not a fantasy. I desperately tried to remember what I'd be doing if this were happening in my head. *He jerks off in his car, shows you the pictures, takes out his dick—what do you do? You, the good-time girl.* I could hear her pathetic begging and whining sounds, first in my head and then coming out of the depths of my throat like a soul channeled. These sounds triggered an arching and writhing and saying of the words *Fuck me. Please, yes, yes, come on, fuck me.* As with Audra there was a sort of salty-and-sweet combination of body and mind that made a brand-new thing, like alchemy. Or sex. The real estate card photographer was really responding to all this, he pounded me and the new deep ache that wasn't a polyp or a cyst surged hopefully. Everything was building and getting more and more raunchy and unbridled and it was all possible with this guy, this Asian photographer who didn't really know me. I couldn't help thinking Harris would be so embarrassed after he came.

But he wasn't—he wasn't embarrassed and he wasn't Harris. He wiped his cum off my chest with his boxers and lay back, reaching his arm around me. It had been ten hundred years since I'd lain in these arms. He told me about all the things he usually photographed besides houses and nature. He photographed cars for car ads. He did headshots for actors and models. He did still photography for porn movie shoots and sometimes he photographed pets.

"We got a dog recently," I said.

"What kind?"

"Sort of a mix."

"A mutt?"

"I guess so. It's more the dog of my husband and child." I hoped this wasn't going too far. After a while he said he was a cat person and fell asleep. I went down the hall to my bed.

When I called Jordi to tell her about last night's surprising turn of events she breathed a huge sigh of relief and said, Make-up sex is the best.

It is. It *is*, I agreed. I pressed my forehead against the garage wall. I had thought it was more than that, something that didn't already have a name.

I walked in a circle; a bubble suspended in oil.

I re-pinned the real estate card above my desk, studying the woman in the robe who had started all this.

The Jungian "provisional self," that's who she was. Like a caterpillar or a tadpole she wasn't meant to last forever, but maybe from her a new thing could be made.

I drove to the Goodwill where I had donated the eleven black garbage bags—the first ten were ancient history, but the eleventh had sat near the front door until just a couple weeks ago. What were the odds of the robe being in the eleventh bag? I searched Nightwear and Lingerie. I checked Children's, because it was small, and Dresses, just to be safe.

"It might not be at this store," a staff member said. "The donations get dispersed. It could be at any Goodwill in California. Or more likely someone bought it already."

"So you think this is hopeless?" I said, eyeing a pair of ceramic lions.

"Pretty much, yeah."

"Is *this* it?" said another staff member, holding up a plastic hanger with my robe on it.

"This is my robe," I told the cashier.

"It's cute," she said.

"I mean it was my robe before and then I donated it to you guys and now I'm buying it back."

"Okay," she said, wrapping the lions in newspaper.

"It's weird to have to buy it again, almost seems like I should be able to just take it, since it's mine."

She glanced at me but kept wrapping.

"It stopped being yours when you donated it. And it starts being yours again when you pay for it. No special deals."

I hadn't been angling for a special deal. My point was: what makes something yours? I guess *paying for it* was her answer.

While Harris tucked Sam in I cleaned the lions and put them in front of the fireplace. They looked nice there. Slowly turning, I scanned the rest of the living room, looking for something else I had contributed, anything. But there was nothing. In fifteen years I'd never changed a thing about the décor. Or I had tried, once or twice—a new dish-drying rack, a basket—but Harris had cringed at my choices and I hadn't pushed back. (Why argue? Less fussing with baskets meant more energy for my work.) So these lions were only my eleventh and twelfth contributions to the home, the first ten being all the spoons.

I hung out in my room for a while, then took off my clothes and put the robe on. Its familiarity made me light-headed. Harris was flossing when I came in. He looked me up and down. Had I been too literal? The robe was nothing special unless you remembered the picture on the card.

He didn't sit in his car this time; the photography part was implied. The sex was the same but more so—it was their second date and it was clear there was something between them, an intense chemistry that I hadn't felt with anyone before. And it wasn't just sex. Feelings were beginning to develop.

"I can really be myself with you," I said afterward, in his arms again.

"That's nice," he said lazily. "You're a great girl. A catch."

"I'm really not, not in my regular life."

"I find that hard to believe."

I stroked his chest, thinking.

"Do you think we could ever . . . make a go of it?" I said finally, caution to wind thrown. The telephotographer seemed taken aback but not shocked.

"Would you really want to leave your husband and this nice house?"

"I mean, it would be hard. But I'd like to feel this way all the time."

"And you have a child, right? A son?"

"They're nonbinary. They/them pronouns."

"Okay. *That's* new," he said.

I almost laughed, but his total commitment made that impossible.

"You're right, I couldn't do that to my child. They have enough on their plate without divorce."

"Yeah, I wouldn't want to mess up a kid's life like that."

"But in theory, would you want me if I was available?" I couldn't let it go.

"I would. But it wouldn't be like this if we were together all the time."

"Right. Eventually I'd probably have an affair."

We were quiet, looking down this never-ending hall of mirrors.

"And knowing me, that affair would probably be with my ex-husband, Harris. I always want what I can't have."

"I mean, I would be okay with that," said the telephotographer.

It seemed in this moment that we had cracked the code. Marriage would always be chasing us, but with this trick we could outrun it forever. I couldn't think of any reason why this wouldn't work.

"Let's give it a go," I said. I was worried he'd be insulted, that Harris would be, but the telephotographer just tightened his arm around me and kissed the top of my head.

"I'm game, but are you sure you don't want to just keep meeting like this?"

"I want more."

The next morning, Saturday, was a little awkward. We obviously weren't in our roles because that would be confusing for Sam. But there was a politeness, a little extra energy. A small altercation about rotting lettuce was quickly abandoned. We were waiting for nightfall. The sun toyed with us, setting and then rising back up a little, sinking then lifting until finally it fell once and for all.

I almost thought we might skip the sex and just jump right into conversation, but of course there was only one way through the looking glass. And there was a new thing tonight: me pressuring him. He wanted to keep his pants on and I shoved his hands away and yanked them down. He suddenly "wasn't sure he was comfortable with this" and I didn't care, just wanted what I wanted. How this fit into the telephotographer's psychological narrative was anyone's guess; it just felt really good to run roughshod over his feelings and boundaries, and of course ultimately his own body betrayed him and he came around.

"I told my husband," I said, recovering in his arms. I had been planning to say this all day; if I didn't push the story forward then it really was just make-up sex.

"Really?" said the telephotographer. I could feel Harris become very still.

"Yeah."

"How did it go?"

"He was furious."

"Understandable."

"I know. I'm having second thoughts."

"Because he's so mad?"

"And hurt. I don't want to hurt him."

The telephotographer was silent for a long time. I wondered if he could feel my heart pounding.

"Well, in the long run it hurts him more to stay with someone who doesn't want to be with him."

This was almost exactly what he had said right before our big fight. Was this like dying in a dream and real life at the same time? Could our marriage dissolve in this fictional place?

"Hey," he said, "don't get too much in your head."

I took a deep breath.

"That's right. Let it all out."

He asked about my youth, where I was from, and I ended up telling him about working in the peep shows. Squirming around in lingerie and less. Despite fifteen years of careful downplaying, I didn't actually have any particular shame about this job; it felt like other things, a mixed bag. Unlike Harris, the telephotographer liked hearing my stripper stories; he said he'd dated a lot of women "dancers" and he actually preferred them because they were more free with their bodies. I was quietly stunned by Harris's convincing portrayal of this kind of man.

"But you wouldn't do that anymore, right?" he couldn't help adding.

"To be honest"—and honesty was suddenly the whole point—"I still think of it as my fallback."

Both men needed a second to process that. I didn't mean stripping per se (I was probably too old), just that I was still the same person who might give a stranger a show. She couldn't be tidily filed into the past.

"You know what?" he said finally, "I think that's cool. It's your body, you do what you want with it."

"Thank you." My eyes welled. What you wanted to do in your dream was not *die* but fly—levitate—and hope that the ability carried through to the next day. The next day worried me. Harris and I were falling behind these two; the gap was getting too big.

We avoided each other for the whole morning, which was easy to do— first one of us was with Sam and then the other, like shared custody within the same house. There wasn't a sexy tension, it was just strangely dead. I didn't see how we could come together for a fourth night—this couldn't go on forever. I wondered if I should let Sam be on a screen so I could go to Harris and say Let's talk. I was considering this, very grimly, when he came into the room carrying the dog in his arms and looking shook.

"I think we need to take Smokey to the vet."

We'd cuddled with him and sang to him but hadn't brushed him every day. Or at all really. So he had developed clumps of matted hair, hidden ones that couldn't be seen but which felt disturbing when you petted him, like cysts. I knew this—dog groomer was on the to-do list— but Harris showed me how a clump had formed over his anus, effectively basketing it shut. There was shit trapped between the clump and the anus; mixed with the frizzy hair it formed a very solid material, like adobe or sod.

I'd never heard of such a thing, but I could really imagine how terrible it would feel. Each time he opened his anus to shit, the previous shit was pushed back up inside him. Sam looked at our alarmed faces and called out, JESS! A family joke, the wonder-nanny, but neither of us laughed.

"We can do this," I said, running for my round-nosed scissors. "It's gonna be fine." My emergency voice was always low and sturdy like this.

Harris held Smokey on the kitchen floor and we began talking to him tenderly, the way we used to talk to baby Sam. My poor sweetie, we said through our plugged noses, you're gonna be okay. With my bare fingers I gently pulled apart the dog-shit hair. Harris pointed out where to cut. I carefully trimmed clumps and masses, always testing first to see if the dense mound had any living flesh in it. After most of the hair was removed there was still a surprising amount of impacted shit. I pinched it away, adding glob after glob to the monstrous mound on the floor, but each layer removed seemed to only give room for the whole territory to expand. I sat back on my heels, reconsidering. It seemed like there would be no end to this. Harris, still holding the dog's legs, looked up at me. *Keep on going, hon,* he whispered.

I refocused and leaned in, digging through the shit with new commitment, pinching and trimming, and constantly murmuring, I've got you, baby, it's gonna be okay. Smokey looked up at me, wide-eyed, and I wondered how a dog like this ever survived in the wild.

"They don't exist in the wild," Harris said.

We kept at it, together, on the kitchen floor. And lo. Suddenly a pink anus appeared, pulsing and oddly clean like the sucking lips of a tiny baby. What a dear sight. I gently wiped the area with a wet rag then Harris took the dog to the bathroom and gave him a bath. I threw the obscene pile of shit-hair into the outdoor trash can, washed my hands, disinfected the floor, washed my hands again, and then stood beside Harris and watched our very clean dog bound around the living room in weightless confusion. We would take him to the groomer tomorrow, but it went without saying that this terrible event was one of the most important things that had ever happened between us. Second only to that time we put on our shoes at dawn and rushed to meet Dr. Mendoza at the hospital.

Who the fuck had we been? Starving hunters? Had we crested Donner Pass together? Or had we tried to and died trying. And now in this lifetime we only felt right when we were saving a life together, fixing a flat tire by the side of the highway; we only became us against insurmountable odds. The rest of the time we respectfully forgave each other for utterly failing to be what we felt we deserved and then some of the time we were fucking furious about this and it seemed impossible to continue, but this itself was a sort of emergency and thus brought out our lifesaving skills, our diligence and seriousness. And so we were condemned to a very rigorous, if joyless, life that was profoundly meaningful until suddenly one day it wasn't. Because I had felt joy. Stupid, pointless joy. Sam was wrestling with Smokey now. We watched the two of them moving like a little tornado from room to room.

"I didn't like that dance," Harris said quietly, looking straight ahead, out the window.

I couldn't believe it.

He was picking up the conversation exactly where we'd left off before it had blown up, and his position hadn't changed. All the telephotographer's sexy understanding had been an act.

Bleakness rose up around me.

What could I say? It would be silly to ruin a whole marriage over a single, booty-shaking Instagram post. Sam and Smokey ran past, screaming and barking. I shut my eyes and saw myself in the Excelsior parking lot, lit by headlights: raw and extravagant, erotic and wholly consumed by a ceremony of my own invention. For months I had trained for it as if I were preparing for Mount Everest or some other death-defying challenge. I had believed my life depended on this silly, slutty dance and I still did; everything had changed that night.

The barking and screaming stopped.

Suddenly the truth was simple and clear.

I had been honest in the video—I'd been myself—and Harris honestly didn't like it. And this was his right; a lot of people, maybe even most people, wouldn't like it.

"It's just not your scene," I said quietly.

"Right," he said, kind of gasping. "It's not my scene."

We kept standing there, side by side, though Sam and Smokey were in the backyard now. After a while Harris cleared his throat.

"It seemed like that dance was probably . . . for someone."

My stomach dropped and I made the mistake of glancing up. Our eyes met in the reflection of the giant window, a cold, desolate world.

"Did you see someone that night?" he asked, and in the blurry glass his whole body seemed to be streaming, spilling, though in fact his eyes were dry.

Given everything at stake the obvious answer was no.

Yes, I said. I had seen someone that night.

"A woman or . . ."

I tried to remember what an old therapist had once said about honesty versus kindness. He just needed to get the general idea, not every detail.

"Yeah. A woman."

The relief on his face was plain. It was as if I'd worked out the whole chess game in advance and now all I had to do was move the pieces, answer the questions. Or else this was what it felt like to tell the truth. It *had* all been worked out in advance; in reality.

"Is it going to happen again?"

No, no, it won't happen again; I'm so sorry, can you ever forgive me.

"Yes," I said. "It's probably going to happen again."

I had thought my time with Davey was the halfway point of my life—the apex of my ascent into the unknown—but actually, this was. This yes, said on a Sunday afternoon.

He asked me if I could keep it in Monrovia and I said I could, on my Wednesdays.

"I figured."

"What do you mean?"

"Just that you were doing more than working in that motel."

I didn't protest; true enough.

"And . . . favored nations, right?" he said, looking down at his shoes.

"Favored nations?"

"The same rules apply to me."

Oh. The foldout couch in his office; he probably hadn't done anything on it but he wanted permission to now. I waited to feel a rush of overwhelming jealousy and rage. Indeed, I was shaking. But—and it took me a moment to realize this—only with surprise. One could even call it hope. He, Harris, the telephotographer, had seen me, or more of me anyway, enough, and I wasn't being cast out. I could remain with him and our child in this house, as I really was.

"Of course," I said, the same way I said *I do* at our wedding—no way of knowing for sure, but here's hoping.

CHAPTER 23

Jordi was gobsmacked. For the first time in years she felt the need to smoke a cigarette so I walked with her to the corner store, where she bought a pack of yellow American Spirits. After exhaling a few streams of smoke out her studio window she started in on me.

"You can do whatever you want one night a week?"

"And so can he."

"But you're not getting divorced?"

"No. I mean, that wasn't mentioned."

She paced around the big room, weaving between her sculptures.

"So you did it. You were honest."

"Well, I was honest with the telephotographer, first. Sort of a cheat."

"Sure, sure; that was your Third Thing."

After pluming out some more smoke she explained the Quaker concept of Third Thing.

"It's a topic of conversation that doesn't belong to either party. The soul, usually so shy, can speak more easily through this Third Thing, at a slant."

The fucking Quakers. They'd invented chocolate bars and maxipads and now this. But could the Third Thing stay? Could the telephotographer become our third, making us a thruple? I was grasping, looking for anything to hold on to. The marriage dream might have been a fallacy, but it was old and familiar, like Santa Claus. Something had to replace it. Although, come to think of it, nothing had replaced Santa Claus, just reality, growing up.

"How will you meet people?" Jordi asked. We looked at each other blankly. "Just walk out onto the street? Ha, this is so surreal! Does it feel surreal? Why are you so calm?"

"I'm probably still in shock," I said, looking at both sides of my hands.

"Who would you want to fuck? Just throw out a name."

"That's not how it works for me." I frowned. But my eyes slid to a card Jordi had pinned on her wall. It was for an exhibition she'd gone to more than a year ago; I'd been out of town.

She laughed. "Lore Estes?!"

After talking to Nazanin about her fantasy I'd finally opened the book on our coffee table.

"Not literally her, but someone that butch."

"Take it," Jordi said, unpinning the card from her wall. "I wonder who Harris will date. And he's so traditional—won't he just fall in love and want to get remarried?"

I looked away. For some reason the way he had said it, *favored nations*, had made me think he was going to be dating various women, women of all nations. For a moment I wondered if all this could have been avoided simply by having a project to do, something in the future to prepare for. Without that, everything had unraveled. Or maybe this leap had been dangerously *delayed* by my work; maybe it would have happened years ago if I hadn't been so satisfied by risks taken in art.

"Well, if Harris is dating, you should be dating," Jordi said.

"He's not!" I assured her. "It's more about the feeling, the *idea* of freedom. It's very subtle."

It stayed subtle for almost two months. He spent Monday nights at his office and I spent Wednesday nights in the Excelsior. We were careful with each other, as if we'd survived a car accident together, and each morning, no matter where I was, I opened my eyes and thought: I can do anything I want. It was like so many dreams I'd had, but I woke up *into* it instead of from it.

Then one night, Harris waited for Sam to fall asleep, poured a scotch, and nervously informed me that he'd had a date with someone last Monday night. Dinner.

I took a deep breath.

"Was it Caro?"

He spit his drink with a squawk.

"She's *twenty-eight*! She's closer to Sam's age than mine, she—"

"Sorry," I said. "My mind goes crazy."

Never in a million years would Harris have considered Caro; I'd known this all along. She was too intense and unboundaried. *I* was the one who needed to swirl together in a churning, dangerous cauldron, and for a short time—while Sam was in the NICU—we did. He was taking small sips of his scotch. Seeing him so clearly felt like tripping. But every day was like this now; I was perpetually waking up and then waking up from *that* and then—

"She's your age," he said, about his dinner date.

I tried to picture her based on this single piece of information.

"Was it just dinner, or . . . ?"

"You want me to say?"

"Yes."

"We went back to her place."

"*Okay.*" I stood up. "Okay then." I sat down. I put my hands to my cheeks and then clasped them in my lap. "All right. All right then."

He watched me, braced for whatever was coming. I crossed my arms and looked away. So, this was the cost of that free feeling each morning. Brutal. But there was enough hypocrisy built into life, one shouldn't choose it.

"I think this is good," I rasped.

"Yeah?"

"Yeah."

We looked at each other in shock, like two people hovering in the air with nothing holding them up. No scaffolding, no strings, no wings—but not falling.

Two Mondays later he said the woman my age, the dinner date, was now his girlfriend.

"You guys used that word? *Girlfriend?*" I was aghast.

"Yeah; it's quick, I know. But I'm not like you—I have no interest in *exploring* at this age."

I wept, remembering when *I* had been his girlfriend, not yet his wife. For a moment I wanted to punch this woman in the jaw. Then I saw myself dusting her off, buying her a drink.

She was someone we'd been acquaintances with for years. Paige—a ruggedly beautiful, red-headed therapist who specialized in neurodivergent teenagers. She had famously impeccable taste; her home had been in *Architectural Digest* (family money). Divorced, no kids. She called me the next day, as one should when one becomes the girlfriend of an acquaintance's husband.

"This is funny," I said. I was trembling but guessed she was even more nervous.

"Yeah," she breathed. Laughter. It started to rain and she said *It's raining.* She only lived a few blocks away.

We tried to remember when we'd last seen each other.

"Maybe a brunch at Erin's?"

"Or after that Christmas fair—on the street?"

Having never been in this particular relationship before, I found our phone energy hard to place. It wasn't flirtatious, obviously, but we desperately wanted to come off well, having been randomly seated together for God knows how long. *Don't worry!* my tone said. *I'm not going to be a problem!* We were both abundantly kind, sane, not-boring, with an occasional flash of the knife: *I'm in a position to destroy you, but I won't.*

She was a little wary of our unusual marriage. She was looking for stability, she said. She'd been through a lot in the past few years.

"Your divorce?"

"It's more that—maybe you heard—both my Airedales died within a month of each other. That was over a year ago but I've been a little bit of a wreck ever since. I still have trouble sleeping."

"Really," I said. "Do you wake up at two a.m. as if it's morning?"

"Yeah. Even after a year!"

"It might not be the Airedales. You're my age, right?"

"I'm forty-six."

"Have you gotten your hormone levels tested?"

"You mean thyroid stuff?"

"Perimenopause."

"Okay, wow. But I don't have hot flashes or anything."

"Some people don't. What about"—for the record, I *did* pause here—"vaginal dryness?"

The uncomfortable silence that followed was the mother from which all other uncomfortable silences are descended.

"Sorry. It's just, my ob-gyn . . . I'm trying to . . . 'share the knowledge' . . . "

"Huh. Because it seemed almost like you were asking how wet I get. Like a big dick contest but for women."

It took a lot of apologizing to get back to dry land, and even then I couldn't ask her to not tell Harris. This was a moment of stark clarity about my situation: she could tell him whatever she wanted. I had one kind of primacy, but she had another. In fact, primacy, the whole idea of it, could not be wielded here. Everyone would have to do the right thing based on some other system.

If I'd ever wondered how monogamous Harris was, it now became evident. After a lifetime of stomping around naked I suddenly began wearing the pink robe to and from the shower and to the dryer when looking for clean underwear—he didn't ask me to, it was just palpably obvious that he would not be comfortable dating one woman while looking upon the nakedness of another. It wasn't dead between us (we could have gone from telephotography to telepathy to pornography), but something had to be sacrificed. He needed to feel like a committed, trustworthy boyfriend, and I needed to feel free.

"No more sex for us, right?" I asked one night, just to confirm.

He held up a finger and I watched his face in the mirror as he finished brushing his teeth; a little storm passed through his features, then they became placid, resolved.

"Right." He wiped his mouth on a towel. "I think that's over. Are you dating someone?"

"No. But I will. And it could be a man. Probably not, but—"

"I know. *I know you.*"

I blushed. Did he?

I pinned the Lore Estes card above my desk, next to the real estate card and the cross-country map—it was a photo of a kitchen counter on its side with the cupboard doors clumped and hanging together; a large rubbery bubble or tumor was barnacled onto one cabinet corner.

"What's that?" said Sam, immediately noticing the new thing. The change in our marriage was happening right under their nose, but we agreed we didn't need to tell them yet, it was too soon. Though sometimes, when I was tired or hungry, I grew confused on this point. My parents had told me everything about their relationship because I was unusually wise and special, possibly clairvoyant. It was a big honor to be confided in, not unlike when an ordinary child turns out to be the reincarnation of the next Tibetan lama (another thing I'd learned about from my parents). Wasn't Sam deserving of such respect? It was sometimes hard to remember that this version of reality had been debunked years ago, in therapy.

"It's a sculpture," I said carefully. "The artist is a . . . role model."

"Can I print out pictures of role models for *my* room?"

Printing out pictures was one of their favorite things to do, but it was very boring and endless and maybe a waste of paper.

"You can print out pictures of two role models."

"Three."

"Okay."

They found three pictures on the internet and printed them out. Charlie Chaplin, RuPaul, and, somewhat disturbingly, the Apple logo.

CHAPTER 24

How often does he see Paige?" Jordi asked as we drove. We were headed to an opening in North Hollywood; Lore Estes was in it but we guessed she probably wouldn't come down to L.A. for a group show.

"Once a week? Sometimes he's gone for two nights."

"So you can be gone for two nights, too, then." Jordi was eager for me to catch up with Harris.

Before we ran across the street to the gallery I floofed my hair and reached under my skirt to pull down my blouse. But, as predicted, Lore Estes wasn't there.

"That's her ex-girlfriend, though. Kris. Her longtime muse." Jordi nodded toward a handsome smoker we'd passed on the way in. "This is her piece."

It was a kitchen table with dozens of extra legs, weirdly similar to Lore Estes's work. Was that awkward? Maybe not. What did I know about the life of a muse? Kris was younger and taller than Lore Estes, but dressed in the same kind of sloppy, chic suit. Stringy, shaggy, shoulder-length hair. From time to time I found her eyes on me, or maybe mine were on hers; it seemed we were weaving a delicate, shivery spiderweb as we moved around in relation to each other. When, for a moment, we ended up in the same cluster of mutual friends, neither of us said a word—introductions would have been uncouth given everything that had already passed between us. Unless this was all in my head.

"That's the great thrill of it, right?" Jordi whispered. "It could be nothing."

You didn't have to ask for people's numbers anymore because of social media.

While Jordi drove us home I followed and DMed Kris, asking if she would still be in town on Wednesday night. That was my shot and it felt pretty long.

"Who even cares if she writes back," Jordi said. "You asked someone out on a date and it's *completely aboveboard*. How does it feel?"

I couldn't answer because my head was out the window, the wind blowing my mouth open as we flew down the freeway. But I pulled it in real fast when my phone buzzed.

I held it up so Jordi and I could read the message together. We didn't crash only because it was so short.

| Yep.

I read fifteen or twenty lube reviews, ordered two different kinds as well as special bottles to decant them into. I bought three strains of pot that women reviewers had said were good for sex: Do-Si-Dos, Trainwreck, and Dutch Treat, all in vape form. I tested them out to make sure they weren't too psychoactive or sedative by masturbating on each of them and trying to compare the body highs. I bought mouth-moistening lozenges for after vaping. I did facial massage throughout the day, upward and outward, and worked out like a Navy SEAL, making hut! hut! sounds. I got a pedicure, buff, no polish. I steamed a skirt that could be ripped open by the snaps running down its front; I practiced ripping it open, slowly, snap by snap. I prepared for Kris as thoroughly as I had prepared for my cross-country trip, as I had prepared for Davey, as I had prepared for the dance.

There was no need to prepare the room—thanks to Helen it was always pristine and ready. I waited on one great chair and then the other, ran to the mirror, then sat down again.

Where's Sam's thermos? Harris texted.

| My date is about to arrive

| Sorry! Good luck!

| I think it might be in Leila's car

About ten minutes before Kris was due an eerie calm came over me. I felt nothing, for her or anyone. Nothing mattered. This was probably how I would feel right before dying; all that worry and anticipation and then right before the end: nothing. Thank God she wasn't late.

"Quite a place," she said gruffly, glancing around with a blue backpack on one shoulder.

"Thanks."

"The contrast between the exterior and interior."

"Yeah."

I waited for her to say more, but she was done talking, so I took over. Yammering away, I went back and forth in my mind about whether there was a charge between us—I wasn't overcome by lust, but then, she didn't seem to be, either. She was sober so I decided not to vape. If I wasn't aroused by the time things got physical I could astral-project myself into a more taboo situation, clamp the invisible screen over my face. Of course some people didn't have sex on first dates, she might be like that. Or maybe I was mistaken, maybe this wasn't a date, given that it had been three hours now and neither of us had laid a hand on the other. By one a.m. and with great disappointment I started to give little hints that we should wrap it up. I yawned and she said, *God, I'm not usually this nervous; come over here.*

The crossing of the threshold. One moment she was respectably over there and in the next I was, impossibly, lowering myself onto her lap, legs spread, my hands on her broad shoulders.

She said I was a queen and she wanted to serve me for the rest of the night. Yes, my queen, she said when I suggested we take off our clothes and move to the bed. For a moment I found this annoying, then the meaning landed: I could do no wrong. So I did the riskiest, most daring thing I could think of: nothing. I didn't crank up a fantasy, I didn't perform my lust; I just lay next to her, feeling the warmth of her unfamiliar body as it breathed in and out beside me. After a long time, or maybe it was only a minute, one of my hands migrated over to her hip, completely of its own accord. She was long-limbed, sinewy, and it was a deep pleasure to run my palms over her shoulders and arms, hips and thighs, again and again, with no known goal, as if I was starting the whole sexual project anew. I thought this might be enough, plenty, but then kissing was invented. From scratch. First stabs and grabs and then snaking kisses that had no beginning or end (was this how Harris and Paige kissed? Did he ever think of me at the wrong time, as I was doing now?—how strange this all was!). Then we downshifted into a new kiss pattern, slowly turning our heads back and forth so that our wet lips could slide over each other. It was only now that my pussy began to awaken, reflexively humping whatever was near it, and my imagination swelled involuntarily, aggressive and greedy—it didn't care that this was a first date, it just wanted what it wanted. I bent my lips to her ear.

"What if you were my"—I breathed the word—". . . daddy?"

Her face turned abruptly stern and I reddened. What had I done.

She jumped up—oh no—and grabbed her backpack.

Unzipped it.

Dumped a pile of dicks on the bed.

"What do you like?" she said, looking at me severely while preparing a holster. "I bet you're small."

I couldn't help smiling, with pure glee. *What confidence*. That grim look—that was Daddy. I picked the most medium one and whispered, Tuck me in.

It turned out Daddy was pissed that I had done this to him. Made him so hard.

"It's not right," he said, jerking off and pulling down the sheets so he could see me. Good fucking Lord. My cunt jolted on so hard it was like being bitten, venom attacking the nervous system. My tongue thickened, brain slowed. By the time he was showing me how to have sex, easing it in, I was so completely within the scene that I kept squeaking, Am I doing it right? Am I doing it right? But when he flipped me over and came in hard from behind I made a sound that was less like a girl and more like a two-hundred-year-old starving beast finally being fed. Nothing compared to a rubber dick worn well; the invisible polyp, Dumbo's feather, was gored.

She left at dawn. I had gotten a soft molasses cookie for after. I ate it in the bath, sore and happy. *This is the part I'll remember when I'm old,* I thought, *eating this cookie in the bath.*

The next evening I tried to tell Harris in the way he said he wanted to be told, without too many specifics. I said I'd had a date.

"Okay. Is it someone I know?"

"No. Her name's Kris. She's an artist. I didn't get much sleep."

I watched this land; there was an old-school flicker of outrage and horror—we were just animals after all. Then he ran both his palms through his hair a few times and said, Got it, thanks for telling me. He was ice cold for about a day. I mantra-ed through it—*not my problem not my problem not my problem*—and by the next night it seemed his curiosity had gotten the better of him.

"So we both have girlfriends?"

"No . . . I don't think so. I don't feel head over heels." Which was new. I'd only thought of Kris now and then since Wednesday, happily but with no obsession. "I just want to be thinking clearly, for Sam's sake."

"We're both here for Sam," Harris reassured me. "You can feel whatever you want."

"Thank you." I leaned against the counter. This was just like talking to a friend! "She's great, *so* handsome, but I'd like to have lots of romantic experiences and *learn* about myself, you know?"

"Actually, I changed my mind. I don't want to hear about this."

I saw her once a month, usually in the room, but sometimes after Harris got back from Paige's I took the quick flight to Oakland, just to spend the night in her shingled cottage. We mostly did what we'd done at the start, lie around naked, touching and talking (me) and kissing, for hours. I whispered I love you one night, it felt natural enough—also preposterous. Who was the you in that sentence? I'd said it like cowboys say *Yee-haw!* Meaning, *I'm really on this horse right now and I wanna make some noise about it!*

I ate blueberries out of all her holes, fucked her with a cock bigger than my arm, jerked off with my face buried in her perfect, tawny ass. I'd forgotten the nonlinear, open-plan quality of lesbian sex, but it came right back.

Her orgasms made me think of a whale breaching out of the water, so unexpectedly huge.

We liked to order in and watch shows on her laptop.

We didn't hang out with other people or go to events. When we got up to take a walk or shower or eat, it was only to enjoy returning to the bed.

After four visits she took my hand and pushed a delicate gold ring onto my pinkie. Where a stone might be was a tiny buckle.

"I'll never take it off," I whispered, in the same spirit as I love you.

"You might want to, one day."

I was tempted to say, No, never! but instead I forced myself to make a brief speech about *my brand-new freedom* and *not wanting to re-create my marriage*. Each word was hard to spit out, but if I didn't put something on record now she might take it personally later. *I'm not interested in random fucking or polyamory*, I said, *but I have a journeying soul. I need to remain fundamentally autonomous.* Her listening face was completely blank, an inscrutable piece of paper. How tempting it would be, I thought, to draw something on it. What would I draw? A face. Whose face? Hers. Ah, this was why she was everyone's muse and I wasn't. My own face was a sweating, anxious mess. I could feel it emoting, molting.

"You mean nonmonogamy?" she said, neutrally.

"No, no, no." I was now so nervous that I was almost tearful. "It would be our own thing, not that! We'd have to really talk about it, down the road. Make rules. When we know each other better." I saw us sitting on the living room floor in front of her cozy fireplace, drawing up our bylaws. Old wounds would be tenderly revealed, kinks admitted; there would be laughing and crying and pauses for self-regulation. Then, given all this information (and in the context of Harris and Sam), we would know what sort of specific, customized relationship was right for the two of us. And it could change! As *we* changed! I didn't say any of this, but I thought about it while she kissed me. Frankly, I was proud that I'd said anything at all and that it had gone so well—apparently, based on this kiss.

"Seems like it's getting serious," Harris said after I'd been dating Kris for a few months. "Just say if our situation needs to change."

"Change how?"

"You might want to eventually live with her?"

I must have looked at him like he was deranged. He laughed.

"That would defeat the whole point," I said. "I'd have nothing to look forward to! Nothing to prepare for."

The future itself was another lover, reaching backward in time to cup my balls. Instead of dangling in the present I was held, I was safe; I was gently squeezed and aroused by my never-ending preparations.

CHAPTER 25

Except for Jordi, I didn't tell anyone about Kris or my husband's girl-friend, it felt too soon. But word got out, as it tends to. Rumors began to swirl around Harris and me—most people thought we were getting divorced. This made me irate.

"Divorce only reinforces the supremacy of marriage!" I complained to Jordi as we drove to the gallery where her headless women would be exhibited; she was worried about the floor plan. "You're either married or you're not, it's a binary. Whereas if marriage is important but not the organizing principle, then it can keep changing, the way the parent-child relationship does. That's actually a good model: it starts out primary, then it becomes less central—that's considered healthy—and then it often flips and becomes primary again at the end."

"You might have to be okay with being in the minority on this," Jordi said. She and Mel were always primary to each other.

The minority, how lonely.

We parked and walked into the gallery. I saw the issue immediately: it was too small. Jordi had made pieces so grand and substantial they could only be shown in some sort of temple or cathedral.

"Or even just a bigger gallery," Jordi sighed. She made some measurements using her feet as a ruler, heel to toe. Then, from across the big-but-not-big-enough room, she said she was quitting her advertising job.

"Really?" I called out.

She waited for me to walk to her, then explained her five-year plan; it was risky, she wasn't going to deny that. "But if you think of the graph," she concluded, "it really matters how we make our way down the cliff. It determines the second half of our lives."

"The graph?"

"The hormone graph."

Without really noticing, I'd stopped worrying about hormones falling and libido waning, such that right now I wondered if perimenopause was even still happening in there. I put my hand on my stomach where I thought my uterus might be. Was it possible that in reshaping my domestic life I had also reversed course biologically?

Of course it was still happening. Sudden bloodbaths, ghost cycles with cramps but no bleeding, thick black blood eels—the perimenopausal period was too erratic to ignore. It was only my alarm that had vanished, replaced with a mild, occasional interest. Maybe the bioidenticals had done this, or maybe the drop in my hormones had transformed me into a person who wasn't worried about her hormones.

Jordi was searching for the graph I had texted but couldn't find it; neither could I. We looked up "hormonal decline over time" and scrolled through dozens of diagrams, some gently sloping like playground slides, some jagged like steps, but none with the near-vertical drop we both remembered. It was as if the internet provided scientific evidence to mirror any anxiety, no matter how arcane, so it had shifted to reflect me as I was now. In any case, the cliff had served its purpose. The cliff, the fork— each woman would find the version of perimenopause they needed, if they needed it at all.

"Let's go," said Jordi. "It's dessert time."

We walked across the street to the grocery store; she wanted pound cake and vanilla ice cream. "And maybe some little potatoes . . . and eggs." I laughed. Now she was just doing her grocery shopping. We couldn't remember ever having been in a supermarket together, it felt like we were roomies. She had a weird way of arranging the items on the checkout belt, in a line like a train. As she was explaining the logic behind this I was watching each item roll by and noticing that the beeps and dings of the cash register were joined by a weird ringing in my ear. The whole sound-scape of the store seemed to be shifting up an octave. So familiar. Jordi made a funny face, I guess mirroring mine. But where had I heard these sounds before?

That dumb moment of disorientation right before it happens.

The cashier rolled my empty cart behind her and the newborn Sam was in there, covered in cords and wires, gliding away from me in the isolette. The beeps and dings came from the blood pressure monitors and pulse oximeters of all the babies in the NICU. What's that alarm? Is the baby desatting? Is their blood oxygen too low? Why isn't the nurse doing anything? *Nurse!* Stay calm, don't plead, but seconds matter—*nurse!* Shaking, I reached for the isolette. The cashier rolled it lazily toward the bagger, a gesture she did a hundred times a day, and I gave her an incredulous, stricken look. She blinked with confusion.

I apologized.

With one hand on my back, Jordi paid and walked me outside. We stood in the parking lot. I shut my eyes and faced the sun.

"A flashback?"

It was never not a shock, like falling down an open manhole. We ate the ice cream and pound cake in silence.

On the drive home I opened babytalk.com/fmhmomschat on my phone.

"It's kind of a ritual. I like to check in on the other moms."

"Maybe you can read a few of the posts to me."

I said nothing to that. This was the only thing in the entire world just for us FMH moms—it wasn't very much, but it was ours. It didn't matter, though, because the page was having trouble loading.

"Probably because we're driving," Jordi said.

I didn't bother telling Harris about the flashback, but I tried fmhmomschat again after dinner. I squinted at the error message. Safari could not open page because server stopped responding.

I tried again in the morning and again before bed: same thing. The page was gone. It had probably disappeared months ago. I imagined myself and all the other hemorrhaging moms spinning away from each other forever. Because the comfort was so modest I had assumed I could keep it; I had taken it for granted. One should always be asking themselves What if I lost this? How much would it matter? And then secure it, at least screenshot it.

The next time we met, Kris was a little late to the room so we immediately got into bed to make up for lost time. We kissed and cuddled, I pressed my face into her crotch, inhaled, and whispered hi. We looked at a video of Sam being cute and she told me about a famous collector she'd just met, a woman in her midsixties named Elsa Penbrook-Gibbard. Have you heard of her? Kris asked. I hadn't, but I snuggled up and put my head on her chest; it was a special treat when she had something to say. This woman was incredibly wealthy and owned a spectacular house in the Marina District filled with art. She was in the process of buying several of Kris's pieces—works that weren't even technically available.

"She's being quite aggressive about it."

Good, I said. I liked to hear about the nuts and bolts of her success. Kris had thought she was going to a dinner party at the house in the Marina District, but no other guests were there.

"It took me a while, but eventually I realized it was a *date*."

I grew still on her chest.

"A date?"

"Yes! It was so awkward. I guess because it came through my gallery I just assumed . . . So now I'm wondering if she even really wants those pieces or if she was just trying to get in bed with me!"

I sat up. We hadn't finished or even really begun the conversation about the terms of our relationship.

"Are you attracted to her?"

"No, she's . . . older."

"I'm older."

"She's older than you."

I got out my phone and looked her up. Not the best style, but she was reasonably hot with one of those pulled-back northern European faces, always looking into the wind. She dabbled in art herself, I scrolled; most of her work was portraits of beautiful young men.

"Does she want to paint your picture?"

Her cheeks turned red and I smiled, shaking my head; once they called her a muse Kris would let the most psychotic people into her life. Now she was describing the portraitist's house. It was truly phenomenal.

"Not garish, you know? Some rooms were real spare, nothing in them but, like, a giant, round, incredibly soft . . . I guess it was a bed"—so much talking all of a sudden!—"and then one major piece of art, like an actual Guston, and then the view . . . the window was open and the fog . . ."

After she had reassured me that she had no interest in this collector and I had reassured her that the collector admired her work, not just her, we fucked. I was so turned on by this story, this threat, I could barely see straight. I imagined Elsa Penbroke-Whatever masturbating with frustration after Kris left and then Kris coming back—maybe she forgot her sweater—and finding her like that and taking pity on her, fingering her, and then getting into it.

"You can't help it," I panted, "you feel guilty, but you're so wet and she's so hungry for you, she's like, whimpering pathetically." I whimpered pathetically. We sweated and twisted, trying to actually eat each other's necks and faces and tits with wide-open mouths. It was the kind of climax that needed another one right after to scoop up the leftovers and then another to lick the plate clean.

Afterward I felt kind of terrible.

"Too icky?"

"No," I said carefully, "but only because I trust you."

That was a question and she answered by giving me many gentle kisses like I was a sweet little baby. I held her as tight as I could, for dear life, and a cotillion appeared before my eyes, a courtly dance of couples.

Kris and Elsa.

Davey and Claire.

Davey and Audra.

Harris and Caro.

Harris and Paige.

Robert and Elaine, my parents, having sex right next to me, thinking I was asleep.

"They did that?"

"A few times, when we were on a trip, staying all in one room. The real relationship, the great drama, was between the two of them and my role was to watch and listen."

"Kinky," said Kris, stroking my hair.

This struck me as profound. A kink, yes. I wrapped my arms around her and considered all the kinky triangulations I had orchestrated, forever trying to avoid both entrapment and abandonment. All leading to this: my girlfriend. She was kissing my neck. My eyes pinwheeled; I was no longer alone in this crucible. I had a willing and wise companion. We would play on the edge of every fear, try some very safe and boundaried cuckolding. Negotiate specialized relationships with other people. Hallucinogens. The Mexico City art scene. Therapeutic French hot springs. Hello, journeying soul. I thought of sending Audra a thank-you note. *I'm in reality!* I'd write. *I made it out of the dream!*

"How did you know the bed was soft?" I whispered.

"What?"

"The bed in the empty room with the Guston, you said it was soft."

"Oh. I snuck in when I was going to the bathroom," she said. "I laid down really quickly, just to cop a feel."

CHAPTER 26

There's a girl in gymnastics named Paige," said Sam at breakfast one morning, "the same name as Papa's best friend!"

Best friend? It was time. We had to tell them that families could look all different ways.

It was easy to imagine us earnestly saying too much or the exact wrong phrase—something accidentally but unforgettably disturbing—so we wrote a script together, making edits in a shared Google doc. On Friday, immediately after dinner, I would give Sam their Popsicle and then begin. *Papa and I had a long, long time of being romantic together and we still love each other so much, we always will, but now our love is more like a super-deep friendship.*

"Does that sound creepy?" I said. "'Being romantic together'?"

"Well don't say it like *that*. Say it more neutrally."

"Being romantic together. Being romantic together."

After Harris said the part about our new friends Paige and Kris, I would jump back in with *We're a nonconforming family, but we'll always be a family, forever and ever.*

"What if we get divorced one day?" Harris said. We were kneeling on his bed with our laptops. "Will all this seem fraudulent in retrospect?"

"Only if we got divorced within, say, two years. I don't see that happening—do you?"

"No, no."

Divorce, just the word, used to feel serrated like a knife, something to wave around dangerously. Now I associated it with taxes, paperwork, bureaucracy. It might make sense, eventually, but what a headache. Marriage, too.

"We should memorize our parts," I said, "so they don't come off stilted."

"Yeah, it has to feel casual. I might ad-lib some lines."

"Well, don't ad-lib too much; don't make it longer."

"No, no—just to keep it fresh. And the cue is—"

"Can I have a Popsicle."

I reviewed my half of the speech on and off throughout the next day. I said it to Jordi and she was very moved. I whispered it to myself in Dr. Mendoza's waiting room while waiting for my yearly. When my name was called I quickly jumped up and the nurse said, You dropped something, pointing at the floor behind me. My script. I imagined another woman finding it and reading it with shock and admiration for the radical new family concepts. Or with disgust, pity for our child. I stuffed it into my purse.

When Dr. Mendoza asked if I was doing weight-bearing exercises I was finally able to say, Yes, in fact I am.

"Good. That helps protect against osteoporosis."

"I know." I knew so much more than a year ago.

Was I sexually active? And how!

She slid the cold metal beak in and I studied her face as she studied the inside of my vaginal cavity. We'd been through so much together, but we'd never be close—maybe that was on me, though. Maybe she was more chummy with her other patients, whereas I cast myself as a passive child around doctors. While she checked my breasts for lumps I told her about my grandmother's and aunt's midlife suicides.

"So I kind of freaked out after our last appointment, about perimenopause."

She nodded, now kneading the other breast.

"Everyone—all my patients—think they're supposed to play it cool about these changes"—now she was checking my moles—"but 'freaking out' actually plays an important role in transitions. Picture how the vaginal canal squeezes the water out of a baby's lungs—it's the shock of this squeezing and the sudden cold air that makes the baby cry out and take their first breath!" She inhaled so I inhaled, too. "The trauma itself prepares them for the next phase, life on Earth."

The next phase. Right. Now that I wasn't crying out about the cliff (the slide, the stairs, whatever) I could wonder about what came after.

"What's the best thing about being postmenopausal?"

"Best?"

"Yeah?" Maybe there was no best.

"Hmm, let's see . . . well, a woman's mental health postmenopause is usually better than it's been at any other time in the life of that particular woman, other than maybe childhood."

What.

"Is that really true? Is it because our periods stop?"

"Mm, it's more that we aren't cycling anymore between estrogen and progesterone and FSH. And, of course, in a patriarchy your body is technically not your own until you pass the reproductive age." She said this offhandedly, less like feminism and more like a scientific or anthropological fact. None of this squared with my friend Mary's dire descriptions, her numbness, but then I hadn't asked her what she *liked* about menopause. I'd reached out to her in fear and she'd dutifully scared me.

After the appointment I sat in my car and did a quick round of opensourcing, sending a group text to all the older women I knew. What's the best thing about life after bleeding? I asked them. Just let me know when you get a minute! But the first response, from Sam's old kindergarten teacher, didn't even take a minute:

My chronic migraines stopped completely after menopause.

Right on the heels of that, from a former producer:

| I feel like my true self. Like I'm 9 years old and I can do whatever I want

Then nothing, so I pulled out of the parking garage. But at each stop-light there were new ones to read.

| I, a lifelong Catholic, lost the ability to believe in God post menopause. God just no longer made sense to me. It was like a switch that had turned off. This has allowed me to explore parts of life that my faith didn't permit.

| I never had or wanted kids so I feel excited that there is no possible way I could make one now

| What other people do, think or say has become kind of irrelevant since I stopped bleeding. Worldly concerns feel like a hectic fever dream of youth

| No more endometriosis pain

In the driveway I turned off the car but didn't unbuckle my seat belt. These were all busy women, I couldn't believe how quickly they were responding—as if they had been waiting for someone to ask this very question. When there was a lull I used the time to review the post-Popsicle script for tonight, pausing with each buzz of my phone.

| You don't know me but Kat forwarded your question. My depression and anxiety and disassociation symptoms greatly improved after menopause and lifelong relational avoidance patterns became conscious, visible

| It felt like my hips narrowed

| I heard about your survey from Joslyn! As someone treated a certain way their entire adult life because they were voluptuous and pretty, it's become a joy to be unseen. But it was a bit of a journey, letting go, and boy how I wish I could tell other women struggling with the fade of their bloom how great life is once you let go of the flower.

Are you coming inside? I'm making dinner—that was Harris.

| I'm in the middle of something, can you text me when it's ready?

| If I'm sad it's because something is actually sad!

> I've contributed 4 people to the world. I've done my part. My body is now mine because it can't be anyone else's

> I lost weight after menopause, following a lifetime of struggles with my weight

> Menopause coinciding with the death of a family member has brought to me the lesson that to live, truly and completely, you have to be willing to let go. Of everything and everyone.

> All of the hormones that made me want to seem approachable so I could breed are gone and replaced by hormones that are fiercely protective of my autonomy and freedom

> Dinner's on the table

> > Coming!

As I cleared the dishes Harris asked Sam if they wanted orange or pineapple.

"No Popsicle," Sam said for the first time ever. "Not tonight."

"Really?" I said.

"Just have a Popsicle," Harris pleaded.

"It's okay," I said, taking a deep breath. "Papa and I have something we want to talk about with you."

Sam's head jerked up suspiciously and as I spoke they looked slowly back and forth between me and Harris, who was ripping his napkin into smaller and smaller pieces. After my last line, *We love each other, but we also choose to love other people*, Harris swept the napkin bits aside and jumped into the part about Paige and Kris and then I concluded and then the speech was over and we waited, as we had agreed to, for Sam to speak.

"Will you marry Paige and Kris?"

"No, we want to live together with you."

"It would be funny if Papa's girlfriend was the girl from gymnastics."

"That would be funny. It's not her."

A long silence. Harris asked if they had any other questions. "Anything. You can ask anything."

"Okay. Do I get extra screen time now?"

"Why would you?" I said.

"The vibe of this conversation . . . it just seems like I might."

The vibe. They were growing up. As we were becoming ourselves, they were, too, and the main thing, really, was not to steal their thunder.

"No extra screen time," I said. "Sorry."

This too could be yours was my energy as I finally began to tell everyone I knew about Kris and Paige and the new shape of my marriage. I braced myself for jealousy and got ready to help other women find a similar path.

"What if Harris leaves you for good, though?" said Cassie, frowning.

"But don't you see?" I said. "De Beauvoir was wrong. You can not only want what you want, but have it, too."

"But I really only *want* to want," Cassie said. "That's the whole point of desire."

Nazanin said she was happy for me.

"You could have a butch dyke, too!" I said. "I bet Kate would be open to it if you brought it up in the right way."

She looked at me like I had tricked her.

"You told me it was just a thought exercise."

"I don't even like to dance!" Talia exclaimed when I encouraged her to diversify her human biosphere, like me. "Neither does Evan!" Evan was her husband. "That's actually something we bond over."

I got it. It sounded nice.

It was like we had all agreed to sneak into the haunted house together but once inside, giggling and full of nerves, I looked back and discovered I was alone; everyone else had chickened out. Or else they were all more sensible than me, or well attached. Maybe they were curious about the haunted house but not so curious that they wanted to risk their own home becoming haunted.

Only my mom had the right reaction when I told her on the phone.

"I think that's what most people would want if they could have it," she said.

Which made me feel very good for a moment, very accomplished. Then I remembered all my friends and thought, *Is* it what most people want? Or is it just what *you* wanted, Mom?

And did she? Really? I suddenly recalled her visiting my first studio apartment. I had felt sure she would envy and admire me—I had really left! Look at my fancy hand soap in a pump! But no, she slipped away to call my dad every chance she got, like a sneaky teenager. She found my life upsetting and wanted to go home.

There was one person who really got it.

"I wanted exactly what you guys have, I even proposed it to my ex, before we got divorced," Paige said. "But he wanted a clean break, i.e., to never see my face again."

We were walking in the neighborhood. She pointed out a pile of dog shit and I jumped over it. We looped around the block a few times, chatting about mutual friends and drawing out our return to the house. She and Harris were going to take Sam out for pizza, a first, and I reassured her that this was totally fine with me. Actually, I was hoping she and Harris might model the sort of intimacy that he and I were done with; a warm, easygoing physicality, admiring looks. Kids picked up on these things, it's how they learned to be.

"I'm a pizza spoilsport," was how I put it, making myself sound like a health nut. "Sam will love the chance to pig out."

We were at the front door now, time to transition from two women chatting to this home where I lived with her boyfriend. It was her first time here; I was embarrassed by the clutter in the foyer.

"Oh, those are great," she said, pointing.

My ceramic lions.

They were wedged behind a bike and a scooter; Harris had moved them there "temporarily." "Why are they there?" she continued, now hugging Harris hello. "They should be on display—put them on top of the piano!"

There was no way she could have known the import of what she was saying, but it was crystal clear: she had my back as I had hers. We must expand now, at this age, *and despite all our fears, there is plenty of room*, she was saying, psychically. Or at least that's how I took it.

Harris suggested we stop referring to each other as my husband / my wife and this felt okay because meanwhile the three of us were making a family coat of arms. This was something we had always wanted to do, but it had never happened, probably because we'd never had a particular relationship credo other than what the state had issued us. Now we drew with black Sharpies on the back of an old David Bowie poster to make something that looked like a sign for queer recycling but represented our commitment to being honest with each other about who we really were, even if we thought the other people wouldn't like it. There was a big spoon shape for capacious holding. There were three black hearts for the three of us and the letters *M* and *P*, which meant we would keep being Sam's Mama and Papa no matter what; this would never change. Harris was adding what looked like paws to the right and left corners.

"What's that?"

He touched his forehead with the side of his hand. Our old salute. Still comrades, in life's trench together. Sam added a frowny face with an *X* through it that represented a commitment to more fun times and less boring times; making this coat of arms was their example of a very boring time.

It didn't happen right then, but a little while later I was trying to explain why I liked a movie he thought was silly, and Harris said, I've never understood your taste, and I said, You really haven't, and as we went back and forth about this movie I realized we'd done it: we'd broken through. Harris and I. Finally.

The exhausting formality that had been there since day two had simply lifted like a depression, a cloud of steam, and what remained was a pair of old kids who knew each other very well. We stayed up too late, chatting in the kitchen, or met for lunch in the middle of the day because there was suddenly so much to talk about—not just Sam but Paige, Kris, Caro's album, my elusive next project (any time now, God!). We didn't try to resolve old beefs, but as old beefs were reincarnated with new people we watched very carefully. *Eye-opening*. But we did not gloat, what would be the point of that?

On good days it seemed obvious that we would tend to each other on our deathbeds (both of them, somehow). Other days I felt sure we were only gathering our strength before making two homes—I could see mine: a gay place where friends might take baths. Either way, Harris and I agreed that this sort of marriage could only lead to more change, but that didn't scare us anymore because, as I told Jordi, we'd broken through.

"You should feel proud," she said. "Not many couples could pull that off."

"Well, who knows." I shrugged, lest any gods think me foolish. "I'm sure there's more surprises to come."

"Just enjoy it!"

Okay, I said, and did a little dance, a silly jig, like Humpty Dumpty or a lesser-known egg.

CHAPTER 27

My next visit with Kris was in Oakland; I flew up on a Friday. Staring out the airplane window I remembered a game Sam and I had played when they were a toddler. They would walk away from me with wide, mischievous eyes as I pretended to sob and tear out my hair with despair—and then suddenly run into my arms yelling, *I'm back!* It was my job to hug and kiss them with histrionic relief. *I'll never let you go again!*

Could I play this game with Kris? Could I have sex with her as Elsa Penbrook-Gibbard, like last time, then become myself again so Kris could "confess her liaison"? It wouldn't take very many words, she could just say *I had sex with Elsa* and I would enact the agony, the horror of abandonment, and then, when I couldn't take it anymore, I would yell a safeword and we would hug and kiss and stare into each other's eyes knowing that the void had been touched, the phobic core, and yet here we were, safe and sound. I wondered if she would go for it. Probably. She was so game. And beautiful. I gave the flight attendant a lesbian smile and felt rich.

Her mood was a little off when I arrived. Or, not off (who was I to judge?), just unfamiliar. She took a long time hanging up my coat.

"Are you okay?"

But she didn't do well with direct questions like that.

As per our ritual we immediately went grocery shopping—provisions—so we could hole up. In the store I pointed out special treats—chocolate? mango sorbet?—and she just shrugged, like I should get whatever I wanted, she didn't care. Walking home from the store, silently carrying too many bags, she wouldn't even meet my eye. I stared glassily at the people we passed, businesswomen, groups of teenage girls laughing and screaming *Vanessa! Vanessa!*

I started doing several different breathing exercises at once that all canceled each other out.

We didn't even put the groceries away, we just sat down—not side by side, not me in her lap, but opposite each other. She hung her head and after a long time she said, I feel hopeless about us. We're not compatible.

I almost laughed.

I mean: what? In what reality was this true?

Her reality. By way of example, she mentioned a time that I hadn't wanted her to kiss me because I was wearing fresh lipstick.

My mom was like that, she said.

I felt heartened—if this was the problem then there was no problem: I wanted to kiss her! I loved kissing her. I said this, but it seemed to have no effect.

Are you breaking up with me? I said, kidding.

She said nothing. Just looked at the floor.

I began shaking uncontrollably. *Keep it together,* I told myself. *Hold her. Just hold her.* I put my arms around her and she immediately began crying. Thank fucking God. Next she would say what was really going on; it would be a long night, but we were on the road now. We'd be home by dawn.

"Maybe we should take some time apart and talk in the morning," she mumbled into my shoulder.

I dropped my arms and reared back.

"You want me to leave? I just got here. Where would I go?"

"Sharon's."

The Bay Area friend I'd mentioned once. She'd thought this all through.

I jumped up like lightning, grabbed my purse, pulled up the handle on my wheelie bag—click-click. My ears were popping; my brain and muscles were flooded with thin fluid. She watched as I took off the gold buckle ring. It was the worst thing I could think of to do. Surely she would snap out of it and understand what was happening—she was losing me! But she just watched as I struggled, twisting it, then dropped it on the floor and rolled out the door. I walked a block, listening for the sound of her footsteps—would they be running steps or just fast walking? Would she grab me from behind and say *Wait* or would she walk alongside me for a long time until I finally stopped.

I sat down on the sidewalk; it would be easier for her to find me if I wasn't too far away.

After a while I walked back to the shingled cottage.

I knocked, then pounded.

She swung the door open and looked at me like a stranger—*Yes?*

She had showered and changed. In the time I had been waiting she had done these things. She was about to go out.

I staggered backward, apologizing for the intrusion.

At Sharon's I was incoherent. I didn't sleep for even one second. I forced myself to wait until ten a.m. before texting, I guess to prove how calm and stable I was.

> I regret taking off the ring and being so reactionary last night. Would it be okay if I came over?

Sure, she wrote, but I'm really tired. I might not be able to talk.

Hallelujah.

No talking necessary, I wrote.

Talking was left brain, masculine, overly intellectual. We could just hold each other; soothe and reconnect. I had been so dramatic with the ring. Why hadn't I taken a moment to calm myself? What an idiot, running off like that when all she needed was a little space.

Are you sure? Sharon said. You don't have to go back there. You can stay here.

I smiled. The only reason I was still here was because of time and physics. I had to put on my shoes and walk, stumbley dumbley, and one of my feet was being extra difficult, it had grown too large for the shoe. I chuckled, squeezed it with both hands to make it smaller. My phone buzzed in my pocket.

| Before you come over I should mention I had sex with Elsa.

The air was loud and crispy; there was a shuddering pulse as I moved. Sharon was saying *What? What did she write?* But I wasn't sure I should bother responding to these questions since they were already ancient; she had asked them years ago—that's how fast my mind was moving. Or slow. I was having trouble tapping Kris's name on my phone with such a shaking finger. It took all my focus. *Hey,* she answered.

"I got your text." My voice was tinny, that of a small metal child. I asked if it would happen again, the sex, with Elsa Penbrook-Gibbard.

"Probably," she said casually. "I imagine so."

A long silence.

"Was it better than *our* first time?" I squeaked. Maybe if I reminded her of when I was her queen, the profundity of our immediate trust—

"You really want me to answer that?"

"Please."

"Els is more . . . into it, you know?"

Into it. Sharon was anxiously watching my face.

"Do you have anything else to say?" I murmured.

"Hmmm. Nope. Nothing comes to mind."

I changed my flight and went home. I told Harris and Jordi, and I actually thought, on that first day, that I might be okay. My shock was so great that it was a sort of high, the energy mothers lift cars with.

"I want to kick her ass for messing with you," Harris said, looking truly pissed.

I laughed through streaming snot; I'd never heard him talk like this.

Then the moon rose and I found myself wanting to tell Kris about the terrible thing that had happened earlier that day. I knew she would understand because it was with her that my fear of abandonment had surfaced, my kink. Wait. Was everything that had happened today just a role-play? A very sophisticated type of therapy? I sat up in the dark.

This is really intense, I texted. We'll definitely have to do a lot of processing.

I thought she might not write back because it was two a.m., but she did, almost immediately.

Are you gaslighting me?

I could see why my dad called it the deathfield rather than primal panic or phobic core. It was a sphere apart from life. The atmosphere was thin; I couldn't take a full breath. There was a brittle, sarcastic edge to every sound—if I dropped a plate it crashed to the ground caustically, a clatter of ridicule.

Is she your girlfriend now? I texted the next day. Am I not?

She didn't write back to that although she did write a few hours later asking for the name of a bakery I'd taken her to. I stared at her question with my nose in a pair of my own used underwear. It wasn't hard to convince myself that this was the warm smell of *her* pussy and that I was between her legs again.

Nabolom, I wrote, inhaling; maybe this bakery name would be the start of a longer exchange about us. It wasn't and because of how scent interacts with the brain this was a very damaging experiment, psychological warfare inflicted by some maniacal despot. Sleep was off the table. Progesterone, melatonin, Benadryl, THC, CBD, a nibble of borrowed Xanax—if I took all these things at once I could black out for an hour or two, but it wasn't worth it; waking up to reality was worse than already being there.

"Can you get outside?" Jordi said over FaceTime. "Can you touch the ground? Take off your shoes first."

"Write that down for me," I said. "That's something I'd like to do in the future if I ever get out of this."

Scarlett texted me on Tuesday and again on Thursday about putting me in the gym schedule, but every time, I told her I was still sick :(. I spoon-fed myself with no help from my rubbery mouth; my stomach was so small that after three bites of anything a fourth was unthinkable. How Kris had looked at me like a stranger when she opened the door—*Yes?*—that's what haunted me the most. If my own mother had looked at me this way it could not be more chilling.

Can we talk about what happened? I texted, after five days.

I'm sorry, I don't understand the question, she replied, like a customer service bot.

There was no indication that we'd ever lain in bed for days at a time or been planning a trip to Paris or spent hours discussing how and when she would meet Sam.

Jordi FaceTimed every day, just to check in. "I don't want to minimize," she ventured cautiously, "but you did say several times that you weren't in love with her."

I frowned. Harris had tried this, too.

"That doesn't lessen the shock. It was so *abrupt*, like—"

"Like being startled out of a dream."

"Exactly, a shared dream, only to find you're alone. I'm always trembling now—look at my hand." I held my hand up to the screen.

"I think . . . the lag time . . . ," Jordi said.

The lag between the plane crashing and the radio news report about it.

Right. That was a shared dream, too; my dad had shared his nightmare with me.

By the time he sang "Ol' Man River" in the Slavic accent I was too old to join him, but until then I'd mostly lived inside his terror. It was cozy in there. Cozy *and* upsetting, nothing could be more intimate.

Of course, Jordi meant the screen was laggy. She was being polite about why she couldn't see the minute tremor of my hand. I was still holding it in the air. Back when Harris and I slept together I would often whisper, *Let's dream the same dream*, right after we turned out the lights. He took it as a sweet sign-off, but I yearned for this joint dream so hard my teeth hurt. He didn't understand that you could create a world—a fantasy, a nightmare—and bring other people into it, not just artistically but in life. I was pretty good at getting people to meet me in my mind, but ultimately no one wanted to stay there.

Wet-faced, mouth hanging open, I spent the next few hours staring at the artifacts I'd pinned to the garage wall—telephotographer note, cross-country map, real estate card, etc. I had entirely misunderstood the assignment, the scale of what life asked of us. I'd only been living second to second—just coping—this whole time. White-knuckling it until the next shared dream, emergency, premiere. And in between these I'd whipped myself into a froth of longing—or worked, created fictions. Fuck. My "conversations with God"—even God was in on this. Was there any actual enchantment or was it all just survival, ways to muddle through?

But it got worse. When I woke the next morning I found, to my horror, that I'd lost the ability to fantasize or dissociate. Having seen myself I could no longer be myself. It was like having your eyelids pinned open or not being able to cough when the urge to cough came; a reflex interrupted. I demonstrated this to Harris, croaking with bulging eyes.

"I get it," he said, disturbed by the enactment.

"Instead, I have to endure the given moment. Moment after moment, it's awful. Is this how *you* live? What's going on in your head, second to second?"

He gave me a tired smile. Unlike my friends, he never indulged this sort of question. But there had to be an alternative to my approach. Surely one day someone would say: *Wait, you've been taking the stairs this whole time? You didn't know there's an elevator?* And to that I would say: *Oh. Duh.* But in the meantime, here I was, suspended in the present with no illusions, no ambitions, no obsessive preparations, and it wasn't going well. I weighed 106 pounds. Aunt Ruthie came to mind, rail thin and telling me the plot of a movie called *The Heiress.* How much did she and Grandma Esther weigh when they opted out? Once you get really threadlike you're halfway gone already, the rest is just residue, trash.

"This is all positive," Harris said. "People pay good money for this sort of insight. You should thank Kris!"

"You think I should thank her? In an email or a text?"

"I was kidding."

Dear Kris. My Kris. Kris. How to begin? And what combination of kind words would lure her to meet up with me. Ideally in person but I was open to FaceTime. It was the only way out of this. Resolution. Closure. Some sort of concluding ceremony. Sam padded into the bedroom.

"Do you want to do Legos, Mama?"

I stared at the child. They should be in their pajamas.

"You should be in your pajamas."

I texted Jordi a draft of my email to Kris.

"Hmm. This is very generous," she said from the screen.

"Thank you. See, if we could just be tender with each other, platonically—I get that it's over—but if we could just talk about what happened, the shock, and say goodbye—"

"Don't send it," Jordi said.

"But it's the only way out of here."

"What about rebound sex? Remember Audra?"

I blinked. Sex?

"Nazanin and Kate are having a potluck next week," she said. "Maybe we go to that together?"

I sent Kris my email, leaning into regret and remorse so she could only do the same. I said I'd believed what I'd wanted to believe, creating a relationship that was ninety-eight percent imaginary. I said I didn't blame her for choosing Elsa, a portraitist whose gift was really seeing the person in front of her.

This did not elicit a similar apology or any response at all.

But a week later, on a rare trip outside the house (dog park), a long-haired butch woman introduced herself as a friend of Kris's. I started shivering.

"I really need to talk to Kris," I said to the woman. "Maybe you could tell her."

She put her hand on my shoulder and said, "There's no need. *Kris forgives you.*"

I laughed.

What twisted humor!

But the woman's face was entirely serious. In Kris's version of the story *I* was the perpetrator and the violence in my face right now only confirmed this.

Don't shoot the messenger, the woman said, I'm just quoting.

I smiled quickly.

There would be no concluding ceremony. The last airplane had left the island; I was stuck here forever.

After two weeks of this (102 pounds) Harris wanted to spend a couple nights at Paige's and I said Go for it, absolutely, I'll hold down the fort. Hadn't I been making dinners and breakfasts and reading bedtime stories? I could do these things with blood gushing out of both ears, an ax in my back; he had nothing to worry about.

"You're sure you're okay with Sam?" he said at four p.m. "You're feeling up to it?"

I smiled and shut the door behind him.

Sam was playing with Legos and eating carrot sticks on the living room rug. *Hi, guys,* they mumbled to themselves, *welcome back to my channel.*

"Just going to the bathroom," I said. "Then we'll do something fun."

I sat on the edge of the tub and tried to come up with a path through the next four hours. To bedtime.

But thoughts don't work like that—you don't pick them like pears from a tree, they just fall on your head:

The dinner-party-that-turned-out-to-be-a-date at the spectacular house in the Marina District: that's when it began. In the very soft, round bed. Just kissing probably, that first time. Then it escalated. *I* had escalated it by pretending to be Elsa Penbrook-Gibbard.

I covered my mouth with my hand.

Should I text her? No, that was over.

I was shivering again, my thin bones trembling. I glanced at myself in the mirror; my hand was still over my mouth. I quickly dropped it. Had I been in here a long time or a short time? I had to come out of the bathroom, but how? What if I couldn't stop shaking? How had my dad parented from the deathfield?

I peeked my head out.

"You okay, Sam?"

"I'm making something incredible, but it's not done yet so don't come out!"

See, there is a God.

My dad would have brought me into it. Of course. A child was an especially good person to bring in because they really believed, hook, line, and sinker.

Deathfield? (Sam would say) Is that a real thing?

Yes. It's *the only* real thing. It's time you knew.

I could make it worse than it even was; I could dramatize. I wondered if my dad did that. Did he really believe my mom's plane would crash or did he amp it up a bit, bring the agony to a sharp point so he could be sure I really felt it? I could see how that would be a relief, especially since I was just dangling in here alone, forever.

"I'm done!" Sam yelled. "You can come out now!"

It was time.

I flushed the toilet.

I walked out to the living room, one foot in front of the other.

Sam was holding their Lego masterpiece behind their back with a big smile. But their smile wavered when they saw my face.

"What's the matter, Mama?"

Here we go. Deathfield.

"Well . . ." Deep breath. Count to three. "I was having a tough time in the bathroom."

"That's okay! Sometimes it's not ready to come out. Maybe it was too soon."

"I think it was. I'll give it a while. Let's see what you made."

It was a tower, perfectly smooth on all sides and instead of a hollow core it was solid Lego all the way through.

"It's wonderful, hon. So blocky."

"But there's more," Sam said.

With great solemnity, they showed me how the tower fit perfectly into the corner of the living room.

"But also . . ." Now they slid the tower against the glass of a framed picture, clicking it into the corner of the frame: perfect fit, again. And— they walked me into their bedroom—the corner of their sock drawer: click.

With each corner I felt a light-headed fizz of familiarity, like déjà vu. It fit into all the right angles of the bed frame and the windowsill and while I continued nodding and exclaiming—"What a discovery, hon!"— I began a parallel conversation with Sam in my head.

I know this is important, I said, but I don't understand.

It has to do with scale, said Sam. We weren't in the deathfield but in another field, one we'd always shared. It was from here that they'd cried wake up wake up wake up to tell me it was time to go to the hospital.

Scale, I said. Okay. I'm thinking.

You're in a corner . . .

Yeah.

. . . but there's corners everywhere.

Huh.

See, even a tiny corner—Sam was showing me the corner made by the dollhouse bookshelf—is still a corner the tower can fit in.

I stared dumbly at the miniature books.

I'm afraid I don't get it, hon.

Sam sighed, in both worlds.

Maybe you will later.

CHAPTER 28

Jordi and I went to Nazanin and Kate's potluck; I had to do the things people suggested because I had no ideas of my own. We brought a banana cream pie that looked disgusting but which Jordi vouched for. I wouldn't know; I still had no appetite. "Don't leave me," I begged, but when Nazanin made an announcement about the neighbor's driveway Jordi went to move her car.

I stood alone holding a plate of tortilla chips.

Within seconds a blond woman with a squirmy baby told me she was a "mega-fan" and that we'd never met but she was friendly with my manager.

"Do you still work with Liza?"

"Yep." I was used to this; everyone loved Liza.

"I love her!" said the woman, giving her baby a ring of gross keys to play with. "She was one of the people who encouraged me to have a baby on my own and not wait to meet the perfect guy."

I smiled and nodded. At least this woman was shielding me from other interactions. I bit a chip and asked her where she worked. Film festival was my guess, based on her sweatshirt.

"Well, I quit for this little guy, but I used to be Arkanda's personal assistant." She said it casually, rolling the words around like pearls on her tongue. She had my complete attention now.

"What was your name again?"

"Tara."

I couldn't remember which of the assistants this was, but my face reddened anyway; they all knew we had chased Arkanda long after she'd ceased to be interested. I half-heartedly thought about playing it cool, but why bother. Not just with this woman but in general. It was too late.

"I was so excited when she first reached out," I began, "but then she just kept . . . *canceling*." My voice cracked; I took a breath. "Sorry, I went through a bad breakup recently."

"Oh, I'm so there with you, sister. I had one of those in the spring and the littlest thing would make me cry! A car ad!" She laughed and I wiped my eyes.

"You probably can't tell me what Arkanda was reaching out about, right? Because of confidentiality?"

"You don't know?" said Tara, looking genuinely surprised.

"I mean, I know it was about a potential project."

"You two had the same birth . . . issue. I think she just wanted to talk to you about it."

The baby was gumming a plastic cup. Birth issue?

"You mean Fetal-maternal Hemorrhage?"

"Yeah, that."

"How would she know that I—"

"Her nanny."

I thought it and said it at the same time: "Jess."

"Jess," she confirmed. "What a superstar. Have you been to her macrobiotic restaurant? Arkanda helped her set that up."

Between the two of them, Tara and Liza had no trouble scheduling the meeting with Arkanda; the magic word was FMH.

"Is she going to cancel again?" I said. "Because I don't think I could handle that right now."

"Tara says we got off on the wrong foot but that shouldn't happen again as long as it's clear there's no creative collaboration on the table," Liza said, suddenly the expert.

"It's clear. *She's* the one who said potential project."

"I might have added that," Liza admitted, "that particular phrase."

Maybe I was no longer beholden to Liza; maybe it was time to get a new manager. She was suggesting Geoffrey's in Malibu.

"There's a hotel in Monrovia," I said. "I'd like us to meet there."

There was some back-and-forth with Arkanda's team about this; they said hotels were generally hard to lock down in terms of paparazzi. Tell them it won't be a problem, I said. This hotel is different—for one thing, it's a motel. I found myself wanting to tell Kris about all this.

"Why?" Jordi said, rubbing her newest sculpture with a big chamois. "Was she a particular fan of Arkanda's?"

"No," I whispered. There was no reason to tell Kris.

Though I tried not to talk about it anymore, privately I remained in shock, broken. My dad had confirmed this was the deathfield. You've actually always been in it, he said, but now you're aware. That's progress, in a way. Most people never even know.

"I think I'll get Arkanda a gift basket," I rasped, "a nice bottle of wine."

"Great idea," said Jordi.

She probably knew I was still crawling through my days, but what could anyone say at this point? She stepped back to assess her work. I glanced at the sculpture and, startled, tripped backward over my feet.

"Is it new?" I said.

"What do you mean?"

"Have I seen this one before?"

"It's been here for months. You've seen it at every stage."

We stared at the green marble figure together. It was veined with black, highly polished.

A headless woman on her hands and knees.

"Everyone thinks doggy style is so vulnerable," Jordi said, "but it's actually the most stable position. Like a table. It's hard to be knocked down when you're on all fours."

A giant black SUV was idling in the Excelsior parking lot and two more black cars were parked on the street in front of the motel. Liza texted that Arkanda was already safely inside; her people had come early and scoped it out first. I was nervous but not too nervous because of the room. She had probably stayed at Le Bristol, the hotel it was based on, so she'd feel right at home. It was almost as if I'd designed it for her, the perfect celebrity hideout—discreet on the outside, exquisite within. What a strange feeling to stand in front of room 321 holding a gift basket, and knock on my own door. No one answered so I knocked again and when no one answered I went to the front office.

"Okay, so, funny story," Skip began before I even opened my mouth. "This couple booked the room so far in advance that I was still using the old software, so when you called—"

"Where is she."

"I put your friend in room 322. She was fine with it. Lots of cars, right?"

I was speechless. But there was nothing I could say that wouldn't put me in the spoiled brat department.

"The couple came all the way from Portugal by way of Seattle so I hope you didn't knock on the door," Skip said, handing me a key to the other room.

"Well, I did."

"Hopefully they have earplugs in."

"We can only hope!" I said angrily, and marched off to 322.

When Arkanda opened the door I was suitably wowed—it was really her—but also vaguely disappointed. Seeing her famous face didn't miraculously make everything okay; she wasn't actually a god.

"My, that's nice, thank you," she said, taking the gift basket and putting it on the laminated dresser. I had forgotten about that dresser, the same one used to be in 321. The nylon curtains, the dingy white walls, the bad painting—it was exactly like my room when I first arrived, just a crappy motel room.

"I'm so sorry for the room," I said, and began to explain that the room *next door* was exquisite; I'd redone it in the style of Le Bristol? In Paris? But these people who came from Portugal by way of Seattle— Arkanda waved her hands, shush, and said she liked it.

"It's cute. DTE."

"DTE?"

"Down-to-earth."

She was wearing workout clothes that didn't seem particularly special except for all the jewelry—rings, bracelets, four or five necklaces. And her nails, makeup, and hair—a long pony of box braids—were all immaculate, but they probably always were. I had worn the most unique, special outfit I owned, a chocolate silk jersey dress. I was dressed for a splendid party, she was dressed like a mom meeting with another mom after Pilates.

She had taken the wine out of the gift basket and was squinting at the label.

I asked her how old Smithie was now: "Four? Five?" I'd done my research—that was her FMH baby; the younger one, Willa, was adopted.

She raised her eyebrows.

"Smithie? You mean *Smith*? Maybe let's chill first, right?"

I could have died.

We drank the bottle of wine and she told me about the intention behind her new album, which was about land, both meanings of the word land. I nodded, Yes, wow, incredible, and asked about her studio setup, which was something I knew about from Harris. The studio was legendary, actually, and after recounting its history, she gave some quotes about her producer, her "ride-or-die." How long could this go on? Or had she forgotten why I was here? Now she was describing her process, how she sent voice memos of lyrical ideas to the ride-or-die producer. She started to take her phone out to play me the voice memos, but then stopped, perhaps remembering this wasn't an interview for *Rolling Stone*. She stood up. Her eyes cast about as she stretched.

"You think this is abstract?" she said, leaning into the green-gray painting over the bed. "Or is that a figure?"

Maybe she herself did not know how to shift to the topic of Fetal-maternal Hemorrhage. I sat on the bed and obliged.

"It's a woman at the entrance to a cave that's sealed up. She can never go back in so she's just hovering near the entrance for the rest of her life, mourning."

"Mourning, hmm." She traced the darkest area, the cave, with a long, lavender nail. "She does seem very . . . set. She's not going anywhere."

Would we talk about the painting for the rest of the night? Funny to think I had waited *years* for this meeting. No matter. It was still a fine way to pass the time.

Arkanda suddenly clapped her hands together and said, "Okay, let's cut the crap. Stand up."

It took a few seconds for those words to register, then I stood up.

"We're gonna pat each other down, okay? With both hands, like this." Her hands hovered in the air. "Every little bit of each other's bodies but never stopping. No lingering. This isn't foreplay, got it?"

Nope, but I nodded.

"I'll go first so you can see."

She began to pat me down. First my shoulders, my collarbones, my breasts, all the way down, pat pat pat, my crotch, my legs, then, walking around to the other side, my back, my butt, pat pat pat, and then around to my face, where she carefully patted my cheeks and forehead with the pads of her fingers. Despite what she'd said I kept waiting for it to turn flirtatious the whole time; I mean, she patted my groin for God's sake. But it didn't. In fact, each area she touched was immediately neutralized, like lights going out all over a city.

"Now you go."

I tried to do it with the same efficient professionalism. It was surreal to touch all these parts—her round, possibly fake breasts, her stomach, her thighs—without the silky cloaking of a sexual charge. Like throwing money into the trash; perverse.

"See?" she said when I was done. "Way better now."

"Is that . . ." I tried to form a question. "Do you do that often?"

"I mean, if I want to talk to someone for real then, yeah, there's always going to be that bump to get over, if I don't know them. Because of the level I'm at now. It's not your fault, it's the media. But, like, what am I supposed to do? If I have to go outside my circle?" She took a sip of wine. "No offense, but you're, like, waaaay outside my circle."

"Right, I am," I agreed, mildly ashamed.

"But you *feel* like you know me—that's the media—and you're revved up from that, which makes this tension that's, like, not my problem. Except when it is, like tonight, because of the vulnerable topic."

Revved up. I saw what she meant. The way I'd dressed, all my preparations—they were like those of a suitor. As if I thought we'd end up in bed together.

"Sex does the trick, it cuts through and puts two people at the same level." It was like she could read my mind, or I was just that unoriginal. "And believe me, when I was younger I used sex for that. Then Chessi taught me about the pat-down."

Chessi. The only singer more famous than her. I thought they were enemies; I guess not. I wondered if this pop star pat-down thing was something less famous people could use with each other, too.

"We're good now," she said. "Right? Just two people? Two moms?"

We were good. We'd crossed the intimacy threshold without sex.

I leaned the back of my head against the wall and stared at her. A woman a little shorter and thicker than me. Not much younger. We were here because the same terrible thing had happened to both of us and no one else we knew or would probably ever know. I asked her if she'd ever looked at the FMH moms chat on babytalk.com and her eyes lit up.

"There's a chat page?"

I regretted mentioning it.

"Not anymore. Sorry. It was all mothers of stillborn babies, though. No one like us."

"We're so lucky," she said.

"Yep." I nodded. But we weren't here to talk about how lucky we were.

She sat in the chair, then realized there was only one and moved to the floor. I slid down the wall, sitting.

"Smith was gray when he was born. Only three grams of blood."

"Same with Sam. Two grams."

"They need six—"

"Six grams to live."

"Right."

We looked at each other, blinking. I had come to believe that this part of me was fundamentally unknowable, unshareable, like any other interiority—a dream, as it were. But no, it had really happened, to both of us.

We talked about their neurological differences. I didn't usually get into this with people; not everyone understood how bright and shining such children were. We tossed around diagnoses and therapies like sports fans discussing their team. Perfection had abruptly lost its value the moment we became mothers, dead being the most extreme of all the ways a person can be different.

"It's been four years, Smith is four, but I still get . . ." She looked up at the ceiling. "I don't know if they would technically be called—"

"Flashbacks?"

"It's like I'm there again." Her face suddenly looked about to crumble; I turned away.

I get them, too, I said to the wall.

"Oh. I thought maybe, since your kid is older . . ."

"No, I just had one a couple months ago, in the supermarket." I took a sip of wine. "Did you have an accident or . . . they say sometimes FMH is caused by a sudden impact."

"No. Did you?"

"No. I guess sometimes there's no reason. I remember the nurse saying that."

Arkanda laughed. "That's fucked up, right? No reason?"

"So fucked," I said, my laughing mouth twisting bitterly. "No reason" was turning out to be a major theme in life. Generally speaking, when real pain was involved, there was no reason. No one to hold accountable. No apology. Pain just was; it radiated with no narrative and no end.

"There was a chat page and I didn't know about it," she said, shaking her head. "It's crazy, 'cause I *looked*. I looked for exactly that."

"Would you have posted?"

"Not as me, but yeah. I would have written . . . something like . . ."

She shut her eyes, thinking. I waited. She was, after all, one of the great poets of our time.

"*I can't believe . . . this happened.* That would have been my post."

I nodded, saying it back.

"I can't believe this happ—" The last part snagged in my throat for some reason.

"I can't believe this happened," she repeated, her eyes locking with mine.

"I can't believe this happened," I said.

"*I can't believe this happened,*" she said, her face suddenly stormy, enraged.

"*I can't believe this happened,*" I repeated again.

"I can't believe this happened," she said.

I was getting nervous. The words were the same, but the meaning was changing.

"I can't believe this happened!" she said, louder.

"I can't believe this happened!" I yelled. I wasn't sure I meant the birth anymore. Maybe I was talking about Kris. Or my marriage.

"I can't believe this happened," she gasped. It was expanding for her, too; I could see it on her face.

"I can't believe this happened," I said, speaking for my dad, for Grandma Esther.

"I can't believe this happened," she said, sorrowfully. Eyes still locked, we were spinning in space. There was some fundamental incredulity that we were closing in on and it was terrifying.

"I can't believe this happened," she said.

"I can't believe this happened," I said.

I felt like we were falling and the only way to stop was to look away, but I couldn't do that; it just wasn't an option. She was too strong and she had come all the way here and now we were doing this.

"I can't believe this happened."

"I can't believe this happened."

She took my hands in hers, and we both squeezed, not gently but as hard as we could, as if we were about to hit the ground. She leaned toward me and our foreheads pressed together.

I can't believe this happened.

I can't believe this happened.

And then it was just the birth again and I was terribly, terribly sad. For little Sam. That dying was their very first experience and that one day they would have to do it again.

"I can't believe this happened," I said, as if for the first time.

She blinked, mutely, and looking into her sad, sad eyes, I loved her baby Smith just the same as if he were mine. This was probably presumptuous, but we had landed and were still holding hands and Arkanda's face was all sweaty and tearstained and my heart just went out to her. As hers went to me.

We hugged, still sitting on the floor, then I went to the bathroom, unrolled some toilet paper, and brought it back. She wiped her face; I blew my nose. She pulled the clementines from the gift basket and we began peeling them.

They smelled unbelievably good, that citrus.

She asked if I had any other kids. Just the one, I said. I knew better than to ask about Willa or anything personal; we weren't going to be friends. Married? she asked. I explained about my situation and she said, I like it, very modern. I tried not to but couldn't help blubbering about Kris and all my recent heartache. Arkanda said, This lady sounds like a ho, and I agreed.

"You get hyperfocused, like me," she said, neatly spitting out an orange seed. "We gotta keep moving! Don't get stuck. *Don't keep staring down the well when the well's run dry*, that's what Carter always says."

I had no idea who Carter was—former president Jimmy Carter?—but I jotted down the thing about the well on my phone while Arkanda went to the bathroom. When she came out she picked up her giant, wine-colored purse.

"Hey, so, I'm gonna hit it," she said, crossing her arms in front of her. "But this was super special, thank you."

She was leaving? I couldn't believe it. But then I never can. I suddenly thought of Sam clicking the Lego tower into every corner. My old feeling of stunned abandonment (or perhaps at this point it was a monument to abandonment, a tower) fit any loss, regardless of size. Kris didn't want to talk about it, but other people did; Arkanda did. I could have this conversation again and again if I wanted, for the rest of my life. I get it, Sam. There are corners everywhere.

"I guess it's late, isn't it?" I said, looking at my phone. Almost midnight.

"Nah, not for me. I'm headed to the studio!" She clapped her hands together. "I don't use clocks or calendars. Every time is now; every day is Tuesday."

I swallowed. All of a sudden, at the last moment, I was completely and utterly starstruck.

She gave me a sisterly hug.

"Maybe *you* stay here, though! You look pretty beat."

"No, that would be weird," I said quickly. "To sleep next door to my room."

"Your call." She shrugged. Then with one hand on the doorknob she looked past my shoulder at something behind me. "Maybe she's guarding it. That's why she's not going anywhere."

I turned and looked at the figure in the painting. Suddenly it was impossible not to see how straight up and down she was, like the guards in front of Buckingham Palace or some other very important, exquisite—almost sacred—place.

Arkanda waved bye-bye with the tips of her long nails and shut the door behind her.

Motherfucker, I whispered. I was referring to life itself. Always surprising you, always with the curveballs. Room 321 *was* the cave and I was its guard. I had made a goddamn womb and I had oneness in it every week. With myself, with God, with my friends and sometimes lovers. And I didn't own it. Because you don't. Own anything, not even your own womb, your own body. It all goes. But every Wednesday I could get back in there, with or without lust, and be—what was the word? Free.

I slept in room 322 like a stone at the bottom of a well.

I woke up in the past. Through half-open eyes I saw the room exactly as it had been a year and a half ago, my first morning in the Excelsior. The light through the nylon curtains, the smell of old carpet; I was overpowered and I didn't resist. Davey had cleaned my windshield yesterday, at the gas station. Today I would buy a pink coverlet from the woman at the antique mall. Very gently, I took my laptop out of my bag and climbed back into the thin bed. I wrote it as I saw it, alive before my eyes.

PART
FOUR

CHAPTER 29

In the end it took me four years—not six days—to get to New York, and I didn't drive there, I flew. The first stop of my book tour was a reading in Brooklyn. I stared out the airplane window and thought about the cross-country trip that was meant to rigorously transform me at forty-five. Now I was forty-nine. There had been cliffs and caves on this odyssey, a golden ring, a tower, but had there been a labyrinth and a crystal? Was I really any different? A test would have been great, a puzzle or gauntlet that I would have failed at four years ago but now could master.

I looked at the clouds then took out my phone.

I scrolled through my photos for a long time, looking for one in particular.

I still had his number, of course.

I bought Wi-Fi.

I decided not to text him.

I put the phone in my purse, relieved, and looked for a movie to watch. Four minutes into *Moonstruck* I tapped pause and, offhandedly, almost without noticing what I was doing, texted Davey.

Hi. A little belated, ha, but I did eventually notice the tiles! So satisfying! And then the picture I had taken of the space behind the toilet.

By the time Cher and Nicolas Cage went to the opera I was a sweaty mess of regret. Finally, about an hour later, he hearted the picture.

Hahaha, he wrote.

And then:

How are you doing? I saw you have a new book [champagne emoji] haven't gotten a chance to check it out yet

You might, um, *recognize some parts*——I started to write, but immediately deleted. Thanks! I'm actually flying to NY right now [plane emoji] to promote it

When it's been long enough you don't even have to refer to the past, for all he knew I barely remembered him. I chewed ice from my plastic cup.

Full disclosure, he wrote, I saw an ad for your reading and wondered if it would be weird to go?! Dev and I are here doing a little thing. You should come!

And then an ad for his event with a picture of two cartoon dancing tigers. I stared at it for a long time. It was tomorrow afternoon, well before my reading.

Cool! I wrote. I'll be there! And then as if it was an afterthought, I added: Oh and I'll put you on the guest list!

It was rush hour when I landed so the closer I got to the city, the slower we went. Ninety minutes in I suggested to the driver that there could be some kind of buoyant forcefield around Manhattan that we "might not be able to penetrate." I said it to be funny, but it came out frantic and insane. He offered me some gum and later he found some hard candy in the glove compartment. I was starving, that was now obvious, and there was another problem. I couldn't put my finger on it.

If I'd been less hungry I would have noticed it had to do with my blinks.

My room was on the thirty-fourth floor, an endless ascent. I staggered inside, threw my bags down, and ate minibar snacks while waiting for room service, but even after a giant bowl of pasta Bolognese something was still off. When I climbed into bed the problem became violently clear. The moment I shut my eyes I felt as if I were falling from a great height such that I immediately sat up and threw my eyes open with a shout. I got out of bed, drank a glass of water. Surely this couldn't be. I lay down again and nervously shut my eyes. Again, a nauseating plunge, as when an elevator drops too suddenly. I turned on the lights and sat on the edge of my bed. If I couldn't shut my eyes then I couldn't sleep. If I couldn't sleep then I wouldn't be in any shape to read in front of an audience or be seen by Davey tomorrow; this was some sort of nightmarish, mythological riddle. I stared at my pillow, panic creeping.

I didn't want to wake up my girlfriend; it was five a.m. in London and we were a little new for this degree of shit-losing.

Harris and Paige were camping with Sam.

"Put me on speakerphone," Jordi said. "And can you open a window? Get some air?"

Dear God, thank you for this woman.

The windows didn't open, but I pressed my forehead against the plate glass. Empire State Building. One World Trade Center.

"Try to take long, slow breaths. I'm looking up your symptoms."

I breathed in; I breathed out. From this height the people on the sidewalk weren't distinct, only the yellow of cabs, tops of awnings, bigger trees. Labyrinthitis, she was saying. Or vertigo. A tiny crystal in my ear was out of place.

"It says flying sometimes causes this, the change in air pressure. Or, oh: fluctuations in estrogen."

Vertigo, like the Hitchcock movie; it was a real thing. I stepped away from the window.

"Is there a cure or will I have this forever?" I whispered. "Hello?" It sounded like she was watching a video.

"Which ear is it in?"

Ear. "My right?"

"There's some exercises," she said. "You might be able to reposition the crystal if you turn your head in a certain way; it's called the Epley maneuver." She sent a link and asked if I was able to look at a screen.

I watched a woman in a white blouse turn her head forty-five degrees to the right and then suddenly collapse, with her head still turned awkwardly. Now lying down, she turned her head ninety degrees to the left and then, with her whole body, another ninety degrees, into the bed; then she sat up and began again. It reminded me of Yvonne Rainer's *Trio A*, a dance for one person without music.

"I'm beginning," I said.

"Good."

I fell back onto the bed. "What do I do after lying down?"

"Wait thirty seconds, then ninety degrees to the left."

When I was done with the whole sequence I gingerly shut my eyes and immediately, sickeningly, plummeted.

"It didn't help."

"No, it wouldn't," Jordi said, "not after just one time. Five times is a set—it says to check after each set and repeat if the symptoms haven't abated."

Oh, so it was that kind of thing. Ambiguous. Ongoing.

As I turned and collapsed and sat up and turned and turned again, I had the bad feeling that I was getting very far away. Jordi's voice—*That was five; now check!*—was reedy, distant, and the air in the room was too dark and too big, bigger than could really be possible. This wasn't good. My sweat grew cold. I stopped the movements.

They were just out of view, but I could feel them on either side of me. Their intensity, their focus.

Keep going, Esther urged her granddaughter.

But there's no hurry, Ruthie added.

The magnitude of what was happening crept over me, a shudder, and I paused to quietly throw up on the floor. Then resumed.

The movements felt so hopelessly arbitrary and cyclical, but my grandmother and aunt didn't seem to think so, so I kept going, rededicating over and over again with an ever-widening understanding of the task at hand. Head to the right, collapse, head to left, turn, sit up. Eventually I wasn't doing the movements in any one bed or with any particular body; the Epley maneuver could have been any dance or song or prayer repeated, the point was to keep going without a comprehensible end in sight. Head to the right, collapse, head to left, turn, sit up, again and again for hours.

Right, collapse, left, turn, sit up, up, up, turn, turn, turn . . . suddenly it became effortless. Second nature, like breathing. It might have been breathing.

Now check! Jordi said.

Check what? I was done with all this and so very, very tired. I shut my eyes and, mercy, I slept.

CHAPTER 30

There were a lot of people in front of the venue and it seemed like there were a few different events on the marquee, but it turned out there was only one event right now, Davey and Dev's, and the crowd in front were people who hadn't gotten in but were still hoping. All morning I'd moved gingerly, waiting for the vertigo to start again, but it had completely dissolved, like a dream forgotten. I only felt a little raw, uncooked, standing around in a gray suit that was more appropriate for my reading. I'd head there afterward, maybe even with him. Someone yelled my name and I looked up nervously—Claire? His mom? But it was just a woman I barely knew—a friend of Mary's—who was with a big group of people. There was a conversation about if more tickets would be released; I said I was on the list and everyone enjoyed chiding me for showing off.

Apparently a lot had happened in the three and a half years since I'd stopped looking him up. Probably Claire and his mother and sister and sister's boyfriend had posted about his many small victories; they hadn't blocked and muted his name so it wasn't sudden to them. Nor was it unusual to hit your stride in your midthirties, to break out if you were ever going to break out. The press probably loved that he used to work at Hertz, from rental car to superstar. Hertz to Megahertz. The will-call line was long and it was hard to shake the feeling that he was watching me stand there. Would his mother or sister be giving out tickets? No, of course not, there was a man whose job that was.

"I'm on the guest list," I said, too loudly.

As I made my way inside, jostling and weaving through the crowd in the lobby, I wore a mask of faint amusement. This was the only way to set myself apart from the almost manic excitement around me. It was general seating, no special section for people who knew him. No chairs, just bleacher-style wooden risers with high backs surrounding a big stage in the center. There were round cushions, too slippery to sit still on. The lights flickered and then went down. I sat holding the cushion in my lap like a pie.

The lights came up on Dev, not Davey, and applause rose all around me. This was his childhood friend, our alibi. He moved in a kind of repeated hexagon, bouncing sharply as if he was hitting corners we couldn't see, and because some parts of the stage were dark we repeatedly lost and refound him in a hypnotic rhythm and one of the times he reappeared it was with a double, a shadow, Davey. The audience noticed him at different times depending on where they were sitting, so the spontaneous applause for his arrival was stretched, growing exponentially as more and more people saw him.

From that moment on it was clear that every single person in the theater felt exactly as I had about Davey; they were all head over heels in love with him. He was wearing ordinary pants and a T-shirt, like Dev, but in time Dev took his shirt off and then the audience held its breath, waiting for Davey to become bare-chested, and when he finally did, instead of hooting and hollering (this was not a striptease show) the audience fell completely silent, dry-mouthed, not a single cough or sniff for the next ten minutes, just his naked torso, back, shoulders. I wanted to slap everyone in the room and scream *Pull yourselves together, you drooling idiots!* He was as I had been remembering him all this time, but bigger somehow, larger than life. They were dancing like two people in love now, a modern pas de deux that was erotic without doing anything familiar.

He was supposed to be working at a Sacramento Hertz, lost in memory and yearning. Or pacing around their shitty little house with Claire telling him to take out the trash and him saying What? And her saying Take out the fucking trash. Blazing around the stage, doing the thing he was put on this earth to do while encircled and adored; it didn't get better than this. This was the one shared dream that wasn't only a dream.

I prayed for their dance to go wrong somehow. Not an injury, God no, but some kind of creative faux pas that would break his spell over everyone and return him to me. Maybe Davey and Dev wouldn't know how to end it, they would wear out their welcome—or plagiarism. Did they have that in dance? It only took one bad review to ruin a career, especially if plagiarism was invoked.

I was aware that I was being profoundly ungenerous—miserly, small-minded—but that only made me more wretched.

Dev suddenly called out, "All hands on the function!" and bizarrely everyone in the audience sang, "And the function grows!" Hundreds of people singing in unison is always a crowd-pleaser, but this was so out of nowhere and the melody was so high and sweet—it was breathtaking, a choir of angels. Minus me—I didn't sing "And the function grows" because I had no idea what that meant (was it even "the function" or were they saying "devotion"?) and in any case I knew I had a honking, tuneless brick of a voice. *This too shall end* is what I told myself.

But it didn't and instead of becoming tiresome its power grew, now the group-sing became complexly syncopated with the dance, like a sound ladder the pair was climbing. And it was getting faster; they only had to call "All hands" and we (except me) sang "the function!" (or "devotion"). Faster and faster and suddenly *with clapping*, a true hell.

I kept my eyes locked on Davey; the only way out of this was a secret signal from him to me, maybe he'd do my old move, fishing, or something from his goodbye video. But nothing came, they were all new moves, things he'd come up with since we'd last seen each other. The two dancers were streaming sweat as they vaulted and turned; how inconceivable that he and *I* had once done this, danced together, in room 321. And everything I'd done in there after him was even more preposterous. Audra, Arkanda, all my God-filled, sacred Wednesdays. Just delusion.

"All hands!"—"Devotion!"—"All hands!"—"Devotion!"

Then a clap like thunder—I was startled, I jumped—and the room was abruptly quiet.

Droning music curled around us, some kind of dirge. My vision grew dim. I leaned forward. The dancers slowly climbed each other, then Davey effortlessly leapt *off* Dev and twisted upward into the air.

Or no, it wasn't my vision dimming, it was the lights. As he rose, the stage lights were very gradually dissolving into a glowing orange wash. We were bathed in golden light, the color of a sunset.

Or daylight through drawn curtains.

Through peonies and dahlias.

I held the cushion, hardly breathing.

He was still rising as I looked around slowly, smelling tonka bean.

Of course none of the furniture was here, not the great chairs or the pink bed or the marble-topped table, but the theater now felt eerily like the room. Safe and full of holy potential.

I swallowed and sat back.

Suddenly I wanted to stay here and for this to go on and on, but from the music I could tell the performance was almost over; it would end when he landed. Any second now I'd be clapping, the lights would come up. In the meantime he was still rising and the warm, hallowed feeling kept growing; I could feel it expanding beyond the walls, into the street. It would still be there when I got outside, gilding the whole neighborhood, the whole city. Indeed the whole world was the motel room. The whole universe? Yes, everything was the room; you could not step outside of it, not even by dying.

And he was still rising, into the air.

If 321 was everywhere then every day was Wednesday, and I could always be how I was in the room. Imperfect, ungendered, game, unashamed. I had everything I needed in my pockets, a full soul.

He was still rising and now the idea of *having* him was perverse, unwise, like using up all the oil on the first night instead of making it last for eight miraculous nights. On the floor below, Dev was stirring the air, whipping Davey higher and higher, and I understood that my new, big soul was not a thing apart from them; I wasn't just spacing out. Dance had done this.

Gratitude came like a punch in the gut and because it's always such a relief not to be an asshole after all, tears streamed down my cheeks. The person sitting next to me was also wet-faced and we smiled a little bashfully at each other because ecstasy has a kind of built-in ridiculousness. And it wasn't just us. I looked out at the circle of faces and saw that every single audience member was going through some version of my revelation, some reckoning with the self they had been carrying around until now. I had not even been the only one knotted in miserly pain; that was part of the ride. Resistance, then giving in. He was no longer ascending; he reached the apex and quickly fell.

Outside it was early evening. There was plenty of time. I decided to walk.

The sun was just beginning to set.

Golden light everywhere.

Acknowledgments

As I was writing this book I conducted a series of interviews with women about their physical and emotional midlife changes, and while there is almost no trace of these actual conversations in the book, they made writing it more necessary. Thank you for talking to me: Calista Termini, Caterina Sorsonne, Megan Ace, Donna Pall, Megan Mullally, Marya Jones, and Connie Lovatt. Also, Aydin Olsen-Kennedy and several people who wished to remain anonymous, thank you.

I interviewed three doctors whom I want to thank for their precious time: Dr. Ricki Pollycove (obstetrics and gynecology), Dr. Michelle Gerber (naturopathic doctor and midwife), and particularly Dr. Maggie Ney (naturopathic doctor and codirector of the Women's Clinic at Akasha), who read, answered questions, and gave notes.

Thank you to Jennifer McLaughlin, Emily Ross, Sarah Bibb, Kaylee Mansbridge, and Despina Vassiliadou for spontaneously and honestly responding to an intimate public query.

Thank you to Heather Corinna for conversation and for her book about perimenopause, *What Fresh Hell Is This?*, which came out just in the nick of time.

Thank you to Chris Svennson for design support and to Sean Tejeratchi, who made the hormone graph with me.

Thank you to Sheila Heti, for reading an early draft, George Saunders, for reading a late draft, and Eli Horowitz, for reading many drafts;

your notes were crucial and spurred me on. A special thanks to reader and note-giver Maggie Nelson, whose hard questions I had to grow into. Also, Carla Frankenbach, for reading and talking. Thank you to my assistant, Elizabeth Litvitskiy, who proofread every draft and for a long time was my only reader, a sturdy, merry eye and ear.

Thank you to my agent, Sarah Chalfant, for her understanding of this book and ongoing belief in me as a writer. Thank you to my editor, Sarah McGrath, for having such clarity and faith, especially on some dark days in the middle—also thank you to Alison Fairbrother for a sharp pen later on. And thank you to the whole Riverhead team: Helen Yentus, who made this cover by hand, Ashley Garland, Nora Alice Demick, Délia Taylor, Lavina Lee, Sheila Moody, Geoff Kloske, and the extraordinary Jynne Dilling Martin. I feel tremendously lucky to be supported like this.

Thank you to Jacqueline Novak, Margaret Qualley, Kate Berlant, Louise Bonnet, Alexa Greene, Marina Kitchen, Angela Trimbur, Dede Gardner, Julia Bryan-Wilson, Carrie Brownstein, Khaela Maricich, Katie Sá-Davis, Bully Fae Collins, Gina Rodriguez, Natasha Lyonne, Stella Lamar, Harrell Fletcher, Jay Cherman, Nikki Providence, Maya Buffet-Davis, Shana Bonstin, and Rick Moody whose insight, dance, care, and music are all part of me and this book. Thank you to Ali Liebegott for her poetry as I finished.

Thank you to my parents, Richard Grossinger and Lindy Hough, and my dear brother, Robin Grossinger: my first and eternal examples of how to make something from nothing. To my late grandmother and aunt, Martha and Deborah Towers: no idea if I did it right, but I think you wanted me to try.

And finally, thank you to Mike Mills, and to my baby, Hopper Mills, whose boldness has emboldened me.